THE NAPOLEON CURSE

Jim Reay

First published in Queensland, Australia in 2017

National Library of Australia Cataloguing-in-Publication entry:

Creator	Reay, Jim E. – author
Title	The Napoleon Curse / by Jim E. Reay
ISBN	9780994377821 (paperback) 9780994377838 (eBook)
Subjects	Incantations – Fiction Jewel thieves – Fiction Criminal investigation – Fiction Suspense fiction

Edited by Patrice Shaw (www.psediting.com.au)

Page layout and cover design by Kirsty Ogden (www.epiphanyediting.com.au)

Available worldwide on Amazon books and Kindle

Acknowledgements

This story is longer than my previous books. It has been many years in the writing, through quite a few iterations and inspirations. It was a challenge to draw the many themes and characters, over two centuries and several continents, into a cohesive whole … but I like it now.

Thank you to Patrice Shaw (psediting.com.au) for her careful editing as well as her challenging questions. Over the several books that Patrice has edited for me, she has shown an understanding of my thinking process and she is skilled at expertly suggesting ways to improve my writing.

My appreciation goes to Kirsty Ogden (epiphanyediting.com.au) for her eye-catching cover design and clear page layouts. She has also broadened my perspectives into exploring the range of opportunities in the wider publishing world.

If the book reads well, Patrice and Kirsty deserve a lot of the credit.

I thank my wife, Brenda, and my extended family for giving me the space and encouragement to write my stories.

My brother, Lewis, has helped me with research, insights and wisdom in this book, as in my previous stories. He has a good eye for continuity and for finding inconsistencies.

To you, the reader, may you enjoy the tale and I hope it resonates from your own perspectives.

www.jimreaywriter.net

PART ONE

The Mohács Blue

The name of the Romany spy is not to be disclosed. Indeed, Suleiman the Magnificent has placed his personal guards, the *Janissaries*, around his tent because no word of this ceremony is to be revealed.

The Romany bows before the great Suleiman, scarcely able to believe the words of thanks and praise being bestowed on him. He has saved the Sultan's life. He understands that ... but not this lavish reaction.

The Romany is but a very minor member of the great Suleiman's *Rumelian* Army, which is made up of Balkan conscripts. He is a spotter, a spy for the Ottoman Empire. His insignificant appearance and manner usually enable him to be unnoticed – a valuable skill in a spy and a product of his station in life.

He had managed to infiltrate the tents of the enemy –Hungarian troops – being led by their commander-in-chief, Pál Tomori. He learned of the devious plan for their archers to trick Suleiman the Magnificent into moving forward on his right flank, as his troops sensed success. There, the enemy archers were to be lying in wait, to cut him down.

He was the prize. Tomori was prepared to lose the battle if he could kill the great Sultan.

The Romany got the message back to his side, just in time.

As it happened, the *Janissaries* scarcely managed to shield the Sultan as he moved away from the danger. Even so, Suleiman's *cuirasse* armour was hit by the arrows, which were intended to end his life.

But he lived and he is grateful beyond words.

As the Sultan presents the sapphire that he is calling the *Mohács Blue* to the Romany, he explains that the large gem was traded to his empire from an island kingdom called *Kotte*, in the east.

The leader adds a blessing that the brave Balkan Romany's people would always be protected from illness, as long as the startling blue sapphire stays in the family's possession. The Sultan's message should be passed down the generations to maintain that sanctity.

The curse

Napoleone, tu sei un ladro saccheggio! Ti maledico!'
Napoléon, vous êtes un voleur piller. Je te maudis!

The Emperor of the French and King of Italy glances from his coronation carriage at the call – a woman's voice – given in two languages. He is fluent in both. 'Napoleon, you are a plundering thief. I curse you!'

He understands her words.

The woman continues to shout, as foot soldiers move to restrain her. 'You stole my family's sapphire – the Mohács Blue. I curse you forever, *Il Grande Ladro,* and any others who choose to show their power by stealing sacred sapphires.'

Napoleon glances at his Empress, Josephine, who sits beside him in the carriage. Despite the celebratory artillery salvo and the cathedral bells, she couldn't fail to hear the clamour on his side of the coach but she continues to wave, unaffected, to the cheering crowd.

Her twenty-four-year-old son, Eugène de Beauharnais, the newly appointed Viceroy of Italy, is in charge of the French and Italian grenadiers that are escorting the thirteen-carriage convoy to the Basilica of *Sant'Ambrogio* for more prayers. The Viceroy pulls his horse close to the newly-crowned King of Italy's coach.

In a side-mouthed whisper, the emperor/king instructs his step-son. 'Find out what that was all about. She called me *The Great Thief.'*

* * * *

'Well?'

The emperor has seen his Empress off, after all the celebrations, on her journey back to Paris and he is now awaiting the Viceroy's report on the woman who shouted out at the ceremony.

'The woman is deranged. She has been moved to the *mad house*.'

'She placed a curse. What happened?'

'It is a long story, *Mon Empereur*. It is about a sapphire given to her family by Suleiman the First after the Battle of Mohács in 1526. It will take time to tell.'

'I have time. The sapphire interests me. And the Mohács battle was against the Hungarians. I know my history. We still battle them; and the Austrians. Tell me her story.'

'She claims that our troops, on *your* orders, plundered their Romany camp at Pavia in May, 1796. Among whatever else happened, they stole the sapphire known as the Mohács Blue. That stone had come from what is now the Kingdom of Kandy, off the south-east coast of India. It has sacred properties and was given to her ancestor by Suleiman the Magnificent in 1526 to protect the extended family from illness.

'You have apparently stolen this jewel and she has placed a curse on you, *personally* – that you will not enjoy your success, you will be branded a thief in the eyes of all your subjects, that you will lose your power and you will be banished from the eyes of civilisation before you die in shame and isolation. And that will happen to any future thieves of such blessed sapphires. She is cursing the world. She's mad. I told you.'

'Do we have the stone? What is it like?'

'Apparently, we do. You will recall that we shot the leaders of Pavia in that campaign, executed for not surrendering on request, and we let the troops take looted rewards as part of that penance.'

'That is correct. Our *armée* is underpaid and deserves reward. I have authorised that by decree.'

'*Absolument. Bien sur.* But the soldiers realised the value of the stone and it has been sent back to Paris with our art adviser, Dominique-Vivant Denon. It is apparently nearly seventy carats – and a wonderful blue. It should be at *Musée Napoleon* very soon.'

'Then ensure that it is headed for my private collection, not *Le Louvre.*'

'But the curse?'

'What curse? Woman's ramblings. What we have done is perfectly legal.'

'And the woman?'

'She stays where she can do harm.'

'*Oui.*'

Napoleon

Saint Helena Island, Atlantic Ocean. 1820

It is as real in his mind as if it is happening now. The emperor had glanced from his carriage as the woman continued.

'You stole my sapphire. I curse you forever. Il Grande Ladro, and any others who choose to show their power by stealing sacred sapphires.'

Napoleon Bonaparte pulls the collar of his greatcoat round his neck and adjusts his distinctive two-pointed hat. His heavy leather boots tread the thick moist grass, as he climbs back up the misty slope to Longwood House – his current place of detainment during what has been a five-year incarceration, so far, on this Atlantic island prison.

As he reaches the crest of the ridge, a shaft of rare autumn sunshine parts the clouds, seeming to create a spiritual ladder to the heavens. Is this God trying to communicate with him – the same God that has deserted him in this forlorn place?

The words of the old Romany woman's curse fill his consciousness. It was back in 1805. The woman's precious sapphire had been stolen. Spoils of war. Of course, she would be upset. It is both the custom and the law. How did she think Suleiman the Magnificent acquired the jewel? It would be in the booty of war or a tribute to his authority. And the Mohács Blue is indeed a beautiful stone. He expects that it is safe where he has left it in the care of a trusted lieutenant.

Back then, the French armies had just defeated the Austrian Army and liberated the whole Italian Piedmont and the Papal States to be part of France. The people should have been grateful to be free from the Austrian and Roman yoke. He was the crowned King of Italy.

His troops had acted honourably. They collected booty from the vanquished, as required. They knew his love of deep sapphire-blue and they had effectively presented him with the gem as a tribute for his victorious conquests. His code of moral and legitimate behaviour was being respected. The soldiers could have kept the stone but *no* ... they chose to have it sent back to Paris with the art director, Denon. How honourable.

And he, Napoleon, has left this legal code as his legacy to Europe. It is the way of the modern world and he would expect that his judicial system would continue long after he has left this mortal world.

He is determined to think no more of the gypsy's hex – but the bolt of sunshine is now searing the words back into his mind with a clarity that surprises him.

The curse said that he would lose all his power and be banished from humanity – and he had ignored it at the time. Why would he not? He is Napoleon, Emperor, ruler of most of Europe – albeit in current banishment. Look at the victories he has achieved. He introduced a justice system separating the emperor or politicians from influence. He lifted France from its post-revolution malaise and brought pride back to his people. His armies loved him – and still do. He was the ruler of all he surveyed. Why would he listen to an old Italian hag shouting abuse at him. He is way above all that pettiness.

* * * *

As he enters the hilltop Longwood House with a nod to his assistant, he feels the miserable damp in the air and hears the rats scurrying under the floorboards again.

The peeling wallpaper is now covered with white muslin drapes to hide the seeping water – but he senses the wet mould; cultures of illness waiting to grab him.

In the billiard room, his campaign maps are spread over the table, protected by covers from drips, as he analyses and re-analyses his tactics for the many victorious conquests. Even his last 1815 battle at Waterloo is scrutinised in the detached methodical manner which characterises his whole persona. He is seen as a risk-taker by the masses, but that image hides the diligence of his planning and his bravery in putting himself in harm's way to find that extra single drop – of luck – which makes the cup overflow, tips the balance, and allows victory to be achieved.

Il grande ladro, the hag had called him – The Great Thief. How dare she? It is the entitlement of all victors in war. It has always had been so.

Outside, the shaft of sunlight has gone – and, with it, his window view. For a fleeting while, he could see the cobalt sea stretching to every horizon as he sat high above the steep cliffs of this old volcanic intrusion into the middle of the Atlantic Ocean.

Africa is to the east and north; South America to the west and the ice of the whaling seas to the south, he presumes. His beloved France is north, over the equator and weeks of sailing away. This banishment is a sad torture but, perhaps, his France will continue to grow and develop despite the external threats from Britain, his incarcerators.

Has the gypsy been right? Will he indeed perish here? He has insisted with the intransigent British that, on his death, he be interred in Paris as a true Emperor of France – but they continue to refuse. His supporters are ready. They will ensure that *Les Invalides*, that most prestigious military museum and hospital for veterans, will accommodate his mortal remains in a manner befitting his contribution to the greater France and Europe.

But the English? They insist that he will be buried on this despicable island. That is why he is prepared. He has chosen a potential tomb on St Helena – a peaceful spot, if his passing should come

10

soon. He has told the English that he wants only *Napoleon* carved onto his tombstone as would befit an emperor, but they refuse that too. They offer *Napoleon Bonaparte* and *he* has refused. That is a commoner's name. He would rather have nothing on the stone than be demeaned in death.

He has just returned from his regular walk to the site and back. No guards are necessary. He is an honourable man – an emperor in exile. He accepts his fate, as a valiant soldier must. How could he flee anyway? Even if he could get down to the settlement, Jamestown, and then slip past the garrisons of troops. He would still have to get onto a ship. The British fort on the High Knoll has a view, in every direction – at least when the mists lift. He would be blown out of the water.

His last few years have been spent writing his memoirs – his version of history, flaws and all. It is a positive tale. He has achieved so much. He only ever lost two battles in his whole military career and one was through underestimating the weather, with tactical battles already achieved. He has lifted the whole of Europe out of its revolutionary depression. Now, they have structure, processes, systems, a code to live by … if the English don't ruin it all with their hubris.

But, strangely, he is haunted today by the curse of the Romany. He tosses his *bicorne* hat onto the floor.

It has taken time … he won't admit it to others, but he realises now that he *has* lost all his power and he *has* been banished from all that he has known. And his beloved sapphires are no longer with him. It has all gone to *merde*.

He hopes that, at least, the Mohács Blue is safe in its hiding place. His trusted ones will guard it. It is a beautiful stone.

At that moment, his *bicorne* starts to move across the damp floorboards. He kicks out at it and a large rat scutters away from its temporary shelter.

Napoleon raises his good hand to wipe his brow. Outside, the moist mist is swirling again, like the cloud of despondency fluttering down on him inside.

Cecile

Cecile's eyes have a distant look; absorbing the view over her estate parkland without really registering.

Her mind is on other matters – more dangerous matters.

An inner anguish suddenly makes her wince – howling voices float to her on the light breeze; wailing laments over the tranquil lake. But there is no-one around, only ducks.

Stretched back in the deckchair, her lustrous grey hair shines in the sun. She knows she should have extracted herself totally from this business thirty or more years ago. It had started as a game; an intellectual challenge for women who had shown their talents in times of war and had been expected to fit into dutiful ladylike roles thereafter.

The name had been Merri's idea; fashioned from the quaint French that she had learned as a schoolgirl. Cecile had told her that the correct word would be *connaisseur* or *collectionneur*. But, no, Merri wanted to use a word for a person who collects dogs or stray tennis balls. Anyway, it had worked out quite cleverly in the end.

The old willow tree shelters her from the early-morning sun. The sudden roar of the plane's engines bursting into life startle the ducks. They shoot like slow feathery rockets on a low trajectory from the chateau lake, their energy far too excessive for their effectiveness in defying gravity. The twin-engined aircraft appears over the tree tops at the far end of the south lawn.

She watches, relieved that *he* is safely off to London.

The fuselage gleams fleetingly as it catches the sun's rays before it soars away to the west, banking northwards as it goes. He will be away for a couple of days. That should give time for Cecile to handle her business. She is feeling tired – surprising her, so early in the morning.

She has to work on the exit strategy – too old for this business now. He isn't being particularly helpful. It is getting out of hand. Hopefully, she can distance herself from it all at last and whatever needs to happen will flow from there. Strangely for her, the solution won't come. Usually she knows what to do. Usually she is very sharp.

The plane has disappeared from being even a speck in the clear blue sky. A wave of cottonwool clouds slide sedately over the Loire Valley as she turns her eyes to the north.

There is no doubt that the chateau is impressive. The lake glistens blue from Cecile's sheltered seat for about thirty metres till it licks quietly at the end of the pale-yellow driveway. Thirty metres of sculpted poplar, privet and cypress frame the drive and take the eye over to the garden lawns on either side. Flower beds shimmer in the breeze; keeping time with an invisible hand; moving reds, mauves, whites and yellows in a rhapsody of colour.

The chateau rises behind; three storeys to the roof with neat rows of mullioned windows. Curved redoubts break the rectangular form of the structure giving an artistic suggestion of military defence, though this is a stately home, never a castle. The roof is adorned with a thick, young forest of dormer windows, turrets and towers, making a jaw-dropping spectacle.

Cecile is enjoying the reflection of the building in the lake. This is home; family heritage; a place of peace – so different from when the jackboots had requisitioned this paradise as a barracks for German officers. A time when a young Cecile, just a girl, had helped her parents hide the family treasures behind the old wine barrels in the cool cellars; when the child of privilege carried messages to the

Resistance fighters; when she was appreciated for her quick mind, her solutions to problems, her bravery.

Hard times they were, followed by the joy of liberation – and then; nothing. Gone was the excitement of the life and death struggle. The value which women had added to the cause was disregarded. The men returned from their battles expecting the social order to be as it was.

Where had the *joie de vivre* gone?

America in the early fifties had been good. She had felt some appreciation there. It was a different attitude to women's roles in *the land of the free*. The GIs were happy that the war had ended. They were prepared to party and to try new ideas. That had been a good three years in the US capital for a young Frenchwoman seeking adventure; and it included that very special friendship which was always a treasured, if painful, memory.

Then on to London in the later fifties – a depressing place; grey clothes, grey buildings, grey skies. Only the lights in Piccadilly hinted at life. Faces were drawn. The spectre of the war lingered on and the discipline of rationing haunted all who moved, just carrying out their little daily functions like drones in a dismal hive.

Goodness, she thought, *they hadn't even been invaded*.

The blitz, she knew about; she had been told, time and again. But that was not like here in France where the real deadly bullying had permeated every aspect of living. The all-pervading culture of division as people were shipped onto transports; *off to the work camps* they were told. No sensible people believed that – but they looked away because the old order was changing.

Maybe right *was* wrong. Maybe this *was* the way to survive. The leather coats, the swastika badges; there was no escaping. Yes, they had been under the *real* pressure. Yet the French had managed to rebuild with a passion, looking for opportunities. What was wrong with these Londoners?

But that was where Cecile had met Merri; in London. Two like minds; a French woman and a Briton, both mute anonymous heroines of wartime – needing a challenge, resisting the pressure for them to conform as obedient women in a male society. That was when the plan had been hatched – as an intellectual game, no more.

* * * *

The flurry of ducks landing in the lake ruffles the chateau's reflection and brings Cecile back to the moment. She has a rowing boat to carry her over the lake to the chateau. She enjoys the exercise. Her mind had been at its quickest in the 1950s and '60s but she can still show the young ones a thing or two.

Ramas

His veins thrum with exhilaration – a shadow, frozen in silhouette; broad shoulders hunch over the keyboard in the ill-lit room.

Only the gentle irritation of his obsessive finger-tapping breaks the silence. His eyes bulge in the eerie glow of the computer screen; the focus on waiting for the signal that will set it all in motion.

He knows that thousands of kilometres away, others are ready; secret tentacles threaded across the globe; watching, anticipating the action which will follow.

The Fijian adventure is poised to write a whole new chapter in the *Ramas* legend. It might well be Napoleonic in its daring. Or so he is being told.

The scale of the operation fuels his adrenalin surge.

It will take nano-seconds to mobilise everything when it starts.

Ramas will finally come of age or … ?

A shiver of fear. Too large, too crazy? Why didn't he just veto it at the start?

Too late now!

The signal. Moving. Too late now!!

PART TWO

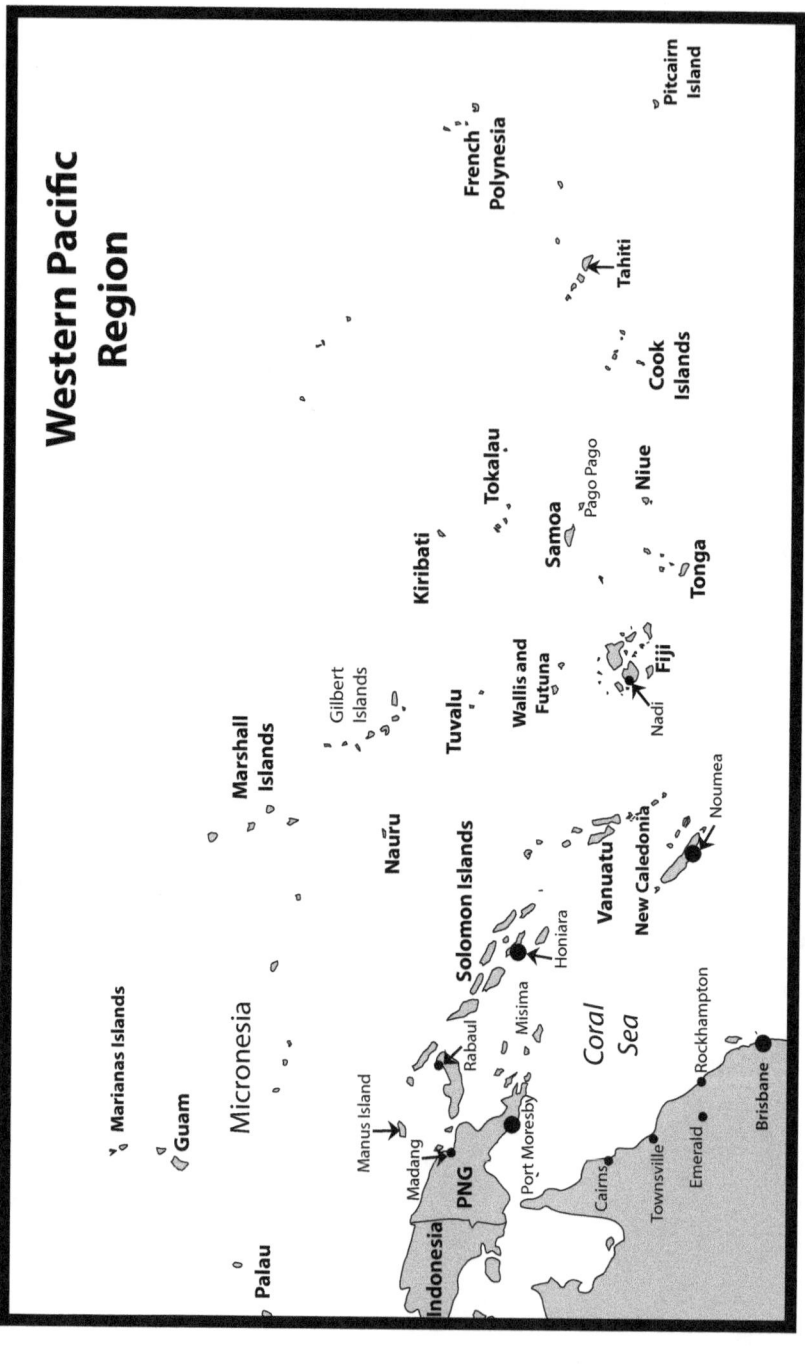

Western Pacific Region

Marianas Islands

Guam

Micronesia

Palau

Indonesia

PNG

Manus Island

Madang

Port Moresby

Rabaul

Misima

Coral Sea

Cairns

Townsville

Emerald

Rockhampton

Brisbane

Nauru

Marshall Islands

Gilbert Islands

Solomon Islands

Honiara

Vanuatu

New Caledonia

Noumea

Tuvalu

Kiribati

Wallis and Futuna

Fiji

Nadi

Tokalau

Samoa

Pago Pago

Niue

Tonga

Cook Islands

French Polynesia

Tahiti

Pitcairn Island

Steve

Fiji. Tuesday 16 January, 2007

A jumble of unwelcome images roll through my brain. They are a painful kaleidoscope of rattling guns, pain and helplessness.

'Steve!'

I hear her. The voice is faint but it is drawing me back to the real world. I smell the tropical humidity in the air. The warm Fijian breeze is gently whispering over me.

'Mr Flynn? You okay?'

I hear her. I am alive and conscious. It has been that bad dream … again. I must have been sighing or twisting. I open an eye and smile to thank her.

Cheery Lani's firm hands return to massaging a blend of coconut oil and frangipani blossoms into my back.

I look out over the turquoise-green of the lagoon. Farther out, a pulsing white line flags the surf, booming rhythmically on the outer reef.

It has been a week since I must have crossed that barrier in a semi-conscious state. Just thinking about it brings a throb back into the still raw scar through my hair above my right ear. I hear myself groan with a memory.

Lani pauses again, with a concerned look. I nod for her to continue.

Aldo Pollock and I were security on board the *Sea Spray 2* for Ingrid, a pop-singing sensation in her mid-twenties. Her second album had just gone platinum in the US. She needed space to develop new material. The next album was due in the stores for the Christmas market. Apparently it takes many months to go from inspired idea to final tracks in shops and on-line.

Already wealthy from music sales, Ingrid had also married money. Her husband – decades her senior – was a seriously rich banker who, presumably had a youthful outlook. But neither Aldo nor I asked such questions. We were the hired help.

Our job was to keep the paparazzi away as we cruised past Bora Bora and Pago Pago. And, just a week ago, we had been off one of the small Fijian islands favoured for the exclusive peaceful resorts of the rich and private.

A chop was getting up with a low pressure system rolling in. The *Sea Spray 2* was luxury – a couple of decks and good cabin space for the musical diva to conjure up her new melodies; large cruising sails for the romance of moving like Polynesians between magical islands; and a powerful diesel engine too, for the days when the wind wouldn't blow.

During daylight hours on board, Aldo and I took turns to monitor the computer and radio waves for potential threats. At night, we patrolled the decks. There was little threat from intrusive photographers at sea, although they would try if we were near a main island. No, the threats at sea were mainly from the elements; and from pirates, who saw easy targets in the wealthy yachting island-hoppers.

The Fijian lady asks me to turn onto my back; which I do, with as athletic a motion as my formerly fit frame can manage. Thirty-four last birthday and less than two years retired from active service with the Australian Army in Afghanistan, Iraq and East Timor.

I adjust my towel to protect Lani's modesty. She laughs at my effort – eyes twinkling. She is a good sport.

Is it alright to touch these scars? She uses her expressive eyes to silently ask the question.

Massaging hands work down the right side of my rib cage. They reach the hardened marks which pepper that side and my right thigh.

What a beautiful dark face she has, sparkling teeth and a cap of tight black curls, providing a backdrop for the red hibiscus blossom behind her ear.

She pours more exotic oil over my battered body. The aromas, the thatched roof of an open-sided *bure*, the warm sea air and the rhythmic soothing of aching muscles seem to belie old and recent violence.

I smile to her to say that it is okay, ignoring my memory of the improvised explosive device which had gone off under our Bushmaster in the cold Afghan desert.

I'd been lucky but the scar tissue is a reminder of hard days. Her massaging hands are gentle. The scents and sounds of Fiji are close to paradise ... but my thoughts had gone back to that night a week ago.

We had watched a burnished sun go down, escaping from scudding clouds.

Aldo and I scanned every horizon. Nothing ... nor on the radar and computer screens. Nothing, except the usual parade of large freighters moving through the shipping lanes and the big rain squalls which were coming from the seaward side.

We wore our thin lifejackets and carried side-arms – normal operating procedure. Automatic assault rifles were in easily accessible lockers on each side of the deck, more to give peace of mind to Ingrid than for any anticipated danger.

The clouds brought an envelope of purply-black gloom over the sea. I could see lights winking on the island – some exclusive resort there, on the edge of the private lagoon. The wind was rising, blowing towards the protecting reef. The skipper had several sea anchors out to counter any drift.

Tomorrow – Wednesday – he had told us, we would head for cover in daylight. But for tonight, we would ride out this not too ominous chop.

There had been no warning – just the shock from a stun grenade, almost covering the rattle of automatic gunfire. The raiders had approached on Aldo's side, from the gloom, and he had dropped to the deck. He was gone. Experience tells you that. I fired off two shots at the shadowy shapes.

It had felt like a huge club hitting my head above my right ear but I hadn't seen anyone near me. I was falling into the darkness. The warm Pacific tasted salty with a hint of vegetation. My numbed body rolled slowly to the surface under the control of the lifejacket. Cool air blew across my cheeks pushing the water to the sides of my wet face. Nothing worked. Not arms or legs. Just deadening; as if all the messages from the brain had been short-circuited. My head throbbed, a stinging pain bit into the open wound.

It had all happened so fast.

As my left eye opened, I could see the *Sea Spray's* lights disappearing – and yet the yacht still seemed to be bobbing, straining at the sea anchors.

Then I got it. It was not the boat disappearing. I was being floated away, driven by the rising wind towards land.

Through my one functioning eye and with my dazed mind lapsing in and out of consciousness, I could see figures on the ship and hear the chatter of raised voices – but they were receding fast.

I was being washed towards the shore, towards the barrier reef which surrounded the lagoon. But there was no huge boom of waves crashing – nothing except the wind gradually growing in strength.

When I looked again for the *Sea Spray*, it had gone. Much as I tried to turn to see where I was heading, I couldn't move. No visibility; lost in this turbulent warm ocean; I drifted out of consciousness again.

Alison

Alison Wood is a court reporter. She looks too gentle a woman to be listening to the procession of petty criminals who pass through the magistrate-court system.

She sits comfortably on the padded vinyl cushions in the Emerald courtroom. It isn't crowded. The list has the usual drunks and driving charges.

In the next case though, the police are seeking to have an alleged robber remanded in custody. He has apparently been involved in a mugging earlier that morning, in the area known to every Central Queenslander as the Gemfields, just to the west of Emerald.

He appears a bit rough, unshaven, a few scratches on his face and his clothes look as if they have been slept in – which, it seems, they probably have.

Alison has her thick notepad on her knee as she records only the salient facts. Court reporting can be really boring work at times.

She hears, in the background of her attention, that the magistrate is having trouble clarifying the police request. The man has apparently not spoken, except to say, 'Nein', when given an instruction to move into the dock. Based on that word alone, the magistrate has assumed he is German.

The magistrate says something to the policeman about the accused needing reasonable representation. The duty lawyer says the accused doesn't appear to understand English.

All of this exchange clearly raises the frustration level of the judge who wants *clean processes* when applying for someone to be remanded in custody. He remonstrates with the lawyer, 'Haven't we got an interpreter who can speak with the accused?'

The tone in the magistrate's voice snaps Alison to a full attention. *Perhaps there will be some excitement*, she thinks. She does enjoy it when justices and judges get frustrated with young lawyers who often *cut their teeth* by practising in country court-houses – much better to be bounced in a remote courtroom than to be exposed to a much more public humiliation in getting the protocols wrong in the busy Brisbane courts.

'Is there no-one who can speak German and interpret for this man?' the magistrate asks.

The young lawyer blushes with embarrassment. Why did he think that he would be able to just roll this case through as a routine remand? He should have checked to see who the presiding officer would be. It could make all the difference between an easy or a hard life. They all have their individual quirks. The law can often be a matter of who is interpreting it.

Usually magistrates take the advice of the police and legal aid. This is the routine. Just his luck to catch a judge who wants to be picky. He hasn't thought to get a translator. This isn't the city. There is no list of court interpreters out here. That is why he wants him remanded to Rockhampton. Surely, that is obvious.

* * * *

Alison notices a thin young man stand up in the public pew in front of her.

'I'll give it a try, your honour,' he says to the magistrate, in response to the request for an interpreter.

'Your name?' the court officer asks.

'Mick,' replies the thin man. 'Mick Stone.'

Alison thinks he has the look of a well-meaning farm dog about him; eager to please but not quite sure of the right way to do it – as he shuffles awkwardly from his pew to the waiting welcome of the clerk-of-court. The court officer appears relieved that he has this community volunteer. What a stroke of luck to have someone who can get the glares of the magistrate off him and all the other court officials.

'Thank you, Sir,' says the magistrate with a relieved tone in his voice. He lowers his head to his paperwork. His whole persona and manner give an impression that he is a judicial officer who wants this case dealt with and that he is tired of the slack processes which are slowing the efficient management of his court.

'Please ask him his name, Sir,' he commands without lifting his head.

Alison watches the slim young man raise his body erect, giving him a sense of ill-fitting importance as, she thinks, he is trying to recall his German words.

'Vot isst your name?' says the young man.

There are moments of silence in life which are quite profound. To Alison, that is the silence in the courtroom at this very moment; a pregnant few seconds, as the magistrate's head slowly rises from his papers – the realisation dawning through a bemused mist that the young man has not spoken German at all. Is this a joke? In his well-run courtroom where due processes are always followed?

Even as he looks in those intensely quiet seconds, the magistrate can see there is no joke in the face of the slim man. He has the look of someone who thinks he has asked his question well and is waiting for the answer from the man in the dock – the man with the confused expression on his face.

The lawyer and the policeman stand stunned. Even more so when the young man repeats, 'Vot isst your name?' with some impatience, or is it pleading, in his tone.

Before he can sense the slightest of tittering chortles move into the stifled smiles around the room, the magistrate takes control.

'You don't speak German?' he says, more as a statement than a question – and certainly in a tone that stops any nascent giggles in the audience. The magistrate realises in one glance at the simple young man that he is not a practical joker. Indeed, young Mick appears as a good, if not overly bright, local who has been trying to do the right thing.

Alison can see in his slightly bewildered expression that his television diet of *Hogan's Heroes* has led him to believe that Sergeant Schultz was speaking proper German when he said in an accent, *I know nothing; nothing.*

She gives the magistrate grudging admiration for his sensitive and rapid appraisal of the situation.

'Thank you. This case is adjourned till the afternoon sitting – by which time I expect you will have acquired the services of an interpreter. Thank you, Sir, for your assistance.' He says this with a gentle smile to Mick who seems bewildered, relieved and a little happy as the clerk-of-court ushers him outside.

Alison is one of several who just make it outside the courtroom door before dissolving into a scarcely controlled spasm of laughter. *Vot isst your name?*

Every so often in a court reporter's work there is a gem. She thought it has taken a Gemfields' case to produce one.

* * * *

It had apparently started with the triple zero emergency call which had come straight through to the Rockhampton call centre. It was at 2.05 am. 'It's a fire! Main Street, Rubyvale. It's a fire!' That's what the call had said. It was recorded on tape for the police and the court to check.

Within seconds, the alert had gone to the police station at Anakie, in the Gemfields of Central Queensland. The small town had only a volunteer rural fire service but the police mustered the sleepy men by using their emergency beepers.

The police car, followed by the Anakie ambulance, travelled north, sirens blaring, covering the few kilometres of bitumen road very quickly. The fire engine would be a bit slower and a second engine had been called from Emerald, just in case.

The message, before it had been cut off, had given no indica-tion of how serious the fire might be. Rubyvale is a few kilometres north of Anakie but it always seems farther in reality than it looks on a map.

Main Street in Rubyvale is perhaps the smallest Main Street anywhere. There are only a few buildings with tourist attractions for the many visitors who come to this area daily to look at the sapphire mining and perhaps to find a cheaper than usual gemstone. A longer street runs at right angles across Main Street. There but for a quirk of history, it should have been the main street. Together, the two streets have the full range of gemstone cutting and shops selling souvenirs from the cheap through to the sparklers worth hundreds of thousands of dollars. Security on all of these premises is well maintained. A fire in these streets could be very costly for a community which often regards itself as just a little different.

The settlement has the feel of the prospector; the sense of the self-made man or woman who has found the elusive glistening bluey-green or sometimes bluey-yellow or, if very lucky, the deep-blue sapphire which would set them up for life.

In daylight, the police car and ambulance would have whizzed past old spoil heaps – *mullock heaps, tailing heaps,* they are called – and rusting brown machinery where the waste gravel from small mining ventures has been picked through, washed, riddled and sorted to find any small gemstones. And there are always many small sapphires in the cast-off dirt. If there were big stones to be found, they would be faceted; polished and set in gold, silver or platinum mountings – protected by the high-security of the gem dealers' premises.

But it was dark; and the emergency vehicles only saw the reflection of their red and blue flashing lights bouncing off gum trees, fence lines and occasional buildings.

As they turned the corner into Main Street, there was no sign of a fire.

An agitated mob had gathered in the shadows. A couple of gesticulating men directed the police car and ambulance towards an area where a crowd was milling around.

'Where's the fire?' the constable asked.

'What fire?' came the puzzled response.

'They got one of the bastards down there,' another said, and the two policemen pushed their way through the parting group to find a huge man sitting on top of a pinioned unshaven person whose face was squashed into the dirt. He looked wet. Sweat or water? It was hard to tell. And blood. He appeared as if he had a bit of bark knocked off him by the mob.

'Where's the fire?' the policeman repeated.

'What bloody fire?' the huge man asked back. 'We've got one of the thieves. The other bastard got away.'

As one constable called the fire brigade to advise of a false alarm, the other handcuffed the alleged thief. The ambulance people checked him for injuries. He didn't answer any of their questions nor did he look particularly frightened – more as though he just didn't understand what was happening. A resigned look as if he was letting the world wash by – a world beyond his comprehension.

A lean gnarled man explained that he had been the victim of a robbery. There were two of them. How had they known he was carrying the *Balkan Blue* on him? He had no idea how that could be. They had seized him as he was walking quietly to his car. They weren't casual muggers, he assured the police. They knew what they were looking for – a big sapphire, partially cleaned; found only last week on his little mining claim. He said that his name was Drago. He had named the stone after his European ancestry.

When they had started to clean the gem, it became obvious that this was *a big one*, good quality, maybe worth hundreds of thousands of dollars.

They had stopped work on the stone. The final job would need to be assessed by skilled faceters. No-one wanted to get the cut wrong and reduce a valuable gemstone to a few fragments of industrial quality.

So Drago had carried the stone on him in a small bag, under his clothes, around his waist.

'They knew vhere stone vas,' said Drago. 'Vas all they vas inter-ested in. I screamed. These blokes came and caught vone of them. Other got avay with my stone.'

'Why did you call triple 0 about a fire?' asked the policemen, while noting everything that was being said.

'Vot fire?' asked Drago. 'I said, *It's sapphire! Main Street Rubyvale.* But the phone, it conked out.'

'A sapphire?' The policeman nodded, as he began to under-stand. Not *a fire! T's sapphir*e, he would have said with his Balkan accent and stress on a different syllable.

It was nearly three in the morning. The crowd was starting to disperse. No-one was quite as sharp as they would be later in the day. Anyone on the streets of Rubyvale at this hour was probably *tired and emotional* at best.

The handcuffed man was securely restrained in the back of the police car. The ambulance officers briefed the central emergency control in Rockhampton. A police car was already on its way from Emerald. The alleged thief would be held in custody to face court the next day.

Drago was then being treated by the ambulance men. The shock of what happened had started to sink in. Prospectors dreamed of the day when they would find the stone that would make all the differ-ence. It was what kept drawing them down into their cramped little tunnels, chipping away at the hard rock, recognising the potential in a new seam, dragging the pickings to the surface and check-ing each one carefully. Usually it was only disappointment and the thought of *next time*. But this stone was a beauty. When the jewel-ler suggested it needed someone really skilled to look at it, Drago understood that he had found a blue sapphire of unusual quality. He could feel the weight.

He called it the *Balkan Blue* after its full deep ultramarine colour, after the land of his birth and after the legendary story of the Mohács Blue – a huge deep-blue gem given to his ancestors and stolen by Napoleon Bonaparte. That Corsican thief was cursed and died in ignominy on an Atlantic island. Drago wanted to curse the thief of *his* stone, the *Balkan Blue*.

Whom had he told?

Well, there was the jeweller – but he would have told no-one. Confidentiality is paramount in the jewellery business.

There was Mick, the slim eager young man who stood beside him as Drago received first aid. Mick did lots of labouring jobs for Drago and helped translate for him sometimes. Drago has trouble understanding everything that is said by these fast-talking Australians with their broad nasal accents.

Mick had grown up in Central Queensland. He was one of those young lads who doesn't quite fit; never really knowing the right things to say at times. He is slower than others in understanding the punchlines in jokes – but Drago makes him feel valued. Mick knows that Drago relies on him for much of the heavy work and the companionship that only two committed fossickers can understand. They are more than workmates. They are friends; the wily Bosnian, Drago, and the slower, kind-hearted Mick.

They'd had a drink to celebrate in the hotel over from the railway station in Emerald – a pretty old cream and maroon building with lovely lace iron-work and a wooden façade. It was like going back in time to the beginning of last century to look out of the pub window at the beautifully-preserved, fully-functioning station. No, they hadn't told anyone in the pub. It was just Drago and Mick and a few beers.

Maybe, they had talked too loud. But that was days ago and nobody had said anything. Naw, they hadn't told anyone about the *Balkan Blue*. But, as the policemen came back to the ambulance to check on him, Drago vowed with angry intensity, 'I call curse on stealers of my sapphire. Even French Napoleon had curse on him ven he stole perfect sapphire from my homeland. Greed. Look vot happen to him. I call *Napoleon's Curse* on the thieves.'

And the policemen each noted Drago's words in their report.

Roger

Roger Cavanagh smiles as he finishes the phone call to his *lieutenant*.

It is always a slow process to train his team to have the confidence to make bold decisions – the strategic approach of the Emperor Napoleon – the decisive strategies, the will to do what others quail from attempting, the power of the mind.

His own success is built on making the courageous moves; thriving on the edge, albeit with a persistence and an attention to the logistical detail to ensure a victorious outcome – just like Napoleon did, at his peak.

He taps the phone gently in its cradle as he savours his rise from obscure servility to discrete international power. One of the joys of power – the luxury to reflect privately. And he knew he had arrived by July, 1999. That was the confirmation of how to get where he wanted to go. And Miss Gina Robér would help him along the way.

* * * *

It was the seventeenth of July 1999 – an auspicious day as another significant piece of the domino game fell into place – viewing the coast of Monaco from a luxury yacht.

For Roger, there was a power in his presence at that destination of the rich; and it felt good. He had just received payment for his Mediterranean trading deals – a substantial amount – now safely

31

ensconced in a numbered account in Zurich. But more than that, *Ramas* had relayed pleasure with his performance.

He was about to be offered a new opportunity in the South Pacific – a few months away, at least, with lots of preparatory research to be done, but another step up the ladder.

So there was an extra swagger in his step as he descended the steps from the red-hulled *Ajaccio 3* and boarded the tender to take him to shore. His white tuxedo and gold jewellery would assure that this Englishman would be welcomed as an esteemed guest.

Only very occasionally would Roger let the ghosts of the past sneak through the cracks of his successful persona – and only when he knew he could swat them away whenever he chose. Today, he didn't mind; he felt quite inclined to indulge his sense of success from small-time London battler to the secretive power behind many boards of directors.

South London had been his inauspicious beginning. His mother waitressed during the day so that she could be with him after school. His father, a sailor, had gone back to sea and never returned to his wife or son. Vanished; just disappeared.

Underweight and lonely, the boy was picked on at school. His birth name was Arthur Gaunt. He was clever; the schoolwork wasn't hard, particularly maths, but the bullies had a field day with him ... until he worked out how to stop it.

There was big lad in the class called Bernard that the teacher was giving a hard time because his homework was never done. Arthur watched the boy suffering in silence. He knew the signs, used to such pain himself, just from different tormentors. After lessons, he sidled up to Bernard. 'He's giving you a 'ard toime.' Arthur's thick accent sounded casual. 'Oi cin help you if you want.'

Bernard had looked down. Arthur was only a little fellow. The others had used to laugh at him but Bernard couldn't be bothered.

'Oi cin help you with your homework. Get the booger off your back, oi cin. Lit me show you!' the small boy persisted.

More from curiosity than anything else, the big lad had followed Arthur.

On a bench in the school yard, he watched in amazement as Arthur wrote in Bernard's maths book, copying the writing style. 'There! Hand it in and see.'

Big Bernard was praised by the teacher. All the calculations were correct.

'What an improvement. Let that be an example to all of you, now. If Bernard can turn it around, then all of you can,' said the tactless teacher, illogically.

The deal was simple then. Bernard provided protection from the bullies and Arthur did his maths homework. It was trade.

Trading and protection were businesses that Arthur understood from that day on. To his way of thinking, protection and power went hand-in-hand; and he was on his way to becoming a very powerful person. From school to the Merchant Navy; perhaps he had inherited his father's genes. Now known as Roger Gaunt – he had consigned the Arthur persona to a sealed forgotten past. He loved the sea; the smell of salt, the moods of water and sky, the travel to places anew. He continued to grow taller and stronger, with the manual work on deck. He sensed from his first day on board that he wanted to live on ships, but not just as a deckhand.

Never again would he live in a damp dingy flat on land; not like the one in which he and his mother had suffered; with rising damp, coin-operated gas fire and cooker, the antiseptic smell of peeling gloss paint in the passageway; and the taps, brown with residue from the dirty water that they drank. Living on board a launch would be fine; but with money!

His break came when he was working on a ship, bringing cut-pine from Denmark to a Scottish sawmill. Roger's sharpness with numbers had been noticed by his employers. He sensed they were training him for higher things. The timber vessel was one which gave him the chance to see a deal from start to finish; the logistics, the bookkeeping, receipt and dispatch.

This voyage was his practical experience to watch the transaction right through. The company had told him that they wanted him to understand every part of the process; how it was streamlined to be efficient.

On the first night out from Denmark as he lay in his bunk, he heard the ship engines slow. Interested, he moved up to the deck and saw the darkened shape of a fishing vessel pulled up alongside. Crates were unloaded and two people came on board – all with no talking.

A few hours out from Scotland, again at night, the ship engines slowed and a fishing boat came alongside. The cargo of crates and two men were offloaded while the timber continued its course to port. Roger had his introduction to smuggling – goods and people.

His discreet enquiries uncovered *the game* as those in the know were calling it. His appreciation of merchant-shipping logistics made him a welcome initiate into this careful club.

He only ever knew a couple of people in a network which clearly had to be international, and he served his time. The watchwords were *silence* and *results*.

After a year of conscientious work, meticulous covert record-keeping and a growing bank account, he heard the name *Ramas* mentioned. It was the system for *the game*, and it had its own language, concealed in the jargon of business – product lines, consignments, warehousing, inventories and the like.

Roger had the aptitude, the words and the burning desire never to be poor again. He jumped at the offer to learn about the Mediterranean market. He became Roger Cavanagh, a man with no past, only a future – a star on the rise.

And the lesson of Bernard at school was ingrained in his mind. He employed protection, always – at that time in 1999, two Corsicans known as Antoine and Lucien. He liked the sense of paid employees clearing a path for him to walk. They were trusted; but never too far – power decreed that he must always hold an edge.

He was now a respected trader; legal cargo as well as less legal. He traded anything, but *people* as a commodity had been providing a discreet and handy profit; people who wanted to enter countries illegally for a better life and people whom others wanted to enter a country illegally – being traded into servitude of some form or another.

That was where Lucien and Antoine came into the picture. Roger never dealt with the physical side; the danger, the enforcement, the debt-collection, the shipment – that work went to the hired help. Roger's role was in planning; routes, paperwork, transshipment methods. He cut deals, worked on the percentages, the financial numbers. He was the brains not the brawn – and it was a very good life.

* * * *

As the tender had approached the Monte Carlo jetty, Roger was at his dapper best, resplendent in white tuxedo and with the confidence of a man whose sharp intelligence has taken him to heights far beyond the station of his birth.

Leaping onto the jetty, he saw a woman gazing out to the *Ajaccio 3*. She was slim, tanned and with long red-auburn hair. As she turned to notice Roger landing on the boardwalk, he saw the deep-blue eyes. This was a *wow* moment. Stunning.

'Bonjour,' he said cheerily.

She replied uncertainly, 'Bon joor.'

'You're English.' Roger grinned.

'Is it that obvious?' She smiled back. 'I was just looking at the ship out there. Are you off that red ship?'

'I am indeed. Would you like to see it? I can take you out there.' His polished accent bore no resemblance to the rough pronunciation of his Arthurian school days.

Beauty and impulse are powerful forces. His mother had always said that he was impetuous, although he has usually been more disciplined in recent years. 'I have a meeting just now – but in two hours? What's your name?'

'Georgina.'

'I'm Roger. In two hours then? Pack a little bag. I'll see if the captain will take us for a sail overnight.'

He left it at that. She would either be there on his return or she wouldn't. Fun. That is what they would be having today – and damn the consequences.

Alison

A week later Alison sits in the Rockhampton court listening to the police recount of the fire-alert misunderstanding. Now she watches the German Gemfields robber about to be sentenced to several months in jail.

She has already posted her original story from the Emerald courtroom. No doubt it has brought a smile to those who read the legal news and the court reports. But the joke had not been picked up by the usual sensation-seeking television or radio talk shows. There have been too many other big news items to deal with at the start of 2007 such as Britain announcing the withdrawal of its troops from Iraq, with commentators feigning renewed shock at *operational failure* in that theatre of war. The American news chat is all about the battle for the democratic nomination. Can the US be seriously contemplating a potential president who would be either the first woman or the first African-American? The lady seems to be the favoured tip if you believe the pundits. So Alison's humorous report was only read by a dedicated few.

The prosecutor advises that the German has not said much, even assisted by a proper interpreter. The robber has not named his accomplice. Maybe, he knows little and it is really he who has been the accomplice. No matter, he maintains his silent, obstinate approach. The only useful or new comment mentioned in court

37

is from the duty policeman who states that the German has said, translated into English, that *'It was for Ramas!'*

The policeman says that he doesn't know who or what *Ramas* is.

Alison notes the comment, and the fire-alert humour, for her follow-up report for the local paper. Cross the 't's and dot the 'i's. Routine – but don't miss the key facts. She learned all of that in her undergraduate years.

Her heart isn't in it – this court reporting. It gives her freedom of movement and a degree of distance from demanding editors but Alison wants to be a serious investigative journalist. She is working on an exciting project; even as she earns her *bread and butter* by reporting the routine cases of the judicial process.

That is right! Alison has an interest in the prevalence of piracy in the South Pacific. As an investigative story, it has the potential to be the one that could make her name. Even now as she finishes her reports, she is planning to head to Brisbane to speak to a man who should be able to help her.

She would be an innocent listener, observer, questioner and reporter. She doesn't want to be in the firing line of people who are involved in piracy and violence on the high seas.

Chris Legrand and Norman Brown

London. Tuesday 30 January 2007

'If it's so important, why hasn't it been reported all through the press, Chris?' the Minister queries gently, sipping the café latte, while watching his guest stare blankly at the foggy scene outside. Even on a murky Central London morning, the views through the vaulted Parliament House windows still seem to mesmerise the American *cousins*. Perhaps, there is some historical mystique about the sluggish River Thames.

The American ignores the question. His mind is on a roll. 'It just shits me, Norm, that some of our own people could be protecting those criminals.'

Chris Legrand is a US Congressman, chair of the powerful accountability committee, the challenger of ethics, the watch group which monitors the processes of government agencies in the States on behalf of the American people.

It is a measure of their close co-operation that The Right Honourable Norman Brown, Minister of the Crown, is *Norm* to his American colleague.

The Minister smiles patiently. He is well aware that there have been more than enough other big news items for the press to deal with at the start of 2007. So, why would the congressman's issue of the moment make the news anyway?

'An American citizen is peacefully cruising the Fijian seas,' Legrand pauses in his diatribe only long enough to gulp another mouthful of his requested extra-large mug of latte, 'when her boat is hi-jacked, held to ransom ... and then thirty million smakeronies are paid to these goons through the electronic airways, so fast that our law enforcers can scarcely track it, let alone stop it.' Another gulp almost polishes off the coffee. He licks his lips and glances towards the bottom of the mug, as if he would need another one before long. 'And no-one is a bit bothered. No-one is even investigating it seriously. It just gets lost! Doesn't that just shit you, Norm?' No diplomatic talk on this occasion.

'Indeed, Chris. It certainly does seem to be a bit of an anomaly that, in international waters, pirates – effectively they must be pirates – can plunder an innocent vessel, and nothing happens.'

'An anomaly! Shit, Norm!' Chris Legrand has a head of steam up. 'The United States is supposed to be the most powerful nation on Earth, and your Great Britain ruled it all in the century before – and we just let these low-lifes pick away at us. Some bastard is protecting them. I can't get a straight answer anywhere.'

'Do you mean within government?' asks the Minister. 'Are you talking about obstruction or some sophisticated protection?'

'Pree-cisely, Norm. Either or both. It's about time we got on the front foot with these bastards. Put them under a bit of heat. Smoke 'em out. What do you think? This Fijian thing is just a symptom of the much wider malaise, Norm. Maybe if we focused on solving that one, we would flush a whole lot of vermin from their burrows. What do ya think?'

'I think you are giving yourself an impossible task, old son,' replies a very measured Norman. 'Do you think that you can set up some *Eliot Ness and the Untouchables* scenario? It would have to be international or it wouldn't work.'

'Norm, I would be surprised if it was any different in your Britain – deals being struck behind closed doors, a cut in the profits for those who turn a blind eye or slow things up. But most of all, it is about bucket-loads of quiet power for someone or some people.

'And didn't Fiji used to be a Brit colony? Don't you still have lots of interests in the South Pacific? The British are still respected down there. Why couldn't we get a tight little investigation group together, in the States and here in your country? Talk to your Prime Minister. Geez, this is about national pride. These crooks are bloody laughing at us.'

The Minister raises a querulous eyebrow. 'You want me to talk to the Prime Minister to set up a little police group to investigate international crime, is that it?'

'No! No!' Chris's tone suddenly changes to calm but assertive. 'Interpol can do that. No, that's not what we want at all. This protection is very high up – maybe already infiltrating … God knows where; I shudder to think. We just need a budget and a bit of top-level political immunity from early disclosure for a small group of – I like your term, *Untouchables* – to probe and to stir, with the clout of our Congress and your Parliament behind them, so that these smug power players can't stymie us.

'I want to get at the big fish; the sly protectors of these outlaws. Thirty million dollars. Shit, Norm! That's no *Mickey Mouse* operation.' The voice is rising again. 'And hardly anyone knows about it. There are big operators around, secretive players – and the bastards are bloody laughing at us just now. And they know the victim won't complain too loudly – adverse publicity and, maybe, something more.'

'Mmm.' Norman muses. 'It certainly is a great deal of money to stay quiet about – a great deal of money, indeed. So you want something like an ethics committee investigation, eh? Perhaps? Small, elite, untouchable? With real high-level clout, as you put it?' He takes in the urging expression in the American's eyes. 'Perhaps you might have something there. Yes, indeed! You *could* just have something there. Well worth considering, old chap. It is only going to get worse the longer it runs, I suppose.' He nods, as some pieces seem to fall into place. 'The PM would like the international co-operation angle. He likes that world stage. I'll … I'll sound him out.'

'Good on ya!' roars a happy Legrand, slapping his English counterpart on the back with the familiarity of the great grizzly bear hug. He is nothing if not effusive, this passionate American. 'To the untouchable team.' They drink their toast with a smile and the last remnants of the latte.

Ben Brennan

Alison Wood approaches the man carefully. He is sitting on his own at a bar in the older part of the Brisbane city business district, just back from the river.

'Ben Brennan?' she asks quietly.

The man has greying hair starting to weave its way through the short brown. His skin is craggy; a weathered tan with deep creases that look as if water would flow in little rivulets through them. Dressed in a good-quality checked shirt, jeans and leather boots, he gives an impression of composure; like an uncle who has lived a lot of life and is tolerant that others won't understand.

'Well, you are a pretty young lass to be asking the question,' replies the man, gently ignoring the question. 'Who would you be?'

'Alison Wood, Mr Brennan. I am a freelance journalist. I am doing an investigation into some sea vessels which have gone missing over the past few years. I thought you might be able to help me.'

The man's voice is scarcely audible. 'If I were to be this Mr Brennan, what makes you think I would know anything of interest to you?'

'I'm investigating fraud and hi-jacking,' Alison whispers back with a growing melodrama in her voice. 'Ships that go missing and claim insurance; ships that are held up by pirates for ransom. I'm told that you have experience around some of these bandit gangs. Would that be right?'

'Who would have told you that?' His dismissive look belies a gentleness in his tone.

She responds tauntingly. 'A London insurance investigator who told me your quiet network exposed the loss of a freighter as fraud, not the vagaries of the weather as claimed.'

'I think you have the wrong man, lady.' The greying man is looking at his beer glass. 'I'm no detective. I'm just an old merchant seaman. Retired.'

'Mr Brennan, close to sixty percent of all piracy in the world over the last twenty years has been in the South East Asian region,' she says. 'I'm trying to help chip away at those who operate by stealth and surprise.' She is persistent; earnest.

'It sounds like you are trying to get yourself killed,' the man replies, deadpan. 'How do you make your living just now?'

'The court reporting circuit.' She gives a downcast smile, as if looking for guidance and support.

'My advice is to keep reporting on the court circuit,' says the man flatly, 'and stay away from this sort of stuff – this piracy, as you call it. There is nothing glamorous in that.'

'I will follow up my story whether or not you help me.' The quiet vehemence in her tone causes only the slightest reaction in the old seaman – a subtle change in the expression in the eyes, a flicker of doubt, a glance in her direction. 'I was told you would understand what it means to someone like me, *particularly like me*. That's why.'

The peppery-haired sailor looks at her for several more long seconds. He is seeing her soft brown hair, her unblemished complexion, her slim almost fragile frame and he thinks of the danger that inhabits the world that she wants to enter.

'My advice is to go back to the court circuit,' he says calmly. 'Remember that advice!'

Then – after some pause for thought and another long look into her youthful silent pleading eyes; just a hint of a long-remembered expression – he says, 'If you must earn your spurs on this topic, look for a ship called the *Lerna*. It will be docking in Cairns in late February. The owner is Roger Cavanagh.'

'Thank you, Mr Brennan. I won't forget this.' There was quiet gratitude in her voice.

'I *want* you to forget this. This is foolishness. You will be in danger.' He writes a number on a yellow Post-it note and passes it to her.

'If you find out something you think I should know about, text this number. Don't ring it. No-one will ever answer – just text.'

Alison looks at the number with no name attached, and nods her thanks.

'Give me your mobile number,' says the man.

She gives him her business card with the numbers attached.

'And if I want to speak to you?' she asks.

'Ring the number on the back,' he says dryly.

She turns the sticker over, to reveal a blank sheet. 'But there is no number on the back!' Her gaze looks for clarification.

'Exactly,' is the only explanation. 'Be careful,' says Brennan. 'You are about to swim with the sharks – and they bite. *Go back to the court circuit* is my advice.'

'Thanks,' says Alison, appreciating his concern for her. 'Can I buy you a drink?'

'I don't drink,' he says and she looks at the glass of beer in front of him.

The pennies are starting to drop into place. She had heard the word that Ben Brennan could be found in this bar at this time. He was there on this day in some weeks. People came up and spoke quietly to him and then left again.

She takes her leave with a genuine 'Thank you!'

He scarcely responds.

The thought of this old seadog doing this clandestine work raises a slight smile at the edge of her mouth. He gives the impression of being a grump but he is more like a caring uncle. *Well, you would have to be grumpy to stay in this business of intrigue and corruption,* she thinks.

She looks back to the bar and a scruffy man has sidled up to him, speaks very quietly and then sidles off again.

Brennan sits inscrutable, resting his arms on the bar surface, appearing to drink but nothing passes his lips.

Court humour

Canberra, Friday 2 February 2007

'Have you seen this, sir?' Sergeant Bill Jones chortles to his Australian Federal Police Superintendent, Jeff Fowler.

One of the sergeant's daily tasks is to check the scanning reports of all the daily news outlets in Australia, checking for anything which might flag a threat to national security.

Jeff Fowler has a special interest. Based in Canberra, he has an important anti-terrorism role in the law enforcement of Australasia; a key liaison with the Australian Security and Intelligence Organisation, ASIO, as well as with overseas Intelligence and police agencies.

'What is it?'

'It's a court report on an incident in Emerald in Central Queensland,' Jones replies. 'It appears that a prospector was robbed of a big sapphire on the Gemfields but the emergency services thought he said, *It's a fire* when he actually said *It's a sapphire*, with a strong Balkan accent.'

Fowler smiles tolerantly. He needs humour. His world is too often one of darkness.

'But it gets worse. The robber was apparently a German and they didn't have an interpreter in the Emerald court. So a slow-witted member of the public volunteered to interpret for the magistrate. He thought he was speaking correct German when he said to the accused, *Vot isst your name?*'

The two policemen burst into laughter – the mental image of this happening in a serious courtroom.

'Bloopers of the highest quality.' The superintendent grins. 'Is there anything in it for us beyond the laughs?'

'Not really. A couple of queries I suppose; when it reached the Rockhampton court, the German robber apparently said that it was stolen for *Ramas*. No-one seems to know what that means. It sounds a bit Indian to me. Anyway, it's apparently the motive for stealing an expensive sapphire.'

'Let me know if that name emerges again. Was there another thing?'

'Yes, the report says that the Balkan man invoked *Napoleon's Curse*. Apparently, Napoleon was cursed for stealing sapphires.'

'Oh, that'd be right, Bill.' Fowler gives a cynical shake of the head. 'And, no doubt, he eventually died because of it.'

'Well, he did lose a battle or two, and then get exiled on an Atlantic island.'

'Okay. You believe what you choose.' He pauses as they both grin again. 'Oh, anything else on that yacht that was hi-jacked off Fiji a few weeks back? The one the maritime police flagged for us.'

'The singer's yacht with the two security guards killed? No, nothing significant, as yet. The Fijians have forwarded statements but they lead nowhere. We are checking our sources – mainly waiting for *Nemesis* and Ben Brennan to get back to me. See if they have any whispers. But he seems to have gone to ground. He's often out of contact in the islands. Why? Has something happened?'

'Just a question from above. Someone wants to know of progress, if any.'

'Mmm. Wouldn't have anything to do with a wealthy pop-star being on board?' The sergeant shrugs at the lack of response to his question. 'Okay, I'll check back into the file and follow it up for you, Boss. Early January, wasn't it? *Sea Spray 2*, from memory. Wouldn't mind being in Fiji in January.'

He stretches back for the manilla folder from the cabinet, while logging into the filing system … for January 2007.

Jeff Fowler and Ben Brennan

Canberra, Australia. Thursday 8 February 2007

'Have you ever heard of *Napoleon's Curse?*' Jeff Fowler, Superintendent with the Australian Federal Police speaks quietly into the phone. 'Something to do with stealing a sapphire … I'm guessing …?'

'Who mentioned the curse?' Ben Brennan replies.

'My sergeant picked it up. It was quoted in a Central Queensland newspaper report. It was a story about a sapphire stolen from a prospector out on the Gemfields, beyond Emerald.'

'Maybe. Maybe I have. If it's what I'm thinking. But that's not a short story, Jeff. Too long for this conversation.'

'The short version, then?'

'Okay. The quick version is that Napoleon Bonaparte was a plunderer wherever his armies conquered. The Italians called him *Il Grande Ladro*, The Great Thief. He was a collector of art, sculpture and jewellery. Stealing cultural valuables in war didn't start with the Nazis; and it continues to this day, whether in war or not.'

'So, the curse, Ben?' Fowler's voice is quietly encouraging.

'Yes. Alright. Maybe I have a connection. Patience. A couple of years ago, I was trying to identify a private collector, that's a collector of art valuables; but this one also deals in human misery … not sure where he or she lives … but I'm pretty sure I would have made one-way contact. As part of that process, I was researching any hoarders of looted art and Napoleon's name came up. The sapphire is what makes me think of him, just now. He was famous for his love of those blue gems. His engagement ring to Josephine was a sapphire and the Ruspoli Sapphire – 135 carats of it – was part of his crown jewels. And, yes, there was the story of a curse – a Romany put the hex on him; at his Italian coronation, I believe. He was to lose all his power and be banished from humanity.'

'Why?'

'Because his troops stole a sapphire belonging to the Romany family. The jewel had been given to them by some Ottoman Sultan, to keep the family in good health, in recognition for a special service – and old Boney nicked it. Not very nice. And he didn't give it back, either. He ended up on Saint Helena in the middle of the Atlantic. And he died there; so maybe the curse worked.'

'Ben Brennan, surely a man of your experience doesn't believe in gypsy curses?'

'You asked if I'd heard of it. That's all. Mind you I wouldn't mind putting a few curses on some of the low-lifes we are tracking. Roger Cavanagh, for one.'

PART THREE

Steve

Fiji. Wednesday 10 January 2007

I am alive.

The light is slowly bringing shape to the images around me. Sharp bleached coral jabs at my skin through my wet trousers and shirt. I can hear the chatter of voices but my unresponsive limbs won't move.

The right side of my head aches terribly. Through my left eye, I can just see palm trees and part of the lagoon. The tide has gone out. The wind has dropped. How did I get there? How did I get through the reef?

Strong hands lift me like a baby. I hear a familiar, *Bula* – the Fijian welcome greeting – and then, someone is tending my weak and bashed body.

Fiji. Tuesday 16 January 2007

I remember the doctor saying it appears that a bullet has ploughed a furrow along the edge of my skull, just above the right ear.

The medical staff patched up my many coral scratches but some angel must have guarded me on that night because the chop had apparently floated me over the outer reef at high tide. A few minutes difference either way and there would have been insufficient water – I would've been sliced as cheese in a grater.

'You were obviously meant to survive.' The doctor had laughed; the expression lighting up his Indian features.

* * * *

The realities have now sunk in. I had been washed unconscious onto an exclusive island resort. There are few guests. Most had left a week before, to avoid the squalls, expecting that they might be stranded. Fijian workers had found me on the beach and brought me to the medical *bure*.

My full eyesight is returning as my strong constitution starts to mend my body.

The doctor – one of the few Indian-Fijian people on this little island – produces my sodden wallet. 'It was in your hip pocket in the passage to shore and now, sadly, it is a wad of congealed paper and some credit cards.'

It is the only identification I have, apart from my name on the flotation jacket – Ingrid's nice touch to personalise things. My passport and other documents had been on board.

The doctor only knows what I have told him – I was a security guard on board a yacht and I must have fallen overboard. I haven't identified the *Sea Spray* but he is a clever doctor. He can add up the signs.

'Don't rush to the mainland, Steve.' His smile is now a frown. 'Without knowing any details, a bullet wound on a man who has been a security guard – just washed up on a shore – will raise questions.'

I look at him, querying.

'Fiji is under military rule. Without a passport, you could be embroiled in bureaucratic and diplomatic red-tape for weeks or months.'

I get it. 'What do you suggest?'

'I could call in a favour to let you hitch passage on a ship called the *Lerna* which will berth off the island in a few days. The owner is a Mr Roger Cavanagh,' the doctor says. 'A nice man – English, I think. Very wealthy. I have treated him in the past. I look on him as my friend. He will take care of you well, I'm sure.'

It seems like good advice – much better than the alternative.

* * * *

And now the beautiful Lani continues to massage my body back to health. I won't mind at all if the *Lerna* takes many days to arrive. I can handle this pampering; happy smiling people; luscious fruit; healthy walks along the beach and smiling aromatic massages.

Could Nirvana be any better than this?

Roger

Malaysia. 17 January 2007

'Naleen, how good to hear your voice again, even if it is only over the telephone and not in person.' Roger's friendliness oozes from every syllable. 'How is Fiji treating my favourite doctor?'

'I am well, Roger. And how is my special patient? No recurrences of your bad experience here, I trust,' the Fijian doctor replies. He is flattered that Roger Cavanagh chooses to call him by his first name, Naleen, rather than an impersonal title like *Doctor.*

'I have been as good as gold, Naleen. You saved my life that day. No doubt about it. Thanks for asking. I got the message that you wanted to speak with me. Can I help you with something?'

'Yes Roger, I believe so. A strange request, perhaps. An Australian, I think, needs your help. He washed up on the shores of our little island last week. He tells me that he fell overboard. I have been nursing him back to health, just as I did for you.'

'What does he need?'

'He has no passport, only a saturated wallet with credit cards. And Roger, he has a bullet scar above his ear. He tells me he was a security guard on a yacht when they were attacked near our island, over a week ago. Pirates, I suppose. He is very vague about the incident – a bullet creasing the head can do that sometimes. Anyway, if he goes to the main island, he will get caught up in all the paperwork. I thought the *Lerna* might take him through to your next port and he could get a passport there, with less fuss. He seems like a man worth helping, if you understand me.'

'Mmm,' says Roger. 'I'm in Malaysia at present but the ship, as you realise, is near Fiji. I won't join it until Noumea but I'll speak with Peter Carter. What's this Australian's name? I'll get a check run on him. I wouldn't want to get involved in anything *too* illegal, you know.' His tone smiles with a polished flippancy. 'If anyone else had asked, Naleen, you know that the answer would have been a straight, *No!* But for you, my good friend, I'll see what we can do.'

'Thank you very much, Roger. I am most flattered. Steven Flynn is his name. He seems a bit lost – the effect of the attack and the coral as he washed over onto the beach. I really think he is alright. He doesn't seem *illegal* to my eyes – more just a shipwrecked man needing help.'

'Naleen, Peter will be in touch. Stay well my friend.'

* * * *

'Peter,' says Roger over the scrambled line to the *Lerna*, 'The Fijian doctor, Naleen, who saved my life from the marine sting there; he wants me to take an Australian shipwrecked man off his resort island and through to Noumea.'

'Is that what you want to happen, Roger?' asks Peter Carter suspiciously. 'Who *is* this man?'

'That's the catch, as well.' A suspenseful pause. 'The security guard from the *Sea Spray 2*, I would guess, apparently wounded by a bullet and washed up on Naleen's island,' comes Roger's impassive words.

'Jeeesus! You want me to take the security guard from the *Sea Spray* onto *our* ship and look after him?' Peter Carter's stunned tone precedes his short silence. 'Does he know about us? He's probably a plant.'

'Perhaps … I'm sure you will watch him.'

Roger is smiling quietly as he pictures the expression on his associate's face, thousands of kilometres away. He has had the advantage of time to think the problem through. Peter, however, is hearing it for the first time.

'Think on this though, Peter. He would have been on that yacht long before we had any interest in it. It would be hard for a plant to read my mind now, wouldn't it? More likely he actually *is* a wounded, displaced Aussie in need of assistance – and won't that get us some persuasive brownie points for future leverage? I owe Naleen, Peter. Never forget the people we owe. It always works to our advantage. Let's just take it at face value. Help this man Steven Flynn with his passport; usual process, call in an Australian favour. We'll get him on his way – and watch him, Peter.'

The *Lerna* and Steve

I am impressed. Even at anchor out in deep water, the *Lerna* makes an impact. Her sixty metres of deep-blue hull sparkles on the tropical swell. The radar and satellite dishes above the bridge give the appearance of almost military sophistication. Even the gem-blue nine-metre tender looks luxurious as it negotiates its way over the glittering lagoon to the jetty.

I am ready; patiently waiting in the shade with Dr Naleen, of the unpronounceable surname. The doctor has informed me that Mr Cavanagh is not on board in Fiji but *his trusted representative*, Mr Peter Carter, will make me very welcome.

A small crew come ashore and head off to collect supplies for the next stage of their voyage through to Noumea. Two men separate from the group and head for the *bure* where the doctor and I wait.

A welcoming *Bula* and I listen to the doctor giving the visitors his brief assessment of how he had found the *shipwrecked* Australian.

Peter Carter has to have been a military man. It is in his bearing, his walk, his gestures. Officer or a sergeant-major? British Army?

It is not the clothes, because they are casually appropriate for island cruising. It is more the way he carries himself; the strut.

'Mr Flynn?' says Carter, without expecting a response. 'The good doctor speaks highly of you. You have conducted yourself well since he found you. So, I understand that you no longer have a passport and you need passage away from Fiji.'

I feel like I am being reprimanded by the headmaster, so I smile politely and say nothing.

'We always like to stay within the law,' continues Carter. 'Good relations with all the islands are very important to us.'

I give him another weak smile. There doesn't seem to be an opportunity for me to speak. Not a sergeant-major – definitely an officer.

'We are heading through to New Caledonia.' Carter talks on like a BBC announcer. 'We will apply for your passport en route so that Australian officials can meet you in Noumea. Then, hopefully, everything will be in place for you from there on. Is that alright, old boy?'

'Thanks, mate.' I make sure that I am sounding as ocker Aussie as possible. 'Really good of you all. Appreciate it. Happy to work my passage, if you like.'

'Oh? And what can you do on ship?'

Keen to keep some powder dry for the future, I suggest, 'Deck hand? Cook? I'm a handy cook.'

'We have a chef on board but no doubt he can manage with an extra assistant.' Pompous bastard. He pauses, and then continues his briefing.

'Our owner, Mr Cavanagh, and his guests are not with us on this stretch. They will join us in Noumea. So it will be light duties for you. Help you recover from your ordeal, what?'

'Yes.' The less said the better. He is the sort of man you would want to snot but he also looks as if he can handle himself, for an older bloke.

Carter's companion is standing behind him. He hasn't said a word, nor has his facial expression changed. And he is big, as in rugby second-row big.

I extend my hand. 'G'day, I'm Steve.'

The man looks surprised. 'Len'. The handshake is not a bone-crusher but it exudes power. The face hardly changes. The skin seems very tight across his cheeks, preventing the mouth from opening very far. A car accident maybe; plastic surgery on many small nicks?

No more is said.

I board the tender and wave *Bula* to the Fijians under the trees. Even from a distance, I can see Lani's smile. I will miss her soft-handed ministrations.

The *Lerna* is a big boat; really long and at least ten metres across the beam. Len shows me to a small single crew-cabin to drop my solitary soft bag. Then he gives me the censored tour.

'Seventeen crew but currently operating well with only thirteen.' His restricted mouth gives a squeaky whispering sound with, what I'm guessing, is a Cockney accent. 'And it can handle an additional ten guests, not including Mr Cavanagh's suite of rooms.'

It seems superfluous for me to say anything, so I don't.

'You don't go near there.' The unsmiling Len has an edge to his voice. I am getting the distinct impression that I am not a really welcome addition to the ship. Is it me or is this just not a happy crew? To the bridge, for more introductions.

The skipper, Captain Rodriguez, is dressed immaculately in a pressed white uniform with gold epaulettes and designer-cut shorts. Long white socks and fashion white shoes complete the sartorial effect. As the rest of the crew appear, they are similarly uniformed, just with different insignias of office on their shoulders.

Some laundry bill. Say nothing. No point in encouraging ideas for *light duties* or exciting the serious Len.

The tour continues with the gym, sundeck, jacuzzi, wide screen televisions everywhere, an onyx bar in an entertainment room. What would my mother have thought if she could see me here? All her life she had scrimped to provide. This is bizarre.

I had thought the *Sea Spray* was luxury – but not like this.

* * * *

The ship sails away from the island within the hour and builds up easily to a cruising speed of thirteen knots. The knife-edge bow cuts gracefully through the gentle swell as I listen to the chef, Marcel.

Clearly, I will be learning some new dishes – and some new words. Marcel is a chef with a short temper. He hasn't asked for an assistant. He already has access to crew members to do his bidding with menial culinary tasks. He has no intentions of being a tutor to an apprentice. I will be expected to pull my weight.

It is going to be an interesting trip.

The passport application

I have been at sea for a day. My kitchen chores are complete – but there really is very little to do. I have just settled in my cabin as I hear the quiet but measured tread of what I assume is Peter Carter's approach. You can take the man out of the military but you can't take the military out of the man.

'Talk? Let's try the sundeck,' Carter suggests.

Is this just a casual chat? There is always an agenda. The deck has several sun loungers, a spa/jacuzzi and a few plastic chairs round a table. He indicates that we should sit at the table, with just a flick of his hand. I'm obedient – watchful, but obedient.

'The doctor told me you'd been running security on a yacht. Glanced by a bullet? Is that right?' Carter opens. Nothing like cutting to the quick. His superior sneer speaks volumes. He doesn't believe the story but there is more to it than that.

'Yes.' I lift my hair to reveal the bullet's track. 'It was at night. We had no warning. I'm not sure why we didn't detect them. They came up on my partner's side. I think he bought it. I got a couple away but a shot knocked me overboard. I ended up floating over the reef and onto the beach. Some locals found me in the morning.'

'Mmm. And you didn't see them coming?' Carter pauses. He is willing me to talk. Piss off – so predictable. I shrug.

When he doesn't get a verbal response, he follows with, 'Take a ship like the *Lerna*. How would you protect it against an attack – any type of attack?'

I need a passport and a lift to Noumea so I try not to be too much of a smartass. Besides, what else is there to do? It is a sunny day on a luxury ship. I'm fairly bored. Painful though he is I humour him.

'You have electronic surveillance.' I start in my most polite Army briefing mode. 'I assume you have radar, sonar. Computer chatter over the networks. You should see an attacker electronically from a long way away; side-on, above or below. That's your first line of defence.

'Then you have visual surveillance – watching for anyone trying to get under the electronic detection. That works even at night with infra-red glasses. So, an attacker would have to jam the electronics to get in close, undetected. That's not easy without setting off all sorts of alarms. So the only other way is to by-pass the detection systems. There aren't many ways to do that, are there?' I smile at him, with just a hint of *up yours*.

'No!' he agrees. 'So how would someone board this ship, avoiding its detectors?' He is watching me intently.

'You haven't shown me your systems, but the easiest way would be as a trusted member of the crew,' I suggest with a grin. You can't take the bastard seriously.

'Precisely, old chap.' He has the look of a schoolmaster who's been given the correct answer. 'Which brings me to you? Here am I in charge of Mr Cavanagh's super-sophisticated security system when suddenly I am asked by his old Fijian doctor friend to take on board a castaway from another ship – an Australian castaway at that – and the boss agrees. It must be some favour that the boss feels he owes the Indian doctor, eh?' His nostrils flare with obvious distaste.

I try not to smirk. He is so full of himself – such a hangover from a colonial age with his superior attitudes. Australian and Indian indeed.

'Now I don't know this castaway,' he continues, 'except that he looks ex-Army, allegedly ran security on a vessel taken over by

64

pirates. Why could you not be a dangerous person, on board to by-pass my security system?'

His weak smile hints at the underlying danger. He is not a fool.

'Do you have something to hide?' I ask, probably too cheekily.

Carter forces a slow smile. It doesn't extend to his eyes. 'Touché.' He looks at me for a few long seconds, as if considering his words. What is he thinking? A cocky Australian? A threat? He is looking at my recent bullet scar; easily visible even as the straggly hair slowly grows to obscure its path.

'Okay. Let's just take you at face value … for the moment.' His attitude seems to change like the flick of a switch − straight into business mode. But I am wary. 'We need to get your application in for a passport. Come down to the office and we will get the process moving.'

* * * *

The office is good. Very good. A bank of multiple monitors fill one wall. They are close fitting. I'm guessing that the operator could flick to many closed circuit shots, using the monitors as independent screens. Or, they could combine to show a huge whole screen image.

Lots of different wavelength radio gear. You could talk to the moon with this little lot. And neat. Everything with a place. Carter's wave shows off the implied sophistication of his security system.

* * * *

Linked through to the Australian Department of Foreign Affairs and Trade, he speaks to a senior official in Canberra. The Australians seem to know him. The wheels of bureaucracy move astonishingly quickly as he flicks through computer screens.

I enter the required information on-line, as instructed, and then Carter tells me that officials from the consulate-general will meet me on arrival in Noumea to finalise my passport.

That is it. Slick. Very slick!

Then, presumably, Carter will piss me off the boat ... with another weak smile.

But I can't fail to be impressed at how effective Carter has been in making this happen. How wise my smiling Indian-Fijian doctor has been to advise me not to get tied up in the Fijian bureaucracy.

There is one part of the ship's office which seems out of place. It is an oil painting on the wall – a Degas by the signature, not a print; the brush strokes are clearly obvious – bright, impressionistic, clearly French.

It is undoubtedly very attractive and not usual, in my experience, to find in a ship's office.

'It's a copy? Right?' I ask.

'Oh no!' replies Carter, with complete seriousness – almost a reverence in his tone. 'Mr Cavanagh is a collector. He likes to acquire beautiful things. That is a real Edgar Degas.'

'Amazing,' is all that I can manage.

Roger and Gina

Noumea, Sunday 4 February 2007

The green tree-cloaked mountains of New Caledonia are an impressive sight after days of flat ocean.

I marvel at Isle of Pines as the *Lerna* rounds the island on the south of *Nouvelle Caledonie* and heads smoothly up the west coast to its mooring in the *Baie de la Moselle*, beside the capital, Noumea.

The French-speaking Customs officials come on board. They are jovial – greeting old acquaintances. Clearly the ship's company are valued visitors to *Nouvelle Caledonie*. The paperwork formalities are completed quickly. I am mentioned to the officials and they say, in their heavily-accented English, that Australian consulate people will be visiting soon.

I watch the tender go ashore and, with it, a sense of urgency can be felt on board. If anything, the ironed creases in the crew's uniform are even more pronounced.

Surely, my passport hasn't produced that effect?

The non-smiling Len stands close to me.

'Somebody important arriving?' I ask.

With an almost dismissive sneer, he replies, 'Mr Cavanagh and Miss Gina, for your information.' There is a tone of admiration in Len's voice and so I realise that the sneer is for me while the adulation is for the *about to arrive* owner of the ship, with his guest.

I add chirpily. 'What? Has he been living here?' pointing to the red scars on the green mountain slopes. These bastards are up themselves.

New Caledonia is an important nickel mining island and the freighters, covered in their red dust, sail from the neighbouring *baie*. New Caledonia has done well to mask the unfettered mine processing of previous generations. Most of the dirty industrial plants are shielded from the tourist areas with their water sports and French culture – but, from the *baie* where the *Lerna* is moored, the industrial area is quite obvious.

I know it is a low shot but I am getting tired of the put-downs.

'Mr Cavanagh and Miss Gina have just flown in from Singapore,' Len replies disdainfully.

* * * *

The tender draws up alongside the ship and there emerges a laughing blond-haired man – not tall, glowing with health even if a bit on the well-fed side – in a blue silk shirt over cream knee-length slacks. The casual brown shoes look Italian to me and match his belt, only visible at the buckle. The thick gold chain as a necklace is clearly very expensive.

His confident presence appears to have cast a charismatic spell over all the crew. They look genuinely delighted to see him, and it seems to be mutual. Two steps behind the man, who is presumably Mr Roger Cavanagh, there emerges a striking woman.

She is tallish, about my height in her shoes; slim, almost statuesque. She has a brown-red shade of hair, falling to her shoulders. A silk dress in turquoise, orange and yellow tones sets off her consistent golden-olive tan. The shoes are definitely Italian – I had an Army mate who always wore Italian shoes on leave. I know the look. The lady's shoes have a low heel in orange and yellow material, with something sparkling.

Eye-catching – presumably, this is Miss Gina.

When her sunglasses are removed, she reveals haunting blue eyes.

She is a stunning woman as she meets the crew in the way royalty might greet them; not much of a smile – more an imperious expectation of acknowledgement.

The entourage of servants carries suitcases up to Mr Cavanagh's private suite. I am not introduced. The emperor has arrived. All hail to the emperor!

The ship is certainly busy now. The word comes from Marcel for me to get to the galley. There is kitchen work to be done now.

I have to give it to Marcel. He is a marvellous chef. Three courses are prepared and served upstairs, with quality and care brimming on each dish. The choice of wines is sent up, selected; and the unselected bottles are returned on their rejection to the chilled wine cellar below.

* * * *

After the bustle of the regal arrival, it might seem like a non-event, for everyone, but me, that the officials from the Australian consulate-general have arrived on board – on a Sunday too.

We meet in a small plush meeting room near the gangway.

They have a passport for me. Some routine forms. They ask how I came to be in the water and separated from my passport. I am vague and non-committal and the officials don't seem to mind. They have asked their questions. The procedure is complete; all very routine. Impressive. Smooth process.

Either Mr Carter or Mr Cavanagh must carry some clout in the corridors of power in Canberra. My money would be on the latter.

Miss Gina

'Come with me. Mr Cavanagh would like to meet you.'

Len is almost civil as he knocks on the cabin door. Is that a smile on his frozen face? He makes quite a fair impersonation of a butler.

I have been quietly sitting in my cabin in the crew's quarters, studying a map of Noumea, matching the features I can see through the porthole. Now I fall in behind the slow-march of the butler, Len. There has been value in all those years of square-bashing, after all. Anyway, I am about to get my imperial audience. I am curious to meet this man who has offered me the lifeline out of Fiji.

Roger Cavanagh greets me with a warm handshake and a cheery smile in the plush stateroom. He asks after *the good doctor* in Fiji and enquires after my health from my ordeal. He seems genuinely interested in my work on board the yacht. It is almost as if he is pleased to meet me. What a surprising contrast to the suspicious condescending treatment dished out by his hired help on the voyage over.

Peter Carter and Len stand to one side looking distinctly uncomfortable at the apparent warmth of my welcome from their boss.

I watch their eyes widen when Mr Cavanagh says, 'Steve, a task for you, if you want it?' He looks at me for a few seconds as I try to guess his thinking. 'I have some guests coming shortly for an important meeting. I want you to take Gina ashore. Look after her. Take her shopping, you know. Okay?'

What do you say? I am stunned. What is this all about? He has only just met me.

I look again at the astonished expressions on his assistants' faces and decide immediately. Up yours, bully boys. 'Yes, Mr Cavanagh.'

'Oh, you haven't met Gina. Peter, please ask Gina to come in. Thanks.' And Carter went dutifully to collect Miss Gina from her rooms.

* * * *

She arrives in a plain grey silk dress with grey low-heeled shoes. The plainness of the dress sets off her model-like beauty. She is eye-catching. I look again at the blue eyes, golden-olive tan and red-brown hair. Maybe too much make-up for my taste. But then ... what has my taste got to do with it?

Cavanagh makes the introductions. 'Gina, Steve Flynn. Steve, Miss Gina Robér.' He pronounces the surname with the accent on the second syllable.

Gina gives me a polite smile.

'Gina, I have asked Steve to take you ashore and to look after you for a couple of hours. I have a meeting.'

Miss Gina looks surprised, disappointed and annoyed, within seconds. Perhaps, she had wanted a say in the matter or perhaps she doesn't like the look of me. No matter, she doesn't argue.

The saddened expression morphs smoothly into another polite smile. She simply looks at me and says, 'Five minutes.' Then she says to Cavanagh, 'Have a nice meeting, Darling,' and she returns to her rooms, without the escort.

Things start getting busy and I am effectively but politely dismissed back to my room to grab my wallet and hat.

On the way, I am accompanied by Peter Carter. He is not quite the domineering officer now that the emperor has returned. Indeed, he looks as if his nose is distinctly out of joint. Perhaps escorting Miss Gina has been Peter's role on previous occasions. Maybe, I

71

have unwittingly stepped on a sensitive toe – like entering the officers' mess uninvited. That wouldn't rest well with Carter's need for order, protocol and superiority.

'Some advice, Steve,' he says quietly. Is that a little menace in his tone? 'Miss Gina is the boss's lady. Make no mistakes – no bloody mistakes at all.' His piercing look is one of *don't argue*. 'Your role is only to protect her. Anything more and you will be walking with a limp for the rest of your days.'

I give him my best imitation of how I imagine an English officer might smile. 'My dear Mr Carter.' I suddenly enjoy affecting his posh accent. 'My intentions are entirely honourable. Now if you don't mind, old chap, the lady awaits.'

I impassively absorb his dark look. I don't mind one bit. His uppity dismissive manner has been tolerated for the whole voyage from Fiji. Now that my passport has been delivered, some of my old jovial confidence is back too; and I seem to be in some sort of favour with the boss – just as effective as the old Aussie single finger gesture, as I leave him with a smile.

* * * *

The tender takes Gina and me to shore. The crew are clearly waiting to ferry some guests over to the ship for *the meeting*. I can't see who that might be.

Gina doesn't wait. She takes off up the street. Shopping must be beckoning. But it is Sunday.

I catch up and say, 'Hello. We are supposed to stay together.'

She stops and turns to look at my cheery smile. Her look, however, suggests that I am either a very bad smell or that I've just crawled out from the primordial slime.

'I don't think so,' she says, in a tone expecting to be obeyed.

I have been in the personal protection business for some time, and before that in hard situations as a frontline soldier. This is not the first time that someone has tried to dismiss me without having the authority or the ability to do so.

'I know so,' I say, continuing to give her my patient painted-on expression – tolerant and polite. 'My instructions are to stay with you at all times, to look after you, to protect you.'

'And who is protecting me from you?' she snaps back. 'Who needs you? Who asked for you?' But she is rattled. She had expected to be able to just walk away from the hired help.

She tries again and starts walking off. I catch up and walk beside her. 'Do you know where you are going?' I ask casually. 'Have you been here before?'

She keeps walking without a word.

'Well, since you haven't been here before, I will keep you informed of the sights from my trusty guide map.' I chirp away gaily. 'You will soon approach the *Place des Cocotiers* – the place of the coconuts. There's a note here to say that many of the coconut trees have had to be cut down to stop the nuts falling on people's heads. Ah, what is the world coming to? I think I'll sue. I think I'll sue you!' I laugh frivolously.

She stops and looks at me. 'Are you going to carry on that guidebook prattle all the way along these streets?'

'Only until you stop.' Two can play her game. 'And show me the respect that you should to a fellow traveller who has done you no harm – and might even do you some good.'

'What did you say your name was?' She suddenly looks bemused. 'Steve.'

'Right, Steve,' she says with a forced patience. 'Let's start again. We have a couple of hours to spend in this place. Where would *you* like to go?'

'Well, there'll be few open shops on a Sunday. We could go to see the cathedral. Take in the local culture? What would *you* like to do?'

She gasps an exasperated sigh.

'Let's find a street café and sit down for a cup of coffee,' she says surprisingly.

* * * *

73

We settle at a café and I order in my schoolboy French. I had waited for Miss Robér to speak in fluent French but she just sits quietly, distracted in some way.

We watch the throng of people walking along the street. The colourful patterned dresses of the women – red prints of ocean creatures on white cotton; blue prints; yellow prints. Head scarves in more colourful designs – contrasting happily with the dark faces and toothy smiles. And the language – French; almost no English.

The coffees arrive. She makes no effort to pay and so I pay with the limited money my generous doctor had given me back on Fiji. *You'll need some New Caledonian francs for when you arrive,* he had said with a knowing wink. What had he known?

'I never carry money,' she says casually.

This is one lady headed for a fall. We sit quietly for a while longer, just watching.

Gina eventually says, 'Who *are* you? I mean, I know you are *Steve* but *why* are you on the *Lerna?*'

'How much do you want to know?' What should I say to a woman like this? 'I lost my passport overboard near a Fijian island. Given the political situation in Fiji, I didn't want to spend these next months trying to deal with government bureaucracies to get a new one. I got the chance to join this ship on my way back to Australia. I had my passport replaced today. Okay?'

'No, not okay! I don't understand how you could suddenly *join this ship* as you put it when I can't even leave the ship without a guard. So who *are* you?'

'I told you,' I repeat. 'A doctor on the island must be a friend of your Mr Cavanagh because he made a phone call and here I am.'

Gina doesn't speak. She just takes in the information.

'How will we know to return?' I ask. 'Do you have a mobile?'

She nods. 'Peter will ring when the tender is ready.'

'What does Peter do in the scheme of things? He is very protective.'

She gives a wan grin. 'He is Roger's executive officer.' She sighs. 'Peter is the organiser. He books hotels, plans itineraries, ensures

74

that the supplies are ordered. He signs for everything. I never buy anything. I have no money. Peter signs for everything.'

I listen quietly. It sounds almost like a plaintive cry for help. Or could it just be clever manipulation by a lady who is accustomed to attention?

I am immune. I am the hired protection. I don't ever get emotionally involved with people who are my clients, in any form. It just takes a little discipline, no matter what they look like or how they behave.

'What about Len?'

'Laughing Len,' she says with almost a grin which quickly fades to a faint wail. She looks straight at me, her blue eyes searching my face. 'Len is the enforcer, the tough guy. He can't smile. Some damage to the nerves in his face, years ago. He is cruel and unpredictable. Sometimes you would swear that he wouldn't hurt a fly and then on other occasions he is just pure nasty.'

A big admission; too much information. We need a subject change.

'I noticed a Degas painting in the office when we were sailing over here. That is quite a purchase?'

She looks at me again. Clearly puzzled. She doesn't know how to take me. I find her pretty – in a cosmetic rather than a warm way. She doesn't radiate warmth. It is her manner, not her appearance – like a distant cat-walk model.

'Roger is a collector. He has lots of valuable things. He is a compulsive gatherer of things he likes. He needs to possess them, to own them.'

Peter had said something similar. A collector.

'Who are *you*, Gina?' Who is the lady I am accompanying?

'Me?' She laughs as a gasp; clearly surprised to have been asked. 'I don't really know who I am any more.'

'Aren't you Gina Robér?' I smile. 'You must have a past to have got to this point in life.'

'A past,' she says vacantly. She seems to be drifting away with her thoughts. I just watch her quietly. We sip the last of our coffees.

'Come,' she says suddenly. 'Take me for a walk round the bay – along the boardwalk. Come on. I want to walk.'

She crooks her arm in mine. We walk steadily in the sunshine, looking at the boats in the marina and moored out in the *baie*. Then looking back inland, there are the old French colonial buildings – large stone structures with red roofs, interspersed with colourful modern designs. It has the air of life and progress about it.

The aloofness seems to leach away from her as we walk on. She laughs from time to time – at a seagull swooping for a scrap; or at a near-accident as the car drivers whizz too quickly; or at dark-skinned children in gaily coloured clothes laughing and jumping at play.

'I haven't walked like this for years, Steve,' she says with a girlish grin. 'Thanks,' squeezing my arm. Suddenly, just for a moment she isn't the painted, dyed or manicured model. She is the girl behind the mask – the girl with the happy giggle. 'I think I have forgotten how to laugh!'

We walk back slowly, enjoying the sunshine and the gentle sea breeze. To anyone looking, we would appear to be a happy couple. I am wary but confident that I can handle this mercurial beauty – and then the mobile buzzes.

'Yes, yes. Right!' Her face returns to the haughty pseudo-aristocratic look. The giggling girl has gone; evaporated away – in an instant. 'That was Peter. The tender is coming to get us. Ten minutes.'

The bubble of happiness has burst. She walks half a metre from my side. Her model mask has replaced the uninhibited laughter. She is going back into another world.

* * * *

I can see Peter's eagle eye watching us as we approach down the jetty. Is that relief that we are back in one piece or that Gina is walking with a distant gaze, about a metre away from my side? It has been a strange day.

The untouchables

'I want *you*, Angus.' The Minister, Norman Brown, fixes the Scottish policeman with a steely eye. 'I need someone *untouchable* to head this unit.'

'And if I say *No?*'

The Minister gives a patient smile. 'It's your right, of course. But I have asked specifically for you because of your background. It is my belief, Angus, and the belief of the Americans, that some people very high up – perhaps here and across the Atlantic – have developed such an ingrained system of corruption that no-one can get near them. I need you! International justice needs you.'

'Minister, you are offering me a special assignment task with a few staff to crack something that, even you are saying, is ingrained international corruption. I'm waiting for the Monty Python punchline.'

'Angus, we are dealing with criminal activity. That is police work. No punchline. I'm proposing a small select unit with access to whatever resources will prove to be necessary – with commensurate remuneration for you and your staff. The Prime Minister is right behind this. The United States Congress is setting up a similar tight group. You would be working closely with them, and other national security groups, as needed. We'll give your unit a grand title, the *National Police Authority*, to give you a status and a lot of clout over senior people, backed by executive order. You will, in fact, be an independent group reporting to a respected retired Brigadier, one step removed from the process of government – then, through me to the PM and to Parliament, when and if appropriate. The implication in what I'm saying is that some senior enforcers of the law may well be corrupt – politicians too, pillars of society, business execs ... and we don't know who they are.'

'And in the States too, you say?' Angus Forbes lowers his chin, gripping it in a pincer-grip of thumb and forefinger. 'High stakes. Lots for them to lose. What's to stop those pillars of society just contracting some heavy to put a bullet in me and my American equivalent?'

'This is police work, Angus, fundamentally – but clever work. I think it is about unsettling some powerful people who are thumbing their noses at society. We don't know the *why* or *who*, but I suspect it is about power – most things are. You will have whatever protection and special response teams you want, as and when they become necessary. But first, I think the task is to get under the skin of a few people, induce them to make a mistake or two. This will be an international effort – but a discreet one.'

Forbes runs his hand through his short-cropped greying hair. 'And you say the main clue is the hi-jack of a yacht off Fiji?'

'Well, more the slick blackmail operation which followed. Thirty million US dollars, delivered in nano-seconds to defy detection, for the release of the yacht and its US citizen. And more again, that the US Congress congressional ethics committee chair cannot get a straight answer out of any of their Intelligence agencies over there.'

'We have no jurisdiction in Fiji. Indeed, it appears to be under martial law.'

'There is an Australian connection, just come through – an Aussie security guard, thought to have been killed in the hi-jack, has applied for a passport from a ship owned by a British citizen, with an elusive past. We have that much initial connection.'

'With respect, Minister, that's really an Australian policing matter or Interpol. You don't want me chasing boats in the South Pacific, surely?'

'No, Angus. The Prime Minister has a soft spot for our historic links with Fiji, but *No*. I think we need you take a close look here in London. We are getting bagged in the press for the ethics and integrity of our Intelligence gatherers and police. If that continues and the people lose confidence, then our whole system of the *rule of law* goes out the window.

'Someone is back-grounding the press. I don't know if they are intercepting phone messages or email or it is just old-fashioned lobbying. Take that Sir Terence Sedgewood, for example. Spruiking on the weekend, like he is some self-appointed spokesperson for the agencies that purchase Britain's goodwill and strategic alliances overseas. Old money and title – and he thinks he is omniscient.'

'Yes, I saw him on the TV – something about there being shades of grey, subtleties of negotiation.'

'Indeed, Angus. He was arguing last week to a select committee that *diplomatic nuances cannot be strait-jacketed into the inflexibility of legal precedent and the integrity values of purists.* Unquote.'

Forbes gave a cynical laugh. 'A pretty dim view of diplomats, lawyers and the fundamental rules of law.'

'That's what I mean. And he is just one of many, no doubt.'

'A good place to start though. I don't think I would mind ripping a few questions at him.' He pauses for about five seconds. 'Alright, Minister, I'm in … for a limited time … and subject to all the arrangements being put satisfactorily in place. My brief can develop from whatever this hi-jack business and a bit of stirring might uncover. Give me the details of the Americans and I'll contact them to see what their view is.'

Washington, USA. Monday 5 February 2007

Kyle Broderick is unusually angry. Not at Angus Forbes. They have not long been hooked into their first secure video link-up. It is early morning in Washington.

Broderick is the head of a newly-formed United States law-enforcement department, *Veracity Section, Versec* for short; very similar in concept to the unit which Forbes is now heading for the United Kingdom.

Congressman Legrand and the British Minister, Brown, have set their early terms of reference. The brief is to investigate high-level illicit activities across international borders.

Part of that is aimed at people involved in such matters as global fraud or piracy. The attack by pirates on the *Sea Spray 2*, just off the coast of Fiji, is their starting point.

Ultimately, the politicians want preventative measures to be in place because, at present, the most powerful nations on Earth seem to be unable to do anything about it.

'I'm not surprised that a kidnap and ransom could be carried out so successfully off the Fijian coast,' Broderick says. His voice is a slow east-coast drawl .

Angus Forbes watches the round, nuggety face on the video screen. The American looks like an old-school cop – short-cropped hair, the facial lines of experience, a scar or two, cynicism – from the school of very hard knocks. And there is an edge to his voice – unhappy?

Kyle Broderick continues. 'Piracy is on the rise in many parts of the world, the South China Sea, the Indian Ocean off Somalia and Yemen … and in the Melanesian western Pacific.'

'I agree,' replies the Scot. 'The details are not even abnormal. The entire ship and crew are held to ransom. That happens. It is police work to solve the crime scene or the Navy, to prevent it happening in international waters, or the diplomats to find a negotiated solution.'

'Yeh,' replies Broderick, as his voice rises some more. 'But, there are a couple of little problems for me, my Scottish friend. One is the skill of the robbers that carried out the operation. It was very polished. These are not opportunist thugs. There was no Navy to be seen. It was in Fijian waters. And two – it's an even greater part of the problem – is the squabbling between government Intelligence and enforcement agencies. It has virtually paralysed any attempt at capture, or intervention or resolution – not a diplomat to be seen.

It is as if some bastard has put a fix in. Even my congressman can't get answers.'

That is why Broderick is unusually angry.

'Really,' Forbes says, with surprise in his tone. 'So what happened?'

'I've read the parts of documentation that exist – and that is not a lot. The ransom was tens of millions of dollars and it was paid – and yet the inquiry notes are just tied up as completed, with little bows of red official tape. It's not so much … I mean, it's not obvious deliberate obstruction. The investigators were just frustrated at every turn, no matter how hard they pushed. It is more that nothing happens. No-one is helpful. It just gets lost in the slowness. I don't like that. It's like politics. It smells.'

Forbes's face is unmoved as he watches his American colleague flare his nose. He takes his time to respond. 'The ship was hired by the singer, Ingrid? I've heard of her.' He waits for Broderick's nod. 'Two security guards, an American and an Australian, are reported missing, presumed dead. Is that right?' Another nod. 'Big dollars demanded and paid. Okay.'

'Angus.' Broderick's tone is back to being quiet but tense. 'The demand was made to the pop singer's husband. He is very wealthy, as is she. To that extent, the money is not the issue. He pays up and the ship, with Ingrid on board, sails safely into Nadi harbour two days later, with the singer flying out to Los Angeles within a couple of hours. The problem starts after that.

'Ingrid's husband informed the state police immediately, as he should, who then informed the FBI. However, their jurisdiction only applies within the United States. So the information floated out into a scatter of our agencies with overseas interests, presumably to liaise with Fiji. But it just fizzled out. These agencies seem to operate on a timescale more appropriate for geological research.'

'I see, Kyle. Passive obstruction?'

'Since 9/11, the Director of National Intelligence, *DNI*, has authority over all the US Intelligence community. Maybe that overview works at the strategic policy level – global issues or homeland security – but at the level of the policing of criminal activities against American citizens beyond its borders, it doesn't work.'

'Or,' Angus Forbes suggests, 'like you say, the fix is in.'

'Mmm. That's how I am seeing it.'

'Well, our two agencies, you and me, are working together. Your congressman and my Minister want us to be ahead of these crims rather than in catch-up mode.' Forbes pauses. 'Easier said than done, I know. But as long as they give us the tools and don't back out when the going gets tough ...' The Scotsman pauses again. 'Because, if your assessment is right, then this could get very hot when we start poking around, shaking up those sleeping coals again. We have been promised whatever we need, with the highest back-up in both our countries.'

'Angus, these parasites – at the street end or high up.' Kyle Broderick certainly seems to be a passionate man. 'They have been given far too much room; time to scheme. They prey on the world community with impunity, using the confusion of shared zones of international waters.'

'Well' Angus Forbes responds. 'Credit to your congressman and our Minister. It is a decisive, even courageous, high-level endorsement; a statement of faith. Not thinking small.'

'Yes, Angus. Well, let's get on the front foot. I have direct reporting accountability to the Vice President and the Congressional accountability committee, headed by Congressman Legrand, himself. There is parallel, but not immediate, advice to the DNI.' He smiles at the last comment. 'The rules of the game have now changed.'

'Good, Kyle. We have a budget; operational guidelines around ethics; and, within those parameters, the speed to move ahead of the criminals. Let's use it well.'

'Who have you got helping you, Angus?'

'Police inspector, Catherine Weston – a Yorkshire cop with lots of experience. She'll be fine. And you?'

'Larry Kennedy. About the same police level. A good man from all accounts.'

'Okay, Kyle, let's work on a need-to-know basis. Keep it in close. No passing on information beyond our brief.'

'Absolutely! My thinking is that it must be some high-level officials who received the intelligence early, in the past. They are the ones using it to stymie progress. But, we are the serious players now.'

Forbes juts his chin and nods. 'We need to make quiet contact with people in the South Pacific. I know of Jeff Fowler, Superintendent of the Australian Federal Police. His role is in counter-terrorism. My Minister has heard good things about him, recommends him.'

'Okay, but, like you say, let's keep it in tight. I'll see who else might be useful at this end.' Broderick gives a theatrical growl. 'Angus, I'm starting to feel a bit more positive now – just a little bit. We will be a good team. We are going to get these coyotes. We will flush them out. I can feel it.'

Chris Legrand and Norman Brown

Washington. Monday 5 February 2007

Congressman Legrand is speaking to Minister Norman Brown on a secure line from Washington.

'Norm, I've been having a think – now that we have our *Untouchables* in place. Carrot, smoke and stick. We will get on with smoking these *Sea Spray* bastards out of their dens through good old-fashioned police work; and then clobber them as they come out. But it would be good to have some insurance – some back-up to be sure we get the big guys. The carrot. To tease them out to make their play. They'll be feeling pretty cocky, is my bet. A sting is needed, if you like.'

'A sting, Chris? We don't even know who they are.'

'Ah, but we know where they are active – in that western Pacific part, down there around Australia, Fiji, all those islands, roughly. It's a bit lawless, I expect, in those islands; all around those newly independent nations – especially after you Brits pulled your control out. But you still have influence; and *we* do too – good memories of our efforts at Guadalcanal and the Coral Sea pushing out the enemy in World War II.'

He pauses, waiting, imagining the reaction from the British Minister. You have to shake the branch, he thinks, if you want to win in these matters. On the front foot, against some smarter-than-your-average crims.

'Chris, we have only just put *Versec* and the *NPA* in place. They've hardly put their feet under a desk.'

'All the better, Norm.' He works at sounding upbeat, but measured. 'No time for any of them to mix with whoever has been leaking on us. They are untouchable. We are unexpected, unpredictable and, I'm sure, our team will be underestimated by our enemies. But we have to be ready to move and move fast. Agreed?'

There is another pause as Norman Brown comes to terms with the effusive American's style. But he doesn't get the chance to demur before Legrand is speaking again.

'The Solomons, Norm? Guadalcanal? Could you set up something there? I'll do the same quietly out of Guam and the Philippines. We need a preparedness process that can move in a number of ways. It's about readiness for whatever might come up. Probably best for you Brits to take the lead in that southern part of the target area – you protected the place until 1978. A bit more recent than *our* wartime involvement. The Aussies have been in there, even more recently. I don't really want to involve more people than you and me, if I can, at the moment. We don't know the Aussies, yet.'

'Chris, I know your brain is sparking in a whole range of directions. I'm not sure I'm fully with you yet. The Solomons? Guam?'

The Minister is trying not to be dismissive. He has the sense that the big American's enthusiasm might morph into an actual practical proposal – eventually.

'Norm, okay. Sorry, I've been working this through for a while. This is new to you. In stages, what I'm suggesting is that we set up a scenario in the Solomons – and/or north out of our US base on Guam – like possible bait. It might be another yacht with money involved – although I think they'd smell a rat with that. It could be some other form of temptation. I don't know what yet – but we need some teams of special forces down there, ready to react. If it is on water, your Special Boat Service boys would be good. We can send Navy Seals, if your folks can't handle it.'

'I'm sure our people can handle anything of that nature.' Brown tries not to sound miffed or haughty. He does sound unimpressed at the imputation. 'We won't need your Seals. The Australians have a very capable Navy who patrol those international waters regularly. Just for your awareness.'

Legrand doesn't seem to notice. 'Now Norm, it has to be super quiet. Just us, for the moment. No disrespect to other countries. We don't want to lose our initiative by letting too many players in, any of whom could be compromised.'

'Chris.' An impatience develops in the Minister's tone. 'You want the impossible, by yesterday. The Solomons is a sovereign country. We would be deploying troops. Approvals have to be sought and granted. There are some logistics involved. This is not *a barge in without any permission* scenario.'

'Norm.' Legrand's tone reverts to patient and tolerant. He pauses as if to acknowledge the Minister's point and to show respect, before continuing. 'Norm, we are on the front foot. Apart from you and me, your Prime Minister and our Vice President, only the *Untouchables* can know anything.'

'That can't work, Chris.'

'Norm, just settle and listen. This is about preparedness – not an attack. Let's just have our people on location with a range of possible plans in the bottom drawer. We may well have to react to something happening between Fiji, Australia and the Solomons. It's guesswork. But we need to be on-site. We can't react from the States or Britain.

'And all the military need to know is that it is a training exercise – under wraps. That's normal for these special forces blokes. The Solomons will probably be grateful … or do they even have to know?'

'Do they even have to know?' The Minister splutters. 'These are sovereign nations, you are discussing. We are not their colonial masters any more. Not in any shape or form. Not only do they *need* to know … but they have to give their *permission*.'

'Norm, somewhere high up in our United States Intelligence system or yours in Britain or both, there are people with access to confidential information which they are feeding to these crims. All

I am suggesting is getting people in place, just in case. I'm sure that can be easily explained as co-operative training exercises. They don't need to know the truth. There is too much probability of leaks. Can you see where I'm coming from?'

The Minister speaks slowly. 'I hear what you say. And I understand your strategy. We may be able to find a suitably delicate and diplomatic justification for the presence of some of our special forces in that vicinity – for supportive training purposes. Out of Honiara, possibly.'

Legrand's appreciative roar booms down the line. 'Well done, Norm. I think you are probably the smartest Minister in your government – and I'm proud to call you *my friend*. This is just about preparedness. But ... only with Forbes, Broderick, you and me. Loose talk costs lives.'

'I'll see what I can do, Chris. And for your part ...'

'If you handle a base in the Solomons, I will get something working out of Guam, to handle the Philippines area and south to the Bismarck Sea. Happy. Can do?'

'I think we will be able to manage that,' the Minister replies softly.

Australian Federal Police

Canberra. Tuesday 6 February 2007

'They particularly wanted to talk to us about a hi-jacking which occurred off Fiji on 9 January,' Inspector Fowler explains. 'They are using that case to test the investigative problems in their operations. There's been a lot more politics impacting on them than we are used to here.'

Some wry smiles greet his comment but no-one wants to touch the topic. This is a federal election year.

Superintendent Fowler is briefing his key team members about the contact from two newly-formed departments within the British and the American enforcement systems. Angus Forbes and Kyle Broderick have been in touch over a secure line.

In the room are Sergeant Bill Jones from Australian Federal Police; Derek, a senior ASIO agent – security Intelligence within Australia, Mary from ASIS – the Secret Intelligence Service for overseas matters; Inspector Eileen Lewis from maritime policing and Inspector Jack Power from Special Response.

'There was an Australian security guard on board the ship, the *Sea Spray 2*. His name is or was Steven Flynn. Ex-Army. He, along with his American counterpart Aldo Pollock, was reported missing, presumed dead.

'The ship was attacked by a pirate raiding party, we assume. The two security men went overboard, shot, according to the accounts.

The boat had been hired by a singer called Ingrid. She is apparently big in the States.'

His team laugh. 'You need to get out more.'

Derek grins. 'She is enormous among teenage girls. Biggest thing happening at the moment.'

Jeff Fowler smiles back. 'Yes, my teenage daughter would cringe, no doubt. I'll need to get home more. Anyway, Bill has been aware of the hi-jack for a few weeks, from Eileen's team in maritime policing.' He acknowledges Eileen Lewis with a nod. 'And he has turned up an interesting anomaly, just as we walked in here. Over to you, Bill.'

'Thanks, Sir.' Sergeant Jones takes up the narrative. 'Steven Flynn, or someone claiming to be the missing security guard from the *Sea Spray 2*, has returned from the dead. Yesterday, in fact.' He pauses for effect. 'In Noumea. Our Department of Foreign Affairs and Trade office has just issued him a new passport.'

Jack Power says, 'Interesting. What's his story?'

'Not very clear, yet,' Jones replies. 'The consulate-general people didn't know what questions to ask. The application had been made from a ship called the *Lerna* en route from Fiji – but no-one advised us in advance, despite the priority flag on the name.'

The superintendent makes the slightest sigh of frustration but says nothing.

Jones continues. 'The ship is owned by a South Pacific freighting company. As yet, I don't know how Flynn came to be on board. He told the officials a story of being washed overboard and the passport being left on board. They thought that he might be trying to hitch a lift back to Australia.'

'Is he injured? Bullet wound, for example?' Power raises upturned palms as if asking the obvious.

'No information. But the ship hasn't left Noumea, yet. Seems in no hurry.'

'Not worth checking him out, in person?' Power asks.

'I'm guessing,' Fowler intervenes, 'given this new delicate scenario with the Brits and Americans, that some care is needed. We could speculate a whole range of reasons for him being on board … and what his plans might be. Assuming worst case, we probably couldn't get much out of him until he feels safe back on Australian soil. If he has indeed been shot and thrown overboard, as in the original story, then he's probably more than a little skittish. Very interesting though, as you say, Jack. The proposed route, provisionally registered in Noumea, is for them to head for Cairns, at some stage. I'll make contact with the Queensland Police. Mary?'

Mary from ASIS has made some mental calculations. 'If he stays on the ship and depending on when they leave, I'm guessing he should berth in Cairns around 12th to 14th – not too long to wait.' She smiles with the patience of her profession.

'Okay, so far,' Derek says. 'Let's keep listening and looking. Tell me, did Flynn's original passport get handed in from the *Sea Spray*? When it docked?'

'Don't know that either! I'll check.' Bill Jones makes a note.

'Alright.' Fowler is running through the options. 'Broderick, the American, has accessed the Fijian police witness statements. They state that the crew and passengers commented on being treated well, albeit after the trauma of the hi-jack. We have some descriptions – the most distinctive one about a large hissing man.'

Jack Power's eyebrows rise, eliciting a response from the superintendent.

'Early days, Jack. More statements to be sent on. Anyway, a ransom demand was delivered by an email to Ingrid's husband, a merchant banker of some resources. That email address was confidential and protected – so someone was able to hack in, possibly. It lifts the case above the level of your uneducated pirate.

'The husband paid the ransom, tens of millions of dollars, into a Hong Kong bank which instantly transferred it to a bank in the Caribbean, which then instantly transferred it to a Swiss bank – transactions moving so fast that they couldn't be tracked immediately, let alone – intercepted.'

'Jeez,' quips Derek. 'And the Swiss have lost their tongues, even to deny that it happened. Incredible! It takes two working days at best for my bank to clear transactions.'

Fowler scarcely pauses. 'As soon as word was received on the ship that the money had been paid, the robbers disabled all the external communication systems and the rudder, leaving the captain to navigate into Nadi using first principles.'

'Neat operation!' Bill Jones confirms.

'Agreed,' adds Jack Power.

Fowler holds up his hand. 'The main issue though … the frustration for Forbes and Broderick … is that the investigation teams not only couldn't get moving but they actually seemed to be obstructed.'

'By whom?' the maritime policewoman asks.

'They don't know, Eileen,' Fowler admits. 'But they now have Ministerial and Congressional approvals to by-pass any bureaucratic stone-walling. And that's also where they are seeking our help. They want us to be active partners, through their encrypted systems. They want to catch the perpetrators in this *Sea Spray* case but they also want to set up a new Intelligence process to preempt their activities.'

Fowler pauses to let the information be absorbed.

'Wouldn't that be double handling?' Mary asks, with exaggerated politeness.

'I can see the workload ahead,' agrees Bill Jones.

'It may well involve that, but for a while only. They suspect very high-level tampering with the Intelligence coming through the normal channels. They're guessing that senior people are protecting some extremely influential crooks.'

'I take it that *we* are not suspected of being high-level obstructers, then?'

'I trust that we have not embarked on that path.'

'What do you want of us, Jeff?' asks Lewis.

'All right. Steven Flynn, first. Let's each run our own checks on what our systems have on him. How did he come to be doing security on the boat? Was he perhaps a player in the hi-jack? He's one of ours, so we all need to make sure our house is clean.' He grins at Mary's look.

'Then we have Ben Brennan, new perhaps to a couple of you, but a very valuable resource when it comes to knowledge about pirates in the South Pacific. Over to you, Derek.'

'Indeed.' Derek speaks quietly. 'Ex-Australian Navy, ex-Special Boat Service with the Brits. He has set up a very effective listening network right through the South China Sea and into the South Pacific; known as *Nemesis*, but the name is really only used among themselves. They don't advertise widely.

'It's based on the simple premise that crims fall out and talk. Government has made a budget available – through our ASIO office, I believe.' He gives an innocent shrug. 'And Brennan now often hears chatter before something happens. He could be a key to our staying ahead of this particular opposition. He has money for information but most of it comes free. He is the defender of the powerless. People want him to solve their problems. So they volunteer to help.'

'A handy person to know,' says Power admiringly.

'Handy for sure. But difficult,' Fowler adds. 'I've known him for years. And there's more; Ben has led several attack parties against pirates. Clandestine affairs.

'He is a motivated man. He particularly goes after traffickers in women. To my knowledge, he has saved several shipments from slavery, rescued hi-jacked fishermen, crews and the like. These people are eternally grateful. Their extended kin groups are now part of his information system. We haven't been able to make contact yet. Maybe, he is out of range. Like I said, he can be difficult but we'll try again and see what he knows about attacks on rich people's yachts.'

The superintendent finalises his briefing with, 'The link with the British is Catherine Weston, seconded senior regional policewoman, inspector level. And with the Americans, it is Larry Kennedy, a major in the US state police. They will share what they have on a timely basis. I've agreed we'll do likewise, so keep me informed as you hear it.'

The team nods, knowing he means exactly that. He does want to be kept informed, day or night. No wonder he doesn't have time to know who Ingrid is.

Ben Brennan

Brisbane. Tuesday 6 February 2007

Ben Brennan is thinking about Alison Wood, the young journalist.

Sending a lamb in among wolves. What had he been thinking to give her a lead to Cavanagh? Impulsive – like *her* approach!

She seems a nice kid – so like the daughter he once had, even in looks. You can't tell anything to the headstrong young ones. They have to make their own mistakes.

It isn't easy having the benefit of experience, he ponders. We know the problems they'll face but they'll still walk into the same minefields!

How could she be aware of what might lie ahead?

At least he knows where she will be heading. She will be off to Cairns to greet the *Lerna* when it comes in later in the month. He will have *his eyes* watching out for her. He'll get word when it leaves Noumea.

His mobile is showing a text message. *Jeff Fowler. My, my! He is being persistent.*

He wonders what the Australian Federal Police might be wanting with him ... but he can't get the *Lerna* out of his head. What has been happening on that ship? What do they want in Cairns?

Nemesis

Brisbane. Thursday 8 February, 2007

'G'day, Ben. Good to hear your voice again. You're a hard man to catch.'

'Moving target. Safer. And you, Jeff? Are you travelling well in the constant fight against evil?' There is a flippancy in the reply, but no disrespect.

Fowler smiles at Brennan's rough diamond manner, an Aussie larrikin – easy to underestimate. Although he is ex-military, he likes to give the impression that he doesn't have time for authority or government. Yet, in his own way, he is very organised, having developed a sophisticated, yet simple, information-gathering network – *Nemesis*; based on trust rather than structure or lines of command. *Lots of layers of listeners, who want the change to happen,* is how he describes it.

'Doing okay, Ben. Always busy. It's never simple.'

'What do you need, Mate?' Brennan asks simply.

'We have a situation; happened off Fiji in January. Luxury sailing boat hi-jacked for ransom. Two security guards allegedly shot and thrown overboard. Everyone released on payment of a huge ransom.'

'*Sea Spray*, wasn't it?' replies Ben. 'Pop singer with a rich banker husband. That the one?'

'Yes. Now, here's the twist. The Aussie security guard has turned up, travelling on another luxury boat to Noumea. He has just applied for a replacement passport, saying the first one was lost when he went overboard. The Department of Foreign Affairs and Trade apparently jumped to replace it. The boat owner is a very influential British businessman.

'The guard's name was flagged for our attention. When my sergeant asked why the passport process moved so fast, scarcely more than a couple of days, he was told the administrative provision existed to fast-track applications in cases of hardship overseas.'

'You think this guard was part of the hi-jack?' asks Ben blandly.

'It's an option. There's been no sign of the other guard. It was a multi-million dollar operation. Lots of pay-outs for everyone.'

'So what do you want from me?'

'Some meat on the bones of this story. There are too many variables at the moment. The Brits and the Americans are interested in supporting us to solve this one and then, if we get the jump on this case, we might prevent others from happening. We're in the same business, Ben.'

Brennan is silent at the end of the line. Fowler senses the wariness – past promises of support, only to be disappointed when politics intervened to do the opposite.

'Do you have a name for the security guard?' Brennan asks eventually.

'Steve Flynn, ex-Army. Clean record.'

'Would the boat be the *Lerna*?'

Ben's casual question lifts Fowler's alertness. This man is very good. He usually sought a bit of information to give a bit. Together they might put the jigsaw together.

'Owner is Roger Cavanagh,' Fowler offers.

'What do you have on our Roger?'

'The Brits are chasing him up. British citizen. Trader. Boat registered in Tahiti. Makes his money on the world financial markets. Investment trading. Apparently worth enough that he can live on yachts during the year. We believe that there may be other boats in the Med and the West Indies. Do you know more?'

'Oh, I know more,' replies Brennan slowly. 'Probably not in a form that you can use though. Just hearsay … through the people who give me information. I wouldn't want to malign an upstanding international trader who is so important that the Department of Foreign Affairs and Trading would jump at his every request.' His voice drips with sarcasm. 'So how much do you want to know?'

'A lead. We need to get started. We can't talk to Flynn till he lands in Cairns. That could be a week. Give me anything that the American or British agencies could track down for us.'

Ben umms thoughtfully.

'Tell me,' he says suddenly. 'Does the name Alison Wood mean anything to you?'

'No. And she is?'

'An investigative journalist trying to do an exposé on piracy in the South Pacific. Cute young lass. In way out of her depth.'

'Means nothing to me. I'll let you know if the name surfaces.'

'Thanks,' says Ben, thoughtfully. 'That would be appreciated.'

More silence.

'Cavanagh *is* a very wealthy man,' says Brennan at length, 'but he won't appear on any *rich list*. Ask your American and British agencies why that is? I'll tell you what I think. I think he has many, very many, small buckets of money scattered all round the globe – never enough in one place that a tax return or share holding would show him as being one of the really wealthy ones. But I think you might find that he has access to the kinds of money and power usually the domain of those in technology or resource development. It will be well hidden. Your searchers won't find it easily. He likes to stay low profile.'

Fowler waits for the next considered thought.

'I also think some powerful people are protecting our Roger Cavanagh – and, for that to happen, he must be providing a very valuable service to them. I don't think it is necessarily money. It's probably more to do with information or power.'

There is a silence again.

'At my level,' Ben continues. 'Cavanagh seldom gets his hands dirty. He is a *hail fellow, well met* type of bloke. Everybody's friend. Bit of money splashed here. Favour done there. But he has a network. It's complicated and no doubt illegal – although well enough disguised to look legitimate.

'Get your agencies to check up on two of his offsiders. One is Peter Carter. Ex-British Army officer. The other is Len Williamson, former London thug sometimes known as *Laughing Len* because he can't smile. Some damage to nerves in his face. Nasty piece of work. Probably a split personality because some have told me he can be as gentle as a kitten – but I know another side to him.

'These fellows appear to administer his street level operation out here. Carter and Williamson are the names they use – probably not their real names. That's about all I'm comfortable to share at present. You'll keep me up to speed on developments with the *Sea Spray* or Flynn or this Alison Wood, won't you?'

'Thanks, Ben. Stay safe, old mate. Oh, one out of the blue as it were: have you ever heard of Napoleon's Curse? Something to do with stealing a sapphire … I'm guessing …?'

Roger's offer

New Caledonia, Thursday 8 February 2007

It is a moist tropical morning in Noumea. I can hear the tender being lowered. Through the cabin porthole I watch Peter Carter and *Smiling* Len stepping on board the tender, with a travelling bag each. I wave them a Steve Flynn farewell, with one finger.

The powerful boat sweeps away to the shore where the men are collected in a vehicle and whisked away.

Interesting. May they be away a long time. The Army teaches you to handle long boring spells but this is now five days with no indication of when we might head for Australia. I am keen to be on the move – but beggars can't be choosers. Still, too many days of just looking at the tropical view, tourist brochures and reading the only book in the room – the life of Napoleon Bonaparte.

I leave the cabin and head for the galley. Marcel is quite civil. Perhaps it is the ambience from so much French culture around him in this port.

'Can I help with anything?' I volunteer. He amiably points out a few small tasks – but, really, everything is quiet. The chef is on top of the tasks.

'Will we sail today?' I ask, hopefully.

'Today! Tomorrow! Who knows? Soon. Monsieurs Peter and Len have left from Tontouta so there are no hold-ups now – no reasons for delay.'

'Tontouta?' I query.

'International Airport,' explains Marcel. 'They will catch up with us in Cairns.'

Cairns. That had been the whisper I'd heard from one of the crew. I'd been staying quiet, making myself invisible, and reading about bloody Napoleon – interesting for an afternoon's read but you can only take so many old-style battle stories.

No-one had told me to leave the ship with my new passport.

I'd intended to bluff my way to stay on board and eventually get to Australia – a forlorn hope, perhaps, but it was heading in the right direction. It would save having to walk the marina trying to cadge a lift, with no money to offer in return.

Now, with Carter and Williamson gone, I am actually looking forward to a very pleasant few days sail, if I can swing it – perhaps make myself more valuable than a non-paying passenger.

'So who will carry Mr Cavanagh's messages?'

'Oh, one of the crew.' Marcel is non-committal – but more communicative this morning than he has been since we met. Maybe the departure of Monsieurs Peter and Len is already lifting the tone on the boat.

* * * *

A message comes from a white uniformed crewman that Mr Cavanagh would like to see Mr Flynn. I am duly ushered up to the master suite. The crewman's nod indicates that I should knock.

I thank the crewman and wait till he leaves. I hesitate at the door, just in case Laughing Len is waiting to pounce. I knock and a distant male voice invites me in – to a sitting room-cum-office.

'Come on in,' repeats Cavanagh, facing away and tapping something into his laptop. 'Sit down. How are you this fine morning?' He looks round and smiles briefly in welcome. His manner is of a man, fresh from sleep and on top of things. Seated at the computer, he gives a short portly appearance.

'I'm good, thanks.' I sink into the padded lounge chair.

Cavanagh finishes at the desk, turns and sits facing me.

'Tea?' he asks, with the teapot in his hand.

It would be impolite to refuse. 'Fine. Just black, please.'

With tea served, he starts, 'Steve, are you comfortable if I call you Steve? Mr Flynn seems so formal on ship.' I nod. Am I supposed to call him *Roger*? But the offer isn't made.

'Have you settled in? I have scarcely had time to be even an adequate host so far. The passport is received? Yes? Okay? You managed the walk with Gina alright on Sunday?'

He isn't looking for more than acquiescent nods – clearly a preoccupied man.

'Good. Good. We will be sailing for Cairns today.'

He pauses to look carefully at me, as if forming a more detailed impression. 'I hope to be there in three maybe four days, weather permitting. I have made the assumption that you would be travelling with us. Will that be alright with you?'

'Very kind of you, Mr Cavanagh.' Be gracious and polite. A memory of my mother's warm voice from my childhood floats through my thinking. Pleasant thoughts.

'Oh, please call me Roger on board,' replies the smiling ship owner.

There it is. Something is amiss. I have suddenly gone from cleaning the slops in the kitchen to *please call me Roger*. Something is not right.

'Now tell me about this business off Fiji, overboard, the passport and all.'

I take him through the general story, keeping it simple. No lies, no speculation.

'Fascinating,' responds Roger.

Am I being had? Is this just a joke and Laughing Len will come in with his round-mouthed chortle, having had so much fun at my expense?

'Would you mind if I run a few checks on your past, Steve? I may have an opportunity for you.'

'Not at all.' I am definitely not comfortable to be calling this man *Roger* yet.

'Good, good. I'll get back to you. Go and relax up on the sundeck for a while. The captain will cast off in a couple of hours.'

I look at his smile as I leave. Bewildering.

The sundeck offer sounds good. It certainly beats the cabin and walking the corridors.

* * * *

In the beach shorts which I had acquired from the Fijians, I head up to the sundeck, towel over my shoulder. The view is magnificent.

Out to sea, varying shades of green and blue reflect over sand, coral and deep water. White beaches fringe the tourist settlement to the south, as the land of the island rises behind in steep tones of deep green. Shadows created by the knife-sharp ridges glower right up to the crest. Blue sky is crowned with small cauliflower-white clouds. An idyllic spot, if you ignore the nickel dust and the red scars from the old mining leases.

'Good morning!' The voice comes from the bubbling jacuzzi.

I turn to see Miss Gina enjoying the frothing bubbles.

Which Miss Gina is she, today? The laughing girl who walked so happily along the boardwalk with me or the pretend-aristocrat who sought to rule over her servants? It has been a few days since I have seen her. Still easy to look at, but so hard to be with.

She has been drinking, a wineglass dangles empty in her hand.

'Come on in,' she beckons. 'It's beautiful at this time of the day.'

'I'm just happy to sit in the sun. Thank you. You enjoy your soak.' Perhaps she'd take that as meaning she is a lush. Thankfully, it seems to have gone over her tipsy head.

'Peter and Len have flown off.' She slurs her words a little.

'Yes. I saw them leave. Where have they gone?'

'Australia. We won't see them again until Cairns.' Her face doesn't record a particular expression.

I lie quietly on the lounger. What is this all about? Roger has sent me up here. He knows Gina will be here. There are so many unknowns on this ship.

She raises herself from the jacuzzi and lightly towels off. I discreetly look away. This is the boss's girl. She wears a one piece swimsuit, tailored to reveal rather than conceal; she's a stunner, in a swimsuit-model sort of way.

My eyes stay skyward, even behind the sunglasses, as she settles down on the next lounger to me.

'Thank you for Sunday,' she says, so quietly that it can hardly be heard. 'Sorry I was so difficult.'

'No problem.'

'Speak very quietly,' she says. 'The area is covered by closed circuit television. They won't pick up quiet words over the jacuzzi.'

Shit! My adrenalin is suddenly pumping again. I am back on patrol. A casual rolling of my head picks out the CCTV cameras.

'Three of them. Is that right?' I mutter quietly.

'Mmm,' is the only reply as she raises her glass to her lips – but she doesn't drink.

We lie quietly for a while.

'What are your plans?' she whispers.

'To stay on board till Cairns. Roger says he may have a job for me.' I can hear her quick intake of breath.

'Be careful,' she whispers. 'You don't understand what you're getting in to. Just be careful.' She adjusts her sunglasses and sits up on the lounger. 'Well, I'll see you around, I expect,' she says loudly, as she rises to her feet and, with a sweep of her towel around her waist, she is gone into the stairwell.

What have I landed in, indeed?

Versec

Larry Kennedy walks into Kyle Broderick's office.

'Kyle, Pollock's flotation jacket has been found – a line of bullet holes across the front. His name is on it. Floating a long way south from where the *Sea Spray* was hi-jacked.'

Broderick nods sombrely as Kennedy adds, 'So I guess he's a goner. His Aussie partner is in Noumea though, having travelled there on a boat called the *Lerna*. He apparently got a replacement for his lost passport in New Caledonia.'

Broderick props his chin on his hand as he listens intently to Kennedy.

'The owner of the boat is a Roger Cavanagh. British citizen. Seems he also sails on boats registered in the Caymans and in Corsica. Money from investment banking and share trading. The Aussies and the Brits are following up.'

'How long before someone can talk to this Aussie guard? What's his name?' Broderick quizzes.

'Flynn. Steven Flynn.'

'Yes. How long?'

'He's on the ship in Noumea. Probably not for nearly a week till it berths in Australia. He might have little more to add anyway.'

'Ooo!' replies Broderick with a theatrical grimace. 'I think I want to know how a man, who people said was dead, has suddenly appeared on a luxury boat in Noumea, claiming he lost his passport overboard. That will be an interesting tale when it is told. Yessirree! What else do you have for me?'

'We are working with the Fijian Government to establish what ships were in the vicinity of the *Sea Spray* on that night. Those inflatables must have come from a ship to approach the *Sea Spray* undetected at night in a choppy sea.'

'Anything yet?' asks Broderick.

'We have some of the vessels identified and we are running elimination checks on them. We're also running checks on the background of all the crew and passengers. It has to have been an inside job in my view.'

'My money would be on the Aussie guard,' says Broderick, with the flat world-weary tone of experience. 'He seems to have landed alright out of this. Keep at it, Larry, and I want to be informed as soon as anything new comes in. Talk to Catherine Weston in London too. We need to tick-tack closely on this. I have a gut instinct that it is much bigger than we think.'

National Police Authority

London. Saturday 10 February 2007

'I want to know about him, Catherine.'

Catherine Weston takes in this request as Angus Forbes points at her. He is slowly pacing a track across the patterned carpet.

Sir Terence Sedgewood has been discussed previously, in passing. He is an important man in the civil service – a former special adviser to select committees, very well-connected politically, outspoken on civil service standards, independently wealthy through banking and heritage.

Catherine watches as Forbes continues treading slowly, with his chin in the fork of his fingers.

'He has approached the Minister, Catherine, wanting us either shut down or out of his hair. *No Mr Plods stamping their simple-minded boots into the delicate world of diplomacy*, he told the Minister. Cheeky bugger! I want to know why he feels so threatened that we are moving to clean up some of the slack processes that let crooks get away with white-collar crime.'

'Or the unbiased answer might be,' responds Weston with cheery impartiality, 'that he is being the devil's advocate for interests who feel we might undo decades of their work in international diplomacy. Couldn't he be correct?'

'Phooey.' Forbes snorts. 'Their work needs to be *seriously* undone.'

She gives a tolerant smile. Today clearly isn't the day for a debate with a tetchy boss. 'I'll see what we can find,' she placates.

This is a huge task that they have embarked on with the US agency, *Versec*. She understands that her gruff Scottish boss will get so absorbed in the complexities of it all that he would be difficult. He has a reputation – for many things; but he will make a very good *untouchable*. His history of leading ferocious national integrity units attests to that. Catherine's role will be to keep him calm – the talented, ethical bloodhound on the scent of a crime.

'Now, Broderick has been on to me about that Fijian hi-jacking,' continues the Scotsman. 'That case of the American pop singer. Husband paid a huge ransom and she was released unharmed. Really? That simple?'

Catherine Weston listens. Clearly, this would be a focal point in their analysis of the policing processes. Angus will give her the direction and she will run with it.

Forbes feigns surprise as he speaks again. 'It seems that the Aussie security guard has turned up in New Caledonia. He's not dead after all.'

'What's our source?'

'Australian Federal Police. Superintendent Jeff Fowler. Seems like a good man.' Forbes pauses. 'Here are the details, Catherine, as we know them.' He clearly doesn't go for all that formal stuff in a close-knit team. 'Steven Flynn is ex-Army. Been in security since he retired two years ago. Wounded in Afghanistan. Clean military record. Fowler's crew has turned up nothing adverse.

'Both Flynn and his American partner, Pollock, were reported as being shot by the hi-jackers and tossed overboard. Pollock hasn't been found but the American cousins say his bullet-ridden lifejacket has been found. They had their names on their life jackets.'

'Interesting.' Catherine muses.

'Flynn apparently travelled to New Caledonia on a luxury cruiser called the *Lerna*. It's registered in Papeete, Tahiti; operated by a Roger Cavanagh, a British international citizen. He spends his life on that ship and others. We don't know much more. He's technically ours, being British. We'll need a good brief on him.'

Catherine doesn't need notes. She is taking it all in. 'Where is Flynn now?'

'He was given a replacement passport in Noumea by Australian officials. They weren't aware of our interest. However, the replacement was moved through extraordinarily quickly because apparently this Cavanagh has some clout down there. Benefactor? Importance to trade? Who knows? The Aussies will track that down.'

Catherine nods and watches Angus mentally trawl through the known information, before continuing, 'So, as far as we know, Flynn is still on the *Lerna*, heading soon for North Queensland, due to dock sometime next week. For our part, Catherine, we need all we can get on Cavanagh. He must have a bob or two. Who is he? Where does he make his money? What are his connections? What is his past?'

She nods; her mental notes clear in her mind.

'Finally,' he says. 'Broderick thinks there is a financial mastermind behind this because of the speed of moving millions of dollars across the world on a route definitely intended to deter trackers intercepting the transaction. Get Techs to run some cross-referencing to see who we might have on our suspect list. Must rush now.'

He waits for Catherine's nod that she has understood everything. Then he grabs his folder hurriedly; off to his next meeting. That is apparently his life – a blur of meetings and analyses.

* * * *

Catherine reflects; there is a fair list of detective work to be carried out. The Minister has been as good as his word. They are a small team but they have access to some twenty secure assistants to help, as necessary, all with their specialty skills.

Techs is the nickname for a talented ex-hacker – a man who loves computers, world-wide networks, encryption and the shadowy world of people whose lives are only illuminated by ghostly screens and creative programming.

He is security-cleared to a high level; recognition of his having proved himself time and again in both military and policing situations of considerable sensitivity. Catherine will brief him immediately and then his personalised scanning programs can begin searching through all the data banks.

After that, there will be Sir Terence.

That might be the harder nut to crack. Politics always gets in the way of good policing, she thinks.

She picks up the phone.

Sir Terence Sedgewood

London. Saturday 10 February, 2007

Sir Terence Sedgewood emerges looking just a mite weary.

The two-hour morning board committee session of the South Mercantile Investment Bank of London had been draining. Sir Terence is the chair and certainly feeling too old for holding on to the reins of aspiring young egos. Weekends had once been sacred, times for family peace ... but no longer.

They have been embroiled in a progress assessment against several key performance indicators in their strategic plan. The meeting had degenerated into arguments over a potential opportunity for the bank to leverage a considerable sum in a new venture. The expectation was that a market rise would deliver a healthy profit. And they all wanted to have their say. It was all a question of risk appetite.

Sir Terence has been advising caution. Expectation of the market movements in these times is really just hope. He is a banker by training and bankers should always confirm equity before entering into well-considered new opportunities. But the new breed don't have that disciplined cautious background. They are impulsive.

Arguments between lawyers, bankers and accountants can go on for ever, without anything ever being achieved. It had been one of those meetings.

However, he is now standing at the desk of his executive secretary, Janet, to check his commitments for the rest of the day.

'Well, Sir Terence,' says Janet. 'You have the teleconference with the Board of South Pacific Freight Alliance starting in twenty minutes. Then you have the board link-up with the Grey Bear Investment Bank in the States after that. The rest of your day is clear. It is Saturday, after all. Oh, and a lady from the National Police Authority called to make an appointment for an hour, as soon as convenient. Her name was, let me see, yes, Catherine Weston – an inspector.'

'Did Miss Weston say what it was about?'

'No sir. Only that it was for the Minister. She thought you might understand. A nice lady, Sir. When should I book her in?'

'When do I have space? This afternoon, don't I? Let's get it over and done with, if she is available on a Saturday,' replies the knight.

'I'll tell her – 2.00 pm. Done, Sir.' She smiles. 'I'll contact the NPA. I'm sure she will be available for you, Sir. She wanted it as soon as it was convenient to you. Enjoy your teleconference.'

* * * *

The South Pacific Freight Alliance is an amalgam of sea and ocean trading companies in the South China Sea and the Pacific. Their freighters ply their trade from Taiwan down through the Philippines and Indonesia, through Micronesia into Melanesia – the Solomons, Vanuatu and Fiji in particular – and over as far as Samoa, even to Tahiti in French Polynesia, as well as south to New Zealand and Australia.

Their ships carry any type of freight as long as it will fit in holds or containers. They are the worker ants who keep the system thriving.

Sir Terence lends his name to this board which is effectively run by Chinese, Filipino and Indonesian lawyers, accountants and traders.

He dials the teleconference number and finds only one person on the end of the line – Roger Cavanagh. It is to be expected. The booking in his diary is just a cover if anyone checks with Janet.

This would take only a few minutes.

111

'I'm here. Let's do this by computer,' the voice says.

The line goes dead.

Sir Terence pulls his keyboard over onto the boardroom table, types in the pass codes and starts to send. All of the typing will be automatically encrypted and then decoded on the *Lerna* which is at that moment at anchor in Noumea.

Likewise, the process works in reverse, giving totally secure communication between the two men. And it needs to be secure. They want no eavesdropping on telephones, even scrambled lines. This is the system, safer than banks.

T – I'm told that Versec in the States is searching all shipping in the area of the Sea Spray.

R – Thanks. Nothing to find there.

T – NPA wants to visit me.

R – Fine. Keep me informed on any unanticipated questions. Cargoes moving as normal in SPFA.

T – Stop them while this is on.

R – No way. It would blow credibility. No-one knows. P and L are out securing the network.

T – Repeat. Stop the cargoes till this blows over

R – Negative. We are moving well.

T – Do you have any pieces for Ramas?

R – In hand. Stay strong. Hold the line. Over and out.

The encrypted line goes dead.

'Fool. Arrogant upstart,' mutters the chairman. 'There is too much at stake. Too much risk in this plan of action.' Sir Terence is nothing if not skilled in the ways of company directors and his risk appetite is low at this time.

* * * *

Sir Terence has always thought that the Grey Bear Investment Bank, GBIB, is an interesting concept.

He dials the silent number for the board.

Some people go to casinos. Others go to the races. GBIB meets that need in a very different way for some ultra-rich gamblers.

It is indeed a successful bank, at least on the surface, and a social club for wealthy bankers who get their adrenalin rush by gambling on short-selling assets.

It takes the skill of a gambler to read the market, to listen to the chatter of boardrooms and then to buy up assets cheaply with borrowed money, gambling on the expectation that they will make a rapid growth, in hours rather than days. Good fun! More of a rush than horses or cards – and it uses skills which bankers value; but which they can't use openly in the mainstream commercial banking industry.

The Grey Bear Investment Bank is also a major vehicle for processing the considerable sums of money which came in through the *Ramas* structure from a huge range of business ventures – most of them have a veneer of respectability and which the board members choose not to put to any seriously rigorous scrutiny.

Those ventures survive because no-one notices. That is part of the system. They are esteemed bankers, pillars of society, with wide ranging portfolios of transactions; and a record of invariably clean audits.

Sir Terence is nominally the chair of the GBIB board. In reality, he is there to provide the title of respectability. He is a late-comer to this company. It had been *Ramas* who had set up the structure – *Ramas* and Aaron Rossiter, decades ago.

The late Aaron Rossiter had been the managing director before Sir Terence. It was he who had trained the directors in the culture of GBIB – *the game* – over decades since the sixties.

'Sir Terence,' the cultured American voice crackles over the speaker phone – encryption noise. A worried tone continues, 'There is a lot of tension around Fiji at the moment. Extensive inquiries.'

'I've heard,' replies Sedgewood. 'But I'm told everything in the Pacific is calm.' That appeals to the dry humour of this classically-educated diplomat.

'We need you to be active, Sir T,' the voice replies. 'Get into those committees and settle them down.'

'I'll try.'

'You'll probably need to come over here to do the same task, before too long,' the disembodied voice continues. 'A British knight will soon settle the Congress committees back down.'

'Sit tight,' replies the Englishman. 'I will keep you all informed. Just hold the line steady. Consistent story. No panic.'

'We need this hosed down, Sir T, just like in the old days. You know how it works, as it always has. We are relying on you. We have done our bit. Now it's your turn.'

There are a lot of skittish people around, thinks Sir Terence. They've had it good for so long. Now, when things are a little tight, they are as nervy as racehorses. All very skilled bankers and gamblers with financial contacts second to none, they have an entree into any significant banking operation anywhere in the world. Anyone who is wealthy is on their private mailing list.

And yet to them, now replete in their many millions, banking and gambling are just fun activities; a game to provide an intellectual challenge. The humdrum of commercial transactions is all in their past. Now, they get their kicks from playing the high stakes on the political financial scene – they have done so since the Rossiter days.

Sir Terence is rapidly tiring of their cavalier attitude to global finance.

To him, financial dealing is serious; important business and a solemn national responsibility. He is a knight of the British Empire after all.

This is a new world. But, surely, standards of banking ethics are constant across generations? It is that deep-seated value framework which is causing Sir Terence such conflict at the moment.

He looks at his left hand with its recently acquired tremor. He has never had any nervous conditions before – but he is over eighty now. That would be the reason, he convinces himself.

Catherine and Sir Terence

'Ah, good afternoon, Ms Weston. Do come in and have a comfortable seat. Tea?'

Catherine takes his offered handshake and unobtrusively studies this powerful figure. Sir Terence is tall and still slim, with wavy locks of coiffured grey hair giving him a distinguished look. He has the presence of a man used to dealing with senior politicians and civil servants – that whiff of elegant education, social poise and avuncular grace. He looks like the Chairman of the Board.

'Thank you,' Catherine replies.

Sir Terence nods to Janet to prepare the refreshment.

Settled in their chairs, the chairman looks gently at his guest. Clearly, he has had some warning of this visit. The querying intrigue is on his face.

She guesses he wants to know more about this fledgling police group, the *NPA*, and what might have brought one of its senior operatives to visit him so promptly.

She reads his eyes to discover his thinking, because the rest of his posture is well-practised polite blandness.

She wonders. Is he thinking that the *National Police Authority* are worried by his frank assessment of their low potential usefulness? No, that would be too charitable an interpretation. Is he surprised by her presence? Again, no. He would know that this meeting would happen at some stage. Does her early appointment suggest to him that the NPA are much more assertive than he had given them credit for? But she sees arrogance in his eyes. Most probably, he is thinking that the NPA are just acknowledging his importance in the scheme of things; his years of international experience in dealing with the sensitivities of government.

'Now, Miss Weston. How might I be of assistance to you?'

Her thoughts don't appear on her face. She smiles politely as she holds eye contact with the knight. A knock at the door.

The tea and *petits fours* arrive, courtesy of the ever-polite Janet, sparing Catherine from an immediate answer.

She takes her time to watch Sit Terence casually take in her appearance. His eye movements are polished, practised. He would note that she wore no rings; dressed in the dark tones of business attire with solid high-heeled shoes. He would assess her as mid-forties. What else would he know? That she is an inspector from Yorkshire and is now working with the no-nonsense Scotsman, Angus Forbes. That the *NPA* has the backing of the Prime Minister? That would challenge his sense of propriety.

'Sir Terence,' Catherine starts. 'Thank you for giving me your valuable time this afternoon. I am looking forward to getting the benefit of your wisdom from dealing in international business.'

He nods his appreciation at the comment, as Catherine continues, 'You know who I am and the charter of the organisation that I represent. So I won't insult your obvious intelligence by going over familiar ground.'

The board chairman smiles politely at the flattery.

'We are working closely with *Versec*,' she continues. 'I apologise for the acronyms. *Versec* stands for *Veracity Section*. It is a branch of *international enforcement* in the United States. Its role is similar to ours in Britain.'

She notes his polite knowing bow. She is quietly betting that he thinks *NPA* has no role.

'We are investigating international fraud,' she says. 'Very clever operators who are being given some high-level, albeit discreet, support.'

His expression does not change. Not a flicker.

'Tell me, Sir Terence, you are chairman of the boards of a number of national and international companies. Could you give me your perspective on the prevalence of illegality in international business practices?'

His thoughtful look changes slowly into a patronising smile as he starts his long dissertation on the state of Britain's economy – with only a few nostalgic glances back to the glory days of Empire. He talks fleetingly about the dangers of high-risk speculators and about the need for Britain's enterprise to be a steadying influence; but at the forefront of opportunities; in technology, in innovation, in walking beside developing nations.

A nice touch, Catherine thinks cynically. *Walking over developing nations might be more accurate.*

The elegant knight continues his impressive colonial monologue of all that Britain had done for the world and how, for Britain to continue to be *Great* Britain, business needs to be at the cutting edge.

'It can't be done by the all-conquering British Army any more,' he says. 'No, we have to be sensitive to the feelings of other sovereign nations. It needs great delicacy and diplomacy.'

'Is that why you are opposed to the *NPA*, Sir?' she asks sweetly, to break the train of platitudes.

Sir Terence seems startled – as if it is impolite to interrupt him in full song.

'My dear Miss Weston.' He blinks, having regathered his thoughts. 'With all due respect to yourself, it has taken generations of quiet persuasion and respectful negotiation to build the alliances that Britain enjoys with the rest of the world. It is not a place for law-enforcement officers to come in and ride rough-shod over all these years of diplomacy.'

'Oh.' Her steely Yorkshire charm resonates in her tone. 'I wasn't suggesting our shoes would be the rough work of some amateur artisan. No, our shoes will be polished; good strong soles of professional police officers for stamping on anything in breach of international conventions, laws and understandings.'

After a nod to emphasise her point, she continues with her quiet assertiveness. 'You see we think that maybe, just maybe, there are some sophisticated criminal minds out there who are plundering the wealth of nations and causing abject misery for many, by their actions. And we also think there are influential people in this country, and others, who are endorsing this plunder; who are protecting the perpetrators and who are complicit in major crimes against international society.'

She pauses only long enough to note a fleeting flicker of worry cross the knight's expression – not anger, but definitely worry. 'We intend to expose those grey players behind the scenes; the puppeteers who pull the strings; and those who, by turning a blind eye, are guilty of allowing the greedy exploitation to continue unabated.'

Catherine has delivered the speech she wants Sir Terence to hear.

Angus had said to her, 'Go and throw the cat among the pigeons. Stir them up. Then they will make mistakes and we will be watching.'

But, to his credit, Sir Terence calmly and slowly acknowledges her. 'Quite a speech. You should be in parliament with such oratorical skills.'

She knows he is being gallant. She has rattled him. The small twitch at the corner of the eye and in the slight tremor in the hand are the involuntary evidence. But, all in all, he has remained very composed.

The hot conversation is over. The façade of pleasantries return. The talk continues for the allotted time.

Yes, of course, they would be in touch if anything develops. Yes, it has been lovely meeting you for the first time. I can see why you have been appointed to such important work, he says.

The meeting ends as it had started, with the precise politeness of the English establishment.

Steve's job offer

Coral Sea. Sunday 11 February 2007

'Your background checks out, Steve.' Roger nods with a seemingly grudging acknowledgement.

'Pleased to hear it,' I reply. His stateroom is slowly growing on me.

'And your background interests me. I could have an opportunity around the security of this ship. Interested?'

I watch him intently, keeping my non-commissioned officer expression in place, while I tell myself to be careful. Never volunteer.

But Roger is launching into his prepared pitch. 'Peter Carter has been looking after the ship's safety, as you might have realised, but I have other work for him now. You seem to have the right mix of skills. What do you say to a trial over the next few days until we dock in Cairns?'

I keep my face in control. What *can* I say to an offer like that? I am unemployed and cadging a lift to Australia. I nod. 'Yes, thank you.'

'Good show!' Roger gushed. 'Jolly good.' He seems to be such an enthusiast. 'Let me take you round how it all works.'

* * * *

We go down to the same office where I had filled out the passport forms only a few days before. I now look with fresh interest at the banks of computer screens.

Roger is a child showing off his new game: the radar, the sonar, the closed circuit television – taking care to show how to toggle from one camera to another.

'Is there sound as well as vision?'

He gives a huge guffaw and then drops his tone to a quiet conspiratorial level. 'Peter and I told everyone on board that the CCTV picked up conversations as well as pictures. You should have seen everyone being so careful about what they said.' He roars with laughter again. 'No, there's no sound, but don't let anyone know that. They're so well behaved as long as they think I can listen in.'

I smile as if to share his humour. Does he realise the fear that his *joke* has engendered in Gina? Is that the angst I sensed permeating the ship, from the moment I stepped on board?

Gina has told me. I can't say I haven't been warned.

'Now look at this.' He continues. 'This is the infra-red vision.' A screen with greenish shapes comes up. 'It doesn't work well during the day but you get the effect in that corridor where I have turned the lights off. It picks up body heat.'

I can see a crewman feeling his way along the darkened corridor to find the light switch which Roger has turned off remotely.

'It picks up heat, up to half a kilometre away over the sea.' He is starting to sound like a salesman. 'You just point it in the dark and anyone approaching with body heat, or an engine, will be picked up.'

'Very impressive.' I have used that type of equipment before in the hills of Afghanistan, but I didn't expect to find it on a luxury cruiser.

'The CCTV, Roger? Is it in the rooms as well?'

Another burst of hilarity.

'Goodness no! Only on the decks and in the corridors. It is security vision, not surveillance. People need their privacy.'

He chortles again at some thought passing through his mind but he doesn't share the thought as he takes me through the radio communication networks, call signals and emergency procedures.

'What do you think? Can you handle all of this and keep us safe?'

'I will be happy to handle it.' I am feeling nervous that I have suddenly been elevated into this position of trust – but then what have I really been shown?

'The money will be good,' my new boss assures me. 'If we get on alright, I might have other openings for you.'

'Thanks.' I hope I sound genuinely impressed. 'You have taken care of me very well.'

Roger grins, clearly happy with his recruitment.

'I have another task. More delicate perhaps,' he adds. 'You seemed to get on fine with Gina, on shore. Am I right?'

What does that innocent comment mean? I shrug my shoulders, not game to commit to words.

'Well, you didn't get into arguments,' Roger continues, 'and you brought her back safely.'

'Yes!' Where is this conversation heading?

'Not everyone has been able to do that.' He grins. 'Our Gina can be quite a handful if she gets her dander up.'

'She was okay with me.' But I understand that scenario. I have seen the arrogant version of Gina.

'I want you to look after her till we get to Cairns.' It comes out in an impersonal tone. 'I'm tied up in lots of business just now – and I just don't have the time to entertain her on board ship. I need you to talk with her, be around her, keep her calm. Can you do that?'

This is dodgy. 'Roger, Gina is your lady. You're asking me to look after her. You're my boss. Won't there be a problem with that?'

He laughs at his sudden appreciation of my comment. He is like a child sometimes. 'No, no. Don't misunderstand me. She's still my *lady*, as you put it. I don't want you to take over that role. I just need you to keep her entertained during the day so that I don't have to deal with a complaining woman when I have important work to do. Okay? Can you see the boundary now?'

He is such a confusing man – danger and charm, intermixed – and my survival instinct is telling me not to antagonise him. 'Yes! I'll give it a go.'

I can see the relief shine in his eyes. Bizarre.

'Good chap! Let's have a drink to seal the deal!'

It is a very expensive bottle of vintage red which emerges from his wine cabinet. This ship never ceases to produce surprises.

Steve and Gina

Coral Sea. Sunday 11 February 2007

The *Lerna* is knifing its way westward through the gentle open-sea swell.

Gina reclines on a lounger as I emerge from the stairwell onto the sundeck. She is just in the shade, getting the warmth of the day and the ozone air but without the burning rays. That golden tan is not from the Pacific sun.

'Good afternoon.' My cheery greeting causes a sleepy movement from behind the large sunglasses. 'Oh, sorry if I woke you. I thought you were awake.'

Well, she is now, whatever.

'Hello, stranger,' she says, now that she has focused her eyes on the interruption to her boredom. 'Have you been busy?'

'As it happens, I have,' I say, with a little smugness in the tone. 'Roger has given me the job of ship security, in place of Peter, until we reach Cairns.'

She doesn't look either impressed or pleased. 'Congratulations,' comes the flat response, as she replaces her sunglasses.

'Mind you, the ship is pretty secure out here,' I say, maintaining my cheeriness. 'I can see to every horizon.' She is not going to get to me with her imperious ignoring. 'So, it is nice to be employed again. It beats voluntary kitchen duty.'

No response.

'And I have had a complete tour of the radar, communications and the CCTV. It appears that the cameras are vision only, no sound.'

'Did you look for the volume control?' comes her bored voice, without any movement of her body, or the eyes, from behind the large sunglasses.

She is not impressed. I can tell.

'No volume control,' I continue, 'just misinformation. Ah well, don't believe me, if you choose. If you must sleep the day away, I'll just go off and be important somewhere else.'

I rise to leave. She sits up. Her eyes take in the CCTV cameras – and she turns her best profile to each, just in case anyone is watching.

'Well, well, there you are,' she says. 'You'd better go off on patrol. Check the screens again. I'm going to the jacuzzi.'

* * * *

I carry on round the ship. What a sense of freedom to have a role and not be supervised by Laughing Len. I wander up to the bridge where Captain Rodriguez looks as elegantly immaculate as ever.

He gives me a welcoming smile. 'Congratulations on your promotion, Steve. Can I call you Steve?' The word is clearly out among the crew already. 'I haven't seen you for a while. Are you enjoying the voyage?'

'It's beautiful, Captain. I like the sea air – and the calm seas. Is everything going to plan.'

'Oh yes! This is a beautiful ship and we have an excellent crew. It should be a good voyage to Cairns.'

* * * *

At the office, I am keen to check on Gina's comment about volume controls.

Sitting down, I methodically work my way through each screen and camera. There are volume controls on the screens, for every function – except the CCTV.

I find the camera with Gina in the jacuzzi. There is no sound – and no provision for sound. Always best to be careful … and maybe my benefactor has been lying. Trust no-one.

What sort of person is Roger? He makes little sense.

I am struggling to read his expressions, the meanings behind his suggestions, his relationship with Gina – and what he meant by more opportunities for me.

Obviously I am not getting the whole story. Even more likely is that I am being set up for something.

* * * *

'Security officer on patrol,' I call out as I approach the jacuzzi, not sure what mood I will find the lady in this time round. Is that a smile there? Hard to say. The big dark glasses mask most of any expression.

'I have watched Madame on the television,' I announce with a grin, as I sit down on the chair by the jacuzzi.

She gives a slight smile. Hard not to relax in the face of such foolishness.

'The volume controls definitely don't work on the TV. I can confirm that.'

'Just keep your voice down,' she says quietly, 'or they won't need a volume control.'

I whisper, doing a great act with my eyes. 'I'm now a free agent. I can go where I like on the ship – with Roger's approval. And I have just left Captain Rodriguez on the bridge – everything is in hand.'

Gina giggles.

Progress!

'Okay, Chief Security Officer.' She grins. 'You're an important man.' Her smile lapses into a worried frown. 'I hope you know what you're doing. There is danger here.'

I return a cheeky laugh – which draws another small smile.

She removes her sunglasses and lays them on the edge of the pool.

'Steve, when we get to Cairns, will you take me for a walk along the boardwalk – just like we did in Noumea?' It is a little girl voice.

Are her eyes looking misty? What is she up to?

'Sure.'

'Promise me,' she says, with some intensity.

'I promise.' I reach out and hold her offered hand, before releasing it slowly. I could be on television. Her frown suggests a disappointment that I had let her go.

'You make me laugh,' she says softly, sadly. 'I told you in Noumea I thought I'd forgotten how to laugh.'

She looks like a lost lonely girl at that moment. Normally, I would reach out to a woman in such obvious distress but the atmosphere around the ship is making me very wary. It is an unsettling sensation.

'You look good when you laugh,' I say as an alternative. 'Your eyes light up. You have the most beautiful blue eyes.'

A true statement; sapphire-blue.

'You say the nicest things, Steve,' she says, still in that quiet voice. 'I like your company. You are easy to talk to. I haven't had anyone to speak to for such a long time.'

Again, I look into those plaintive eyes. 'Gina, we have a few days before we dock. I have nothing to do except repel all boarders. Roger has told me he is really busy, so even *you* probably won't see much of him. If you want to talk, I'm happy to listen. I don't provide solutions. But listening? That I can do.'

'Thank you,' she whispers as a slow tear rolls down her cheek. 'Sorry. I'm usually in control,' She dabs her eye. 'Thank you.'

She rises from the jacuzzi, wrapping a towel round herself as she does.

'I'm just going to freshen up. I'll meet you on the deck in a little while, if you like.'

She gives me an encouraging smile.

Alison Wood

Cairns. Monday 12 February 2007

Landing at Cairns International Airport on a sunny day is always a beautiful sight.

Green waters glow bright around the islands, merging with the tropical blue of the deeper sea. Steep forested hills seem so close to the settlement. The port city of Cairns shines its welcome, nestled white among the cane fields, in contrast to the misty gloom of the Bartle Frere and Bellenden Ker mountain block to the south.

It is hot, with a cloying humidity, as Alison Wood emerges from the plane.

The birds seem quiet and even the fronds on the palm trees hang limp. Yet, while dark clouds gather far out to sea and over the peaks, it isn't raining.

'Might as well be lashing down,' she mutters outside the terminal doors, at the immediate rush of perspiration as her skin reacts to the humidity.

The air-conditioned taxi covers the distance to the city in a few minutes.

After checking into her motel, she decides that it is pointless to change the damp clothes; everything would be soaking again in minutes in the saturated air. She walks the two blocks to the esplanade and stares out to sea.

Boats are slowly wending their way towards her, in an even-paced late-afternoon procession; making for the safe shelter of the marina and harbour.

She strolls out along the jetty, taking in the colour-splashed view of luxury power craft. Most of them are Australian but there are others registered in the Pacific islands and some from Asian ports.

It shouldn't be too long now before she would expect to see the bow wave of the *Lerna* heading along that same channel. Maybe a couple of days? She would be checking the shipping info on the web and be a regular daily spectator on the wharf, until it arrived.

In the meantime, she has court reports to complete.

The *Shinwuan*

'G'day Jeff. Ben here!'

Jeff Fowler walks immediately out of the committee room to take the call. It is rare for Brennan to phone him, so it must be important. *Mind you*, he wonders, *the Nemesis man can be a puzzle to figure out.*

He listens to the familiar laconic voice asking him, 'Do you have anything for me?'

'No. Nothing yet,' says Fowler. 'What about you?'

'My whisper is that the boats that raided your luxury yacht came from a passing merchant vessel.' He speaks in a slow dramatic voice.

'Go on.'

'I'm told it was the *Shinwuan*, a two-thousand tonne freighter, moving from Port Vila to Apia.'

'Your source?' asks Fowler, in the vain expectation that he might be told.

'Someone who knows someone who was on the *Shinwuan* when three demountables were launched into choppy seas under cover of darkness. Over to you now, to deliver. See you later, mate.'

Brennan has hung up before anything further could be said. Not even time for a *thank you* from Fowler.

National Police Authority

London. Monday 12 February 2007

'I think you have stirred them up good and proper, Catherine. Well done!'

Angus Forbes leans back in his chair with the fingers of both hands touching in a steeple shape. He nods quietly. He has listened to Catherine's account of her Saturday afternoon meeting with Sir Terence Sedgewood. 'That has set up a very good start to the day and the week.'

She smiles in thanks. Take praise when it is offered. Who knows when the next time might be. 'I imagine that the Minister will be hearing from *The Dark Knight* very soon, if that hasn't already happened on the Sabbath. I'm glad we have the Brigadier on our side to deal with the Minister's questions. He would be good at running interference, I'd imagine. Yes?'

'The Brigadier?' says Angus. 'Oh, yes. He'll be more than a match for all those politicians, lobbyists and complainers. He won't flap. He'll just be Mr Calm, Mr Reasonable – but with a lot of Mr Steel.'

'What's the Brigadier's background?'

'Military man obviously. Douglas Candow is his name. Long history in action. He retired after the Balkan conflict; involved in Intelligence work latterly but also in coordinating the undercover activities – counter-espionage, messy stuff.'

'He seemed happy to retire. Experienced amateur pilot. His own plane. He's not poor. He married a Frenchwoman about a dozen or more years ago. A countess, I believe. They have a chateau in the Loire Valley. Lots of money. Vineyards. Wineries. I haven't been there but I'm told that it's quite a place. Heritage antiques, old French cars. Like the stately homes of England or our Scottish castles, where all that history is preserved.'

Catherine tilts her head with an impressed smile. 'Sounds like he doesn't need to work. Earned the right to retire to leisure and luxury. Dealing with all that wealth would keep him busy enough.'

Angus gives a nod. He is keen to explain some more.

'Except that he was very good at what he did in the military. He had good contacts, networks, and a fine analytical brain – and he was used to dealing with the politics of the grander strategic picture.

'So the department approached him to work in an advisory role only a couple of days a week. He liked it. It gave him the intellectual stimulation he needed – as well as the opportunity to pilot his plane as a weekly commuter between France and Britain.

'And now we've been lucky enough to have him overseeing our operations, as an advisor and a troubleshooter, on a few days a week. He was the Minister's suggestion.'

'A good way to retain his skills and services,' agrees Catherine.

'And just you wait till you see the Brigadier take on the Sir Terences of this world.' Forbes has a Celtic smirk on his face as he pictures the scenario. 'He'll stand toe-to-toe, look them in the eye and taunt them to take him on. And they'll hear his campaign medals rattling, figuratively, because he's been in the tough fights while they've been shining their trousers on the leather seats of the boardrooms. It'll be interesting to watch.'

Australian Federal Police

'Sir, we have a report on the *Shinwuan*,' Bill Jones advises Fowler. 'She's registered in the Philippines and was chartered by the South Pacific Freight Alliance. The alliance is a group of shipping companies. The directors come from many Asian countries. The chair is a Sir Terence Sedgewood of London.'

'Do we have confirmation that the vessel was in the vicinity of Fiji on the date the *Sea Spray* was attacked?'

'Yes, Sir. En route from Port Vila in Vanuatu to Apia in Samoa; she would have been close to the north of Fiji on that date.'

'Excellent, Bill. Well done! Get that intel through to the Brits and the Americans as soon as you can. Thank goodness for Ben Brennan. A breakthrough, at last.'

'Oh,' says the sergeant, 'One other thing. You asked about the name, Alison Wood. I thought it rang a bell. She was the court reporter who wrote about the sapphire robber at Emerald. Do you remember? *Vot isst your name.*'

'Yes, I remember.' He chortles at the recollection. 'Do we know anything about her?'

Jones shakes his head.

'She means something to Ben Brennan. I don't know what but if there is some connection with the *Lerna*, that might mean Cairns. Alert the Queensland Police to keep an eye out for her, please. Tell them not to intervene, just observe. We don't know what this is about yet.'

'Done.' The dutiful Jones smiles. 'I feel as if we are starting to make some headway. I'll get back to the cross-checking and monitoring team.'

Ben Brennan

'You have something for me?'

Ben Brennan has just rung Fowler's mobile number in response to a text message.

'Yes, Ben. I think so. First, Alison Wood wrote a court report last month about a stolen sapphire out on the Gemfields beyond Emerald. It was a witty story and she quoted a comment attributed to the German robber, *It was stolen for Ramas*. It might have lost something in translation. We have no record of *Ramas* – as a person, or a thing, or an event. Bill thought it sounded Indian.

'That's all we have on the Wood girl, at this stage. We don't know where she is, at the moment. We're working on it. Does *Ramas* mean anything to you?'

'I've heard the term,' replies Brennan. 'I'll do some listening.'

'Now second, we followed up on the *Shinwuan*. It was in the right place to have been part of the story. We've also uncovered that the Chairman of the Board of the South Pacific Freight Alliance is a British knight, called Sir Terence Sedgewood. We are cross-referencing his activities. Does his name mean anything to you?'

'Not at the moment. Anything else?'

'No, not yet,' says Fowler. 'Stay in touch.'

'Will do. Cheers,' he says and hangs up.

Fowler smiles at the more polite closure than usual.

Ramas? He needs to get that name to the British and American teams. He picks up his phone to call Bill Jones.

Alison Wood in Cairns

Cairns. Tuesday 13 February 2007

Alison Wood looks like a tourist trying to catch a fish. She sits on the warm concrete Cairns jetty, with a blue canvas hat on her head, wearing a long-sleeved pale shirt, knee-length white jeans and leather sandals. A slim silky fishing line hangs off her forefinger with the reel resting in a green bucket at her side.

She sincerely hopes that no fish will bite onto the bare hook, only to be thrown back if it does. There are no facilities for cooking fish at the motel.

In her mind, she is setting up a pattern of behaviour which will look normal by the time the *Lerna* arrives in harbour. She plans to sit for two hours on her folding chair, depending on the tides, and appear to fish.

Beside her, she has a novel to read, as well as, in an embroidered dilly bag, her iPad and the rough written notes for her investigative story on piracy. She has collected a lot about ships being attacked in the Malacca Strait, the South China Sea and through the islands of Indonesia. In the Coral Sea, she has examples of ships being scuttled in attempted insurance fraud and there are a few hi-jacks of luxury boats for ransom. She even has printed transcripts of interviews, which she has made with survivors of pirate attack. But it is the actual names of the people behind it all, that she wants – an exposé.

There had been one attack recently which seemed to have had a clamp on any real information. It had been near Fiji and involved the pop singer, Ingrid. It had only been reported fleetingly in the tabloids, so maybe it was only a publicity stunt. That, in itself, interests her, as a fledgling investigative journalist. Who is controlling the publication of information?

She is in Cairns, having followed up on Ben Brennan's tip of the *Lerna*. She hadn't found much information on Roger Cavanagh. He appears to live on a ship and the only registration she could find said he is a *trader*. Beyond that, he doesn't appear as a director on any boards; he isn't listed with any companies. Really, he scarcely exists. Not a birth certificate, or even a date of birth, that she can source.

The jetty is quiet; just a few tourists taking a stroll out to see the expensive boats in the marina. The marine life isn't biting along the pier. She slowly and methodically starts to pack up her gear, establishing the routine.

The thrill of the chase is enjoyable yet she has a persistent nagging insecurity, a trusting hope that she can actually write this piece – like an actress peeking out from behind the mask of a character role.

She is an independent soul; not wishing to compromise to another's needs … unless …

Her mother has always harped on, *Why don't you settle down near home with a nice fellow, raise a family, be satisfied with your life? Why do you need to go to Brisbane to study? What's wrong with NSW universities?*

Nag! Nag! Nag!

They're all too close to home would have been the answer she would have given if she'd been honest; too close to the suffocating atmosphere of conforming to an expectation. And there is the big sister … the one who had been abused and abandoned in her teens and now, on the rebound, is a single mother; battling. Where is the comfort in that environment? The family hadn't been there for her sister when she needed them. Maybe, that is part of how her strong sense of social justice had developed. Not so much as a champion for the oppressed individuals but more a quiet crusader against the system that sees women in an inferior light, as chattels to be used, owned and abused.

She needs to breathe freely – to follow her dream to do something useful ... and to hit out at the culture of expected social gender roles. Alison wants to strike back – but using her brains, her keyboard and her way with words.

The media scholarship from school to uni was the *get-out-of-this-rut* card. It gave her the start, with the course fees paid and guaranteed vacation work in a news office. But her university studies had disappointed her, as did the media focus on sensation; the scoop story, the smart headline and the disregard for integrity.

She knows that she needs something more ... but in the meantime ... court reporting is at least about writing honest observations. There is no latitude to add a journalistic commentary on the judge's deliberations. It is safe. It earns the money. She can retain her principles. And she needs to satisfy her need for identity, for purpose, a goal beyond self.

Initially, she had formed the idea to do her exposé on pirates when reading about desperate East European women being kidnapped in the Baltic countries. Something about that story struck a chord ... and she started her research.

That has become her psychological support when anyone asks why a nice girl like her is following the court circuit. Well, they have their answer; she is earning her living while working on a much bigger project.

So here she is in Cairns, just a little scared that this could be very *front line*, while she waits for the yacht of perhaps the pirate king – almost Gilbert and Sullivan-like on a sunny day like today.

She isn't sure about the contrasting sources of her adrenalin, from the excitement of such a chase or from the reality of fear. She has no back-up. What does she expect to happen by waiting for the *Lerna* to arrive: that the scoop story is just going to fall into her lap; the journalistic disclosure which will whisk her into a quiet but successful life as a writer? She is depending on her appearance of innocent naivety. Is it ever going to be as easy as that – divorced from the essential stench and pain of criminal piracy?

* * * *

There is no glint from the binoculars. The man is in the shade. The picture in the lens of the glasses is of a girl in a blue hat, pale long-sleeved shirt and white knee-length slacks, fishing off the Cairns esplanade and then packing up to walk back into town.

Versec

'The Aussies have come through!' Larry Kennedy says to Kyle Broderick. 'They believe that they have identified the freighter – the host to the attack-inflatables at the *Sea Spray*.'

Broderick gave his best *tell me more* expression.

'It's the *Shinwuan* and it was hired by the South Pacific Freight Alliance. They have a board headed by a British knight, Sir Terence Sedgewood.'

Broderick's brow wrinkles.

'We did some research on the Brit knight and he chairs a board in America too – the Grey Bear Investment Bank. We're running some more checks.'

'That it? That what you have just now?'

Kennedy nods.

'Mmm. Lots of pieces. A jigsaw puzzle,' says Broderick patiently. 'Is it making any sense to you yet?'

'Needs a bit more detective work, boss.'

'Mmm,' the *Versec* chief repeats. 'Run it past Angus Forbes's group and see what they have come up with. They may see it from a different angle. Many brains might spark some link. Our task will be to check out the Grey Bear Investment Bank. I've never heard of it … but it smells a bit that they need a Brit to chair it.'

NPA and Roger

London. Tuesday 13 February 2007

Angus Forbes is in his familiar contemplative pose as he listens to Catherine Weston's report on Roger Cavanagh. Her team has been tracking down everything and anything about the mysterious businessman.

'From official documents,' she says, 'Roger Cavanagh has been the operator of three million-dollar luxury boats at different times. He is not listed as the owner of any of them in the registration documents. The owners are actually companies.

'His current boat, the *Lerna*, for example, is actually owned by the South Pacific Freight Alliance so technically the shareholders, through the board, are the owners. But Roger Cavanagh is the operator on the registration papers, listed as a trader, with clauses in the agreement to allow him total operative access.

'Cavanagh is not registered as being a director of the company. He's not on any board that we can find, anywhere in the world. His passport also states that he is a trader but, again, he deals through a whole range of companies.

'His tax return in Britain shows only a moderately wealthy income, comprised of a range of commissions from companies for services rendered. We have found no other tax returns lodged in other countries in his name.

'It appears that Mr Cavanagh gets other people to sign documents of ownership leaving him as *Mr Anonymous*. All his travel and accommodation arrangements for the past two years have been signed by a Peter Carter, an employee of the South Pacific Freight Alliance.'

Forbes is mulling over the documentation.

'This makes our task very difficult,' he concedes. 'No paper trail with his signature on it? Hard to sustain a court case in corporate fraud or illegal deals. Do you have anything else, Catherine?'

'We move into more circumstantial information,' she says. 'Is that okay?'

Forbes nods impatiently.

'Of the companies who actually paid money into the declared UK tax assessment, most came from companies which have Sir Terence Sedgewood as the chair or as a director. In particular, we delved into the South Pacific Freight Alliance – often known just as SPFA – and we find out that Cavanagh may well be an ex-officio adviser to the board. We tracked that down from the emailed invitations that he attends board meetings but is not recorded in the minutes as having attended.'

Angus Forbes's eyebrows rise up in surprise. 'Wow!'

'Still with the SPFA,' Catherine continues, 'they have multiple trading businesses across their many companies in the alliance. Cavanagh appears to be paid a commission on many transactions. They are all small payments but, cumulatively, we suspect he may be paid millions by the companies in that alliance, alone.'

Forbes peers in question, 'But we haven't accessed all his accounts as yet, I take it?'

'Only the British ones, for his tax return. Some others appear to be in Liechtenstein from the International Bank Account Numbers, the IBANs. We are tracking where the money seems to be sent by the payers. Others may be in Switzerland, Panama or the Caymans. They all look like numbered accounts so his name is most likely not even noted. Early days.' She waits till the Scotsman's growl ceases. 'Now, when we add the *Versec* investigation information about Grey Bear Investment Bank which, incidentally we were drawn to by the connection with Sir Terence Sedgewood, we find inconsistencies in receipts which have, on the balance sheets, been shown as share-trading profits. The sums don't match and, again, significant sums may have been siphoned off to the Caymans as *commission for services*, I'm guessing ... to a numbered account being accessed by Roger Cavanagh. None of these sums show on his British tax returns. They just get lost in the international nature of his life. His official personal bank accounts are actually quite modest.'

'Well.' Forbes grumbles. 'They would be if he is charging all expenses up to company accounts. I take your point. We might, in time, find substantial sums in his care at banks, all round the world.'

Weston nods. 'I see now why Sir Terence Sedgewood wanted us out of such an investigation. He is in this business right up to his knightly neck.'

Forbes's steepled fingers seem to support his chin. 'To recap, as I understand what you are telling me, we have information that Roger Cavanagh does not have the financial resources to sustain the lifestyle he leads. He will counter that the companies pay most of that – the boats, the travel, the lifestyle.

'We have no documentation that he has made board decisions or carried out executive orders for anything other than trade. It will be extraordinarily hard to pin corporate fraud on him, without written proof.

'We have circumstantial evidence that he is a decision-maker, does attend board meetings as an adviser and is probably very influential but that won't hold up in court because the official minutes don't mention his role. Do we have any hard connection with Cavanagh and the *Sea Spray* matter?'

'No. None,' she replies definitely. 'He wasn't on the *Lerna* at the time of the attack, although the ship itself was only a hundred kilometres from Fiji. An SPFA freighter, the *Shinwuan*, is implicated in the attack by the Australian AFP advice but Cavanagh is only a contractor with the alliance. So he has no provable culpability there. He wasn't on the *Lerna* when Steven Flynn was picked up, not joining the ship in fact till Noumea.'

'Thank you, Catherine. So,' Forbes muses, 'while we have a fair idea that Cavanagh is very likely a major player in some form of organised crime, we can't nail him on anything unless we catch him in the act, eh? A sting operation, perhaps? What do you think?"

'You're out of my league,' replies Catherine, 'but I'm always willing to listen.'

Forbes runs his skeleton of a plan past Catherine, who is then delegated to talk in bare-bones terms with the Australians – just to set the scene as it were.

Maybe, just maybe, it could work if the circumstances were to present themselves – but it is a long shot. Angus Forbes wonders at the high-level strategy which has been floated past him by people in superior positions.

Versec

Larry Kennedy has just read through the law-enforcement analysis on the *Sea Spray* incident, completed in record time. It exonerates most people on board but found the apparent anomaly – a crewman with associations to a ship used by Cavanagh in the Caymans.

The crewman, Bob Curtis, was employed at the last moment before the ship sailed from Papeete, to replace an injured deck-hand. However, he was more than a deckhand and had worked for Cavanagh's associates as a communications operator.

Interesting!

And Curtis had effectively disappeared after the boat berthed in Nadi. There is no record of him flying or sailing out of Fiji. It is a cold trail.

The search for the materials from the missing security men found their clothes and wash bags in their cabin spaces – but no personal papers of any type were found. No passports, no wallets, no diaries, no laptops, no mobiles, no PDAs … Bob Curtis's cabin area had been emptied as if by a professional cleaner.

More pieces for the jigsaw.

NPA and Techs

Catherine is just about to leave the building when Techs knocks on her office door, in the height of excitement.

'I have a match!'

She listens patiently as he explains the different databank cross-checking processes he has been running – just to see if Roger Cavanagh would appear anywhere, linked with any of the other personalities in the case; or maybe he might be matched against some transaction or event.

Most of it is routine and clean – just the boring whirring away of billions of audit calculations and correlations, through official electronic data records and on into more confidential e-traffic files and searches of a mass of ICQs, messaging and chat programs.

'ICQs?' Catherine queries.

'I Seek You,' Techs replies. 'Jargon for messaging systems.'

Then, further on into targeted encrypted systems.

Who is buying these systems? Catherine wonders. *Who is using them in the non-Intelligence market?* The computer scans purr away, night and day.

Using a personalised searching program that he has designed himself, he has gained entry into certain types of encrypted files. He was tracking his cryptanalysis through a massive bank of secure PGP files – perhaps not as secure as the marketers claim – when he had a match.

'PGP?' asks Catherine.

'Pretty Good Privacy,' Techs responds. 'Commercial, personalised encrytpions.'

She smiles, tolerantly.

It wasn't a straight hack. He had come at it from an oblique angle – not by hacking into the personal encryption but rather by finding a record of an installation transaction.

A sophisticated PGP encryption system had been installed on the luxury cruise ship, the *Lerna* – ordered and paid for by a Peter Carter – and Techs' program had recognised the connection between Carter, the *Lerna* and Cavanagh.

Catherine is excited at the match. Perhaps not quite as intensely as Techs, who is jabbering on about the processes he will go through to find the key to that particular encryption system. Given time and a lot of luck, he says, he will crack the code and then he can find out what is being transmitted and to whom.

Catherine isn't interested in the technical chat; the life-energisers of people like Techs. What pleases her is that she now has the start of some documentation that might link Roger Cavanagh, even tenuously, to the attack on the *Sea Spray* and then, perhaps, to a whole rack of illegal activities.

'Well done, Techs,' says Catherine. 'Keep at it and keep me informed. I want to know fast if you can hack into who Cavanagh is emailing in this secret system. Who? When? and What About? You are a wizard, Techs.'

* * * *

Techs looks very pleased as Catherine leaves; pleased with himself, pleased with the praise … pleased that his specialised geek skills are appreciated.

Gina and Steve

Coral Sea. Wednesday 14 February 2007

The early-morning sun has just started to light the sea from the east. I am on my sunrise patrol when I find Gina on the sundeck, staring towards the west, as if Australia might soon be visible.

She speaks quietly, and with warmth, as I join her with my questioning grin. 'Couldn't sleep,' she says. 'I thought I might watch the sun come up.' And then she turns to look at me. 'It's pretty, isn't it? It will be over the horizon soon.' She flicks her hand at the glistening sea and the lightening sky. She pauses for a few seconds, as if trying to find her words. Her expression is serious. 'You've been really kind to me, Steve. You've listened without sitting in judgement.'

I take it in. We've had some fairly happy hours on the deck, chatting about routine things; the ship, world news, clothes, food – even the weather, which has scarcely changed since we left Noumea.

I am slowly becoming convinced that she is speaking genuinely. The imperious aristocrat of Noumea has never resurfaced – at least, not with me. We have scrupulously avoided talking about personal matters or what would happen in Cairns; until now.

But this morning, she is clearly in one of her pensive moods. It happens every so often, when she retreats into her thoughts. Her normally confident front cracks and she looks frightened. At those times, I can sense the need to not interrupt.

'I'm feeling really low at the moment. Do you know why?'

I raise my eyebrows as if to say *Go on*.

'We are nearly at Cairns and, when we get there, everything will change. It will be like Cinderella at the ball at midnight. It has been good talking with you – a release, just by the conversation.

'Normally, people only speak to me on programmed occasions like when Roger is entertaining or I am paraded out as *the beautiful partner*. I have all the material things on this boat that most people would dream of. Clothes, jewellery, shoes, food – a luxury yacht travelling to all the exotic places in the world – but I am a prisoner. This is all just a mirage, Steve, an illusion. I can't *leave*.'

I gave her my *of course, you can* look.

'I have no money, no identity beyond this boat. My passport is held in the office safe. I am a trophy; the once-pretty model, getting older every day; trotted out to show that Roger Cavanagh has collected something else valuable.'

I sit quietly, sincerely trying to provide moral support while she pours out her woes. She is attractive, even with the tears – but not, for me, in any amorous way. I have trained myself not to let genital urges rule my head in work situations. She is the boss's lady. *The sister I never had* is always a good barometer to keep me from falling into honey traps. It worked while guarding a very tempting major's wife too, in a previous life.

'At Noumea, you asked who I was. You said I am Gina Robér. I must have a past. Well, I am Georgina Roberts from Bournemouth in England. I was an aspiring fashion model who won a swimsuit contest and the prize was a trip to the south of France.

'I went to Monte Carlo and looked out at a luxury cruiser called the *Ajaccio 3*, named after the capital of Corsica, bloody Napoleon's birthplace. The ship was dazzling red and white. As the tender came to shore, I was still looking at the ship spellbound when Roger Cavanagh hopped onto the quay and started talking to me.

'He invited me out to the ship and treated me like a princess. I'd never seen such luxury; and the power to make dreams come true. I was hooked, in more ways than one, sadly.'

149

As I look at her in question, she says, 'Yes, there were drugs too, Steve. Lots of them. It seemed like a good idea at the time.' She gives me a plaintive shrug, before continuing. 'About two luxury boats later, I woke up to myself when I realised I was totally snared – a pretty bird in a gilded cage. Got off the drugs after a long time but I couldn't get out of the cage. People look at me and see all the trappings of wealth and pampering. How would they know I can't leave?'

'But *surely* you can leave, Gina? All you would lose are the possessions on this boat. You could walk out and start again.'

'You still don't understand,' she whispers. 'All this wealth, everything here, comes from crime. Roger, for all his charm, is a smiling gangster. He might not fit the bad guy image but things that are done on his instructions are evil.

'I don't know the *ins and outs* but I do know where we have travelled, when, and who we often meet. I know a lot of that casual information. They couldn't risk me sharing it with others. That's why I am never allowed off the boat without an escort. They would never let me leave … and stay alive.'

I see the involuntary shiver as she makes the last comment. Who is it that causes such a reaction? Len? Peter? Roger, himself? Is she over-reacting?

'I have seen too much, Steve. As a captive, I am a submissive alibi. Free from the supervision, I could easily be a crown witness.'

There are no tears now. Gina is emotionally drained. She looks relieved that she has finally been able to tell someone.

I sit silently. I can't say I haven't been warned.

The survival instincts of the former soldier are being resurrected from my past.

Steve's dilemma

Off Cairns. Wednesday 14 February 2007

'We'll dock in Cairns later today,' Roger says to me.

'It's been a smooth crossing,' I reply. 'This is a beautiful ship, Roger.' No harm in praising a collector's toy.

'You've done well, Steve.' He looks at me with a slow head nod. 'The ship is safe.' He smiles as if to say *of course it is*. 'And you have kept Gina entertained. She has even been more sociable than I imagined she would be. It's an improvement anyway.'

'Thanks.' What more could I say without getting into deeper waters?

'Have you thought about what you will do when we land in Cairns?' he asks casually.

'Well, you said you might have work for me. That's a possibility. If it's not on offer, I'll check out the security businesses in Cairns. I'll find work.'

'No. You misunderstand. I *will* have work for you. No, I meant what will you say to the police in Cairns? Have you thought about that?'

'Why would I want to speak with the police?'

'I'd think it would be more them wanting to speak with you.'

I give a puzzled look.

Roger has a patient expression. 'I'm no expert on what happened in Fiji.' He speaks with guileless innocence. 'I only know what little has been reported and most of that seems to have appeared only in

151

gossip blogs. But it would seem to me that the Queensland Police would have reason to be very interested in the security guard from the *Sea Spray* who was reported dead and has suddenly come to life on their patch in Cairns.'

'But it's all explainable.' I am bemused. 'I've done nothing wrong.'

'Is it all so explainable?' asks Roger mysteriously. 'As an outsider, I see that a luxury yacht has been hi-jacked on a stormy night off Fiji, confirmed by you. The two security guards are reported by the crew as having been shot and thrown overboard. Presumably, since the rest of the crew and passengers were unharmed, there would have been a ransom demand, although that doesn't seem to be reported. Presumably also, since they were all released unharmed, the ransom was most likely paid.

'So, now the questions. How did the pirates get so close? Undetected? That they could attack the boat? An inside job? Who was in the best position for an inside job? The security guard? Oh, but witnesses saw both of them shot and thrown overboard. Cold case. No solution.

'But wait! Suddenly one of the security guards has risen from the dead and appears on another cruising ship heading to Noumea. He even applies for a passport and is given one. Normally that process could take weeks. Now he is arriving in Cairns. I think the police will definitely want to talk with you.'

'Okay,' I say defensively. 'But all of my story is checkable. The Fijians on the island can verify finding me on the beach. The doctor, Naleen your friend, can establish my injuries. Peter Carter can confirm that I came on board this ship.'

'Ah, now that is your problem,' says Roger. 'First, the island. Fijian territory. Did you declare yourself to the Fijian authorities? No! Do you expect the workers at the resort and an Indian-Fijian doctor to testify that they encouraged you to by-pass lawful process and to hitch a ride on a passing boat? What do you think the Fijian Army would do with them?'

I can visualise the smiling face of Lani and the men who had saved my life; *the good doctor* who had redirected me from being lost in the passport bureaucracy of the Fijian capital, Suva. No, I won't ask that of them. I won't put them in danger.

Roger continues. 'And Peter Carter is away on other business now. We are a law-abiding ship. We would pick up a shipwreck, a castaway – but we would not condone encouraging a possible criminal suspect to escape the law of a sovereign nation. Now do you understand your dilemma, Steve?'

He has been speaking very quietly, in a friendly yet menacing way. I am not quite sure what he means. Throw me out? Take away my alibi? I can feel my blood starting to rise. I can't say I haven't been warned about this man.

'You are one of us now, Steve. You see that, don't you?'

'What do you mean? One of us?' I can feel my muscles tense.

'Sit down.' Roger passes me a whisky and takes one for himself. 'I like you, Steve. You know that. I've told you that. I'm a trader. We trade in anything generally, anything that will fit in a freight ship. Our boats hop from island to island generally carrying whatever produce or equipment is needed. We keep the locals happy. We make a small profit on every transaction and, over a big business, we make a large amount of money.

'Our company is called the South Pacific Freight Alliance. It is governed by a board of Asian businessmen and is even headed by an English knight. It is a successful legitimate business – and it is growing. I need good people to work with me. I think you could be one of those people.'

I watch him; his charming benign expression, while painting me into a corner. 'When you say you trade anything, does that mean *anything*? Like drugs? Are you in the rackets?'

'Actually, probably the only product we wouldn't touch would be drugs. Not from any moral or philosophical stance but more because Asian countries have very harsh penalties for drug dealers – the death penalty in most countries. Most Asian merchant seamen are very wary of dealing with drugs. It's just not worth the risk.

'We run a low-risk operation. We stay under the radar. We don't want trouble with police or naval ships. Certainly, we would carry things which some countries might not regard as legal, but not drugs.'

'So, I still don't understand what you are offering me.'

Patiently Roger says, 'First, I want you to think about what you are going to say to the police when they interview you in Cairns. I have just given you the context so that you can understand our position and the position of those in Fiji.

'I've been watching you. I like *the cut of your jib*. I am always on the lookout for those rare people with skills we could use. I would like to think you could work in our company. Certainly, there's security work on this and other vessels. But we also have a network of people who look out for business opportunities in most countries of South East Asia and the South Pacific. These networks need people to supervise and train them. Believe me, we have lots of opportunities. Just think about what I have said, that's all.'

He is such a gentle persuader. I can feel myself being carried along on the tide of his argument and the sense of power, which his understated display of financial success suggests.

'I need to be away on business for about five days when we dock,' he says. 'I am offering you the chance to look after the ship's security while I am away. Do you think you would able to do that? Captain Rodriguez and a skeleton crew will remain. The captain can contact me in an emergency. The money is good. So, are you interested?'

'Yes, I'm interested.' I surprise myself with my lack of hesitation. 'Okay. I'll look after the security for the days you are away. We'll work out the rosters between the captain and me. I get on fine with him. We can talk about all these other options, when you have time on your return.'

'Done deal!' Roger's smile has returned. 'Let's seal it with a drink.' He pours new glasses with the very nice single malt whisky, with no ice to dilute the taste.

For some reason, I feel as if I have just been watching a conjurer at work, manipulating the cards, but I can't quite see how it was done.

Gina and Steve

Off Cairns. Wednesday 14 February 2007

She is back on the sundeck but not in the usual swimsuit, for this time of day. She is still wearing the flowing chiffony thing that she had on at sunrise but now with the addition of a broad-brimmed hat shielding her dark glasses. She is staring towards the faint Queensland coast on the horizon, just a faint mountainous line … and we will be there in a couple of hours.

'Okay?' I ask, as I reach her, but she keeps staring ahead.

'I have to go with him when we get into Cairns. That is my work in this organisation. Smile at a procession of nameless crawlers.' She turns to look at me. 'I'm so tired of all this shit, Steve.'

'I have to watch the ship with Captain Rodriguez until you return. We'll have that walk when you get back.'

She gives a wan smile. 'If I get back, Steve.' She removes her sunglasses and rubs her eyes.

I look at her but her eyes stay down as she speaks. 'There is danger here. I'm beyond help now but … Steve, it is something to do with an organisation or person or a group called *Ramas*. Be careful!' Her eyes lift, moist and a little red. Her hand just grazes my arm before she returns to her mournful stare at the coastline.

Arrival at Cairns

Cairns. Wednesday 14 February 2007

Bill Jones, at Cairns International Airport, phones the news to his Superintendent.

'We have a lead on Alison Wood. There's a record of her flying into Cairns from Brisbane on Monday. The local police are discreetly checking the motels to find out where she might be staying. We'll keep you in the loop.'

* * * *

Alison lays down her book and fishing line. The wait has paid off.

The ship looks very grand; the glistening deep-blue hull with the sparkling white superstructure; a big cruising boat, wide across the beam. It has almost no bow wave as it slowly progresses along the channel towards the harbour.

It looks far too big to moor in the marina, unless it is to use the huge *Sailfish* jetty, behind the high black gates … or the dredged cruise ship wharf, farther upstream.

The *Lerna* nudges steadily towards the shore; large square-shaped yellow flag clearly visible, high on the mast; two smaller powerboats accompanying it. The yellow one has the lettering, *Customs*. The other is probably a port pilot, Alison surmises.

She imagines there might be an hour at least before all the docking procedures would be complete. The chat around the wharf is that the *Lerna* would be there for five days at least.

With a sense of satisfaction that her quarry has now arrived, Alison picks up her familiar bucket and strolls off along the pier back to the town.

* * * *

'Ben,' Jeff Fowler says, 'Alison Wood is in Cairns. Flew in a couple of days ago. Seems to be keeping a vigil on the marina pier while pretending to be fishing. I have her motel address. Do you want it?'

'Yes, thanks,' says Ben, lowering his binoculars to note the address. 'Do you have anything else?'

'Nothing more at this stage.'

'Cheers,' says Ben and he hangs up.

* * * *

'That's all the Customs and Immigration paperwork complete now,' Roger advises. 'The Immigration people will return with Cairns police in an hour to talk with you, Steve.'

He gives me a look which suggests a sense of support; that it will all be fine. Routine. As long as I have thought about what I am going to say.

'I'll be gone within the hour,' Roger says. 'I have a flight in a little over two hours so I will get moving. Oh, Gina will be coming with me. You're in charge with Captain Rodriguez until we return.' He gives me a strange grin … as if I have been given a meaningless responsibility.

* * * *

Only fifteen minutes later, a vehicle is alongside and the crew load suitcases into the back. As if on cue, Roger and Gina emerge, dressed for the airport. She looks across at me, with a bland expression.

I smile confidently back and quietly say, 'See you both when you return. I'll know which sights in Cairns you should visit, by then.'

I hope she gets the message.

A weak smile, a small wave; and the limousine whisks them off to the airport.

It has been all action around Roger's needs. I sit down in the quiet aftermath of the grand exodus to prepare my thoughts for the police interview.

* * * *

Inspector Mal Willis of the Cairns Police listens to Superintendent Jeff Fowler. It has been a long conversation but an important one.

They have talked before but never met ... and the upcoming interview on the *Lerna* has high international priority.

The key message Willis has received from the AFP Super is that the interview must appear to be absolutely routine. No interrogation of the facts. Simply listen and form an opinion as to how much truth is being told.

Fowler reassures Willis that the reason for such an experienced police officer attending is that there would only be one chance to assess Steven Flynn's state of mind or hear his view of his current situation.

'We don't know,' Fowler says, 'whether Flynn is on the boat under duress or a fugitive from the scene of a crime. It is very delicate.'

Willis feels both flattered at his selection and nervous at the sensitive role he is about to perform. He will be accompanied by an Immigration official, John Norton.

Cairns Police

Cairns. Wednesday 14 February 2007

An ominous feeling courses through me as the police and Immigration officials step onto the *Lerna*. I won't get a retake on this.

The comfortable interview room near the gangway is provided; all low key. No luxury. No swanking.

Roger has left everything very vague. Given what Gina has said, I have limited confidence that my new employer would support me if the going were to get tough. I am very dispensable. Not a collectible.

I grin wryly to myself.

* * * *

The introductions are made – Inspector Mal Willis of the Cairns police and Immigration Officer, John Norton.

Inspector? A pretty high-powered welcome for a stranded ex-soldier returning home.

'Welcome back to Australia,' says the inspector, on cue. 'You have had quite an experience. Our job is to hear what happened so that we can close the file on the loss of your passport, that's John's interest. How you came to be rescued is my interest.'

'Fine.'

John starts. 'Your original passport. Where was it when you last saw it?'

'In my locker in my cabin, on the *Sea Spray 2*.'

'Has anyone advised you of its current whereabouts?'

'I'm sorry? No. I've been out of all communications since the incident. I've just been travelling back to Australia on this ship.'

'Thank you.' John makes a notation on his form.

'Can you tell me what happened on that night in January when you were on the *Sea Spray*, please?' asks the inspector.

I launch into my explanation. 'It was a dark night with a fairly strong chop on the water, in the direction of the beach. We had sea anchors out. Aldo and I checked the radar – that's Aldo Pollock, my security partner. Everything was clear. Visuals were clear too, but we couldn't see far. The wind was making a bit of noise but we would have heard if any outboards had been approaching. There weren't any. We had lifejackets on as we patrolled the decks. Aldo was on the windward. I was on the leeward.

'A stun grenade went off. I saw Aldo being hit and falling. I got two shots away at the shapes of people. Then I got hit on the right side of my head and fell into the water. Apparently, the bullet scoured a furrow along my head. Here!' I lifted my regrown hair so that they could examine the still-red scar above my ear.

'I have to confess I don't have much more memory of events until I was on the *Lerna*. I'm told they took me on board at the jetty on the nearby island. I don't really know how it all happened.'

The inspector looks at me, encouraging me to continue – so I carry on with my prepared story.

'The owner, Mr Cavanagh, wasn't on board the *Lerna* at that time. His assistant, a Mr Carter, looked after me and I have gradually regained my strength.'

'So do you remember how you were found on the island?' the inspector asks.

'I'm told some locals found me unconscious on the beach. But I have no memory of that.'

'Who patched up your wound?' the inspector points at my scar.

'I assume it was the locals. I think it is just healing itself … with rest, food and nature.'

The inspector looks at my head again, above the ear. There are no dressings on the wound. It is just healing in the air.

'Who arranged your trip on the *Lerna?*'

I shrug. 'I don't really know. I think the ship was looking to the island to get supplies. Someone must have mentioned that I was there, with no passport – a shipwrecked sailor. But it is all very vague to me.'

'What actual documentation did you have?' the man called John asks.

'All I had was my soggy wallet with my credit cards – in my hip pocket – but no passport. I knew I would strike trouble with Customs as soon as we reached Noumea. So Mr Carter contacted DFAT by satellite phone and computer. We organised the pass-port. Mr Carter spoke to someone in Canberra and smoothed the path. The consulate-general officers issued me with a replacement in Noumea. And since then, I have been travelling on the *Lerna* to here, in Cairns. Does that answer your question?'

'Yes,' says the inspector, while the immigration officer makes another note or two. 'Do you know what happened to the other guard?'

'Only what I have told you. You probably know a lot more about what happened than I do. Have they found Aldo?'

'Not to my knowledge,' replies the inspector.

'Poor bugger.' I lean forward. 'Can you tell me anything about how it all ended up? Did everyone get rescued?' I hope I am coming across as man earnestly seeking answers.

'I don't have detailed knowledge of the incident or the after-math.' The policeman smiles, as if wishing he could be more helpful to me. 'There's been minimal reporting and I'm not a party to the investigation. I can tell you that the ship sailed into Nadi Harbour a few days after the incident and that no-one else was seriously harmed apart from the two guards.'

'Well, that's some good news. So what's happening with the case now?'

'I understand that detectives are still working on it, but I have no details that I can share with you.'

I nod slowly. 'Well, I don't think I can tell you anything more about it.'

'Can I ask what your plans are now that you're back on home soil?' Inspector Willis asks. Maybe the hard questions are over. Is that it?

'Mr Cavanagh is away for a few days, so I am assisting Captain Rodriguez with the ship's security until he returns.'

'And then?' asks the inspector.

'And then we'll see. I'm still coming to terms with being alive. It's good to be back in Australia. I'll look for work. Maybe in Cairns. Maybe I'll stay with this boat. I really don't know.'

Inspector Willis quietly finishes noting the answers.

'Well, thanks for your time, Mr Flynn,' says the inspector warmly. 'I'm pleased to be one of the people to welcome you home. This is my card – mobile number on the back. If you should need help in Cairns or have anything that comes back in your memory that you want to share, I am quite happy for you to give me a ring, direct. Please touch base with me before you leave town, as a matter of course, just in case I have anything new for you. We wish you well.'

With handshakes and cheery smiles, the two officers leave the ship and I breathe a long sigh of relief.

* * * *

My heart is light as I take in the precise ordered cleanliness of the bridge. Captain Rodriguez has invited me to join him in a cup of tea as we work out our rosters for supervision.

I will go ashore in the current afternoon and evening and be on the ship for all of the following day. That suits me as I note on the calendar that it is Valentine's Day.

I fancy my chances in the tourist city of Cairns.

The *Lerna* is berthed at the secure jetty.

The captain issues me with a ship's mobile. It works on land and sea – waterproof, taking its signal from satellites, not the land-based mobile-phone towers.

I am to ring when returning to the ship.

Safer than carrying security keys with me. He gives me a wad of Australian dollars from the bridge safe, as an advance on my pay, until either Cavanagh or Carter return. I look at the notes – $300. It could be a good night.

Alison and Steve

Alison Wood is back in her fishing position.

Two men emerge from the *Lerna* and leave the area in a car. Alison is sure at least one of them is a policeman. All these years of observing court circuits hones the eye to recognising the confident walk and the neat haircut.

Patiently, she waits, with the occasional casual glance in the direction of the ship.

Now, someone else is walking off the ship and heading for the security gate. *Could this be the mysterious Roger Cavanagh?* Alison wonders.

He is a handsome dark-haired man; average height but well-built, the nuggety look of a sportsman. He is wearing a casual checked, short-sleeved shirt over neat jeans and brown jogging shoes. A black Nouvelle Caledonie cap and smooth sunglasses top him off.

Through the gate, he waves back to the crewman on the bridge and starts to walk towards where Alison is seated.

With an impetuous surge of confidence, she turns just at the right moment to say, 'Oh, hello!' with her biggest smile. 'Lovely ship!' she adds, nodding to the *Lerna*. 'Do you own it?'

It is shameless flattery – she knows that. But, if he happens to be the owner then he won't be insulted and she won't be at all disappointed.

'No,' replies the man. 'I work on the ship. Just heading ashore to see the sights.'

'Allow me to accompany you,' she smiles with just enough shyness not to seem too pushy. 'I've had enough fishing for one day.'

* * * *

I carry her blue bucket. The age of chivalry is not yet over.

I am feeling good, surging with excitement … with just the smallest niggle at the back of my mind about the words from another woman; and something or someone called *Ramas*.

What was that all about?

I'll keep my ears open for any mention of it when Roger returns.

Ramas? What a strange name for an organisation?

Peter Carter and the *Balkan Blue*

Peter Carter is looking at an uncut sapphire. The deep-blue core of the high-quality gem is obvious even to an inexperienced eye. This stone had been stolen for *Ramas* a few weeks before, from a prospector out on the Gemfields of Central Queensland. Roger will be so pleased.

Carter's boss just loves sapphires – that intense blue. It is there in the colour he'd had the *Lerna's* hull painted, right through to the lustre in Gina's haunting eyes.

It had been an alert agent, trained by Peter, who had recognised the potential. Out on the Central Queensland mine sites, he had overheard a Bosnian prospector chatting to his offsider in a pub on the main street of Emerald. The fossickers had drunk a few beers as they talked about something called the *Balkan Blue* – a Napoleon stone, they had called it.

That was the clincher for the agent. Napoleon was always mentioned at the training days. Someone higher up in the organisation was always interested in things to do with Napoleon. Brownie points were up for grabs.

As the Bosnian mentioned the stone, he touched the front of his trousers as if checking. That gesture could easily have been misinterpreted or just overlooked.

Peter smiled as he looked closely at the gemstone. That was the value of recruiting perceptive watchers, training them very carefully and paying them well.

Peter's man took some German *muscle* out to Rubyvale. They watched and waited. The opportunity came in the early hours of a morning, when the prospector walked to his car after visiting a house. They took their chance and went straight for the waistband of the trousers – and a leather drawstring bag with the sapphire rock inside.

It had been a gamble, but it had paid off. This story would be a practice scenario at future training sessions within the network. This was the type of example that Peter encouraged – and he had learned it from Roger.

Initiative. Training. Observation.

The German unfortunately had dithered at the scene though and had been caught. He didn't speak English – more smart thinking by his man at the mines. *Silence* is so important. Loose talk costs lives.

The only weakness had been that the German had let slip that *It was for Ramas.* He should never even have heard that codename. A slip up from his agent. But the key to the organisation's structure has always been that if someone breaches security, with a name slip, no intruder would get far before meeting an encrypted gateway.

Discrete cells.

But the comment had been picked up by a reporter and printed in the court column of the local newspaper. While it wouldn't mean anything to anyone – it represents poor discipline. It doesn't sit well with Carter's need for precision. It is not acceptable. He has drummed *results* and *silence* into them at all the training sessions.

Len had already dealt painfully with the Central Queensland agent who had let slip the *Ramas* name to the hired muscle. Len would also see that the German didn't walk easily for some time when he is released from prison. They are each examples, so that others in the organisation will always understand. There are consequences for breaches of discipline.

That level of security is time-consuming and expensive, with everything being repeated in each small controlled cell; but it pays dividends if there is ever a breach. The knowledge of others in the chain is very limited.

The other side of the balance is that the organisation looks after people properly – very well, in fact. His team knows their role, with good money paid for results and silence. Trans-shipment of *product* out to SPFA freighters is a simple business as long as you avoid the Customs and the Navy.

Carter sees this as a business just like any other. He brings his skills of military organisation to the operation. There are services to be delivered and products to be distributed.

Roger Cavanagh is amazing. He understands good business processes. He models the need for positive relations to be maintained with all the countries where they have connections. Such a good mentor; thinking strategically and deceptively, beyond the norm, just like the hero he always quotes – Napoleon, the great emperor.

The military analogies apply to business as well.

Strategic thinking; deception.

Sometimes, crews need to be hi-jacked. The secret is to treat the crews well and then the word gets out. If they know that they won't be harmed, they will be passive, co-operative. He is just like Robin Hood, unloading wealth from the rich and spreading it across the little people in the *Ramas* organisation – and all quietly, under the radar.

Influential people are only too happy to cover any potentially damaging situations; a quick persuasive word from Roger and things are smoothed over. He has leverage as well as being so persuasively convincing.

The balance sheets are invariably good, the risks acceptable and Roger's expertise has the high-level strategy in place. The operation remains *commercial in-confidence.*

Peter hadn't even considered crime to be a respectable business until he met Roger. It had been a total revelation to him that all the expertise he had developed as a moderately-paid Army officer could be used in a low-key low-margin but high-overall-profit business.

Only a week in Roger's company had him realising that the difference between legal and illegal activity was only in who had written the rules.

As Roger explains it, the laws only protect the interests of those who are in power. That doesn't make them right. There is no *absolute* in laws – no correct sense of *right* or *wrong*. The lawmakers are just reinforcing the control of the ruling elite.

Too many pseudo-moralistic attitudes being applied.

Roger has always made that clear, whenever anyone has doubts or when they question the ethics of their trade. His words are always so logical

This is a business like any other.

The Brigadier

London. Wednesday 14 February 2007

'Good to see you again, Brigadier.' Sir Terence greets the imposing retired military man affably.

Breakfast toast awaits them on the low table, with their tea. The dark-leather chairs of *The Club* are very comfortable – an exclusive environment.

'And you too, Terry. How's Meredith?'

'Oh, still active in croquet and the hunt, although we don't hunt foxes anymore, of course.' The slight nod and head tilt signifies the joke. 'But the horses and the dogs have to go out each week. Training, old boy – or they will lose condition. Can't have that. And there's nothing quite like the sound of the horn, with the *Tally ho!* eh? I thought Meredith would have settled down to retired life but it seems she's had a new burst of energy in old age. She's always been a sharp one.'

'That's good,' says the Brigadier. 'You inspire me to keep going. I had thought I'd retired too. Goodness, there's plenty to do at the chateau. It's a busy property. Well, you understand. You have a similar situation. And I've had all the countess's interests to maintain in the partnership, you know.

'Always kept my place in Knightsbridge though. I like to fly back and forth. I couldn't live in France all the time. Old traditions and loyalties die hard.'

'Yes! Well,' agrees Terry, 'that is really what I want to talk to you about. This new group, the *NPA*, Forbes and his assistants; they concern me. They report to you, don't they?'

'They do indeed, in a liaison sense. I'm an adviser really. Too old now to be controlling everything. I'm just part-time.'

'Well, they seem to be stirring up a hornet's nest in some of our more sensitive areas of business, like Washington and the Far East. I don't know that it's the wisest strategy for the Minister to have adopted. As you would appreciate, I'm on a few boards and I am getting negative feedback from many.'

'What seems to be the issue?' asks the Brigadier quietly.

'They have a bee in their bonnets about ... sorry about all the apian examples.' He chortles. That *old-school* humour. 'About a hijacking of a pop singer on a yacht off Fiji.' Terry pauses to remind himself of his logical argument. 'Now, I don't know if it was a real event or just a stunt because it only seems to be reported in junk magazines and internet blogs associated with her fan base. Nonetheless, the *NPA* seem to regard the matter as being of *national* importance – nothing to do with Britain, of course, we don't run Fiji any more – and they are harassing legitimate businesses; making them very edgy, you know.'

'So,' clarifies the Brigadier, 'you would like me to use my influence to call them off the hunt, is that it?'

'Well, y-yes,' stammers Terry, pleased that his colleague appears to be in agreement with his understanding. 'It's not good for business to have all this scaremongering going on. Exaggerated out of all proportion in my view.'

'Sorry old chap,' says the Brigadier, without much time for thought. 'The *NPA* is a Ministerial appointment. They are working with a similar group in the States to seek out serious international fraud. I really think it'll come to a head very soon and there will be blood in the aisles. I won't be calling them off, Terry. My advice to you is to review your business connections and to make sure that you're clean. You don't want to get hurt in any collateral damage, do you?'

'I see.' Terry slowly absorbs the Brigadier's assessment. 'Certainly not! Collateral damage, eh? You reckon, soon?'

No point in arguing with someone like the Brigadier. He'd made his case and received a flat negative.

'Terry, as an old friend, I know you're heading up a lot of these boards because they want your expertise and prestige at the top. But, I don't think you can give due diligence to all of them. It's too much work – even at my age, and you have some years on me.

'Take my advice and get out of this multiple board scene before it all goes belly up – because it will, either through the *NPA* investigations or through some of the crazy financial behaviour that I'm seeing in the market just now. Just madness and it can't continue. You know that too. I know you do. Go back to the estate and enjoy some time with Meredith. You have earned the right to be happily retired together. Spend some time with your dear wife.'

'I see,' says a nodding pensive Sir Terence. 'Well, thanks for giving me a hearing anyway.'

They sip their teas slowly and talk of old times, of empire, of nostalgic events. *The Club* has that warm ambience where the leaders of business and of nations can meet, share ideas, float new projects and be assured that the conversations will go no farther than the rich upholstered walls. The Brigadier and Sir Terence have known each other for many years. They are friends; and they part as friends after this discussion.

Cecile

Behind the barrels, Cecile follows the narrow flagstone path to the old door.

She is down in the cellars. The ancient wooden casks hold the jewel drops of the vineyard's best. They will lie undisturbed for years.

Inside the locked door, the flick of a switch brings a growing glow of light from concealed globes. Programmed by her computer control, some lights brighten to highlight the paintings; others stay subtle, coloured, bringing a warm ambience to the room – the renovated treasure storeroom which the Nazis didn't find in the war.

Back then, the doorway had been concealed behind dust-covered rubbish – but now, Cecile visits here daily. This is her private collection. These are gifts from people all round the world; precious gestures of the highest quality; paintings, sculptures, jewellery, artefacts, photographs.

Lonely splendour – but artistic beauty is comforting.

Back in the sixties, gifts arrived as an expectation. But, in the decades since, they come unexpected and unannounced through the disguised transit chain with genuine expressions of gratitude and respect. Senders know that presents would have to be high calibre. Cecile has no need for quantity. She is a collector of only the highest quality or rarity.

The game has taken on a life of its own like the famed *Hydra* of Greek mythology. She tried to kill it off – more than once – but it just grew another two heads to replace the killed one.

It started through boredom – in Washington and then London in the fifties – within secretive government buildings where female expertise was acknowledged, albeit under a veil of faux-tolerant recognition. That was directly against the run of the misogynist civil service opinion of the time.

Counter-espionage was the grand term which applied to their work, where they dealt in numbers, talked in codes and were grudgingly accepted as equals.

In Washington, it had been the E-Street complex in Foggy Bottom. The political capital was also where Cecile met the bankers and the agents; free thinkers, willing to try novel ideas; people to bounce new concepts around. The seed of the structure had been born there, as well as the romance that could never be; that creation, that tangible expression of love, now lost forever.

In London, it had been more about the women. A few had drifted over to the MI5 house on the Thames from Bletchley Park – very secretive ladies but among those who had handled the most secure Intelligence information of the war. Were they really to be expected to go back to supervising the laundering of sheets and idle prattle about children's games?

Cecile's French Resistance credentials, coupled with her problem-solving reputation, had her accepted on the analysts' floor. That was where she had started working with Merri – interesting enough work and these were sharp ladies. Merri was a little older, very English, active mind. Cecile was a lateral thinker, very French, a dreamer but with a need for structure in her plans, an unusual combination of thought processes.

The ideas kept sparking in their minds. The visions had to find a voice. It would be like asking a volcano not to blow.

They started after work-hours to play with imaginary armies and navies attached to different countries. Then they would make alliances, deals, trading equipment in their fantasy landscape.

It was Merri who realised that the deals and alliances would be too transparent unless they were shared in code. Her Bletchley Park imagination ran wild. The trade needed a language to disguise the goods being shared or sold – and the language of shipping logistics covered the whole general scene and the specific cryptic codes concealed the gateways and the pathways through the maze.

It was such fun that the two women became firm friends, sharing many private hours discussing *the game*, its options and its possibilities.

The London work for Cecile finished at the end of the fifties, with the death of her father – her inheritance of the chateau awaited. There were vineyards and wineries to be managed. A whole settlement of workers depended on her business acumen and organisation. But *the game* gnawed away at her. How would the countries transfer their moneys without other countries knowing? How could a country hide its financial resources from another? It was the mental stimulation her mind craved.

Then in the early 60s, with crop harvested and all the vineyards quiet, while her new husband, the Count, was looking after his business transactions, feeling very male and in charge, Cecile wondered what it would be like to trade for real using the labyrinthine structures of *the game*.

It was to be a secret challenge. The Count wasn't to know. They had built codes into the structure but the other fundamental was that players in the chain would only know the next person in the line, not anyone else. Discrete cells. The coded messages would not identify a source. If one part of *the game* was discovered, then the rest could continue in sublime anonymity.

That was how it had started – and now this roller-coaster threatened to come back down the hill towards her.

* * * *

She jolts her thoughts away from the past to relax with all these beautiful *objets d'art*. The Velázquez is lit cleverly, at the end of the room. Cecile appreciates that the artist had such a talent with painting light. As does the Turner, but in a different way.

She feels the calmness that this room always brings her. So many beautiful things. She moves towards the jewel-encrusted Fabergé egg, from the House of Romanov in St Petersburg.

And she stops to admire the sparkle from the sapphire – in *pride of place* display. She doesn't need the explanatory label. The Mohács Blue is legendary.

The Emperor Napoleon had it in his personal collection until his exile. It was spirited away for over a century and half; hidden, protected … until she received it as a tribute some twenty years ago. What an amazing gem. Such deep-blue lustre. And so large.

Legend has it that it came originally from present-day Sri Lanka, way back in the sixteenth century and was even owned by Suleiman the Magnificent.

She smiles.

Jeff Fowler

Canberra. Wednesday 14 February 2007

Jeff Fowler listens carefully to Inspector Mal Willis's assessment of Steve Flynn.

Seems basically honest. Certainly has a nasty bullet scar above his right ear. Looks to be genuinely interested in finding out what happened on the Sea Spray and afterwards.

Quite vague as to how he got from the water to the Lerna. There is probably more to know in that area.

He appears to have become accepted by Roger Cavanagh, the owner.

Steve and Alison

Cairns. Wednesday 14 February 2007

I feel as if we have hit it off from the first few minutes as we stroll from Cairns jetty.

She looks cute in her fishing clothes. I carry her reel and hooks in her blue plastic pail. There are no fish gracing the bottom of the bucket – or bait either, that I can see. No matter – her laughing is infectious as we walk past the angel-fish statues in the scenic swimming lagoon on the esplanade.

* * * *

Half-an-hour after she has excused herself to drop off her bucket and fishing reel, we are strolling cheerily along the seafront. She is easy company, I like her and I need to relax without all the agendas of the *Lerna*.

Perhaps my luck is in … and it is Valentine's Day.

* * * *

Eventually, in a water-view bar with cool air blowing through the rooms, we sip quiet drinks and she tells me her story of being a court reporter.

She has a freshness – no airs and graces.

I don't really consider or question how easily she has picked me up on the jetty. It is some casual fun. I will be gone again in a few days.

* * * *

Alison has worked out her strategy for whomever she might meet from the ship, but Steve hasn't fit the fierce pirate image – too good looking and normal. But, all a bit of fun for her acting role and ... who could know?

Her plan is to be the innocent, asking naïve questions about where they have travelled; what it is like to live on such a fine ship. Then, if she is speaking with any of the seriously nasty ones, they wouldn't take her seriously, writing her off as a light-weight idealist, which perhaps she is.

But the hope is that the person would talk, maybe brag or drop some snippet which she can add to her research ... or pass on, surreptitiously, to the authorities.

Not much of a plan, but a start. She is intending to charm and listen.

After, she will retreat quietly into the background, and her writing.

Just how she is to going to get from the anonymous *fly-on-the-wall* to the successful investigative journalist is not yet quite clear in her mind. There is thinking still to be done.

Hey! It is a journey – although, in principle, she does want to reach an endgame and put the thugs out of business. Most of her research has been in libraries and online, so far. The few people she has interviewed have mainly been victims, not villains.

So, Steve?

He says he has only been on the ship since Fiji and then on through Noumea to here. He isn't really a crew member at all, more just a passenger. He probably has nothing to add to her investigation file; but he is good company so she chatters away to him about her general interest in the sea and her dream of being a serious journalist, investigating insurance fraud.

He seems such a patient listener, so encouraging – fraud wouldn't interest too many good-looking men. She mentions her casual reading about pirates raiding ships in the South China Sea to see his reaction – only mild surprise, and still interested in hearing her say more.

Since he is sailing on an expensive ship, it seems logical to warn him of the dangers she has researched about real South Pacific pirates who actually hi-jack luxury yachts and hold people to ransom, like the case last month in Fiji with the pop singer, Ingrid.

He just sits very still, looking at her strangely.

'I've been out of the country for a while. What was that all about?'

Encouraged, she confesses that it seems to be the strangest of cases. At times, she's even begun to think it has been a publicity stunt. 'It's hardly been reported. I found it in a tiny column in a couple of Fijian papers, as well as one in California. The only other mentions are in internet blogs and most of them are where her fans are asking what actually happened.'

'So, what do you think actually happened?'

She looks at him, wondering whether she's already said too much. Goodness, they have only just met. This is heavy conversation for a quiet drink. But he grins at her and reaches out for her hand. It feels good. It has been a while since that familiar buzz has coursed through her.

He smiles again, nodding for her to continue. 'If you were to guess what had actually happened, what would you say? How would you write it?'

He really *is* interested. 'This is a hypothetical, right?' she says with a giggle in her tone. 'Right. Here goes. Are you ready?'

'Ready,' replies Steve.

'I think … Ingrid hired a yacht to get some peace from the paparazzi. Someone saw a dollar to be made by holding her to ransom. She is rich. Her last album went platinum in the States. I think she might have a rich husband too.'

Steve looks thoughtful.

'Okay.' Alison continues with her theory. 'Let's assume the crook then contacted some people to carry out the raid. Now I don't yet know where you find *pirates*, just like that. It's not like going to the employment agency but I'm pretty sure there are people you can approach to provide *the service*, shall we say.

'The attack was on a dark night and in a roughish sea. So these are not your *I think we'll just attack that boat on the spur of the moment* type of pirates. It sounds more organised, like commandos. They had to get close without guards hearing and they killed both the guards, tossing them to the sharks.'

Steve seems to give an almost imperceptible shiver. 'Alright. If it happened that way, how did they deliver the ransom?'

She is on a roll and happy to attempt another answer. 'This is the trouble with hypotheticals. It's all guesswork. Well, they couldn't deliver the ransom note to Ingrid because she was already on the boat. Maybe they forced her to reveal her husband's mobile number or email and then sent the message that way. But they would need specialist knowledge to obscure where they were sending from. You can track electronic messages.

'My guess is the heavies on the boat informed someone else, somewhere else, of the successful snatch and the other party handled the ransom demand.'

Steve grins as he slowly shakes his head. He seems to be mulling the idea around in his mind. 'Bit thin. So how did they get paid?'

Alison is very logical. She has a clear processing style. 'Well, it would have to be secure and secret. Gold bars or jewels are too messy; too heavy or traceable. Paper money could be treated with chemicals or magnetic traces. My bet is it was electronically transmitted into a lot of bank accounts. No, they would all be traceable too. What about a bank in some safe haven? That would need very specialised knowledge too, because the police or Interpol would have people running electronic traces on any transactions.

'So, I think, this had some master-crook behind it. Someone who knows how to find pirates; how to move money round the world without being detected; how to send computer messages anonymously and then it is someone who can also keep all this from being reported in the press. Sorry, I know it sounds crazy but it's the best I can do or maybe it never even happened.' She laughs, her hands upturned in a defeated gesture.

Steve laughs with her. 'It's a good intellectual exercise though. You like this theorising, don't you? Aren't you worried you might bump into one of these nasty people, if you keep investigating?'

'Yes.' She is still on a grinning high from struggling with the challenge. 'It would be scary if I thought about it. I'm around courts all the time. Maybe I'm getting used to seeing crooks. Mind you, all the ones I've seen have been caught.'

Her cheery shrug indicates that the topic has been exhausted.

'So tell me about you and the ship,' she says.

'Another drink?' Steve suggests.

'Mmm. As long as you tell me about sailing in a ship like that.'

* * * *

I watch her anticipation over the top of my glass, as we both take sips from the new drinks. 'I've just being doing security to pay my passage over from Noumea. The owner and his partner flew out this morning for a few days. I'm looking after the boat with the captain until they get back.'

Just looking after it? Can you smuggle me on board?' she asks excitedly.

'You could be a pirate.' I laugh with mock surprise, 'Maybe you are not just investigating pirates, eh? You could be planning the takeover of the ship. No, I don't think so. I'm not into smuggling people on board ships. The owner wouldn't want visitors on his expensive pride and joy.'

'Huh! Who is this unfriendly owner?' She pouts.

'His name is Roger Cavanagh.'

'Oh, so what is he like?' She enthuses.

'Oh, handsome, rich, charismatic – the usual.'

'I bet he is short, fat, old and bald with no teeth and bad breath, especially if he won't let me on his boat.' She pouts again, managing to smile simultaneously.

'I'll tell him you said that.' I laugh.

We pause for a few seconds, looking at each other.

'Would you like to go out with me tonight?' I ask. 'I envisage a romantic dinner for two overlooking the glistening ocean; some dancing and a walk in the moonlight – if it doesn't rain.'

'I think that would be lovely, Steve. Thank you. Yes.'

We exchange mobile numbers, agreeing that I will pick her up at 7.00 pm at her motel room.

* * * *

I feel unusually tense as I muse over the hypothetical that Alison has painted. There are some tumblers falling into place, maybe. Some of the words she used. Somebody to provide *the piracy service?* Where have I heard someone talk like that about being a *trader* and *providing a service?*

The computer set-up? The office on the *Lerna* would be able to do most things – and probably quite a few that Roger hasn't shown me.

Financial expertise? Moving money across continents?

He owns a luxury boat, maybe more than one if Gina is right, and is a trader.

Finally, the *Lerna* wasn't far away from Fiji at the time of the *Sea Spray* attack.

Gina has said there is danger. She has called him a smiling gangster – his money comes from crime.

Gina? Where is she just now? How is she faring? I recall her worried look as she left with Roger in the tender. I fully intend to walk her along the esplanade when she returns.

What to do about Roger and all these suspicions? I can hardly go to the police. What was the name of the inspector today? I try to imagine what I might say. Excuse me, Inspector Willis, I have these vague ideas my boss is a master criminal. Can you help me please?

Roger is right. I am trapped by the circumstances of the *Sea Spray* – but he isn't right that I am one of them. I'm not a crook or a gangster.

My thoughts wander to more pleasant things.

Alison is a honey, not the beauty-queen style of Gina. It is more an inner beauty – warm gentle hazel eyes, her so-soft brown hair, her ready laughing smile. And, most of all, she is vital and enthusiastic. All the things I have been missing.

I am looking forward to the evening and ... one thing might lead to another.

AFP, NPA and Versec

Canberra. Wednesday 14 February 2007

Fowler emails a summary of Inspector Willis's observations off to *NPA* and *Versec* – to keep them fully informed.

Then, he texts Ben Brennan ... and his phone rings within a minute.

'Brennan here,' the *Nemesis* man says. 'You have something, Jeff?'

Fowler recounts Mal Willis's impressions. The line is much clearer than it often is when talking to Ben.

'I hope Flynn is the good honest fellow the inspector thinks he is,' says Ben, 'because he just spent the afternoon in the charming company of Alison Wood, the journalist. I suspect they'll be out on a date together tonight. I am here in Cairns. Jeff, something is brewing. There is chatter in the network.'

* * * *

Fowler sits back quietly in his chair as the call ends as abruptly as usual. He thinks through all the information which he now has. He needs plans in place.

He is glad now that he'd had the foresight to send Bill Jones to Cairns that very morning, with his kitbag of electronic goodies. The AFP needs to get ahead of this game. They are not dealing with amateurs. These people have money, influence and will play nasty if the pressure comes on. They have shown that on the *Sea Spray*.

* * * *

He calls Inspector Willis and Sergeant Jones. They have the authority to put the proposal into action.

Then he sends another text for Brennan to get back to him.

He is now on the front foot, just like Forbes and Broderick want.

Steve and Alison

They come for me at 7.00 pm, at Alison Wood's motel room, where I have just arrived for my date. There are three of them. Military and police; that is my best guess. What is this?

'Well, Steve Flynn. We meet again,' announces Inspector Mal Willis of the Cairns police, as he introduces his companions. 'Bill Jones, sergeant, Australian Federal Police and Ben Brennan from *Nemesis*.'

I thought so. I can pick them. The solid bloke, my age or a bit older, forty maybe, shortish hair, looks Army; dark shirt, jeans, runners, carrying a sports bag – Bill Jones. With a fit-looking man, maybe in his fifties, salt and pepper brown hair, weathered face, alert grey eyes; ex-service too, by the look – Ben Brennan. And the lithe casually-dressed police inspector, with his silver streaks above the ears lightening a thick, but neat, black mane – Mal Willis. Was it only this morning that I saw him on the *Lerna* – the ship that had brought me back from Fiji to here?

I say nothing and look at Alison Wood, my pretty companion of only a few hours. It is *her* motel room. I am just meeting her here, before we go out for some Valentine's Day fun on the town. That is the plan, until this interruption.

But, she doesn't seem overly surprised by the visitors – she has let them in, as if they are expected – although she is nervy, just a quiver in her manner. But then, I hardly know her.

'We believe that you are both in considerable danger,' Willis announces quietly, as we find seating on the chairs and the bed.

He has my attention. Even more when he pulls a flotation vest out of the sergeant's sports bag and places it on the coffee table. The name, Aldo Pollock, is clearly visible on the personalised jacket, above the row of bullet holes on the chest.

'Missing, presumed dead.'

And my mind has me back in Fiji.

It has been just over a month since it happened … although, given a choice, I would prefer to think about a week later, Tuesday 16 January, 2007… and the scents of Lani's tender care.

But the choice is not mine.

The bullet holes in Aldo's lifejacket have shocked my mind back to the present in the motel room in Cairns. Those torn wounds stare their dead eyes at me as Inspector Willis says, 'It was found last week and flown to us today. Fifty ks from where the *Sea Spray* had been. Over a month from the attack on the ninth of January.'

Alison stares at me; the nerviness has changed to horror in her look. I haven't lied to her. I have just kept my counsel while she told me her story. Anyway, she hasn't been telling me the truth either.

Hardly a great start to a friendship – and on Valentine's Day, too.

But the link has to be *Ramas* … it was she who had told me about *Ramas* and the *Balkan Blue*, the Napoleon stone. Then, to emphasise the seriousness further, Willis places Phillippe Poe's statement on the table … the Tahitian cook from the *Sea Spray 2*. It reads:

Fiji Police Service, Suva, Fiji. Statement by Phillippe Poe, cook, charter yacht Sea Spray 2. Friday 12 January, 2007. Transcribed from interview tape, with clarification by Detective Malakai Tabakau in brackets.

'Il était le Diable lui-même - vêtu de noir, et sifflant!' (Clarification – He was the Devil himself – dressed in black, and hissing!)

189

I, Phillippe Poe of Papeete, Tahiti. I chef on Sea Spray. My English not good. French and Reo Tahiti good.

They came in the dark, Tuesday night at start of a storm. I was in galley, make omelette for Mademoiselle Ingrid – she artiste, créateur (song writer and performer). She composes in the evening.

I hear bang bang. Look through forward hatch. See gardes for yacht (ship security) shot and fall, splash overboard. Many men in black clothes, black masks into galley.

We speak English on yacht so I say, 'Where monsieurs on deck?'

'Gone,' huge man hissed. He Devil. 'No talk,' man at back say. They speak English, not native or French. See?

Devil at front hit me with rifle butt. See – my head? (Interviewee has large bruise on right eye and cheek.) He wheezed, sound terrible, like chien enragé (mad dog.)

Monsieur le Capitaine calmed the crew. I see Mademoiselle Ingrid cry in cabin as I return to galley.

In a few hours later, Devil and men disappear. Le Capitaine sail to Nadi. No radio or electronics – broken by men in the night. Rudder too. Two days to Nadi port.

No-one in crew harmed after me. Devil terrified them all.

That all I know.

Signed Phillippe Poe,
12 Janvier 2007

'So, now we come to you two.' The Inspector looks at Alison and then at me. 'We have a crime committed and you each appear to have different pieces of the puzzle.'

Ben Brennan speaks slowly. His voice is deep. 'Have you heard the term, *Ramas?*'

Alison gives a startled gasp. Instinctively, I reach out my hand to her. I can feel her fluttering in distress, the only woman among four big men. It has only been a couple of hours since she told me her story and mentioned *Ramas,* in passing, as a courtroom joke – the *Balkan Blue,* that the prospector also called the 'Napoleon Stone' and his curse on the thief.

But, it would appear that our meeting on the jetty was no accident. She had been waiting for me. What is going on?

The AFP sergeant, Bill Jones, speaks up. 'We have a strong interest in the ship, the *Lerna.* We want to share some information – to protect you and perhaps for you to help us. Some of our knowledge is easily confirmed, but much of it is still police speculation and projections, if you like. When we have finished, we will walk out. You have the choice as to what you do. This is off the record.'

He looks pointedly at each of us, taking our stunned silence as agreement. 'We believe that the owner of the *Lerna,* Roger Cavanagh, is a wealthy criminal, a kingpin.

'Beneath Cavanagh, his South Pacific operation is probably supervised by a Peter Carter – not his real name definitely. We think he is former British Army. Gerald Hughes may be his birth name, but we will use his *Ramas* codename for simplicity. And the enforcement of discipline is led by a nasty piece of work, a man called Len Williamson – not his real name either. We believe he is Reg Fletcher, wanted for gang crimes in South London.'

The adrenalin wafts through me at these familiar names that have been confusing me throughout the recent voyage across the Pacific from Fiji.

Jones acknowledges Brennan with an open palm. 'Ben, here, has been involved in breaking up pirate gangs in this part of the world for ten years, quietly, no publicity. His listening network supplies discreet Intelligence – and that includes this group. Alison, your research may have thrown up the name, *Nemesis?* Yes?'

I watch her as she slowly nods. She doesn't look at me. Her cheeks seem to redden as she looks oddly at Brennan. I can still feel her fluttering tension as I hold her hand, to give support. There is a lot more going on in this room than I understand. This is a long way away from the promising Valentine's evening I was expecting.

'*Nemesis* is Ben's group; a loose structure of information gathering. Ben joins the dots about what might be coming up … and crimes that have already happened.

'That's where we at the Australian Federal Police come in. I'm attached to the Asia-Pacific area. We're investigating the hi-jack of a sailing boat off Fiji. Now, I know you were on that boat, Steve.'

Shit! I hope my outer appearance is one of calm. Thank goodness for those sessions in simulated capture and interrogation. Alison stares at me again. Her hand grips mine tightly and shakes; an angry puzzled shake.

I manage to say, more casually than I feel, 'I'd like to know what happened.'

'Good,' says Willis. 'I'll continue. Our guess is that Roger Cavanagh saw an opportunity to fleece millions of dollars out of the banker husband of the pop singer, Ingrid. She had hired the *Sea Spray 2*, from a charter company, called *Mer Charte*, based in Tahiti, to cruise the islands; for some peace to write some new songs. The charter company had found the guards to protect her from photographers. You, Steve, were employed along with an American, Aldo Pollock. Is that right?'

I nod.

'Now *Mer Charte* is part of a larger trading group called the *South Pacific Freight Alliance* – often just called, SPFA. The group takes cargo from island to island but it does include luxury charters as well. Roger Cavanagh is connected with SPFA. We believe he is actually the Chief Executive Officer within the alliance but we haven't yet found documentation to confirm that.'

I look at Alison. Her eyes are wide and her mouth is open.

'We think that Cavanagh saw his chance when he noticed Ingrid's booking in his company records. He planted his inside man as a crewman on the ship. A Bob Curtis, I believe.'

Ah ha! Curtis! Aldo had interviewed him. Just a crewman. Employed right at the last minute to replace an accident injury. Experienced. References. Nothing to indicate a problem. Not even a dodgy past. It had all seemed so routine.

'Hi-jacking a boat wouldn't be too difficult for Cavanagh. But getting the ransom money securely from Ingrid's husband is a whole different matter – to do it without being caught or even traced. We think Cavanagh's team, not he personally, launched the attack on the *Sea Spray* using inflatables from a nearby freighter. We believe we now know exactly which freighter it was, through Ben's contacts. Two guards were killed, or at least we thought they were. But then you, Steve, appeared a week or so later, sailing blithely on the *Lerna* to Noumea.'

Alison gasps. I can read her dilemma. Have I been part of this hi-jack?

I had said nothing when only this afternoon she gave me her hypothetical view of what might have happened. I had never once indicated my involvement.

She pulls her hand away and I have the sinking sensation of being painted, for a second time in a month, into a situation far beyond my control.

Willis continues. 'AFP investigators have checked with the resort island in Fiji. They did find you unconscious on the beach. They said it was a miracle you were washed over the outer reef in your lifejacket with such minimal damage. And I have confirmed the bullet scar under your hair this morning.'

I can see Alison's shock going to new levels. Bullet scar? What next? She is staring at my hair now.

The policeman is still talking. 'We believe you might have been the innocent victim of the attack and, through a chain of circumstances, you have ended up being a relatively-accepted member of the *Lerna* crew. Well, as much as Cavanagh would accept anyone. That has advantages for us and considerable dangers for you, as I'm sure you can both start to see.'

It is Ben Brennan who breaks the short silence. 'So Alison, I repeat, what do you know about *Ramas*?'

She gulps and closes her eyes to remember Central Queensland and *Ramas*.

The plot thickens

The motel room walls seem to swim before Alison's eyes. She is totally confused after listening to Inspector Willis, Sergeant Jones and Ben Brennan.

What does she know about *Ramas*? What does she really know about any of this – the *Lerna*, Roger Cavanagh, pirates, hi-jacking, ransoms … ? This has suddenly become very serious.

She can't look at Steve. Her emotions are on a roller-coaster. She senses the colour draining from her face. It is a horrible vibe, being genuinely scared.

She thinks back to the anger of social injustice that had brought her to investigate this story in the first place. Well, what she had found happening is wrong, very wrong; it needs to be exposed.

But, she has only now started to realise what the danger and fear really mean. That there is a price to be paid when you delve into such matters; that this can't be impersonal; at a distance – like court reporting. This is real – and aimed at her. Not some academic assignment into piracy. This is not the swashbuckling investigative journalism of fantasy. This is scary.

She looks across at Ben Brennan. Familiar, and as unreadable as ever, except for his eyes which are saying, *I told you so. I told you to stick to court reporting. You wouldn't listen, you headstrong girl.*

When he had come alone to her motel room only an hour earlier, his old sea-salt manner had made it sound so convincing. It

194

had seemed right to listen to whatever the police wanted to say to her … and to Steve too.

Mal Willis is continuing. 'Steve, you mentioned you were sharing the security of the *Lerna* with Captain Rodriguez. What rostering plans have you made?'

'Today is my day to go to town. I was happy to be out with Alison.'

She hears his words. Is he reaching out to her with that comment? So confusing. What to believe.

'Tomorrow, I'm on ship all day and the captain can go ashore. We'll alternate till the boss comes back. Then, who knows? It's always just a flurry of activity when he's around. Also, Carter and Williamson flew here from Noumea. I expect they'll turn up sometime soon. I don't get on with either of them.'

Willis gives a knowing look towards Ben but Sergeant Jones took the lead.

'Something is definitely about to happen,' Jones says, '… at an international level. Cavanagh is being squeezed from both ends and he is no fool. Many stand to be innocent victims if anything blows or collapses.'

Inspector Willis waits until the message is absorbed. 'We need information, early information. Are you willing to assist us – and, in the process, we will be able to help protect you both?'

Alison looks across at Steve. She is maddeningly confused now. But the anger is returning. No, dammit! She will not be weak in front of four men. She will not give them that satisfaction.

She looks slowly at Steve's questioning eyes, trying to read them. She wants to know what *he* is feeling. A little over an hour ago she was getting ready for an evening out in the warm Cairns evening – meal, a dance, some romance perhaps. It had all looked so promising. She had been excited. Keen to ensure the make-up, the perfume and the dress were all suitably enticing.

Now, she is being asked to assist the police foil some dangerous criminals.

She listens to Steve say, 'What is the danger to Alison?'

She is taken aback. What … a caring thought?

Ben is direct to the point. 'She's been making enquiries into international piracy. Someone will know that. She has spoken to people. Talk moves on. Trust me, that's how I get a lot of my information. She's been seen talking with you this afternoon. No doubt, all very innocent to casual observers; a friendship starting to form. But, you are off the *Lerna*.

'If I was Len Williamson and I saw Alison with you, I would join those bits of information and produce a potential threat. He's not a nice man. Well, you know that already – but maybe not as well as I know it.'

Alison feels a chill shiver up her spine.

'For my part,' Steve speaks quietly, 'I am willing to help you. I would prefer that Alison be safe from any of this. Can you do that?'

How gallant. The only reason he has met her is because she had been waiting for his ship to arrive. But … Phooey! What a patronising comment. Is he thinking she is a poor defenceless woman who can't share risk for the good of the community? Her blood rises with impetuous anger.

'I'm willing to assist,' she says forcefully. It sounds disembodied but it is her voice speaking. She can't believe she has just said those words. What is she thinking? She can see Steve looking at her, surprised – or is he proud? He has just provided her with a way out and she has ignored his chivalrous gesture. Yes, he does look stunned – and he isn't commenting further.

Mal and Ben share a silent expression and then Mal nods to Bill Jones.

* * * *

I look again at Alison. What is going on? All I really want is to get the hell out of here, with a bit of dignity, and now Alison has volunteered to help.

I gave her the way out and now I have to stay involved. And there is the matter of the job on board. And Gina? Frightened woman or another good actress? Bizarre!

No, better to string along with *the boys in blue*, keep my job and maybe take my chances to be able to spend some more time with Alison. We have been seen together now anyway. Carter and Williamson are out of town. We should have four or five days in Cairns yet before anything serious need happen. Why waste the opportunity? Let's enjoy the moment and maybe a way out will present itself. She is attractive. I like her.

Are all my decisions in life made on the basis of love and lust?

Bill has opened his business case.

'First of all,' he says. 'The key to this type of work is to have good *comms* – communications. These two gadgets are tracking devices. You keep them in your underwear.' He passes a small package to Alison and me. 'Don't laugh. Safe, concealed, but easy to discard if danger presents itself. They send a signal so we will know where you are at any time. Just remember to change the device over when you change your underwear – daily,' he adds, as a joke, and then he looks embarrassed. 'Not you, Ma'am,' stammering and resorting to his polite official language.

I am pleased to see that his embarrassment is raising a small smile from Alison. We need some levity in this difficult conversation.

She rescues him. 'That will be fine, Sergeant.'

Bill carries on. 'Now these next little pieces are listening devices. They can be stuck to anything just by wetting them a little – saliva will do it.' He has half-a-dozen tiny beads each about the size of a large ear of corn. 'Miniaturisation of electronic components has been a great benefit to the eavesdropping business. These little beauties just need to be stuck discreetly in a few places and we can listen in. I suggest, Steve, that you take these on board the *Lerna* tonight. You would have the run of the boat, wouldn't you, as security officer?'

I listen, giving nothing away; too long in the Army to get caught nodding agreement. Bad enough that I have volunteered for this.

I am weighing up what is possible, what is risky and even whether I really am prepared to stay involved. There is still time to get out, run for cover and leave the lawmen to do what they are paid to do. Who needs to be a hero? All I really want is the girl. This is the stuff of undercover agents. I've done my bit in the front line, been to war, been shot at and blown up. Given a choice, I would much rather just be curled up in bed with the beautiful Alison.

But she is probably thinking that I am some low-life involved with a hi-jacking. God! It doesn't take much to blow the potential for a romantic evening.

'I suggest you place one in the ship's office.' Jones continues his instructions. 'One in Cavanagh's private office and maybe one other in his living room. Maybe not the bedroom.' He is getting embarrassed again – a big, brawny copper being put off by the presence of a young woman. 'Put one in your bathroom or wardrobe so that you can speak to us with some privacy. Again, be aware that these gadgets will be transmitting all the time. If it is in the toilet, then it will be heard.' He coughed.

Somehow, Alison's gentle presence has shaken his sergeantly cool. I grin at his predicament. At least he is human and decent.

'Do you think you can do that, Steve?' Mal Willis says. 'Practise with one of these. Just wet it with your tongue. Press it up under the bed head.' I follow his instruction, successfully. 'See it sticks and it's virtually invisible. Even if someone saw it, they would take it for just a large piece of grit. It doesn't look like a spying device. Okay?'

I nod. 'I can do that. Roger's quarters, the office and my cabin. Anything else?'

'Yes,' says Bill. 'These miniatures send a signal up to fifty metres. They are already calibrated so we know which signal is from which. Coloured tags, see? Match them to this list and then remove the tag.' He hands over a notepad page. 'Alter the locations if you wish – just tell us the changes, quietly, over the microphones.'

'Next, you need to conceal this little gadget in your room.' He is holding something that looks like a spectacle case, even to the logo printed on the outside. 'This is the transmitter which picks up the messages from the little miniature phones and sends them on to us at headquarters. The signal is also calibrated to roll through several rarely-used frequencies according to a pattern, preset with our receivers – just for extra security – and can be transmitted up to fifty kilometres away. The batteries will last for about six months.

'If the ship goes to sea, we will follow at a distance that won't cause suspicion. The 'spectacle case' can just be in your bathroom or in a camera bag – wherever it will look appropriate and not raise suspicion.'

I pause to reflect on everything he is telling me. 'Okay. Alison and I can be tracked. You will have listening devices on the ship. What then?'

'Then we carry on as normal.' Mal Willis is taking the options away. 'If Roger Cavanagh offers you a job, take it. We need you to be around them. We need you to be in the inner circle, listening.'

'So how do we communicate?'

'If you want to speak to us,' Willis continues, 'speak into the mini-microphone in your bathroom. We will pick it up. We won't contact you. It is too great a risk. It would compromise your safety. Even if something goes wrong and you are caught, you can claim total innocence. There won't be any calls from us for them to inter-cept. You must just trust we are following your trail – both of you.'

I sit thinking and glancing at Alison.

'Any questions?' It seems almost superfluous. We have lots of questions but none that we are going to voice at this moment.

Ben is watching us carefully. 'Steve, you're Army trained?' A rhetorical question. 'Done much with boats?'

'A little. Basic assault and rescue stuff. Did a course in inflata-bles for the security work on the yachts.'

Ben nods. 'It's possible there could be some action down the track. Are you up for that if it happens?'

What can I say when I have been trained for such things? Of course I must say, *Yes* – but it is good of Ben to flag it might come to that.

'Sure. I have no weapons. I'll check on what can be accessed when I get back on board. There are weapon lockers on the decks.'

Ben is reassuring. 'If and when the time comes, we will get gear to you.' He presents as a very serene confident persona. He is either extremely good or extremely naïve. I hope it is the former.

Bill hands over his little gadgets. Mal and Ben thank us both.

'You still have my mobile number?' Willis is checking off a mental list. 'You can use that if you need. It could just be a routine call worrying about what happened to Aldo or something like that. Just be careful. Always expect that people can listen in, if they are on the right frequency.'

'I have it.' I feel like the energy has been drained out of me. 'Thanks to you all,' I manage to say politely, as they leave.

Alison closes the door.

She turns and rushes into my outstretched arms.

Words don't seem necessary as the warmth of our bodies communicate silently. We stand like that for a long time. Thoughts roll around like whirlpool eddies. Still we cling to each other – limpets on coastal cliffs, secure only when attached.

Eventually I say, 'Well, you look too good to be stuck in a motel room. Can I take you to see the sights of Cairns?'

She looks up into my eyes and kisses me. Our first kiss. A long kiss.

'I would love to go out on the town with you.'

'Let's go then.' I grin with relief. 'I only have tonight. Tomorrow, I will be imprisoned again on the luxury vessel so we won't be able to meet.'

'Let's go,' she responds with a rejuvenated happy smile. Some decisions have been made but they are for the future. For tonight, we are determined not to waste the opportunity to enjoy the warmth of Cairns – and of each other.

* * * *

The Cairns evening cocoons us in warmth – velvet sky, a sea bird calling over the rippling water, the distant murmuring of tourists in the gaily-lit eateries along the seafront, the soft embracing esplanade turf beneath our backs – so far from the dramas of the earlier evening.

Cicadas tune in and out with their electric language. I sense I should understand their airborne message – it is like an insect code, maybe warning me. I listen some more but I can distil no meaning.

Alison's innocent face is looking at me, our bodies touching with the fluttering excitement of our new relationship.

I breathe her warm scent as she lies beside me on the grass cushion, behind the sunfish pool, and I hide the taste of fear which is drying my mouth; the dread intrigue which I sense is about to engulf us.

This was never some stark obvious decision – it was always more insidious, manipulative, each step down into the abyss. Did we ever really have a choice?

But, for now, only Alison's slight eye flicker hints at her worry. Her expression is glowing – familiar yet new. It was her brave volunteering that shamed and inspired me into this venture with the mysterious Ben Brennan and *the law*.

I had been warned. Gina told me, days ago.

The healing scar above my ear throbs.

Yet here is Alison, the petite court reporter with a dream, overcoming all sensible fears to insert both of us like covert agents into a world that neither of us could really understand.

I briefly consider scooping her into my arms to head for the airport, away from my instinctive worry. Instead, I cuddle her closer, protectively, as a fruit bat floats silently above our starry gaze. It lands noisily into a darkened mango tree. Frightened lorikeets flutter and chatter around the branches, then settle again.

Damn it! Live for the moment! I can remember too many times walking into dark action – wondering if that night would be the end.

I absorb her gentle buzz – a seductive beckoning to Elysian abandon. To hell with holding back. Tomorrow I might be dead.

The cicadas take up their droning music again – laden with some hidden language that I can't quite grasp.

* * * *

Alison floats back to the motel room on Steve's arm – the distance from the esplanade passing in giggling anticipation.

The bland motel room could have been a colourful treasure house so enraptured is she by the moment; it whirls like an exotic carousel; everything feels right. Nerve ends tingle as their clothes drop silently to the floor and a forgotten flush of energy surges into her hips.

She purrs – gently onto the bed, drinking in his warm manly scent – so comforting, so strong, so needed. A circus of imagined music transports her, with him, into a euphoria of release.

Roger

The encryption warning light flashes on Roger's computer.

He checks his watch. It is late. He logs on. It is Sir Terence. What time is it in London? Ten hours earlier?

T – It is hotting up here. You need to lie low.

R – What has happened?

T – Met with the head of NPA, an old friend. The forces are gathering on both sides of the Atlantic. He thinks it will blow very soon.

R – What do they know?

T – GBIB is being investigated. FBI called in. They are investigating me. Only time before they find you.

R – Thanks for the warning. Keep your head low. It will pass. Weather the storm. Our systems will protect everyone. *Remember the watchwords.*

Roger cuts the connection.

A terrible worrier is Sir Terence. But … time for a contingency plan.

The opposition

'Dammit, Broderick. What is going on?'

The senior agent from the Office of the Director of National Intelligence is shouting at the *Versec* chief. He is clearly not used to being kept out of the information loop and is using the old tried and tested technique of public service bullying and intimidation. But Kyle Broderick does not come under his bureaucratic authority.

'My reports are furnished to the *DNI* and to the Congressional Accountability Committee just as agreed in the charter of *Veracity Section*,' replies Broderick calmly. 'What's your issue?'

'What's my issue?' splutters the agent. 'Senior investment bankers are being harried about their personal investments. Pillars of the American financial industry are having all their personal FBI files requested for your scrutiny. What gives you that power? The integrity of a knight of the United Kingdom is being questioned in the highest circles because he is chair of the board of an American bank. A prestigious investment bank, GBIB, is being thrown into suspicion – and over what? And you ask what my *issue* is?' The senior agent is almost apoplectic! His cheeks are going purple. 'Who the hell do you think you are?'

'I think I'm the head of *Versec*.' His voice is as saccharin sweet as he can muster, 'and if you've an issue with that, take it up with Congress or even the *DNI*, because I am operating absolutely within my charter.'

＊ ＊ ＊

'Not a happy camper,' Broderick says to Kennedy, as the *DNI* agent storms out. 'We must be hitting some of the right nerves. Keep it up!'

Kennedy grins his agreement. 'It's a good feeling to have that Congressional authority behind us at last.'

'Stick it up the whiners.' Broderick laughs. 'They don't like having their power base questioned, do they?'

GBIB

Sir Terence is quietly using Janet's personal mobile phone to call a distressed GBIB director in the States – a quick discreet call to see what is happening. It has been a long and worrying working day. Janet is out of the office, checking on other staff, before tidying up and heading for home.

'FBI and *Versec* are examining all the gambling ventures,' the shocked American director says. 'The board is in panic mode. This has never happened like this before. We can account for the investments as just the sport of financial players. The other monies cannot be explained so easily. If they really start to examine the bank's ledgers and journals, it will go pear-shaped. Time to take the parachute and get out.'

Sir Terence has the Brigadier's advice firmly in his mind – the investigation into the *Sea Spray* is about to blow. *Blood in the aisles*, he said. Now the American connection is being grilled; there can be no logical explanation for the laundered money if they check the accounts, line by line.

The old *Ramas* structure had been set up in the sixties when Aaron Rossiter had been the managing director. Those had been different times and old Aaron – rest his soul – had kept a rein on total stupidity.

It had started as a game with a bit of spice added because they were gambling with real money; borrowed money, the short-term money market – all fun for lots of left-brain thinkers who were feeling left out of the swinging sixties. And not illegal.

Ramas had helped Aaron design the system for the sport – and it just grew from there. Sir Terence had no knowledge of when it would have crossed the line into receiving dodgy money to be processed through a respectable investment bank. He hadn't even been involved until a little over a decade ago, when he had been approached to take over Aaron's role. But, somewhere along the line, GBIB became a significant clearing house for money from the *Ramas* trade – perhaps one of many around the world. He doesn't really know.

Right from the start, Aaron's intention was to make the laundering of a myriad of small deposits look like the profits of their high-risk market gambling.

It wasn't even remotely possible that most of the directors were unaware of this laundering role. That would indicate a combined naivety and hubris beyond Sir Terence's understanding. They were all financial people. His left hand shook again with the returning nervous tremor.

And Aaron has been dead for ten years. Apparently, he had amassed some amazing contacts through his era; the influential ones who had always been able to head off any investigative audits into the business.

The Chief Executive Officer, Ted Hayes, must have been across the daily operations. Ted had been a protégé of old Aaron. It was the logical transition for him to become CEO as Aaron reverted from managing director to being solely board chairman, and then to being just an influential director near the end of his time as Sir Terence assumed the chair.

The former chairman's sudden death had been a shock. Aaron had only been in his late sixties and it had surprised everyone when he had fallen to a stroke, so soon after Sir Terence had been appointed to lead the board. As the new chair, he had hoped for more time to learn this GBIB culture – but he had trusted that his skill as a banker, diplomat and board director would see him through.

Aaron's legacy had been that GBIB continued to prosper, with Ted handling the operations and a compliant board enjoying their continued gambling sport.

So Sir Terence chaired the board, content to be heading an American banking organisation – a compliment, he thought, to his obvious expertise and standing.

Indeed, it had been the GBIB board, through Ted Hayes, that had approached him a year before Aaron Rossiter died – flattering him that his status as an esteemed board chair would have him *head-hunted*; a feather in his cap, being seventy at the time. And he was slack in the monitoring of processes that had always appeared to be clean. He recognises that fully now.

It wasn't long after Aaron's death that he had twigged initially. Members of the board were gambling on the short-term market with the bank's borrowed money. He had bailed up Ted Hayes immediately, confronting him with such a high-risk practice.

Ted's response was that GBIB, under Aaron Rossiter, had perfected the technique of maximising returns and minimising the risks. He showed audited records back to the 1960s of annual reports indicating significant returns including shareholder dividends. Surely, if the risk was as Sir Terence anticipated, it would have faltered somewhere during the previous three-and-a-half decades. But no; the balance sheet, assets and dividends had all continued to progress. There had been no federal or state investigations into their operations.

Ted told Sir Terence that it would be a courageous decision by the board to change such a successful formula. So, he had gone along with the accepted practice – both through a sense of not wanting to rock a successful boat but also that even an old banker, like him, might be able to learn new tricks.

As the months went by, he studied the transaction lines even more closely. By then, he was sure that lots of small amounts of money were being deposited with the bank, in addition to recognisable profits from the directors' gambling activities.

It took some time for him to get his mind round the notion that the bank was being used as a clearing house for unidentified monies from overseas. While each amount was relatively small, collectively the financial arrangements added up to a billion-dollar operation – and the transactions were being lost in the massive operations of a very successful investment bank.

He had confronted Ted Hayes again, who calmly indicated that Sir Terence had been chair of the board now for many months; many presentations of balance sheets to board meetings; many opportunities to query the operations. Nothing had been challenged either by him or, over the years, by auditors or by bank monitoring agencies. It had all been clean.

The realisation was as traumatic as being shot. His reputation; whether or not he had been set up, it had happened on his watch.

A shocked Sir Terence had walked around the tourist sites of Washington on that autumn day. The drying leaves were casting off from their branches and landing in a rustic palette of shades of yellows through to brown. He watched the grey squirrels collecting their linings for their winter nests as he pondered what he should do; declare the fraud and face the humiliation – or do nothing and allow the practices to continue as they clearly had done for decades.

Even quietly cutting out the laundering of overseas deposits would send the bank into rapid decline – the short-selling gambles, likewise. Did he really want to be the chair who had caused the Grey Bear Investment Bank to fold after so many years of apparently unblemished business? What can of worms would that open?

What would it do for his reputation as a chairman?

He was now a knight of the British Empire. He had been chairing GBIB board meetings for a year with no comment at all about operational practice. Ted Hayes was right; it would be a very courageous decision to unilaterally turn all that around.

And Sir Terence had a noble record in international diplomacy – his knighthood was in large part for that role – a trusted party to negotiations between nations, to resolutions of regional conflict; an arbiter of alliances, a confidant of shadowy espionage and counter-espionage dealings over many years. He understood that even black and white are shades of grey. He had contacts with British and American power-brokers in Thames House, Vauxhall House and Langley, Virginia. Favours were owed, discretion was paramount – this issue would pass. It had to. Most things tended to cure themselves if left to heal.

So, as he walked slowly away from the Lincoln Memorial on that day, he was feeling tired, no energy for the sort of fight that might lie ahead if he called the behaviour of GBIB – and he made his decision.

If nothing had been found wrong with operations in over three decades then maybe he was being old-fashioned, too conservative, not adapting to a more modern risk-taking age.

He decided, on that day, that he didn't have the drive to rock the boat. He would go with the flow.

Just to confirm his thinking, he resolved to call *Butch*. It would be a local call. Butch and Sir Terence were veterans of some interesting pseudo-espionage scenarios in the past. If need be, he would drop in to see him, discreetly in the shadows as before.

He would remember that fateful autumn day over the months and years to come as the day he sold out his conscience, his integrity and his duty – and he was compromised.

Then he started receiving the messages to be relayed on to others, in the Caribbean, in the Mediterranean and the Far East – simple instructions to start with, the start of the slippery slide. The directions, he understood, came from the phantom-like *Ramas* – the leader of this elusive international maze.

He was appointed to chair the board of the South Pacific Trading Alliance, the command coming to him through the blind secretive channels from *Ramas*. He was instructed to accept. How could he risk exposure by refusing the order?

The name, *Ramas*, became part of his hidden world as a conduit of coded messages. There were no sources given. He suspected they originated in the United States. That was his impression from Ted Hayes, although it was never actually said. It was more just a sense that GBIB and *Ramas* were being protected by powerful people – and those players were American.

Sir Terence had known what was happening. Yet he hadn't enlightened his fellow directors, in any formal sense. He assumed they could not be so innocent as not to realise that the short-term money markets couldn't make the entire volume of transactions of the bank.

But they were all receiving good bonuses, so everything stayed quietly discreet. They were all having fun, problem-solving in the high-risk game of financial daring. To them, it was the equivalent of playing three-dimensional chess; intellectually exciting, utilising the latest technology and their significant expertise. It was a fantasy; a reason for living; a game with no sense of wrong-doing. The *Ramas* illusion hid the laundered money ... and they didn't check to see. They were naïve rich game-players, on a board synonymous with unquestioned success.

The *Sea Spray* had been a terrible mistake.

The order to comply with the plan had come from *Ramas* but it was Cavanagh who seduced the GBIB board with not only a massive amount of *play* money but also the adrenalin rush of the chance to get away with the joke of the century – the ransom gig on some anonymous banker who wouldn't miss the small fortune. It would still all stay under the radar, he told them, because the victim would avoid any adverse publicity.

Madness! And they believed him because everything they had ever done with *the game* had been covered up by influence in high places.

Sir Terence had warned Roger not to get into overt violence. Then what had he done? Kidnapped a famous singer, killing two guards in the process. Then he had stung the husband for tens of millions using the GBIB board's financial expertise to put the followers off the trail.

It just defied belief!

Of course, important people were going to be annoyed – so annoyed as it happened that they had now formed two special investigative units on both sides of the Atlantic to solve the case finally; political support at Ministerial and Congressional committee level.

The strategy had always been to stay under the radar; that was *Ramas's* template – *results, silence* and avoid raising the interest of the authorities.

Now, they are caught in the radar, like deer in the headlights.

Then, there is the matter of a GBIB director being the source of disclosing a confidential personal email address of the pop singer's husband. They are like overgrown school-boys – except that the man's wife had been kidnapped.

The husband had paid his multi-million dollar ransom using a secure pathway devised by more of these director game-players, thinking they were solving some intellectual problem-solving challenge; and then people had been killed on the boat. Madness!

And now, they want Sir Terence to pull strings to get them out of it.

Probably the only aspect that won't get discovered is how Roger's encryption program disguises the source of the ransom email. All done through the *Lerna*; anonymous on a trackless electronic ocean.

He had warned Roger – done all he could – but how he wished he had never listened to that little persuader's flattery. Every venture had always been made to sound so plausible. He always made an old knight feel so respected and valued.

Twenty years ago, he would have thrown Roger out of the office and called the police. But it had been very subtle when they drew him in – just a little at a time, a little deeper and then a bit more. He supposed he had fallen for the fawning; needing to feel he hadn't lost it. It was a matter of pride.

Of course, there had been a point where he knew that he had crossed the line.

He could have said, *No!* at that time, albeit with more than a little personal shame, perhaps even some significant public disgrace.

Nevertheless, he *could* have pulled back then – that autumn day in Washington.

But he didn't – and now he is the regular courier for messages, from *Ramas*, he supposes. They are always coded, anonymous and untraceable – as they have always been, even before computer technology.

Yes, he is merely a conduit; a façade to be used at directors' meetings. Certainly, still a polished performer in those circles but he now carries the spectre of his dishonesty, like a sword of Damocles, recognising that threatening wraith every time his hand shakes a little.

And there was the time when Cavanagh alluded to laundering the profits of people-trafficking. That smarmy crook had laughed.

'The British Empire and most others were founded on slavery,' Cavanagh had said. 'The Sedgewood fortune too, check it out.'

'You are trafficking in people too?' Sir Terence had responded, aghast.

'Very profitable. Everyone is a slave to something. People need to be moved. Didn't you realise?' And Cavanagh had given his conspiratorial smirk.

How could he tell his family of his deceit? His country had given him a knighthood for services to the community. And it had just been hubris, vanity, the need to feel wanted, respected, belonging ...

He replaced Janet's phone.

Now, they will all have to get out, each in their own best fashion. The Brigadier is right.

In Greek legend, the *Hydra* is a gigantic monster with nine heads, the centre one immortal. The monster's haunt was in the marshes of Lerna near Argos. The destruction of the Hydra was one of the Twelve Labours of Heracles; as one head was cut off, two grew in its place.

The Brigadier and Cecile

London. Wednesday 14 February 2007

It was back in 1990 when Douglas had first met Cecile.

The widower Brigadier and the widowed countess – the old soldier attracted to the elegant lady of the aristocratic polish and the sharp independent mind; she, enticed by the solid reliability of an intelligent senior officer, a man needing a rest from all the demons of his profession, a discreet man, a people person, a fit for the role. Why not?

They were clever people, able to challenge each other's thinking; both independently wealthy, no fragile egos to be nursed. When eventually the Yugoslavian conflict ended, the Brigadier officially retired. With the barriers cleared and the positives accentuated, they decided that their mature companionship would suit them well for their last decades.

They each retained their independence and old networks while sharing their friendship. The chateau with its vineyard operations was a living business needing attention and care. Cecile enjoyed the work. Douglas assisted. He was good with networks and he understood production lines.

They had been married for two years when Douglas found his wife in the cellar gallery with her plethora of paintings, jewels and ornaments. Presents, gifts, he had been told – very expensive presents. An amazing sapphire, displayed prominently in a lit case. The *Mohács Blue*, the label said. Was that painting actually a real Rubens or just a clever copy? No it was real, she had replied – a time for honesty after a lifetime of secrets.

Left over from the Nazi era plundering, perhaps?

No, post-war gifts.

Why are you receiving gifts?

It was then, two years into a happy mature relationship, that Cecile slowly explained *the game* to Douglas, not the other parties involved, but the rules and how it had taken off.

What had been innocent dreaming and fun had become a template for an international criminal trading process, which dealt in many forms of legal and illegal trade, laundered money and now appeared to have a life of its own.

The language, the security, the training, the problem solving – it had all been an interesting challenge in the early days. The financial structures, the normal language of business, communicating by coded messages had all been exciting.

The Americans had been quick to see the potential – all they had needed was the catalyst of the idea and they were ready to run with it. The British were always more conservative – grey hues rather than the bold colours of the States. She had been in charge of the encryption and no-one in the organisation had known where the messages came from. The template was brilliant. The structure was secure.

Then, she had wanted out. *The game* had run its course. It was no longer stimulating, no longer fun.

However, the system was, by then, in place. It enabled each cell to be self-sustaining, even growing. Such was the admiration for her coded title in the early days and the success of the organisation that her followers sent her gifts, a tribute to her skill in setting it all up. That was how the Mohács Blue had arrived – an amazing gesture from a grateful organisation.

She had tried to get out, and she'd had no active role since the early seventies. But she *had* accepted quality *objets d'art* over the years – too good to refuse.

The cellar became a place of tranquil beauty and joy – a solitary place for a solitary woman.

Then, later, she was drawn back deeper by the new challenge of the electronic age and new largesse from people she didn't even know, all sent securely through the blind channels of *the game*.

The new technology age was exciting – digital encryption, electronic funds transfer, even the parallel avatar world stimulated her ageing mind to be really alive again. The gifts continued to arrive through the anonymous channels and the *Hydra* couldn't be killed.

The Brigadier took some time to absorb the enormity of his wife's exploits. It was foreign to all of his training, his ethics, his upbringing. His initial reaction was to declare what he had uncovered and place the matter in the hands of the courts. But which courts? French? British? World-wide courts, because the business had its tentacles all over the globe?

He believed Cecile when she insisted she had tried to escape from the monster she had created decades before, but its addictive lure had brought her back and it was self-generating anyway. She couldn't kill it off; unable to rid herself of the clinging fiend or to get away from its tantalising tendrils.

And, anyway, she would always be morally implicated, even if no-one knew who she was.

What to do?

Cecile's role had been lost in the maze of processes in the system. Such was the security, multiple channels, code names, dead ends, encryption, international operations, dummy companies – that it would be an extraordinarily difficult task for any law-enforcement agency to track anything back to the chateau in the Loire. Besides, the regulations around international waters and international finance were absolutely full of confusions and denials.

Then, there was the simple matter of love.

He had found a charming acceptable companion, who apparently shared a similar mature view of him. That was a rare chemistry to find when in your sixties. To just abandon someone about whom you cared deeply; to walk away from that bond in the autumn of your life. Was that really what he wanted?

For weeks, Douglas said nothing. He couldn't decide. The only people who knew about it were he and Cecile. Why stir up an international incident?

Then months had gone by with no mention of the matter at all. Then a year.

The moment had passed. It was too late to raise it again. He was compromised. He had known; and he had said nothing.

Now he would have to manage the situation as best he could.

Lady Meredith

England. Wednesday 14 February 2007

'Lady Meredith, Sir Terence's car is just heading up the driveway.'

'Thank you, Meg,' Lady Meredith calls back, in reply to the house-maid.

How surprising! Her Ladyship thinks. *Terry doesn't usually come home until the weekend. Perhaps he is unwell.*

* * * *

The car tyres crackle over the gravel on the circular driveway and the vehicle stops in front of the grand door to the Sedgewood family home.

It is an imposing, old, stone building set in twenty hectares of rolling countryside. Sometime in the past, the whole vista, as far as the eye could see, had been farming divisions on Sedgewood lands – a huge manor estate. But generations of death duties had reduced the once grand lands back to its current area. While twenty hectares is not a suburban plot, it pales against the memory of what Sedgewood Manor had once been.

Sir Terence is in a morose mood as he alights from the car. He is indulging in a self-flagellating reflection on his inability to maintain the prestige and tradition of his ancestors.

He hurries up the stairs as Richard, the butler, opens the grand door for him.

'We weren't expecting you, Sir. Welcome home.'

'It's good to be here,' says Sir Terence, automatically. 'Is Lady Meredith home?'

'Just coming down the stairs, Sir.'

'Are you alright, my dear?' asks his concerned wife.

'Can we talk, dear, please? In the library. Yes, I'm okay.' He is aware that his wife knows, from his jumbled language, that something must be terribly wrong.

By the time Lady Meredith closes the library door, Sir Terence has tears rolling down his cheeks. They have been married for nearly sixty years. He can not recall ever being in such a state, in all that time.

'I have let you down terribly, my dear. It's all over.'

He sits heavily on the sofa while his wife pours him a glass of water from the beaker.

The desolate husband allows her to cradle his head in her arms.

'All you have in life is your integrity.' He is rambling. 'And that has gone. I could blame Roger Cavanagh but I must shoulder the responsibility. I can face the pain for my own sake, but not for yours, my dear. You did nothing to deserve such shame.' And he dissolves into racking sobs again.

'What has happened, Terry?'

They sit silently for maybe ten minutes while Terry slowly sips water and they hold each other close. Meredith offers to fetch the doctor but that just starts another wave of sobs.

'Merri,' Terry says, using his wife's nickname, 'I don't know where to start. Suffice it to say that I need to resign all of my directorships today.'

Meredith doesn't argue and says simply, 'Yes, dear. Why?'

'I have knowingly allowed myself to be involved in illegal activity. I suspect perhaps that people may have died as a result of my inaction and ineptitude.' He is suddenly drained of all the teary emotion.

'The main two boards implicated, both of which I chair,' he continues, 'are the South Pacific Freight Alliance and the Grey Bear Investment Bank in the United States. There are two very high-level police committees investigating these matters in America and Britain, as we speak. At the very least, there was a hi-jacking of an American citizen in the waters off Fiji, conducted under the auspices of people who work for SPFA. Two people died in that attack.

'A ransom of thirty million dollars US was paid by the husband of the kidnapped citizen. It was acquaintances of mine on the board of GBIB who showed the blackmailer how to carry it out successfully. It was just a game to them. But it was real, Merri; happening to real people.

'That precipitated the inquiry. The Brigadier and I had breakfast at *The Club* this morning. He heads one of the groups that are investigating the matter. He knows nothing of my involvement. He tells me they are nearly ready to blow the case wide open. *Blood in the aisles,* he told me.

'But that is just part of it. That is the sharp part. But really, I have known for a long time that SPFA has been making millions through laundering the profits of illegal smuggling, insurance fraud and piracy. It went through GBIB, passing it off as profits made by high-risk stock trading. I have known about that too for many years. I turned a blind eye.

'There's more. I suspect that the smuggling might even involve trafficking people into slavery. I don't know that, but I suspect it.

'When the police investigators go through the books, they will find the fraud immediately. It's disguised on the surface but skilled forensic detectives won't take too long to expose it.

'And finally, I think the whole world financial market is about to collapse.' He paused to let out a despairing wail. 'I have been listening to the new generation of bankers now for months. They are gambling like addicts. They are just like drunks, betting that particular stocks will grow and they will be able to sell them fast, making enormous profits. At the surface level, it's just a bit of fun – but I sense that greed has become ingrained in the economic psyche of this emerging breed. There's no prudence of assuring equity and assessing risk.

221

'We have a whole financial structure now which is like a ribbon of dominoes – each relying on the next one's stability to remain upright. But the foundation for the whole edifice is a sham. When one domino goes, the whole pattern will follow.

'Mark my words; it's been worrying me for a few years now. It's just a mirage. It will have to collapse at some stage. Soon. A financial crisis impacting on the whole planet – a global financial crisis. Perhaps the worst ever.'

Lady Meredith nods, rises and slowly walks over to the library desk. Opening the top drawer, she withdraws a small packet of pills before returning to the sofa.

Sir Terence shakes his head slowly, his eyes fixed and staring, as his wife sits beside him. 'I have tried to lead a noble life, my dear Merri. I am a proud Knight Commander of the British Empire and now, through my own fault and actions, I have become a shameless man, devoid of all human worth or respect. I do apologise to you, Merri. I never meant it to end this way.'

'There … there. Is anything public yet?' asks Meredith extracting three sleeping pills as she speaks.

Sir Terence swallows the medicine with a sip of water, lies back on the library lounge, and closes his eyes. His agitated face is relaxing.

'Not to my knowledge,' replies the drowsy-sounding knight. 'It's all over, Merri, all over … Sorry.'

He lies back, asleep.

* * * *

Lady Meredith has recovered from the shock of seeing her husband in such a state.

Her first phone call is to a silent number in the heart of London's decision-making centre, her next to a Harley Street doctor.

Her third call is international, to Washington DC.

PART FOUR

All that is necessary for the triumph of evil is that good men do nothing.

Edmund Burke
Irish orator, philosopher, & politician (1729–1797)

Brennan – a decade earlier

Halmahera Sea, Indonesia. 1997

The sparkling turquoise sea is framed by the jagged volcanic islands of the Maluku; steep mountain slopes are covered in a rough, green, velvet cloak of rainforest. These are the legendary Spice Islands of nutmeg, clove and mace fame. Could anywhere be more heavenly?

Ben Brennan can remember standing on the Tasmanian *Island of Graves,* just off the Port Arthur shore, and thinking, *why would anyone put a prison in such a beautiful place?* Isn't that just double the torture?

Double the torture is the way he is feeling at this moment, standing above the sandy tide line on the island, a *pulau*, hammering two crosses at the heads of the graves. Why it should be crosses, he doesn't know. He isn't religious. It just seems to be an easy shape for the purpose, an appropriate symbol to mark those resting places in his sorrow. He needs to mark them.

He has let them down.

* * * *

The attackers had taken him by surprise. His yacht, the *Pelindung* had been at anchor in a horseshoe bay off a small *pulau*. It had been a perfect sunset. High flecky strands of cloud, tinged with gold over pale purple – a complete dome of colour, gently changing. The camera clicked.

Sarah was nineteen at the time. This was her gap year – sailing the romantic islands with her mother and father; tales of spice traders in the world's primary source of nutmeg trees.

'Sunsets to die for,' she had said. How prophetic!

Her father, a retired Navy special forces soldier, was trained to attack and defend. He had weapons on board and all the right safety communications. They felt secure. He inspired confidence. Sarah's mother was Sonya. They all loved the sea. It was sailing that had brought her parents together – and the dream of gliding silently through the pristine waters of the islands was what had kept them focused until he retired from the Navy.

Pelindung – the name of their ship – meant *protector* in Indonesian. These were blissful days, cruising by sail with a back-up motor if needed. Just the three of them. Sarah told her father and mother that she had never felt so happy. Nor had she seen her father, Ben, so relaxed.

* * * *

He had heard the slight sound and started to turn, but they had approached quietly on bare feet, as all eyes had been on photographing the sunset. The club hit hard – and then it was black.

* * * *

He didn't understand the taste of blood and deck wood as he slowly regained consciousness. The gentle sighing of the boat as it rode the swell drew him up from the mists of the concussion. It was night when he realised where he was – and he called out to Sarah and Sonya. Nothing!

Blood on the deck where he had landed.

A few seats lay askew, but otherwise – so peaceful.

Beyond the yacht, which still lay at anchor in the bay – serene.

Clear seas, reflected in the moonlight. The dinghy was gone! His head throbbed. He felt an egg of a bruise on his head. The adrenalin was pumping through him. What had happened?

They hadn't even landed on the island. They were being careful; staying safely out to sea. He would have to swim to get to land.

No ordeal for him but he is loath to leave the boat unattended. Then he could be marooned on the island. How much worse could it get?

He makes radio contact with the Port of Ternate on Maluku to advise that his wife and daughter are missing. He is going ashore – in the darkness; like operations – as if he has never retired.

The beach. Footprints.

The dinghy has been pulled behind the line of coconut palms. A pencil of light from his waterproof torch shows the trail. It isn't hard to follow. There is a village up ahead.

He circles carefully, his weapons concealed at his back. There are people moving around, a child calls out, unable to sleep; a peaceful normal scene. He looks at the huts. No sign of his wife or daughter. Everything is calm. But the track has led here? Have they passed by?

A man is near. He does not appear to be armed – more a villager.

A decision is made. Challenge any threat with guile, but find out where his family is.

Ben steps out from the trees, with a friendly non-threatening wave into the ambient glow from the moon, the village fire and lights. Two other men appear quickly. He tries speaking in English.

Puzzled looks, rather than fear or anger. Encouraging.

Ben's Indonesian is very limited.

He tries 'women', *perempuan*. Confused looks. *Wanita*. A glint of awareness. 'White', *putih*. '*Perempuan putih. Wanita*'. That gets a reaction, apprehensive looks. Ben points to the bay and to the cut on his head. Sympathetic nods. Looks of worry.

'*Perempuan putih*. Women,' says one man stepping forward, reaffirming his interpretation. '*Pedagang budak,*' he continues, and then repeats it. He points to the headland.

Ben doesn't understand but he knows the headland. He had studied it through binoculars from the bay, when they first sailed in and moored.

One of the men is offering to guide him. Through the darkness of the forest, the native leads him along a scarcely identifiable path which comes out onto a headland. He points to the sea. *'Perahu, perahu.'*

Ben understands the word for boat.

Then the man says, *'Pedagang budak'* which has no meaning for him.

He can pick signs of human movement on the headland.

With a few steps to the edge of the low sea cliff; he can look back into the horseshoe bay where his yacht is still moored, glinting peacefully in the pale moonlight.

* * * *

Back on board, Ben radios for assistance to Ternate. He asks what *pedagang budak* means.

'Slave traders,' is the reply.

* * * *

Now five days later, he has just laid his beloved Sonya and Sarah to rest in the sands of the *pulau.*

The tears have been shed but the wracking pain has only intensified. It is his fault that they are dead. So many errors made. He had the knowledge and the experience, but he got it wrong. From their first capture to his abortive raid on the *perahu*, it was his impetuous action that has resulted in the loves of his life now lying beneath the warm Indonesian sands. How could he have failed them so badly?

The guilt is tangible, knotting his entrails and fuelling his agonising anger.

Revenge! Retribution!

No brutal reprisal could ever replace the loss of everything important in his life but … he could spare other victims from a similar fate.

He would expect no forgiveness and he sought no release from his failure. His death would never compensate. Indeed, his demise for the cause would be a welcome deliverance.

Some *pedagang budak* have died already at his hands but they are the bandits, the pirates at the lowest level. Somewhere high above are the organisers of this trade. They are his target. They will feel his wrath.

With a hand on each of the crosses, Ben Brennan makes a solemn vow while letting out a cathartic roar. He is a man with a mission.

Hillnah

Hillnah thinks it must be night because the air-conditioner has stopped. There are no other clues in the dark.

She tries to roll over on the foul-smelling matting but her leg restraint won't stretch. The woman beside her moans as her right leg is tugged; then the moan moves unconsciously into a low wail. The rest of the chain of women pick up the deep plaintive cry and the whole darkened container resounds to a painful lament of despair.

The stench of reed-matting merges with the rusty tang of metallic paint. Fumes from the chemical toilet waft over the prone women, each tethered to the next by a thin chain-link of plastic.

In the heat of the day, their shipping container prison is air-conditioned to ensure the survival of life inside. At night, the air is switched off.

Eventually, the container door will be opened and the captives will shuffle out onto the darkened deck again, to squat for toilet and then be hosed off.

How could it have come to this?

It seems like a dream – so long ago. Her village. The outrigger ride with Rhyno. But it could only have been a few days ago – when the dream turned into the worst of nightmares.

* * * *

Hillnah is educated – a Solomon Islander who has been to school at Honiara on the main island, but has returned to the Western Islands for her traditional wedding to Rhyno.

He is from Espiritu Santo in Vanuatu. He is a handsome young carpenter, enjoying using his skills in the building industry of the new Solomon Islands after the *RAMSI* regional assistance military forces had restored order.

They had met in Honiara. They wanted to be married in the traditional ways of both their peoples. So they had gone first to the Western Province, to Hillnah's family, as a mark of respect for her culture. There had been introductions, discussions of kula, preparation of their minds to the values of the past and an appreciation of their roles as young islanders in leading into the ways of the future.

As a traditional indication of trust from the older people, Rhyno had taken Hillnah for a paddle in an outrigger canoe. It was to be a short trip, round a couple of headlands and back within a few hours.

They had never returned.

The village search party found the outrigger floating in a calm white-sand bay; paddles bobbing on the surface close by, water containers still on board – but no Rhyno nor Hillnah.

A total mystery. Sharks? Drowning?

The wedding ceremony had changed to a mourning ceremony.

* * * *

It had been two inflatables with powerful outboard motors racing round from behind a headland.

Rhyno had pointed to them straight away, laughing at those foolish young ones with their fast boats. Then he had seen the guns in the hands of the intruders on their peaceful sailing trip. He had raised his paddle in defence of his new bride-to-be, only to be clubbed from the boat circling behind. No shots. Hardly any words. The unconscious Rhyno and the shocked Hillnah. What was happening?

* * * *

231

They had been taken on board a fishing boat which had transferred them, bound and gagged, onto this huge ship during the night.

* * * *

Hillnah was tied to a long line of sunken-eyed frightened women, pushed inside the container. The gag was removed – and now here she lies and cries in her terror. Rhyno must be somewhere on the ship. She didn't see where he was taken.

Her parents? The wedding ceremony? What is happening?

The woman next to her is Chinese. She speaks no words that Hillnah can understand. She doesn't seem to want to speak anyway. The next one speaks an Islander dialect that Hillnah can't follow. There are so many dialects in the islands.

Then, in the inky, smelly darkness of the container, a woman three along in the line, says something in broken English. It is a slow process of communication, Hillnah with her schoolgirl English and the woman with her Filipina, crossing between Tagalog and English words. The message, however, is clear almost from the beginning of hearing it.

Slave traders.

What does it mean? Surely this cannot be happening? This is 2007. What sort of slave? For how long?

The Filipina woman seems to know something about it. This trade has been the talk of her village. Her people know the stories. They know to avoid these traders but still it continues. She was tricked into capture.

How long has she been here? Many days. Weeks probably.

She has not seen daylight. They are only brought out on deck at night. More women have been brought on board and others taken off since she had been imprisoned here.

Escape? No way. They are all tied together. Maybe fifteen or twenty, all shackled by the right leg, rubber and plastic shackles. The plastic ties are long enough for them all to lie down without being twisted but they wouldn't break. There is nothing to cut these tough bonds.

When they come out at night they have to keep their steps in time or they trip over, bringing all the women to the ground. The guards hit them if they fall over, laughing as they do it. Not heavy clubs, but stinging straps. No! Escape would be for all, or none.

What sort of slavery? The Filipina's villagers have known of people taken away. Word had filtered back. They talked of what happened to some of them. Horrible stuff!

Middle East, perhaps. Rich men's pleasure.

India? Thailand? 'Where we would be different,' she said. 'Exotic.'

Or maybe just labourers. Sewing clothes? Cleaning and scrubbing? Who knows? But we are slaves. Men's property.

For how long?

Forever. Your life as you have known it is over. Forever.

Rescue?

This is forever. Who can stop a huge ship like this? Who even knows that you are here? You are no longer a person.

And so Hillnah spends each day, alternating between crying for her family and trying to keep track of her sanity.

* * * *

After two nights, another two women, Islander women, are brought on board and shackled to her other side. Now she is even more trapped – just one more in a line of prisoners.

At times, she can hear wailing from somewhere else, another container perhaps. The Filipina woman says it is the men. They are crying out. She has seen them once being locked up just as the women were being led out onto the deck.

It is the thought that Rhyno is nearby that gives Hillnah the faintest glimmer of hope. She needs that twinkle of purpose to get her through the black times when death seems to be the only sensible thing.

How to do it? Stop breathing? Strangle herself? Use the ties that link them together? She would need to be a contortionist.

There is nothing sharp in the container to cut the ties or to stab. Nothing to bash. How hard it seems to find a way to end it all.

But Rhyno would be going through this too – and being a man, he would be feeling he had failed to protect his bride. Oh, what pain he will be suffering. She has to let him know she is here.

What if she kills herself and then he escapes only to find her dead?

No. She must carry on. *They* must carry on.

They must not give up hope.

But what if the Filipina woman is right? What if her destiny is to be in a harem in some Arabian camp?

May her parents never know what fate has befallen her. May they only think that the sharks have taken her. That would be an honourable end – not this other way!

Oh the shame; the shame; the shame.

PART FIVE

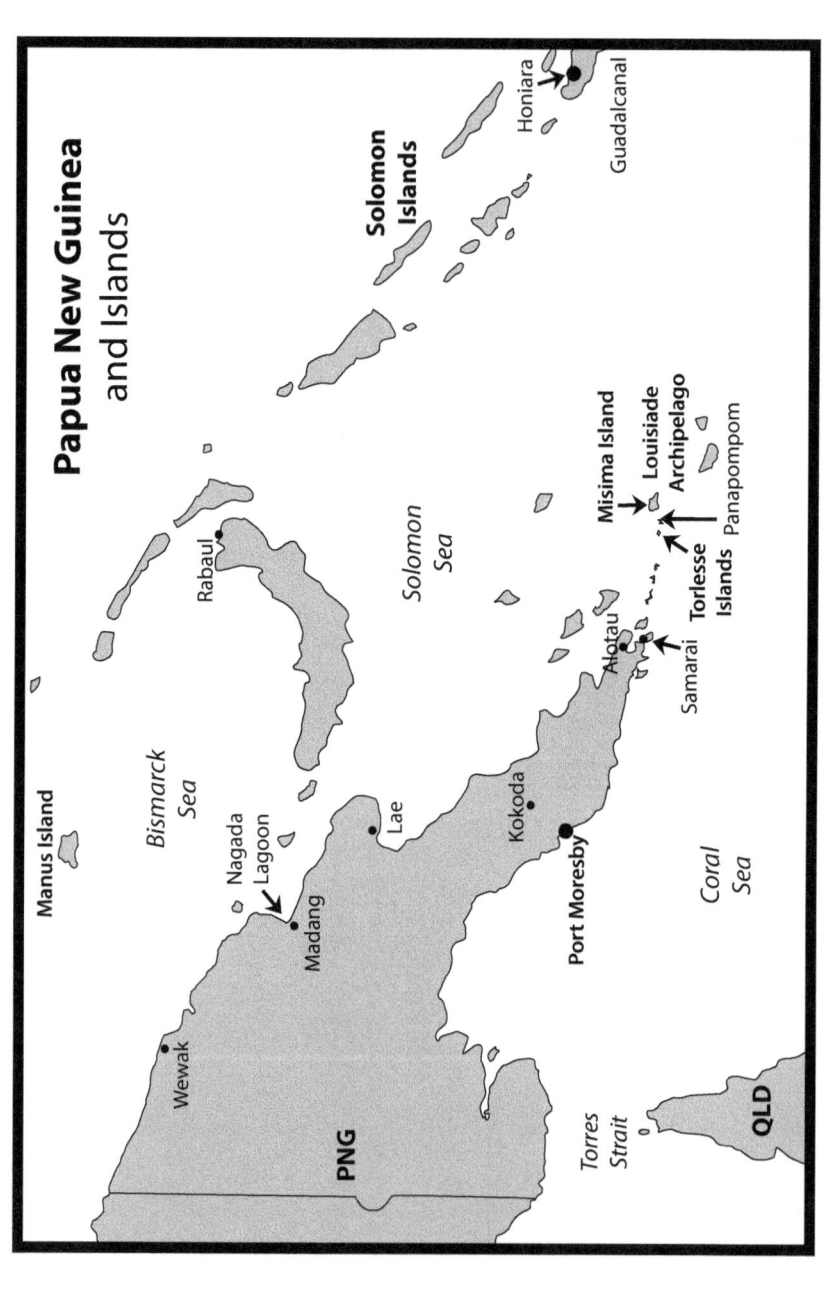

Papua New Guinea
and Islands

Manus Island

Bismarck
Sea

Wewak

Madang

Nagada
Lagoon

PNG

Lae

Kokoda

Port Moresby

Rabaul

Solomon
Sea

Alotau

Samarai

Torlesse
Islands

Misima Island

Louisiade
Archipelago

Panapompom

Coral
Sea

Torres
Strait

QLD

Solomon
Islands

Honiara

Guadalcanal

Steve and the *Lerna*

The gulls are calling. They are heralds for the early morning on the near-deserted ship, now moored at the secure marina jetty.

It has been a *better than wonderful* night. I am basking in the marvellous tingling memory as my mind rolls through ecstatic images, scents and sounds.

Even the crewman is *happy to be of service*, despite being called to open the security gate to the Sailfish jetty for me, an hour before dawn. The world seems so good.

That is why it is such an effort, in the bright light of a wakening day, to come back to the reality of the venture on which we have both embarked.

The 'spectacle case' nestles in my soft clothes bag. It is not out-of-place there. What a clever little transmitter. According to Bill Jones, it rolls through several rarely-used frequencies in a pattern calibrated with the receivers; so that, if someone accidently heard part of transmission, it would have moved to the new frequency before they could track it.

Anyway, it is lost in my bag. I don't have many clothes. I only have the cash the captain has advanced me for my big night out on the town.

It is so strange, this money-less luxury environment. If I want something, I assume someone is prepared to sign for it – and be in control of me. Even after the distracting excitement of last night with Alison, I can recall Gina saying the same thing. It has been part of the process that is trapping her.

Tired, yet euphoric, I set out on my routine patrol of the ship as I have been doing since Noumea. The captain has gone ashore for the day, leaving only a skeleton crew on board – that would be me, Marcel the chef and three crewmen. Everyone else is getting well-earned shore leave, on a roster. It should be peaceful for me.

In my pocket is a small re-sealable plastic bag containing eight miniature microphones.

Only the slight groans from deep in the bowels of the vessel accompany me as I walk the silent ship – a gentle movement against the wharf in the subtle marina swell. It is so quiet.

I prepare to position the listening bugs, carefully coded to match a numbered sequence of the ship locations. Bill Jones has been meticulous with his written instruction note.

In the main communications office, I check the CCTV screens. The captain is already ashore and a crewman is working at the jetty gate. Marcel is talking in the galley to a crewman. The third is cleaning around the big diesel engines. Everyone accounted for. Safe to move into Roger's private suite; the reception room-cum-office.

I place a microphone near where Roger taps regularly on his laptop.

Silently, through a door into the plush stateroom, then back to the office and through another door, into the private living quarters.

It is a surprise; cluttered like a jumbled museum of traditional and modern art. To my eye, it doesn't work – paintings, ornaments, bookcases with old books, a set of biographical works on Napoleon, sculptures, a huge television screen with all the DVD technology, satellite receivers and video game machinery – valuable junk interspersed with modern technology.

I wonder if Gina ever sits in that room. It is so oppressive.

No doubt that is why she is usually on the sundeck, in fresh air and away from the claustrophobia of the collector's chaos.

I place a listening bug in the couch facing the television.

Through a door into the bedroom, I find a huge king-size bed with a television screen at the foot. Huge walk-in wardrobes; one for Roger and another for Gina – hers laden with shoes, cocktail dresses and high-quality casual day-wear. Just viewed from the outside of Roger's wardrobe, I could see tuxedos, white and black; suits in colours from bone to business; silk shirts, casual trousers. Beyond were separate bathrooms and another room – a bedroom too.

I leave without placing any of the gadgets. It doesn't seem right.

Downstairs, beneath the stateroom, I find the cabin which Peter Carter has occupied. I try the door and it opens. On a hunch, I place one bug in that room. I try the same approach with the room which Len Williamson has been in. Another listening device.

Up to the bridge – another bug placed. The CCTV room – another microphone, in waiting mode.

Then back to my own room where I secrete a mini-microphone near my bed head. It's the easiest place in the room to speak quietly into the little electronic gadget to send my regular reports back to Inspector Willis.

To test the system, I send a message to Bill Jones over the bedroom microphone to advise that two bugs have been placed in Carter's and Len's cabins respectively. I'd just have to trust the receivers are working and being tracked. Go with the flow!

Back in the office, I check the screens again. No-one has moved. I put my mind to establishing the location of all the weapons on board. When Roger had shown me the security systems, he made no mention of weapons, although I saw lockers which should hold weapons on my strolls. Really he has told me very little. Was he setting me up? Is this all some sort of test? It has all happened very quickly.

I find it hard to buy this *super-crook* idea. Would Roger have accepted me so easily if he really is this master criminal? Would it have been so smooth?

Maybe he operates above the paranoia that might plague lesser people. He certainly talks with a confidence that fits his command of the situation. Maybe even like the Napoleon in his book-set.

Yes, he is a little Napoleon. I can visualise him in a typical French Emperor pose.

Back to the weapons. I walk up onto the bridge and find a locker, locked, which clearly should hold rifles of some sort. Having found the first, the others are easy to locate on each of the decks. It is a well-armed vessel. I will ask Roger about the keys to the lockers and the maintenance of the weapons. A rifle is no use unless you can rely on it to fire. Maintenance!

I allocate a crewman to monitor any incoming radio messages, in a room behind the bridge. And another crewman to watch the standard deck camera images on the CCTV screens. He can watch satellite TV on another screen, simultaneously. It won't be a boring day for him.

Everything is in place. I retreat to the stateroom where I sink into a comfortable lounge chair with a cool drink – a chance to reflect on everything without the pressure of watching my back for danger.

* * * *

My brain cogs start to freewheel. Thoughts just roll through mental images of life on the *Sea Spray*; Lani's tender massages on the Fijian island; the smart looks of the scheming Carter and the stretched visage of Laughing Len. Lots of images of Miss Gina; the austere snob, the giggling girl on the boardwalk, the lost and lonely rich girl on the deck of a luxury yacht.

There is Alison; a soft, affectionate lady who has suddenly landed in my world; the journalist who wants to write about dangerous people – but is scared at the same time; the girl with the happy laugh. As we lay on the grass of the esplanade watching flying foxes soar overhead and listening to the cicadas' song, I knew we were in for a fabulous night – and my expectations underestimated the reality. Far too good to walk away from this, for at least a few days more.

Then there are Inspector Willis, Ben Brennan and Bill Jones. What is to happen next? It is comforting to feel they are there in the background; monitoring, planning and scheming.

But my thoughts are of Alison. For reasons I can't explain clearly, I want her to be safe. Goodness, I have only known her for just over a day and I am feeling those protective thoughts. But what a day! I sense this is a turning point in my life. It is just that the signposts aren't yet very clear.

I grew up in Perth; an only child. My truck-driving father was a distant figure in my life but imposing when he was there; away a lot, drank heavily when he was not out-of-town driving – bingeing, out of control. My mother was regularly on the receiving end of his verbal outbursts when the old man returned home with a few under his belt.

I don't know if the old man was cruel, maybe just self-obsessed and dismissive of women. He backed down when I was around, at least when I had grown big enough to be taken seriously. But there had been times when he had tossed me around as a little protesting kid.

I was a different proposition in my teens. He knew that; and he didn't push. I'd have dropped him cold. I didn't forget the earlier years. Never have.

Mum was gentle; kind, pretty. She worked in the supermarket and, in the evenings, she told me stories; adventure stories from her reading and from her imagination; of a life beyond my little world in Western Australia – of following dreams, travelling, all the things she had wanted to do herself but had never had the confidence or the means to tackle.

I had seen the military at nearby Swanbourne. I pictured them travelling overseas, on adventures like the stories my mother talked about.

I had wanted to be in the Army from as young as I could remember.

I was seventeen when Mum was diagnosed with leukaemia. It was a swift but harrowing end. The pain of watching her suffering was matched only by the relief of her passing; when she need suffer no more. Even the old man had shown more compassion than ever before; but the funeral was the end of an era for him and me.

Mum had been laid to rest. My father had become a stranger to me. I was seventeen, going on eighteen. The Army beckoned and it became my new family. But the time in service, the regular overseas tours, had tired me of the routine. I wanted a future. I had some money but no skills, except in team combat.

I'd never been very keen on school.

For the present, all I can do is security work and it has passed its *use by* date.

I want to settle down. With someone like Alison, maybe – but it takes two to tango. Early days but, for me at least, she has just clicked – from that first smile on the jetty.

How have we managed to get ourselves involved in this crazy commitment to the police? It is sure to end in tears and pain. Why don't we just walk away? If last night is anything to go by, we could have a blissful time together. Why play at being cops or secret agents?

There are still a few days before Roger is due to return. Maybe we can get out of it all, go away together – leave this world of pirates to others. I am over the hero stuff. I just want to be like everyone else – quiet and happy.

But, for the meantime, I *am* involved, committed. I have given my word to the police and to Alison. Goodness, she said she would be involved too. Not what I wanted and yet, there she is, willing to put her safety on the line. What sort of lame wuss am I turning into?

The Army sense of duty snaps back in. My mind goes to the task in hand. I will be the spy within the crew. Being the ship's new security officer will go over really well with Carter and Williamson when they return. Carter has been suspicious of me from Day 1. It will be very interesting to see their reaction.

I wonder where they are at the moment. Willis has alluded to their roles in supervising the Cavanagh network; training others.

Indeed, I recall Roger referring to something like that role as a possibility for me. What is he up to? Maybe Carter and Williamson are on the outer. Why else would I be brought in? It is bizarre.

My thought doesn't last long because the crewman calls me to the bridge office.

'A call from Mr Cavanagh. He will phone back in four minutes.'

* * * *

I am in the bridge office with one minute and thirty seconds to spare. Life is never dull around Roger. What will he want this time? He still has nearly four days to be away.

The call comes through. Roger's voice sounds agitated through the business-like words. I haven't heard that sense of tension in him before.

He is returning to Cairns today and will be at the airport in about two hours. He wants me to verify the booking of a room in an apartment block overlooking the esplanade. There are people flying in for a meeting. He wants me, his security officer, to attend the meeting.

Wow! What is that all about? The last time Roger held a meeting in Noumea, my role was to take Gina for a walk, to keep her out of the way. For reasons I don't understand, I now seem to have a new status.

Roger gives me routine instructions of where business credit cards can be found in the main office. I am instructed to sign for anything that is required and he, Roger, will do all the confirmations when he gets back to the ship. He even tells me where I can find those bank delegation forms, in the filing cabinet.

I take this all in while scribbling little notes to myself. Clearly my boss is used to just rattling off these tasks to Peter Carter and they would just happen. I have neither the organisational expertise nor the familiarity with the operation to be as effective as that. I am like the duck paddling like mad under the water.

I make good notes as he talks and after he has hung up. I go through each task methodically. I brief the crewmen and Marcel that Roger is returning shortly.

Doesn't that generate a jumping-to-attention? The emperor is returning. The ship is abuzz with only five people on board.

I call the captain on the ship's mobile system. Wherever he is and whatever he is doing, he sounds like the cool Captain Rodriguez. He will be back on board within the hour.

I confirm the booking of the seafront apartment. Roger hasn't mentioned catering. Maybe that would be a rush job when he arrives back. So I consult Marcel over the ship's intercom about what arrangements would be made normally for such a meeting – and I listen to a flurry of French. From the tone, I deduce they wouldn't have been words I would want translated for a mother.

The gist of Marcel's message is that he will be prepared, no matter how inconsiderate the timing might be. How many for the meeting? I don't know.

I hang up as Marcel starts on episode two of the French language lesson.

It is going to be another interesting day.

The Brigadier

London. Thursday 15 February 2007

'Brigadier,' says the Minister in a pre-dawn call. 'What is going on? I am getting extraordinary heat from high quarters. Is there something I should know?'

'I presume it could be about Sir Terence Sedgewood,' replies the Brigadier. 'He has apparently had a medical emergency, Minister. I am not sure of the details. My conversation with Lady Meredith was brief to say the least. She was clearly under a lot of pressure.

'The nub of her call is that Sir Terence is stopping all duties, effective immediately. Resignation from all boards of directors. Lady Meredith is advising all boards by email today.

'He is being admitted on doctor's orders into an exclusive medical facility and she, Lady Meredith, advised me firmly that she would be taking the matter further. Perhaps that meant *you*, Minister?'

'How unfortunate for Sir Terence.' The Minister is all political sincerity. Sir Terence's silence would, no doubt, be a blessing for a while – reducing the work load that his committee room rants tended to generate. But the Minister is not buying that Sir Terence's illness is the only source of the heat from above. 'I think it could be something more than just Sir Terence. Ask some questions around the Intelligence agencies. There is something in the wind. Perhaps the bureaucratic mandarins are on a new tactic.'

'I'll check,' says the Brigadier.

'Thanks. I want to be interrupted for updates.'

The Brigadier frowns as he replaces his phone.

Congressman Legrand

Washington. Thursday 15 February 2007

'What is happening, Kyle?' asks Congressman Legrand.

It is just after midnight – pitch-dark and cold. Clearly, Kyle Broderick's brain is adjusting to being woken from deep sleep because he doesn't reply with more than a cough. So Legrand continues.

'Is it just our investigation into GBIB that is stirring up the raccoons? I have had tetchy calls from above and worried chats from high-powered congressmen, all wondering what you are doing. What is happening?'

'Sir,' replies Broderick, having gathered his thoughts. 'I think we are close to knowing how the *Sea Spray* was attacked and how the bandits got the financial and computing information. A lot of that comes from those directors at GBIB. I've seen more maturity from college sophomores than from some of these pillars of our financial industry. So that might be what is stirring everyone up.

'Also, we have a line on a Brit, a Roger Cavanagh, who is possibly behind not only *Sea Spray* but also a whole catalogue of criminal activity in Asia … and some pretty big financial scams. The whole banking business is on shaky foundations.

'So if Cavanagh falls, others will fall with him. Maybe it's that which is causing the heat. This is the battle we anticipated. Hold firm, Sir. We will get this bastard. He is clever but we are not too far from nailing him and his gang. The Brits are working closely with us on this, as are the Aussies.'

Legrand doesn't respond immediately.

'I think some people are out to get you and *Versec*, Kyle. Get Kennedy to do some beavering in the halls of the Intelligence community. People may be upset at you usurping their power base, but I need advance info to counter their attacks.

'I know that means diverting energy from your current cases but it is necessary if we are to kick ass in the end. We need to be well warned about distractions. Keep me informed, Kyle. You're doing important work.'

'Will do, Sir.' The lawman moves smoothly to call Larry Kennedy. There will be some others he would meet too, when daylight comes. They are so close to blowing this whole thing apart.

Gina and Alison

I see the car carrying Roger and Gina sweep along the jetty and through the black security fence to the *Lerna*.

Captain Rodriguez is back on board and going through the process of recalling all of his crew from leave, so that the *Lerna* will be ready to sail whenever Roger decides it is time to leave. The crew understand. Everyone is busy.

I watch in admiring wonder that the arrival of *the emperor* could cause such ordered, yet frenzied, action. The crew has lined up just as they did in Noumea and the same ritual of smiling greetings is carried out.

This time, however, I can read Roger's demeanour with a little more clarity. His slightly chubby face is not quite as magnanimous. There is an urgent impatience as he passes through the welcomes and heads for his private office; beckoning me to follow. Gina is two paces behind. She gives me a pointed look and passes gracefully off to her room, without a word.

'Welcome back, Roger,' I say, as he bends over his suitcase.

I wait patiently while he unpacks his laptop; plugging it in at the desk. He leaves it to boot up and turns.

'Good to see you, Steve.'

There is a smile painted on his face. He is clearly preoccupied with some serious thoughts. 'Have all the instructions been carried out?'

'Yes, all done. I didn't hear an instruction about catering for the meeting so Marcel is on stand-by if required.'

'Good thinking. Yes, we'll need food. Six guests, me and you. Asian food, tell Marcel. That will get his Gallic anger up. The guests are all Asian.'

'Fine, I'll tell him to cater for eight. What time?'

'Seven pm for drinks,' Roger says absently. His mind is elsewhere. 'Red and white wines. No spirits. Soft drink for the Muslims. Delivered to the apartment by crewmen. They won't need to remain long once the food is unpacked. They just need to usher the guests in.'

'Fine.' I try to appear as efficient as I imagine Peter Carter would be. 'Will I talk to Marcel now?'

'In a minute.' He is now typing into his laptop. 'This will be a meeting of people who are on the Board of SPFA. It will take a couple of hours. They are flying in from all over. I'll get the captain to organise transport from the airport to the apartment for them. You have the keys? Have you been inside?'

'Not yet. I'll check it early this afternoon, or sooner depending ...'

'Good.' Roger still seems partially distracted. 'Can you look after Gina for me again? Take her for a walk. Out of my hair while I get my organisation in place.'

'Will do. Will you let me know when she will be ready?'

'Make it in half-an-hour,' he says, 'and take her for a meal or something. I need no interruptions for about four hours. Can do?'

'Can do.'

* * * *

In thirty minutes, I knock on the door of the office.

I find Roger at his laptop, his back to Gina who is relaxing on a comfortable chair, flicking through a fashion magazine.

'Oh, yes,' he says dismissively. 'Have a good time, both of you. The captain will call you, Gina, when it's time to return.'

She gives a forced smile and says, 'Don't work too hard now.' I feel like a schoolboy collecting a father's daughter to go out for a party. What a strange relationship she must have with Roger.

* * * *

Having landed on the jetty and walked through the security gate, Gina sighs.

'What a relief! Let's just walk side-by-side till we get into the town. We don't know who is watching. Then, take me along the boardwalk as you promised.'

There is just the smallest of cheeky smiles peeking through her strained expression.

I thank my lucky stars for Gina's caution because, as we reach the end of the jetty, who should I see but my amorous companion of last night, Alison Wood, whom I had told I would be unable to come ashore today. Damn! Explain this one away.

* * * *

Alison has woken on this sunny morning, aglow with a pleasant ache from the romantic evening. She is feeling loved and wanted as she takes her shower.

As she is dressing, she even remembers to transfer her tracking device. She grins as she hopes Steve has remembered too. She won't see him today. She understands. He is tied up on the boat till tomorrow.

She plans just to go out for a walk, take in some more sights, a quiet coffee somewhere with a view – a restful day.

She strolls down to the jetty, more by habit than design. The silver angel-fish sculptures over the lagoon are sparkling in the sun; or are they sunfish?

It is hot but the humidity seems to have lifted – an easier heat. In the distance, on the marina, the sleek shape of the *Lerna* is clearly visible.

She is just thinking of Steve doing his rounds on the decks when suddenly there he is, walking down the jetty with a striking-looking red-headed lady.

She stops in her tracks. How can this be? How can he be ashore? Who is this woman with him? She is an eye-catcher. Every male along the jetty is looking at her.

251

There is nowhere to go. She is right in their path. He has seen her. He looks startled. He hasn't stopped walking. They are heading right for her. How embarrassing and how annoying?

He lied to her. He told her that he couldn't see her today and here he is out on the town – and not even on his own – but with a stunning red-head.

What is going on?

He smiles at her – a wave; they are coming over. Keep a straight face. Don't let the colour rise in your cheeks.

* * * *

'Hello, Alison,' I say cheerily. 'I didn't expect to see you today.'

'So I see.' There is no warmth at all in her polite face. 'I thought you were to be on the ship all day.'

Patiently, I say, 'Let me introduce you to Gina Robér, friend of Mr Roger Cavanagh, the owner of the ship.' I am hoping beyond hope that she will catch on quickly if I give enough clues. 'Mr Cavanagh has returned unexpectedly – business. I am just taking Gina for a promised walk on the esplanade.'

Alison seems lost for words but Gina has summed up the situation as many women might, sensing the tension. 'Nice to meet you, Alison. Steve promised me in Noumea he would take me for a walk on the esplanade when we got to Cairns. This is the first opportunity I have had to keep him to his word. Roger is working and we may not be in port tomorrow.'

I focus my gaze on Alison's eyes, willing her to understand

She hasn't spoken and still looks stunned to have seen me, us, together.

'Gina, Alison is a journalist. We met yesterday and had a lovely time together. We didn't think we would be able to see each other today.'

Gina is quick. 'I'm so sorry, Alison, for occupying your friend. I understand.' She has managed to make it sound compassionate, not catty. 'We are just going to walk to the Catalina memorial that Steve says is along the esplanade. Can we meet, all three of us, when we come back – for coffee and a bite to eat? I would really like that. Please?'

Alison is clearly confused. I can see it in her eyes and I am impressed by the way she is holding herself in control.

'I think I would like to have coffee with you both.' Alison tries as friendly a smile as the situation would allow.

'Super,' says Gina. 'How does that restaurant over there look?' She points to a place with a view of the water. 'It'll be on me,' she adds graciously. 'In an hour's time? That will let us walk to the memorial and back, won't it, Steve?' She looks questioningly to me to check that it would be a reasonable time frame.

I nod.

'Thanks Alison,' I say, hoping she can detect the hint of relief in my tone. 'We'll see you at the restaurant in an hour.'

* * * *

Alison watches Gina and Steve walk off, a metre apart, along the esplanade leaving her to ponder what has just happened.

She sits on an aluminium bench, looks out to sea and collects her thoughts. Why did she naturally assume a man was betraying her? Past experience for sure, but Steve is not like those in the past. Goodness, she only met him yesterday. She doesn't own him. He can do what he likes.

No, he can't. Not if last night meant anything. And he couldn't just come ashore with a crewman. It had to be with this drop-dead beauty who also happens to be the owner's wife, guest, partner, companion – whatever she is.

Well that says it all, doesn't it? He must be trustworthy. What man would send his woman out with someone else, especially one as handsome as Steve? And she actually seems to be alright, despite the model looks. Who can help what they look like after all? We are who we are. It was Gina who had asked for the three of them to sit down and have a coffee together – on her.

253

Alison has a logical mind. She can think through situations, given time. Maybe she is letting her emotions run away too much. She knows it is a weakness.

Pleased that she has controlled herself, she pats her shoulder softly. If she had created a scene, that would have been the end of things. What man wants to be possessed – by a woman possessed?

She laughs at her humour and settles back to watch the pelicans soar. Beautiful birds – lovely colouring and graceful flyers in their own way.

* * * *

Gina and I turn the corner and we are out of sight of Alison now. We have walked on quietly since the meeting.

'Tricky situation for you back there.' She smiles. 'Seems a nice woman.'

'We had a good time yesterday,' I say, simply. 'She would have felt some reason to be annoyed, seeing me walking along with this beautiful lady, especially since I wasn't even allowed to come ashore.'

Gina smiles at the compliment.

'Thank you for the way you handled things, Gina. Very sensitive; quick to assess the delicacy of the situation.'

'It's alright.' There is appreciation in her tone. 'I've been hurt before. I know what it feels like – and besides, I think you are a nice man. You deserve to be looked after.' There is that grin again. 'She's a journalist, you say?'

'Yes, a court reporter – follows crime stories.'

'Well, she's come to the right place.' Her smile has suddenly gone. 'Steve, there's something big happening. I've never known him so tense. These people coming to the meeting are coming from all over Asia. They are board members of a freight trading business – but they deal in crime too.

'If Roger says you could be an asset to his business, don't trust him.' She pauses to look at him … and shrugs. 'You're a big man. You can make your own decisions – but don't trust him. You are expendable, if it suits him. We all are.'

There is an ominous tone in her statement.

'We were in Townsville when he got news on his laptop. He has a computer that can send messages in code. After he got the message, he called Peter and Len. They'll be back here tomorrow. I think we might even be sailing then. He's worried – and when he gets worried he gets dangerous. Now *I* am worried.

'He has never ever hit me but I thought he was going to this morning – for no apparent reason. I suspect he doesn't need me around anymore. I am a *collectible* that can be offloaded. I'm sure he is pretty glad he had you on hand to take me away today.'

I just listen. All information is useful in the current situation.

'Is that the Catalina memorial?' She looks up at the flying-boat model on the top of a tall tower. 'It reminds me of a pelican.'

'Yes, it does a bit,' I agree. 'This was a base for Catalinas in the Second World War. They did long-distance reconnaissance and could land on the water – very pelican-like. It would have been a close-run thing in those days, defending against such a formidable enemy; not knowing whether you would win or lose – but knowing you would have to fight anyway.'

Gina links her arm in mine and nestles up close. 'No-one can see,' she whispers, sensing my concern. 'But I think *we* are about to be defending against a formidable enemy. It just feels so comforting to be able to cuddle up against you. I envy your Alison,' she says in a knowing way, 'but I won't compromise anything. You can trust me. In the days ahead, our lives may depend on it. Let's head back now. I would like to listen to a journalist who reports on crime.'

She gives another of her strange smiles, leaving me wondering.

Lady Meredith

It is wintery at Dulles International Airport and still Valentine's Day in the States. She has viewed the cold scenery as the plane came into land. Spring is certainly still a while away, over here. Somehow, England seems warmer.

And Valentine's Day. Terry has always sent her red roses on this day – has done all their married life. Well, that won't be happening this year.

The elderly lady looks dignified as she is escorted slowly from business class.

The flight from London has been on time. To observers, the lady must be in her eighties, yet she insists on walking by herself, with the use of a stick, and she holds herself high, used to being in charge.

She does accept a lift from an internal airport passenger cart which takes her to a limousine, drawn up right at the terminal door.

The dark car moves away almost silently, with orange leaves spiralling up in its wake, into the Washington morning.

It arrives after a short trip at a large, discreet stone building in the hub of the town.

It moves through a solid security gate into the underground park and the lady transfers to another dark car with darkened windows.

In minutes, Lady Meredith Sedgewood is on her way to meet important people in Langley, Virginia.

256

Stepping into danger

I check my watch. 'We have time if we are quick. I need to check out the apartment for tonight's meeting. I have the key. It will only take five minutes.'

The apartment block looks out over the esplanade. I didn't know why they hadn't just used the conference facilities at one of the international hotels but clearly Roger had anticipated the need for a meeting. The apartment had been booked and paid for, prior to the ship arriving in Noumea. The security guard in me assumes my boss wants to be in a place where people won't expect him.

We enter the apartment with the security key for the outside door, as well as the lift and the apartment. It will be safe from intruders, at least.

There are two bedrooms, a kitchen and a huge main room with a landscape window view out over the esplanade to the *Lerna* and then out to Green Island – a blur on the horizon. Occasional boats are still wending their way out to the reef, through the dredged channel.

'Well, this should be sufficiently private for this evening's meeting.'

I glance casually around. Gina is standing back from the window.

I look at her. 'Are you alright?'

She shakes her head as I come over to see what the problem is.

'Steve, I promise I won't ask you for anything again.' There is a quiver in her voice. 'Can you please hug me here while we are private? I'm really scared.'

She rushes into my unsuspecting arms. I hold her tight by reflex and rock her gently.

Under normal circumstances, this would be no ordeal at all – flattering even. She is a beautiful woman. However, today, only minutes away from meeting up with Alison, I have no desire to be deceitful. And here in the hired apartment of Gina's partner, my boss; in contravention of my mantra never to get emotionally involved with the friends of people who employ me; this is not a comfortable moment. It has everything to do with respect, for women, ingrained into me from watching my mother experiencing the opposite as I grew up.

Gina is strung tight; I can feel the fluttering racing of her heartbeat. She is clearly scared … and vulnerable. For me, there is never anything right in taking advantage of a woman's distress – although some of my old Army mates would be shaking their heads at me.

I have to manage the situation. The embrace is a gesture of care not an expression of romance.

* * * *

Gina inhales the animal warmth of his strong body. Long suppressed stirrings are flickering through her, fleetingly over-riding her conscious control.

This has to be brief because he has never reciprocated in the way she expects a man would do normally. Does he not feel for her? He must; he cares; she knows that from the way he speaks and acts.

Does she not attract him? Is he turned away by her looks? Bizarre as it would seem to others who do not have her appearance, she has known men to shy away from her in the past; to quiver with some maladjusted sense of inadequacy when they thought she might find them unworthy.

What is it? Does he prefer men? That doesn't fit with pretty Alison.

Is it Roger? More than probably. Perhaps it is some puritanical sense of claim that another would have on her? Whatever, she senses he is definitely *off limits*. But he is so, so comforting to hold; so reassuring.

Her mind regains control of her urging, slowly, and she starts to feel a calmness wash through her, as her thumping heart relaxes into the reality of her situation. Her feeling of anxiety is settling down.

She inhales one last draught of his manliness.

'Thank you. I have wanted you to hold me since we sat on the sundeck of the *Lerna* – and I couldn't with the cameras everywhere. I wasn't even sure you would want to hug someone as *used* as I am. I *am* scared, Steve, but I'm … much better now. This moment will see me through the hard days ahead. When I smile at you, I will be remembering this hug.'

No kisses. She is in control again as she pulls away.

She gives him a weak encouraging smile. 'I'm sorry if I embarrassed you. You can trust me to be discreet and sensitive from now on.'

They leave the apartment as they had found it, except for a light left on for security.

* * * *

Alison welcomes them with a courteous smile. They find a table and order coffees, with some light snacks. Steve pays on his new company card with a look at Gina. She hasn't batted an eyelid. Of course, the bill has been *on her.*

'You're a crime reporter?' Gina asks, with interest.

'The court circuit,' says Alison. 'It's very routine. Someday, I'll maybe be able to write about something more significant but, for the moment, it's routine.'

'What would be more important?'

'Oh, I've been doing some research into modern day pirates, that sort of thing,' she says, very conscious of the person she is speaking with.

'Have you found much?'

'Bits and pieces.' She smiles. 'Criminals tend not to broadcast their actions.'

'Aren't you worried about the danger?'

'I haven't really done anything to be dangerous to anyone. All my information can be found in court reports and in library archives. I have only spoken to a few people who have had actual experience. They stay anonymous, as journalistic sources.'

Gina looks questioning. 'So these people you have spoken to have been attacked by pirates and survived?'

'Yes.' Alison has a matter-of-fact tone. 'And in some cases, people who have been abducted at sea; smuggled into other countries.'

Gina's eyes widen. Her mouth opens and stays open for a few seconds, as if she is going to say something, but she remains quiet.

Eventually she says, 'I'm sure those people ... would be very grateful to be free.' Her eyes seem far away for a second or two more. The words sound so politically correct, like some platitude that holds no meaning.

Alison changes the subject. 'And what is life like travelling on a beautiful ship like the *Lerna*? I asked Steve if he could get me on board but he said he wasn't allowed.' She gives her smiling pout again.

'It's not all it would seem from the outside. Alright for a short time. It feels good to be pampered and to see exotic places – but you yearn to be just an ordinary housewife going out to do the shopping or walking the children to school.'

'I think I could handle being pampered for a while.' Alison laughs, lifting the chat to a cheerier level. 'Court reporters don't earn too much, you know.'

'If we could swap places, Alison, believe me, I would!' Gina tries a laugh but it doesn't quite work. Steve watches with a polite patience, letting the women talk. 'We will probably be sailing tomorrow, or Saturday,' she continues, 'to who knows where; and the sea will still look blue to each horizon and the sky will still look the same above – and the cabins don't change just because we move over the ocean.'

'Aw, you're taking the romance out of it all.' Alison laughs again. But she has noted that if the boat is sailing tomorrow, so will Steve. These next few days and weeks would test their fledgling friendship.

They sit, eat and talk for a couple of hours. Alison is warming to Gina. The conversation flows easily. There are no obvious tensions. She doesn't feel threatened by the striking eyes. There is a surprising sense of *down-to-earth* honesty about this red-headed beauty; like a wizard's prisoner longing to break out from the constraints of a sad spell.

Indeed, Alison is gradually feeling a little sorry for the pretty rich woman. She isn't even noticing Gina's looks anymore; perhaps because Gina isn't a preener – she is more trying to be, well, ordinary; in spite of her appearance. The reporter laughs internally; maybe there are disadvantages in having a stunning appearance.

They chat about the Catalinas flying free, about the South Pacific islands and an easy-going approach to life. Gina doesn't come across as being some gangster's moll. Her personality doesn't fit. She is nothing like the crooks Alison has seen in courtrooms – she is more … well … sad or lost or stuck – and wanting to get out; appearing quite vulnerable; maybe caught up in something too big for her, too.

If Ben is right and this is all going to come to a head, she might be in the firing line too. Maybe she is on the side of the good guys. If she is, then she is one very brave lady.

Ah, there is the crime reporter looking for a story. Maybe, Alison is missing her calling as a writer of mysteries.

For her part, Gina seems impressed by Alison's independence, that she can pay her own bills with a steady round of court reporting, while chasing her holy grail of a big story which might make her name some day – a reason for living and working hard.

'It is important to have dreams,' Gina says, with a straight face. 'Something to look forward to. A bigger purpose than just personal enjoyment. I envy your goals, Alison. I can see I'll have to work on mine.'

The mobile rang – time to return to the ship.

'I'll wait for you, Steve; at the lagoon pool with the fish sculptures. Lovely meeting you, Alison. All the best with your research. I hope we can meet again sometime.'

* * * *

I watch her walking away and silently thank her for giving me space.

'Do you understand what's been happening?'

'I think so,' Alison says as she snuggles into me. 'And it sounds as if you could be leaving tomorrow or Saturday at the latest. This might be my last cuddle.'

'Only for a while.' I hold her gently. 'It seems we might have important work to do. Are you still okay with us being involved?'

She nods slowly. She *is* brave.

I have given her another chance to get out and she hasn't taken it. There is a tough lady behind that gentle appearance – or maybe, just maybe, she has no idea of what she is embarking on.

'Tell Inspector Willis what has been said, please. Someday, when this is over, we will look back fondly on this time. Take care, Love.'

We kiss tenderly, fondly, slowly – allowing our shared passion to be remembered, to be transmitted softly through our lips; and then we step apart.

'*You* take care, Steve.' A tear is beading at the corner of her eye. 'Go, while I can still control myself.'

She smiles and I leave with a cheery grin, waving farewell.

* * * *

The red-headed beauty is waiting patiently at the side of the lagoon, oblivious to all the admiring looks from the many male eyes.

I am pleased to see her. She *can* be trusted. I would have had a hard time explaining if she had disappeared on me. She is a courageous lady too. She knows she is walking back into danger. We both do.

The die has been cast. There is no turning back now! Adrenalin flutters through me.

The SPFA meeting

In the car, moving to the apartment, I watch Roger ticking off all his checklist of tasks in his mind. As the last mental tick is completed, he relaxes.

'Okay?' he asks, now able to give his attention to the real world. 'Yes, fine.'

'This meeting is with some directors of SPFA. They have flown in from China, the Philippines, Malaysia, Thailand and Indonesia. We have some risks to evaluate – business risks.

'Peter and Len will be back tomorrow, then we will be going to sea again – north through New Guinea to the Philippines.

'I want you to listen to what is said, Steve. It will all be in English. I think you have the potential to be successful in our business, if you are interested. I like the way you operate.'

He is silky smooth but I am hearing his words through new ears now.

'Business is a cut-throat affair. You can only make money in this competitive market if you have an edge over the opposition. You will hear things tonight that you will need to process. Don't judge too quickly. As I indicated, we trade in areas where others choose not to tread or trade. That gives the buffer to the bottom line to carry us through hard times.

'My companies don't fail when others go to the wall. We operate as many lines as we can, seeking small profits over many transactions – and then minimising the taxes that we are required to pay. So just listen. We'll talk when we get back to the ship.'

* * * *

We arrive at the apartment door long before the others are expected.

'The light is on,' says Roger warily, seeing the glow from under the door.

'I left it on to make it look occupied. I checked the place when I was out.'

'Like I said,' his boss notes admiringly, 'I like the way you think. You remind me of myself a few years ago.'

I take the compliment at face value. No way will I fall for the charm but it is an insight into how Roger thinks.

There has to be a reason for his favouring me, so readily. Perhaps that is it; he sees his own perceived qualities in my manner; flattering himself by valuing me. Bizarre, if true, but Roger is indeed a strange and interesting man.

The view from the apartment window is impressive in the early evening. Coloured lights bob along the esplanade, throwing reflections out onto the glistening sea with its specks of ships and their lights as the darkness takes over; a beautiful setting for a meeting.

The food and drink arrive; and is unpacked. The crewmen leave to welcome guests downstairs – a slick operation.

Roger positions himself in the centre of the room. 'Make sure that everyone gets a drink when they arrive.'

The crewmen actually do the waiting and then leave for the ship. Roger is the genial host. All the guests are very respectful to him, as they arrive. Traditional Asian courtesy? Perhaps he is a very important man in the scheme of things?

The group are all present, settled at the large table, with drink and food – the Asian custom is to do business as they eat. The dishes and drinks are organised. Roger nods that he is happy and I mouth a silent *thank you* to Marcel, the chef, in his absence. He is a master of improvisation – and every dish looks expertly presented.

Roger introduces me as *my assistant*; a flattering compliment.

The directors are introduced as Mr Li from Taiwan, lawyer; Mr Gonzalez from the Philippines, accountant; Mr Alatas from Indonesia, merchant trader; Mr Masa from Malaysia, shipping logistics expert; Mr Esobal from the Philippines, political lobbyist; and Mr Yodsuwan from Thailand, technology specialist.

'Gentlemen,' Roger says. 'You are aware that our chairman, Sir Terence has had a serious ailment, perhaps a stroke. He has resigned as chair, effective as of yesterday. I am sure we all wish him a speedy recovery and I will convey the sympathies of the board to Lady Meredith.

'His illness creates some problems for us, does it not, since he was the major conduit to connections in the British maritime policing system? His contacts in the States gave us the investment banking access to process our resources. He was also the traditional link with *Ramas*.' My ears are even more focused at the mention of that name.

'So the agenda as described in your invitation to this meeting includes an election of a new chairman. I am happy to provide all the advice as before but someone needs to be chair on paper.

'Before he fell ill, Sir Terence expressed his concern that some of the lines we are carrying need to be terminated, and speedily. So that is second on the agenda.

'And we need some leverage. Sir Terence was made aware of two investigations into our affairs: one in the United States and another in the UK. We need to assess what they know and what we should tell them. I think we also need some back-up insurance to ensure the investigators don't get too carried away.

'Are we comfortable with the agenda?' After a pause for Roger to see the nods, he continues. 'Then please enjoy your food and refreshment. Just let Steve know if you need anything.'

The introductions complete, Mr Alatas is elected chairman as an appropriate representative of the core business of SPFA.

Item 2 concerns some of the lines that are being carried. As the discussion progresses, I realise that they are not talking about transporting rice or coconuts, but illegal goods – contraband.

They never state what the product lines are. It seems to be understood. The arguments revolve around the risk of being caught as against the financial losses which will be made if they stop. There are questions of disposal of product. I don't quite understand which lines of product are which but I get the impression that the items are perishable. I can appreciate the business processes in the discussion. They must have a considerable fleet to handle the breadth of logistical demand.

I imagine that this could have been a discussion in a directors' meeting anywhere in the world, except for the implication that illegalities were occurring. But Mr Li, the international lawyer, is not flagging any concerns.

The decided action is to terminate the non-perishable product lines to which there is no long-term commitment or which could be placed in secure storage.

The perishable lines are divided into Category A which could be just dumped at sea. Are they talking about fruit or cereals? Category B includes lines for which dumping would cause complications, such as loss of face.

Loss of face would create an unwillingness for partners to reengage in trade when times improve. These are products which can't be returned to the sender. They would have to carry on through the transportation process whatever the risk. The board spends a long time discussing Category B with Roger advising they should take advantage of any unforeseen opportunities, which might become available, to maximise profit from Category B before it is shut down.

As a group, they work through the lines on their inventory sheets – all in code names, some English and some Asian. I get the drift that Sir Terence's turn of health has created international problems which have forced this prioritisation.

Finally, they discuss the investigations into their business practices, which seemed to be associated with a matter around a ship called the *Shinwuan*.

They discuss their ability to influence the investigation agendas in the *Shinwuan* matter – but Sir Terence has seemed to have been the main negotiator. His illness certainly appears to have created a significant problem.

Roger takes on the role to make contact with *Ramas*, to establish what requirements would be needed into the future.

Next, he advises that he needs a freighter to carry cars into Sydney, with docking approvals to offload at the White Bay, Balmain dock, in the next few weeks. It must also have containers bound for Melbourne. Date to be confirmed but the window of opportunity for the visit must be booked.

Mr Masa undertakes to put all those operations into effect.

The meeting continues for over two hours and, by the end, Roger has achieved endorsement for all the commitments he had requested – a smooth persuader.

The visitors leave for their hotels and flights home on the next day. Surely an expensive exercise for a board meeting but money doesn't seem to be a problem.

I have been listening carefully as requested, trying not to be judgemental. Roger is certainly running the show although he has no official director role.

As we return to the ship, he looks satisfied with his evening's work.

'Let's talk about your impressions in the morning,' he says, looking relieved. It reminds me of the Army. The mission would move now with the plans in place. 'Thank you for your assistance today,' he adds. 'We will talk with Peter and Len when they arrive tomorrow too.'

* * * *

I make some notes as soon as I return to my cabin. I need to be able to give coherent responses to Roger tomorrow. Then I lie on the bed to let the brain just relax. It is at that moment I remember Bill Jones saying the miniature microphones are on all the time, for six months.

Very quietly, I mumble my observations of the meeting into my little eavesdropper, hoping the police at the other end are recording my comments.

I also mention the potential arrival of Peter Carter and Len Williamson; possibly sailing tomorrow too – perhaps to New Guinea and on to the Philippines.

These days are never boring. I drift off to sleep thinking of a beautiful court reporter.

Butch

Cliff Butcher looks through the bullet proof, tinted-glass window, over to the Virginia lawns and trees. His silhouette emphasises a strong frame, not unlike that of his father.

Few people know more about him – the real person – than his shadowy profile. His work is loosely attached to the *NCS*, the National Clandestine Service – classified, dangerous, influential.

Many people would have seen him in his multitude of aliases but they would not have realised who he really is; such is the nature of this hidden world. Indeed, Cliff Butcher is not even the name that he is known by, to the majority of staff at Langley.

He is an important person. In his range of disguised roles, he has served covertly overseas and in the homeland, often in diplomatic roles. Valued for his clear-thinking, his networks, his prescience – an analytical anticipator of events – he is known as *Butch* to a very select group, people who understand *silence* and *results*. To others, he has a more conventional persona.

That is why he is pondering at this moment as he gazes from his sixth floor window over the peaceful scene of still-bare trees to the Potomac.

How will this pan out? The settings are in place. It should all work, so why is he concerned?

What would his father do?

He misses the chance to bounce strategic ideas around with him. His mother might well have an answer too but he won't be going there.

His left hand ruffles his thick beard. The window reflection shows the grey speckling through the dark hair as he nods with satisfaction that everything is in place.

Roger explains

'Mr Cavanagh would like to see you in his rooms, Sir.'

A crewman in neatly-pressed whites has found me checking the CCTV screens in the office.

It is another beautiful Cairns morning. A sense of anticipation hangs over the *Lerna*. The word is out that we might be sailing again soon.

The charter catamarans are heading out from Trinity Inlet, teeming with passengers in gaily coloured outfits, heading mainly for Green Island.

There has been no movement from the staterooms. No sign of Roger or Gina. Breakfast has been served and cleared. It is a waiting time; the peace before all the action starts.

* * * *

I knock at the door and enter the office area just as Gina is passing by me, towel over her shoulder. 'I'm going to the sundeck, Roger.' She breezes past me with only a look for a greeting.

'Come in, Steve. Have a seat!' Roger sits in a neighbouring chair. He looks to be at his enthusiastic and refreshed best as he pours cool drinks for us both. 'Tell me. The meeting yesterday. What do you think you heard?'

I am glad that I'd jotted some notes on the previous night and referred to them again early this morning … but I don't need any notes now. This is a casual conversation with my boss, at least on the surface.

'Firstly, you're a very important person in that organisation, though you're not Chairman of the Board. Indeed, you don't appear to want to be the chairman.'

Best to start with a little flattery. It appears to have worked. Roger giggles with delight.

'It appeared to me more like a committee, discussing options,' I continue, 'rather than what I imagine a formal board meeting would be like. Nobody was taking minutes – but then you elected a new chairman; maybe *appointed* would be the more correct term.'

Roger nods his satisfaction with what I am saying.

'SPFA,' I say, 'appears to have a minor crisis with the sudden illness of the former chairman, Sir Terence somebody, and so the directors have had to make some serious business decisions about the product lines it will carry.

'You have them divided into three categories: perishable ones which can be dumped; the non-perishable ones which can go into storage; and the ones, presumably mainly perishable, which would cause too much long-term business damage if they didn't continue through to their destinations.

'You've a problem with an investigation into something called the *Shinwuan*, which needs crisis management. Something has gone wrong.

'The illness of Sir Terence appears to have taken out a communication link with someone called *Ramas*. You volunteered to re-establish that link. Evidently, it is important. In all, I thought it was a slick business meeting covering a lot of ground in a couple of hours. Expensive too; I'm just getting used to the money at this level of commerce. How's that for some initial impressions?'

'Bravo!' roars Roger. 'Braaa-vo! I'm impressed. I have been right about you, Steve. You do have the potential.' He claps his hands together.

'Tell me.' His eyes glow with excitement. 'What do you think our product lines might be?'

I can sense the danger in the question.

'They were in code. You mentioned cars and containers. You've told me earlier that you deal in more suspect products, to give your company an edge.'

'Go on!'

'My guess would be ... not drugs – but some other form of contraband.'

He is nodding, smiling in agreement; a child playing a game – on a high.

'I'd guess jewels or artwork. You have a Degas in the ship's office. But then that doesn't take much space. That could go into storage. Smuggling weapons? But you look for low-profile, low-margin, high-volume goods. Large-scale arms-trading would attract the attention of the law; so maybe it's not arms.

'Maybe items banned in some countries; movies, books, magazines? They could be dumped at sea and make other copies later. How am I doing?' I am watching his expressions.

'Braaa-vo again, Steve. You're good. Very perceptive. Quite close.' Then his face becomes more serious. 'You're right. We have some illegal trade and it's putting us in the headlights of a couple of investigations. Are you repelled by the idea of doing illegal things, Steve?'

'No.' I pause. 'Generally, I try to abide by the law but there are times when it's necessary to do things differently. Otherwise, I would still be sitting in a Suva government office, trying to get my passport back.'

'Well put, Steve. So yes, we deal in contraband. Indeed, we are agents who trans-ship other people's contraband. Right across South East Asia, and I include Australia, there are groups who need their materials, our product lines, moved discreetly between countries. We are in that business, as well as more normal trade. We take a percentage to move product around. Because of high volume, we make a lot of money. There is a huge demand. We are a service provider.'

He stops to see any reaction from his alleged protégé. His eyes are weasel-like. 'Do you have any questions?" He is full of himself. Cocky bastard.

'Just one probably. How do you manage the money you are paid for dodgy deals? Wouldn't that show up on your balance sheets?'

'Bingo!' shouted Roger. 'You *are* the most perceptive of young men. Well done! Small sums can get lost in the volume of reported transactions. That is Mr Gonzalez's job. He's a good financial deceiver. Unless someone goes through each line with all the original invoices, that fudging could never be found.

'Bigger sums don't go through our books. We have a place in America where those monies appear as speculative market trading – which they are in a way.

'*Ramas* set up the system and Sir Terence has been the means of keeping it ticking along. Extra money passes through the investment banking process and comes out the other end as legitimate profit, which is then deposited in the bank accounts of those involved. It never goes near the SPFA books.'

'Very clever,' I acknowledge. He is so pleased with himself. Either I am his new adopted son or he has no intention of letting me live long enough to tell anyone about this. Thank goodness that Alison is well out of this.

'Yes, it is, isn't it?' he says, smugly.

'You mentioned a role for me, supervising. Is that still on offer?'

He nods, steepling his fingers and pointing them towards me for emphasis. 'Good. Good. Clearly an operation as big as this relies on constant input of product lines. You can't be efficient if you have no regular system.

'People who smuggle occasionally get caught, because they don't have tight processes and constant training of their people. It's the system that protects you.

'That's what Peter and Len are doing just now in Australia. They're working with the networks, making sure the skills in the field are up to scratch, checking on processes and fine-tuning the understanding of the expectations. We pay well, very well – but, in return, we expect *results* and *silence*. No loose lips.'

Things are slotting into place.

'You mentioned *Ramas*. Who is *Ramas*?'

His wide eyes change to a piggy peer, again, and he whispers in awe. '*Ramas* set up a sophisticated template for this system thirty or more years ago. It's the copyright that we use today. I have only met our leader twice and I was very impressed.'

I could tell. He is almost genuflecting.

'We keep a clear separation of important people in our organisation. Fewer chances for security to be breached. Very useful in crisis times, like now.

'In our group, Sir Terence was a conduit for *Ramas's* messages but he has never met or spoken with the leader. He couldn't identify our founder.'

Pompous fart! Wetting himself in reverence for whoever this person is.

'It's part of the security. The messages came through coded notes originally. Then, as the technology developed, it became coded emails. Now we have encryption systems so that we can transmit electronically; knowing no-one can accidently be a fly-on-the-wall. We don't need anyone reading our conversations, do we?'

I feel another rush of adrenalin at that comment. Does he suspect there are listening devices all over the ship? How could he? Settle down.

'So what has *Ramas* got to do with your current business?'

'*Ramas* set up the process,' says Roger, 'so, out of business respect, the leader is entitled to royalties on everything we do. Not money. *Ramas* doesn't need more money. Our founder is a collector – in some ways, my role model. I like collecting paintings and beautiful objects. I learned that from *Ramas*.

'So, as part of our training of people in the field, we show them how to look out for the things our leader might like. It's a kind of tribute, a treasured gift, to the person who masterminded the whole system in the first place.'

'I see.' I hope my expression is suitably impressed. This is all wanking.

'I know that's been a lot to take in,' he says, 'but you're doing very well – better than I had hoped.'

Well, pat me on the head, why don't you? I am pleased though that I appear to have lived up to my employer's expectations.

'Peter and Len are returning about midday. I'll need to debrief them. And I've a lot of international matters to deal with. Sir Terence's illness has come at a most inconvenient time. Things are busy. Can you keep Gina occupied again?'

Emboldened by the compliments, I thought I might chance a question. 'Roger? You haven't mentioned Gina as being part of your operations. How does she fit into the scheme of things?'

He stops his thought pattern for a moment and decides some explanation is necessary. 'Yes. It must look strange to you. Gina has been with me for a long time now. She's like a good glove; comfortable. We are used to each other. She isn't part of the business in any way.' I am more pleased to hear that than he would ever have thought.

He continues. 'There are many times when I need to have an attractive female partner. We actually entertain a lot when things are rolling smoothly. In my lifestyle, I can't be spending energy trying to find suitable escorts. I need someone who is always there, looks the part, knows how to behave and can keep silent.

'Gina has shown over the years she can do all of these things. So it is a mutually benefiting relationship. She gets to live a life of luxury travelling the world, never having to worry about what to wear or not being able to buy what she needs. For my part, I have a charming companion to keep everything normal.'

He pauses, clearly appreciating the unasked question.

'Gina and I are friends, Steve. We are past the romance. We both understand our roles. We live together – but we don't need to be around each other, more than required. Gina gets bored easily. I neither need nor want her in the business, but she is a necessary accessory – so when you entertain her as you have been doing, you are doing me a great service – letting me get on with business.'

I now appreciate why the beautiful lady with all the trappings of wealth has been starved of even an affectionate cuddle.

'Thanks. I understand a little better now.'

'Okay,' he says. 'We'll talk later in the day. The ship will cast off during Saturday night, en route to Port Moresby.'

I get the hint. I am dismissed for Roger to *get on with business.*

'Oh,' I say. He irritates me with his regal ways. 'I meant to mention that I talked with the Immigration people and the police yesterday. It went alright. I told them I couldn't remember much about the time in the water before boarding the *Lerna*. When I showed him my scar they really didn't ask any more questions.'

'Your scar?'

'I was hit by a bullet above my right ear.' I lift my hair to show the very obvious red furrow along my skull. 'I'm sorry. I showed it to Peter but you haven't seen it.'

He blanches a little as he looks. 'I didn't realise that you'd been actually shot.'

'Anyway,' I continue. 'The police inspector from here in Cairns thought there would be no problems with my story but he would check it out. He asked me to ring him before I left town.'

I hold up the policeman's business card. 'Are you comfortable if I give him a courtesy call? It might just stop the police wondering why I left without phoning.'

'Good thinking, Steve. Initiative.' He raises his thumb with a distracted smile. No problem.

* * * *

Back in my cabin, I call Inspector Willis's direct line.

'Willis,' says the voice.

'Inspector Willis, this is Steven Flynn from the *Lerna*. We met yesterday morning you might recall.'

Willis picks up on the tone immediately. 'Yes, Mr Flynn. How can I help?'

278

'You asked me to call before I left Cairns just to check everything about my passport was okay. Have you been able to check out all my information?'

'Yes. Everything checked out fine. Your information was very useful. I think it will add to our understanding of the case.'

'That's good because I expect to be leaving Cairns, Saturday overnight. I've been offered a position on the *Lerna*. I was pleased to accept.'

'Thank you for your co-operation, Mr Flynn. I hope you have a good voyage.'

'And thanks to you. You have been good to deal with. Please pass on my thanks to the others in your team.'

I hope that last comment will be passed on to Alison, as well as the officials.

* * * *

'They are spooked. We have them on the run.' Bill Jones smirks as he sits with Ben Brennan, listening to the recording that had been transmitted the day before from Steve's bedroom microphone.

Ben rarely gets excited; always looking for the catches, the problems.

'I'm pleased your miniatures work well, Bill. Good information. They might be spooked but Cavanagh won't go down without a fight. And Carter and Williamson have returned, apparently – another interesting complication. The *Lerna* will sail on the night tide tomorrow.

'We need a pattern of ships to pass the *Lerna's* route. We must have a receiver within fifty kilometres at all times. Not the same ship or they will twig.

'This is the key time now – getting Steve's information and being ahead of them when they get to New Guinea. They arrive there in three to four days, depending on the weather and how fast they want to go. I expect they're heading for the Philippines. That will probably take two to three weeks tops.

'So whatever is to happen with the *product lines*, as Cavanagh calls them, will happen in the next fortnight. My other concern is that Cavanagh is requesting some diversion or back-up as insurance – a boat berthing in Sydney. I suspect a terrorist-type situation; some blackmail. Jeff Fowler needs to be across that.'

Bill notes his jobs list, enthusiasm dampened a little. An alert flashes on his screen showing a recording a few minutes previously from Roger's suite office.

There is also an email message from Mal Willis advising that Steve has phoned in to check they are receiving his messages. They would be sailing on Saturday at the latest. Everything is moving fast now.

Time to brief Jeff Fowler.

Catherine and Techs

'Catherine,' calls Techs. 'I have cracked it!'

Catherine has been sleeping in a room at the office as she co-ordinates all the activities that Angus Forbes requires. There are jobs to be done across a range of time zones. Techs, likewise, has chosen to work in the security of the office – more accommodating in some ways than home, perhaps, and less need for travel across busy London.

'Techs, it is one in the morning.' Catherine had been dozing, fully dressed on the bed, before she responded to the knocking on the door.

'I have cracked it, Catherine. I can read the messages.'

As she opens the door, she sees the excitement on the hacker's face. It is pure boyish joy. Not only has he worked out the PGP code which Roger Cavanagh is using but it hasn't been a fluke. That makes it doubly gratifying.

This is skill – well, not totally lucky anyway. He has been working on his mirror program for cryptanalysis for over a year. This has been the first time he has had the chance to use it *in action*, as it were.

Days of twenty-four-hour-a-day scanning and correlating, generating hypotheses, mirroring how the encryption might work have paid off. It is a phenomenal achievement to find a particular encryption out of the myriad of possibilities.

He was lucky that Catherine brought in Sir Terence's office laptop yesterday. That has eliminated probably more than 99 per cent of the possibilities with that little coup, overnight.

But, although at the back of his mind, he knows that chance has played a large factor. If he hadn't created the program to make the environment for the luck to happen, they wouldn't have the encryption code at all.

'Well done, Techs! Bloody well done,' says Catherine with an amazed grin on her face. 'This is like finding an Enigma code in the Second World War,' she exclaims. She knows her history. The role of the Bletchley Park boffins in cracking the German codes is the stuff of cipher-breaking legend.

'So, emails that Cavanagh thinks are secret can be read by us. Am I right? We are ahead of the game now; listening in.' He nods. 'Bloooody well done, Techs!' she repeats with the Yorkshire accent coming through stronger than ever.

'Well, we can read the text of emails and other comms ... when messages are sent. We can't yet identify the sources or targets – they are still anonymous encryptions. I'm working on that. We need a little while longer. But we are inside their system to know what is being sent.'

Ben Brennan and Alison

'This is Ben, Alison. Can we meet for an update?'

Alison hides her surprise. She had hoped it might be Steve on the line.

'Yes. Happy to meet. I'm out at the pier complex.'

'There's a café overlooking the harbour,' Ben replies. He gives directions to the specific café. 'Meet you there in twenty minutes.'

* * * *

Alison can see Ben Brennan approaching her table.

He looks much fitter and younger than his weather-beaten face would suggest as he sits down quietly with a simple, 'G'day'.

She feels comforted. He has that effect; in control, not wasting words.

'I have information and a suggestion or two. Are you interested?' he asks.

Such a strange way of talking; it is as if he expected she would say *No.*

'I'm interested.' She has ordered a pot of tea, which arrives with two cups.

'For me?' he asks, as if there were ten others going to arrive at the table.

She smiles, feeling that sensation again. He is a very independent person.

'Thank you.' Just a spark of genuine gratitude. 'We got word from Steve. The little microphones appear to work. We can't speak to him of course, but he's an old soldier, he'll handle it.'

She nods, a flutter of worry. 'How is he?'

'I don't know how he is,' replies Ben flatly. 'He's told us the ship will probably be gone by morning, heading for New Guinea. He was at a meeting of the board of the South Pacific Freight Alliance, last night. Roger must really trust him to let him in there. I'm still trying to work out what his game is. Unless, he is trying to use Steve as a wedge to keep Carter and Williamson in line.

'Anyway, from the meeting, they are planning to offload a lot of their criminal activities. Cavanagh knows about high-level investigations into the *Sea Spray*. He is scheming now, ducking for cover and planning his defence.'

She just listens. There is nothing to say, so she pours the tea. He seems to be building up to something.

'Do you remember the advice I gave you in Brisbane?'

'What? Stick to the court reporting circuit?'

'Now is the time to follow that advice. There's still time.'

He looks at her earnestly.

'Don't you want me around?' Her expression is a combination of hurt and anger.

'It's about to get dangerous. Get out now while you can. Go back to court reporting.' His serious expression leaves little doubt that he really means that she should go.

'No! I won't be bullied, by you or anyone else. I'm scared. I admit it. I'm no heroine. But Steve is out there doing his bit, so are you and the police. There's maybe even the red-headed woman on the ship. We're all in this, for better or worse, Ben.'

He sips his tea. 'The red-head?'

'She's called Gina – Cavanagh's wife or partner or something.'

'You've met her?'

'She was with Steve when he came off the ship. Yesterday. She didn't seem like a pirate – more like someone who is where she doesn't want to be.'

'Mmm. Okay. Thanks.' He doesn't flap; always so in control. 'Back to now. Don't you ever tell me I didn't try to get you to leave this thing,' he says quietly.

She just looks at him. There is nothing to be said.

'I've a proposal then,' he says. 'Do you have your passport with you?'

'I always travel with my documents.' She likes to feel she can move anywhere, any time, following her holy grail.

'Good,' he replies. 'I'll be leaving for New Guinea tomorrow and then on to wherever we need to go to sort this business out. I would like you to travel with me – for your safety.'

She looks at him, not knowing quite what he means.

'I suggest you travel as my daughter. If anyone asks why we have different surnames, say you use your mother's name. We'll be going to Port Moresby, flying out tomorrow. I have the money. We need to be in New Guinea ahead of the *Lerna*. I have contacts up there. They'll know the detail of what is happening.

'It's quite possible there'll be some action but I'll be better able to look after you if you're with me. It won't be a pleasant couple of weeks. It'll be planes and maybe boats; the insides of hotel rooms and no tourist things – it can be a dangerous place, New Guinea, especially for women if they are on their own. But you'll be near Steve when he arrives in port and you'll be safe from any of Cavanagh's gang who might work out who you are, back here in Cairns.'

She shivers at the thought. Ben does inspire confidence. She has no commitments, used to travelling and comfortable to be moving as a free agent.

Never one to need people around her, she doesn't feel lost or lonely easily. Her parents are in New South Wales. She contacts them irregularly by phone or email – for their benefit; courtesy. They aren't close. She had lived independently since she came to Queensland to do her degree in Brisbane.

Ben is still looking at her. She works out he needs a response.

'I'll come with you.'

He nods but still does not look happy. 'We'll be in each other's company a lot. You'll have to put up with that. You've nothing to fear from me. I'll respect you as I would my own daughter.' His voice seemed to catch. 'Anything we find will be yours for your story, as long as you leave me out of it. I'm not in this for glory and, believe me, I don't need what I do to be advertised.'

Her turn to nod. 'I'm fine with that.'

He continues. 'Let me give you the abbreviated version of what I think is happening. Cavanagh runs a smuggling empire across South East Asia and the South Pacific. He co-ordinates gangs in most countries to steal, kidnap and run protection rackets. He's a gangster even though he looks and sounds like a well-fed, successful businessman.

'He'll deal in most contraband. He even has attack bands that go out and steal ship's cargoes. Carter and Williamson do the supervisory leg-work and the discipline. They're effective. They've built layers of organisation throughout this part of the world, working with and through established crime syndicates but always with their own brand of security.

'The result is that the whole smuggling operation works like a business. I'm sure many of the people working for them don't even understand they are involved in committing criminal acts. Carter saturates their minds with all the jargon of the corporate world. He talks in euphemisms, as if their smuggled goods are just *products*, and their training is *professional development* and their silence is *commercial in-confidence*. It's a very polished exercise in brainwashing.

'My information is that what is troubling Cavanagh most at the moment is the people-smuggling. He has set routes where his ships transport people, hidden in containers on his freighters. He collects in one port and drops off in another. It works like the branches of a tree linking down to the main trunk, drawing everything into the single route.

'Freighters collect *people*, product, and they bring them down towards the trunk route, the main passage through to India and the Middle East. The ships, which are the branches, offload and onload the *passengers* at sea, under cover of darkness. It's a very efficient system.

'If it was just illegal migrants or refugees, it might have some merit, because they would usually be willing participants. But most of the trade is in women, girls, young boys – into slavery; any of the forms you could name and a few you couldn't even imagine.

'I'm told at least one of the major routes is working at this moment. We've detailed news coming in to our network. My guess is Cavanagh is worried that if he doesn't deliver his cargoes, then he will lose face among his trading customers and then he would never be able to trade in this way again.

'So, he will be debating the risks – whether to cancel the route and jettison his cargo or carry on till the end of the run. The final stage of the route will probably be in the greater Middle East somewhere. Can he afford to take the chance of being caught red-handed by the police or by one of the Navy boats – because he knows we are onto them?'

Alison realises that she hasn't taken a breath through the long explanation. She gulps; and fleetingly thinks she really should have gone back to the court circuits. But, she forces the idea out of her mind immediately.

This is a serious and tragic tale that Ben has just shared.

It is the sudden shocking realisation of what he meant by the jettisoning of a human cargo. She must see this through. This injustice must end. You hear whispers about such things happening, but that is all it usually is, whispers.

Yet she knows from a person she has interviewed that Ben had saved him personally.

He hadn't gone into the detail – the torment really – too painful to disclose; just that Ben had freed him from the clutches of pirates. Perhaps she was just too innocent to understand, fully, the pain in his eyes, now that she thinks back.

'Why do you do this work, Ben?'

'Someday I might tell you,' he replies. She can't read his impassive face.

Then it is all business; flights to be booked, motel check-outs, plans to be made. They are booked to leave first thing in the morning for Port Moresby.

They each have personal affairs to tidy.

Ben arranges to collect Alison in a taxi at 7.00 am and by lunch-time, they would be landing in the tropical heat of New Guinea.

The sting

Trap Roger Cavanagh in a *sting* operation?

Jeff Fowler rechecks his first reaction to the suggestion in case he is missing something. No. His second view isn't any different. How can the Americans and British contemplate such a way-out idea – setting up bait, on the expectation that Cavanagh might be caught red-handed.

It sounds hare-brained, and Fowler tells them so over the secure teleconference link.

He explains to Catherine Weston and Larry Kennedy that the AFP has an informant implanted in Cavanagh's inner circle, recording conversations and reporting back. The plant needs to be protected.

The *Lerna* is expected to leave for New Guinea on the night tide, Australian time. Fowler vehemently vetoes allied agencies from embarking on anything that would alert Cavanagh and endanger their man on the inside.

Since the *sting* brainwave was Angus Forbes's idea, Catherine Weston agrees to recommend that a hold be placed on any plans until they see how the Australian process is panning out. She also advises that her technical section has cracked Cavanagh's email encryption code and so a lot of information should be flowing soon.

Fowler arranges a time on Sunday for a more complete sharing of information on another secure telephone hook-up and he wants all the players on that call.

He sits back to go through all the strategies one more time. The settings are in place to monitor Cavanagh's actions and to give them early Intelligence. He is comfortable with their actions.

His attention now turns to the wharf at White Bay, Balmain. With Bill Jones on assignment in Cairns, he has called upon Inspector Eileen Lewis, from maritime policing, to monitor any applications from SPFA for docking permissions.

Fowler's mind works overtime now, projecting possible uses of merchant shipping to threaten cities. Flynn's early warning has been critical.

His phone light blinks. Bill Jones is on the line.

Broderick and Legrand

Congressman Legrand is patient but firm.

Another phone call from the congressman just after midnight is getting to be annoying ... but, leading into the Washington weekend, it also indicates its seriousness.

He needs Broderick to meet with him and senior people from the Office of the Director of National Intelligence, very early in the morning.

'There have been developments,' he says.

Broderick has no choice; plus he smells a rat.

The congressman is supposed to protect him from this type of interference. Distractions from the main game are interruptions that the head of *Versec* can't afford, particularly as they are close to homing in on the big players.

Surely the accountability committee won't give into pressure?

Would he have to go directly and plead his case to the Vice President himself?

Fowler

It is heating up.

Fowler listens to the detailed report from Bill Jones. These are the times he savours. This is why he is a policeman.

The only pressure niggling him in life is in trying to be a good father and husband, while still being the high-level police superintendent.

His son needs him at the school football fields for his first game in the First XV. He has missed so many of the important occasions for his children; he has promised himself he will be at whatever events come up this year – school presentation evenings, sporting events and even listening to his daughter playing in the school violin ensemble.

But the pressure of this case is increasing with all the updated information on Cavanagh – and moving overseas now. It is possible he will be required to fly to New Guinea, if that is where the action will be.

He hopes other cool heads will be able to handle that connection, leaving him at base in Australia to supervise any anti-terrorism danger. And, for the moment, it would let him watch his son in his first game for the top team.

He needs to speak with Ben Brennan.

What does *Nemesis* know about the SPFA agendas? His fingers automatically text Ben as he thinks.

Tomorrow, he must be able to give the British and American agencies as complete a picture as possible. Their top people, Broderick and Forbes, will be part of that secure conversation.

Roger reflects

Roger smiles. He has been right about Steve Flynn – his instinct told him from the start.

Flynn is just a retired soldier-cum-security guard who has been caught up in a hi-jacking – and he is fresh, unsullied, uncompromised; just what is required. Through pure chance and the good graces of Dr Naleen, he has ended up on the *Lerna*.

Roger prides himself on always having his antennae up for emerging talent; just as wise heads selected him all those years ago.

He has never forgotten the lessons of Bernard at primary school. This Australian is *muscle*, primarily; but he is also smart, perceptive and malleable, with that dutiful sense of service about him. Maybe it's an Army thing, maybe upbringing.

The small signs tell the story. Steve has not betrayed his trust or Gina would have let on; she isn't bright enough to hide things from him. And the Australian has kept her quietly out of his way at this troubled time.

There is always the back-up of checking the CCTV digital memory but Roger has never bothered with that – a time-consuming waste in his view. Gut instinct is a far better guide than trying to double-guess motives in mundane images flashed across a silent screen.

Anyway, Steve hadn't baulked at the business meeting; he was well organised, showed initiative within boundaries, polite – plus he is *security*. He has that military toughness that can be used later on. Freeing up Len and Peter too.

And, if it doesn't work out, then he is expendable. Everyone is expendable.

And he is compromised. His dubious passage on the *Lerna* can always be used to keep him in line. Roger always keeps leverage to ensure that people toe the expected line. Good leverage is an integral part of the protection business.

In case of emergency, Roger's first back-up plan is the one he learned from the example of the father he had never met; he will just disappear. The plans are in place.

Failing that, anyone who stands in his way will be taken out of the equation. He will never be bullied again. Steve is fresh clean muscle – unquestioning protection with no hang-ups, no previous loyalties or grievances. He can be groomed to do whatever is needed to ensure Roger's safety.

Now, the challenge is to deal with Peter and Len. They are clearly not happy with his new recruit. Paranoia? Probably. But they don't understand his bigger picture. Maybe Steve Flynn reminds them that they botched the Ingrid operation. His bullet scar is proof of that. He shudders. You can't fake that!

That is it. So blindingly obvious.

The Australian is a constant flag to them. Their judgement is clouded by the need to protect their own tails.

But to Roger, Steve is a wistful reminiscence of his young self as he climbed the ladder of the *Ramas* network; sharp, willing to learn, handsome even. He smiles at the flattering comparison.

And the business is vulnerable at the moment. As the leader of the South East Asia operation, he has certainly had a positive influence in improving the larger structure of the whole *Ramas* network.

It is he, Roger, who built automatic political protection into the operating fabric of the business model. Payments discreetly made, routinely and constantly, so that key players are always running interference for the enterprise. These people are in government, civil services, enforcement and Intelligence agencies; in many lands – and they are influential.

Sir Terence – the old fool. *Ramas* has used him for many message transfers but there are others, in other lands.

Roger is now so powerful anyway, that he can send messages on the encryption system that would appear to have come from the leader.

The police investigators are a distraction; but his people should force their withdrawal from the scene. They have done it before and they will again.

He has devised a Plan B to give him time, a negotiating position if they ever get close. Given only a few hours, he can escape from his current identity. The Swiss and Cayman accounts are numbered and anonymous. He can walk away, untraceable, from the whole *Ramas* structure and live very well on the interest of his accumulated wealth.

He has his exit strategy. And new employee, Mr Flynn, is the clean recruit; the devoted expendable, if required.

At the very least, he will be the signatory for all documents which will, as ever, leave Roger far removed from any future incrimination.

The Brigadier and Angus

London. Saturday 17 February 2007

'What's this nonsense of holding back for a while,' demands Angus Forbes. 'We are close to having him dead to rights.'

The Brigadier is very calm; the wisdom of years of command.

'There is always a bigger picture, Angus. You know that. The *Big House on the River* has concerns about dealing with international sensitivities. You are not being stopped – only asked to be patient. Continue to collect your information.'

Angus's eyebrows furrow into a frown. 'Sir, I think some big player must have got to the Minister. We have a lot of information now. The Australians have an agent in Cavanagh's crew. We are with them and ahead of them.'

The Brigadier's expression is tolerant and patient. 'Angus, at the end of the day, the decision will be the Minister's. You know that. Obviously there are people who don't want us on their territory – for very valid motives. Espionage and Intelligence are not businesses for bullish behaviour. They are very subtle processes built over years, with lives at stake. Believe me, that *was* my world.'

'I understand that, Sir, and I appreciate that you are advocating well on our behalf. But I'm a policeman. That is why the Minister appointed me, to nail international crooks. We knew we would tread on people's sacred territories. We also believe there are senior people trying to shut us down.'

The Brigadier smiles indulgently again. 'Patience, Angus! Which part of *No!* didn't you hear? The Minister is saying *Hold back for the moment!* Just keep collecting your information for the time when the combined forces of *Versec* and the *NPA* are ready to move on Cavanagh.'

'I hear you, Brigadier,' Angus concedes. 'We'll follow your advice; your directive. But I want it noted that I, indeed we plural in the *NPA*, are not happy with the pause, the delay, the stoppage.'

'Duly noted, Angus.'

The *Lerna*

From the screens in the ship's main office, I can see Gina relaxing with a book on the sundeck – catching the dying rays of afternoon sun, without actually being touched by them. I smile sadly at Gina's ordained life pattern, as I focus again on the sophisticated camera monitoring system.

I know CCTV would have a data-storing provision – it is a standard feature on such installations. It is possible a record of my movements might be stored someplace, to be used later to compromise me. Gina has warned me. Why hasn't Roger mentioned that?

I watch Captain Rodriguez on another screen running through his briefing on the bridge.

Marcel is busy in the galley.

Crew members are moving around with a sense of purpose. Everyone knows the jobs to be completed. This is a disciplined team. The ship is being readied for sea.

Peter and Len appear by car at the jetty. They go straight to their adjacent cabins to drop their gear and then head for Roger's suite.

No doubt their de-briefing would take an hour or so.

Roger, Steve, Carter and Len

Cairns. Saturday 17 February 2007

'Mr Cavanagh would like to see you in the suite office, Sir.'

Why does Roger always beckon me in this way? I carry a ship's mobile phone.

Maybe this is part of his formal style of making the crew feel involved or perhaps it is his imperial demeanour to use a servant to beckon. Evening seems to mean nothing to Roger's priorities. He operates on 24/7, as far as his staff availability is concerned – not too different from the Army. No matter, I arrive at the suite office to be greeted by Roger, Peter and Len.

'Come in, come in, Steve.' There is an efficient busyness. 'I've just been bringing Peter and Len up to speed on your developing role with the company.'

While Roger is smiling, Peter and Len are not showing kindness and welcoming, in the least.

'They have been doing terrific work,' Roger gushes routinely, 'with the people in the field. That's why I value them so much.' The boss's compliment is acknowledged by their appreciative single nods.

'Look at this beauty, Steve!'

Roger is holding up a large piece of glassy rock; an opaque greenish-blue colour mainly. But where it has been cleaned, it is a deep sapphire-blue; clearly a high-quality gemstone material, even to my untrained eye.

'This is a gift for *Ramas*. The network picked it up in Central Queensland. Here, hold it! Isn't it just marvellous? Feel the weight, the power.'

I hold the large gemstone, a solid stone for its size.

'Marvellous,' I agree. '*Ramas* should be very pleased.' I can see a look exchanged between Carter and Williamson. I understand the significance of the secretive name. Their noses must be right out of joint.

Roger beams as if he is handling the crown jewels. He has the collector's joy in his eyes.

'That's the value of a well-trained network, Steve. Such an appropriate gift too. I mean, sapphire! Such a pure blue stone.' His eyes look heavenward and back to me. 'Don't you just love the intense colour of this jewel? It does something to me. Do you feel it too? Our ship's hull is sapphire coloured – not an accident. The sapphire is the logo I would use for the company, if we had a badge.

'Do you realise that the crown jewels of Napoleon Bonaparte had a huge blue sapphire to emphasise the power of the gem and the emperor? The Ruspoli Sapphire. Not everyone knows that but I am a serious student of the great emperor. He had the Parure of Marie Antoinette – that is matching jewellery with twenty-nine sapphires of over twenty carats each – and the Mohács Blue was in his private collection; another magnificent stone that was once owned by Suleiman the Magnificent, ruler of the Ottoman Empire. I have actually seen that one, in someone more recent's private collection.

'Oh, gentlemen, this is *so* good. I will highlight the link with our sapphire-coloured ship and Napoleon when I talk with *Ramas*. Oh, well done, chaps. Well done! This *really is something*.'

He takes the gemstone to the wall where he pulls back a hinged Polynesian mask from its position – revealing a discreet wall safe.

The dial is whirled three times to the right, twice to the left and once to the right again – too fast for me to pick the numbers – and the safe door swings open.

Roger carefully deposits the gemstone inside and closes the safe door.

'Now, Steve.' He is slowly coming down from the high of handling his beloved jewel. 'I've been explaining to Peter and Len that I've moved you into the security role on the ship, to release Peter to do other fine work out in the field.'

Carter receives another affirming look. 'I've asked him to take you through some more of the security for the ship, as well as giving you training on the business-side of the operation – because you'll take over the signing of all documentation from now on.'

Adrenalin rushes through me. I'm about to be set up as the signing patsy. But there is a bigger picture now – and I am part of the police operation. I have to go with the flow and keep my expression the same.

Roger hasn't stopped his chat.

'Len has to leave us for a while to link up with a freighter currently leaving Newcastle for Sydney. D'you recall me requesting access to a ship docking at Balmain with cars and containers? Mr Masa, our logistical expert, has done brilliantly in getting us access to a Korean freighter which was heading to White Bay anyway. That's even better than using one of our own ships – no link back to SPFA. Len will rendezvous with the boat at sea. The captain is being well paid. He knows our business mantras, very discreet.

'Len will join us later in New Guinea. Meanwhile, I need you and Peter to go through all the training and security as a matter of urgency. I have asked Captain Rodriguez to be ready to cast off around 2.00 am.'

Peter is Mr Efficiency personified. 'Give me an hour. Then I'll meet you on the bridge.' Maybe the transition might be smooth after all.

We leave Roger at his desk, his mind already onto his next planning task.

The mole

The encryption light flashes on the *Lerna's* suite computer. Roger logs on.

The message is: *Sir Terence out of the picture, moved into hospital, gone in the mind. Danger! You have a mole in your crew. No ID yet. Be careful.*

He stares at the screen. It is a trusted communication.

A traitor to consider among all his other current challenges? No identification given.

Logic would suggest the most recent recruit – Steve.

He has run through the scenarios many times already: employed on the *Sea Spray* before Roger even had the idea to hi-jack it; then shot – he had seen the scar – only good luck that he had been washed up on a beach rather than being shredded on a reef. None of that could have been planned. His Army background checked out and he'd been on board the *Lerna* nearly all the time so the chances of him being infiltrated as a mole after Fiji are minimal.

Peter and Len? They have been away for days. Could someone have contacted either of them? He seriously doubts either of them would turn traitor. They have too much to lose and nothing to gain. Unless … unless they can see the writing on the wall for the organisation and are trying to turn Queen's evidence, to plea-bargain. He must watch them both closely.

And the crew? Captain Rodriguez knows nothing of the business. He is a career skipper, employed to take the ship where Roger wants it to go. The crew are paid well and, normally, have good leave conditions in exotic locations. Mind you, it has been busy during the last few weeks with all the distractions – less leave than usual. Perhaps someone is disenchanted and has been compromised – but what can a crewman tell?

Gina? No, Gina may be difficult but she has been with him for so long, much longer than Peter or Len. She is so reliable and always supervised. Besides, she wouldn't have the smarts, or the *bottle*, to betray Roger.

But the warning is there. He will be alert.

Carter's briefing

Cairns. Saturday 17 February 2007

'Well, haven't you had a rapid rise through the ranks?' Peter Carter has just a faint touch of respect in his tone. 'I leave you in Noumea as a cook's assistant and I come back to find you have taken my job and are the confidant of the boss.'

What can I say?

To his credit, Peter continues. 'I have no hard feelings. I will be taking over the Thailand connection for the company. Huge task in the making. I am looking forward to it.'

'Congratulations, Peter!' I manage as genuine a tone as I can.

'So, what do you need to know?'

'Roger showed me the CCTV and the infra-red scanning – very effective even with the lights of a Cairns night. I've used the computer set up. What I don't know is about our defensive weapons. I've seen the gun lockers around the ship. I need keys. What is the maintenance schedule for cleaning them? And anything else I need to know to defend the ship.

'Then, there's all the business paperwork Roger wants me to do. My signature is approved but that's all I know. I'm assuming I'll do bookings. Right?'

Peter agrees with a shrug.

He is logical. Same for me. Army admin is meticulous. Handovers and briefing are part of that life.

'Let's start in the ship's office and do the paperwork first. Then we'll do the weaponry and check that everything is working to your satisfaction. We need to move quickly if we are to do everything before sundown.'

He sounds like some mid-Atlantic salesman.

Fowler

It is evening.

Jeff Fowler has returned from cheering his son's performance for the school's First XV – and they won. He has now left his family to bask. He is immersed in the productive after-work-hours type of police *busy* that he enjoys.

He has just been talking to the office of the Deputy Chief of the Navy. Their senior officers are now briefed on the requirements to maintain communications with the *Lerna* north to Port Moresby and to wherever from there. The Navy are experts in that type of work.

Fowler has also briefed the Deputy Chief on the possible need for Navy intervention at some time in the future within international protocols.

Inspector Lewis has advised that there are no current applications for berthing at White Bay, Balmain, by any SPFA ship.

Indeed, there aren't many vessels due to dock at White Bay in the next few weeks.

A large car transporter would be leaving port tomorrow to return to Japan. The next ship due is a smaller Korean freighter, that is currently in Newcastle. It is scheduled to dock in a week and then head south to Melbourne.

NPA

London. Saturday 17 February 2007

Techs picks up the message received by the *Lerna's* encrypted system.

He advises Catherine that Cavanagh knows about a spy on his ship.

The sender is still effectively anonymous. Even the acknowledging reply address is scrambled. Techs is working hard on a way to find the identity of the sender but he hasn't mastered that yet.

Catherine immediately tells Angus, who appears to be deeper in thought than usual.

'Well,' he says in a seemingly depressed tone. 'Now we know how they managed to deliver the ransom message anonymously. Have you had your information-sharing with Australia yet?'

'Tomorrow, with *Versec* as well,' she replies. 'I think the Australians would like you on the line too. They want to know more about any sting operation.

'They're concerned about protecting their contact on the *Lerna*. But he might be compromised anyway now. Or maybe it's a *she*. The leak could only have come from their end. Neither we nor the Americans have information about the plant.'

Forbes raises his thumb in agreement. 'Okay. Put the call in my diary. We'll see how the land lies by tomorrow. The Brigadier has asked us – no, he has told us – that we must just have a watching brief for the moment. No actions. There appears to be some interference happening; maybe here or maybe in the States. I'll tell you more when I know more. We'll say nothing to the Brigadier about the sting. He would only veto it.'

Catherine now understands her boss's manner.

More briefing

'You sign for everything. Roger never signs.' Carter stresses the point. 'It's part of his strategy of keeping fire-breaks in the business. Neat compartments so that snoopers never get the whole picture.'

I am not that naïve. I understand why Roger doesn't sign. He doesn't want any paper trail. But I let it pass.

'Where does the money come from?'

'Do you mean, *which account?*' asks Carter. 'It is called the *Lerna Expense Account*. It is as big as it needs to be. You can essentially order anything Roger requires. The money comes in usually from SPFA and Mr Gonzalez's accountants are expert at finding notations to explain away any strange sums.

'Alternatively, money sometimes comes from an investment bank in the States. I'm not sure how that works. Anyway, there's always money available.'

Peter shows me how the office files work. 'Most of it is electronic. We have a couple of crew who scan documents into appropriate files. Hard copies of invoices are kept here for a month or so. We also have a storeroom in the bulkhead. We store obsolete files there till we land in the Philippines but only Roger, Len and I have keys for that room.'

'So you do that filing yourself?' I ask, surprised.

'We have other gear in that room,' he replies casually. 'It's out-of-bounds to all crew. Yes, *we* file whatever needs to go in there.'

'Do *I* get a key?'

'If Roger gives you one,' he replies, with finality in his tone. 'Now, the boss mentioned your pay. What's your bank account number? He wants me to transfer twenty thousand Australian dollars, as a down payment.'

Impressed is scarcely the word. Roger said that the money would be good. If that is the monthly rate, then I am in for a bucket-load.

I give Peter my Queensland account number and watch the process so that I can do it for others when I might need to.

Having completed the business procedures, we head to the gun lockers. Each has automatic attack rifles, a defensive shot gun and a rack of Glock pistols.

Peter hands me a key to the lockers. 'All keyed the same. Roger, you, me and the captain have the keys. Maintenance schedule is pasted inside. Cleaned and worked every month, perhaps not regularly enough in this salty environment.'

I am unconcerned. 'I'll work my way through them all progressively. Weapons have been my business for a long time – just like you in the forces, I imagine.' Carter shrugs agreement; no sense of flattery or pride in the acknowledgement, as if the memory is part of a little-considered, even irritating, past.

'Is there anything else you need to know?'

'The captain and the crew? How have they been briefed for an emergency? A pirate attack, for example?'

Peter's glance gives nothing away. He takes me through the drills they practise regularly and the training which new crew receive on induction as well as the refresher courses for the rest.

It all seems very efficient.

Steve and Gina

Cairns. Saturday 17 February 2007

Gina is dressed in another chiffony robe thing, enjoying the night sky on the lounger by the jacuzzi as I approach. She remarks that Peter and Len have returned and that Len has left again.

'Yep, he's off to Newcastle,' I say. 'Will rejoin us in New Guinea.'

'Whoopee!' Gina comments with a bored sarcasm and sighs.

'We cast off in the middle of the night. Only a few hours away now'

Gina just gives a casual flick of the hand. It has been expected.

'Two things.' I drop my voice to a whisper as I switch the jacuzzi pump on. The significance is not lost on her.

'One. Do you know the numbers of the safe in Roger's office? It goes three turns clockwise and stops at a number. Then two anti-clockwise turns to another number. Then one more clockwise to a third number. I would like to know these three numbers.'

'I don't know them,' she says, 'but I'll watch next time.'

'Two. Do you have a gun and can you use it?'

'*No*, to the first and *I don't know*, to the second.'

'I think we are moving into dangerous times.' I feel calmly efficient. This is a familiar routine. 'I need you to be able to protect yourself – or even me. I can't pass a gun over openly or it would be picked up on the CCTV.'

'It would be hard to hide in my swimsuit.' She smiles back sweetly. 'Even with my fluffy evening wear.'

'I'll bring a pistol to the chair at the side of the stairwell,' I say, 'wrapped in the folds of a towel. Pick it up innocently as you leave and hide it in your room. In your underwear or your shoes; somewhere where Roger wouldn't normally look.'

She gives me a questioning glance but I am already continuing. 'The gun will be a Glock, loaded and in working order. All you will need to do is point the gun and pull the trigger with a full grip. The safety is part of the trigger mechanism. It won't fire by accident. So just pull the trigger right back, a double click, and it will send a 19 millimetre parabellum shell at your target.'

Seeing the worry in her eyes, I add, 'I'm just being careful. I care about you.'

She gives a grin of appreciation as I leave to get the pistol. No doubt, clarion bells would be ringing in her mind about what might happen. She flagged it herself, long ago.

* * * *

Gina wonders why he is so cool. Perhaps there is more to Steven Flynn than meets the eye; elusive – and attractive.

Wow, how long since she had sensed those thoughts? Whatever; he is caring for her when no-one else is.

Her mind seems to have that automatic default these days; never letting her enjoy too many warm thoughts for anyone. The price of her guilt complex; programmed to protect her troubled conscience.

The happy tingle dissipates; a zephyr of shadowy regret dissolving like a wisp of smoke, as she jolts back to the present. It is a time for thinking of self preservation.

Steve smiles over to her as he lays the folded towel on the chair.

She picks it up casually as she leaves the sundeck and minutes later the Glock is hidden in her walk-in wardrobe.

313

Gina on the *Lerna*

Coral Sea. Saturday 17 February 2007

Gina lies between the scented silk sheets in the seclusion of her private room. The ship will depart while she sleeps – if she can sleep. She is awake for the second time that night in the darkness.

She can picture an image of Steve Flynn's face; cheery and yet very confusing. Such a strange and desirable man – she is trying to remember when genuine stirring thoughts like that had last passed through her desensitised mind.

Normal feminine urges had been repressed for so long in her abnormal world; a withdrawal into a subconscious restraint just to survive. But this new unsettling actor in this perplexing scenario is not playing the role as it has normally panned out. He doesn't react like most men she has met.

Usually any man who had been in her company for as long as she and Steve have spent together … usually he would have tried to crack on to her; and she would have rejected him as she had trained herself to do, over the years, with the haughty manner guaranteed to keep any cocky, speculating suitor at a distance.

That had been her pattern and it just reinforced her sense of loneliness.

But not Steve. He had made no advances at all.

She'd seen no evidence that he preferred men. She was regularly in a swimsuit, yet he always kept a friendly distance – like a brother.

Ah ha! There it is! Suddenly she understands.

That is the taboo. He behaves like a brother. She is out-of-bounds in his thinking – like a sister to a brother.

A brother; now there is another thought that hasn't crossed her conscious mind for such a long time … maybe eight years. She has submerged the painful memory – although the unwelcome ghosts of her raw shame haunt her sleeping dreams in quiet nights, when she least expects it.

Has it been eight years since her brother had come to the ship in the Ajaccio marina in Corsica? He had brought messages from her parents – a plea to come home. Loving greetings which, in her then drug-induced high, she had rejected with a detestable dismissiveness.

Not just that though; worse than that. Through the mists of her then psychedelic memory, she can recall the gist, if not the detail, of the vitriolic language she had used about her parents, brother and past life. No-one deserves to be spoken to like that. She could blame the drugs – disembodied. It was like a stranger speaking on her behalf but she couldn't stop it happening.

To her eternal humiliation, she had not only abused her brother but she had stood back as Roger's goons, Antoine and Lucien, beat him up in front of her and then threw him onto the jetty.

And she had done nothing; no protest, no intervention; just a blank look of indifference.

Her brother's harrowing expression of pain and disappointment comes back in the nightmares which have plagued her over the years. Sadly, her family has been lost to her from that day on. There had been an opening to return to a sane world on that day; the day she had passively, almost unwittingly, signed up with the Devil.

Steve. Yes, he is like a brother; trustworthy, a confidant, a friend – who has respected and cheered her like few others. That must indeed be the reason.

Now it appears that the pretty journalist has taken his attention; another opportunity lost, although there had been no chances with the all-seeing CCTV.

Perhaps Alison would be the best for him anyway, although she seems such fragile thing to be trying to write a disclosure of pirate activities. Maybe that vulnerable honesty is the attraction, coupled with opportunity.

Strangely, Gina feels an almost sisterly affection for her *brother's* friend – none of the competitive shrewishness she might have felt years ago. Has this doldrum-like despair mellowed her or is she past bothering any more? The silent thoughts float carelessly through her mind.

In any event, hasn't she told Steve he can trust her to give him space in his new romance? She will keep her word – about time she did what she believes.

She sighs and rolls over between the sheets, to dream an irrealisable dream; an impossible fantasy curling the corners of her mouth.

Alison and New Guinea – the action starts

Cairns. Sunday 18 February 2007

Alison wakes early – too much excitement and tension to stay asleep.

As she dresses, she again remembers the tracking device. She wonders whether the device will work in New Guinea and how Steve is faring on the *Lerna*. Perhaps he has already cast off on the voyage north.

Ben arrives with the taxi exactly on time.

He asks the cab to go to the airport via the esplanade, hardly out of the way.

A glance seaward towards the marina confirms that the *Lerna* must have left during the night.

Alison mentally wishes Steve well. Ben sits inscrutable as ever.

* * * *

The Fokker 100 is a sleek-looking twin turbo-fan plane which seats a hundred passengers. They settle into their seats and the plane curves out over the turquoise sea, heading north to Port Moresby.

She expects that she might be able to pick out the shape of the *Lerna* but the ascent is too quick for her to focus on the blur of ocean.

New Guinea. Sunday 18 February 2007

The plane swoops into Jackson International Airport at Port Moresby, showing window panoramas of the impressive green mountain ranges to the north and the multi-shaded green-blue ocean to the south.

A taxi trip takes them into the central area of Ela Beach; passing through beautiful tropical vegetation and the cloying heat of the atmosphere, as well as zipping past tired places with boarded windows; and lots of dark-skinned people sitting, bored.

Debris, graffiti – the litter of hopeless decay.

Alison is starting to appreciate Ben's comment about personal safety. But the hotel at Ela Beach is spectacularly modern with views over the harbour and a strand of white beach in the other direction.

In the distance, they can see the white speckles of the stilt villages, built over the water. Ben says they are called Koki and Gabi.

This place has its charm; new world and old world; so different from the Cairns they have just left.

Ben has booked separate rooms and Alison thanks him silently.

He takes her for a quick stroll on the peninsula, taking in Paga Point, the Old Parliament Building, a view of the harbour – 'That's where the *Lerna* will anchor to replenish supplies. I'd be surprised if they stay long,' – and back to the hotel.

That is their tourist activity over.

Four men join them in the lobby as they go up to their room.

Ben welcomes them with a tilt of the head.

Inside the room, he introduces Alison to Tom, Ron, Harry and Mike – all nicknames, she guesses. Mike has the dark skin, features and wide, white grin of a Nuigini native. Harry is undoubtedly of Chinese Asian origin. Tom is Eurasian, white skinned but his eyes and cheeks look more Malay. Ron looks like your fair-dinkum Aussie living abroad – floppy blond hair, casual, lean, with a larrikin grin.

'Alison will be our independent witness,' says Ben as he introduces her.

Little is said by way of explanation but she forms the understanding that the men are part of this mysterious *Nemesis*. They would all be flying out that afternoon to Madang on the north coast. The hotel rooms in Moresby would be there for the return; but tonight, and perhaps tomorrow, they would be sleeping at Nagada Lagoon just north of Madang.

Alison listens to the reports from Mike and Harry. If she understands them correctly, a Panamanian-registered freighter, with a Russian captain and crew, is travelling from Rabaul in New Britain to Davao in the Southern Philippines. It is a trunk ship of one of the people-smuggling runs.

Ben nods at appropriate times in her direction as the briefing continues; reminding her of the analogy he had described back in Cairns.

The ship has come from the Solomons. Its registered route will pass through the Bismarck Sea, then between the Philippines and Indonesian Sulawesi through the Celebes and Sulu Seas; and finally on through the Malacca Strait to southern India and Arabia. People would be brought to the ship and offloaded as required while the ship would maintain her steady course.

Ben and his men are going to attack the vessel in the sleepy hours of the next morning. She is to be an independent observer. The thought has butterflies fluttering inside her.

This is the chance she had always thought she had wanted; direct investigation for her exposé – but now that it is here and real, she is barely concealing her terror. Yet Ben Brennan and his team inspire confidence. They are so controlled and focused.

'We travel light. Even leave our mobiles behind. Most don't work there anyway.'

She takes only a change of clothes, her digital video recorder, spare batteries and her notebook.

Gear organised, they are in a taxi for the fifteen kilometre return drive to the airport and the Air Nuigini plane.

* * * *

Spectacular jagged green ridges wreathed in clouds pass beneath; till they descend over the blue of the Bismarck Sea, into the settlement of Madang.

A driver is waiting.

319

Another short trip north and they are established in a couple of huts, within a group, beside the idyllic lagoon of Nagada; tiny green palm-covered islands, clusters of coral reefs, secluded bays; dive-boat signs and inflatables with powerful outboard motors. This is reef-diving heaven.

A hot cup of tea and then they are in the inflatables, out to a larger fishing trawler. It noses steadily out over the blue swell to the freighter shipping lanes, just beyond sight of land.

The salty tang in the air spray reminds her that she has volunteered for this. She daren't look Ben in the eyes and say she hadn't been warned.

The sun is setting as they move out past Bababag Island and out onto the massive, translucent, molten hills from the steady Pacific swell rolling into the Bismarck Sea.

Dry in the mouth, she listens to the chatter of radio conversations. Little of it uses English but she forms another impression – that Ben has men already on board the freighter. They are going to stop the ship.

Ben tells her she will be brought on board only when the ship is secure.

'No problem,' she replies, controlling her gulp. She can't recall having so much adrenalin coursing through her system at any time before, in her entire life.

* * * *

Two inflatables leave the fishing boat after midnight, leaving Alison on board in the care of Tom, the crew and a third fast rubber boat.

It is quiet and pitch-dark. No stars, no moon, just the faintest strange luminescence on an occasional swell as the vessel rolls gently. There are no lights on the fishing boat.

Somewhere in the distance the intensely-deep throbbing growl of a large ship's engine is transmitting through the water. The sound gets louder. The freighter is coming. She strains her eyes to the east, staring into the gloom.

Suddenly the throb stops. A crackling sound floats over the water.

Then silence.

The fishing boat captain listens to the radio and speaks to Tom. 'Right! They're on board. Into the inflatable. We are off.'

Alison descends into the inflatable and they surge forward.

Holding tight to ropes on the side, she can't see much as they power forward. Then, within minutes, a greater darkness floats over her like a shadow with a little phosphorescence at the water level and the smell of rusting, salty metal. The bulk of a huge freighter is overhanging their small boat.

Tom speaks on a hand-held radio. Then a rope ladder appears. A torch shines down from above – dazzling through the dark.

'Come on,' says Tom, with a tap on her shoulder.

He leads her by the hand to the ladder base and then follows her up so closely it would have been impossible for her to fall off. Then onto a solid ladder, with bigger rungs, almost steps. It is a huge climb. Puffing with the effort, they eventually cross the side rail and there is Ben.

'Glad you could make it.' His dry humour is very welcome. 'This way.'

The deck is well lit – a huge contrast to the darkness of their approach. Alison is aware of a haunting melancholy sound rising into the night air. A sea bird seems to answer with an echoing call.

A huddle of people appears to be seated near several open shipping containers. Harry is with them.

'Get your video camera ready,' says Ben.

It is then that Alison recognises a line of women. She can't understand why they are in a line until she realises that their legs are shackled together.

The binding is a sleeve of rubber around one leg from just below the knee to above the ankle. The leg sleeves are linked by a chain of plastic cable ties which secure the women into a coffle, just as effectively as if they had been locked by the metal leg or neck irons of the old African slave trade. It registers with her that these rubber leg sleeves would leave no marks, no chafed ankles, no reduction in the value at sale.

The women wear only raggy cotton frocks. No footwear. No cloaks. And they are wailing, a low guttural painful howl.

They are thin. Some Filipina, Chinese, Indians but most look like South Pacific Islanders.

Alison scans her camera over the depressing line of captive women. Even from a distance, an unpleasant animal waft catches her nostrils. Then Ben takes her to another coffle of men and boys. Fifteen in that chain – all wailing an unrecognisable lament; wide-eyed and then, as the camera moves towards them, heads down to hide their faces.

'Do you have your evidence?' asks Ben. 'We want to cut them free now. That's thirty-five captives on this boat at this time.'

She nods. There are no words that she can form. The intense smell is causing the gorge to rise at the back of her throat.

The wailing dirge changes to moans of bewilderment as the cable ties are cut. Water and some food are provided.

She follows Ben's lead to the prison containers.

'Air-conditioned,' he says. 'The prisoners are kept sealed in, during the heat of the day. They are brought out on deck only at night.'

A putrid smell hits her at the door of the container. She could not contain the vomit as she hacks the burning spew onto the deck. A chemical toilet at the rear gives off the most retching stench. It challenges the imagination to understand how anyone could survive in there, let alone use that facility when chained in a line of twenty women, in the dark. Maybe they didn't! Aagh, how ghastly!

There is another multiple squat toilet set up outside, on the side of the deck; hardly private, but designed to cater for a dozen at a time. Presumably this is used at night so that the captives could toilet en masse. Large deck hoses were nearby – to clean the people, the mess, the deck … it is becoming too hard to absorb.

Ben's expression doesn't change. Impassive. Challenging. 'Come and meet the captain now. Keep your camera running. Our men will get these people down to the fishing boat. It'll be a tight squeeze but no tighter than they've had.'

She follows him up the steps to the brightly-lit bridge. In there, men with guns guard the captain and the crew.

Sullen looks. Quietness.

Alison pans along the group with her camera. The crew try to look away but to no avail when Ben's men with guns growl.

'They can speak English, although they will pretend that they can't,' says Ben. 'Keep your camera rolling.'

The captain is being asked the questions.

'Why? Do you understand what you have been doing?'

His answers are about Carter. He claims to know no-one called Roger or Cavanagh. Carter had tricked him into carrying captive women in a container two years ago. He had filmed the whole process. They were threatened with exposure; delivery to Asian police and not less than twenty years in a filthy prison. Then he speaks of the *Devil Man* with the stretched face. No name – only the description.

'So cruel, so cruel.'

The captain describes how the *Devil Man* apparently tied one of his crew to a chair – an innocent crewman randomly selected – and tortured him with a knife in front of them all; just as an example, in case anyone thought of breaking the code of silence. The man didn't live through the ordeal; and the *Devil* had tossed the butchered corpse unceremoniously over the side to the sharks.

Alison shudders, the smell of her recent vomit on her clothes adding to her nausea. She has no doubt who the *Devil Man* must have been. She has heard him described before.

'What happen now?' the captain asks, terror obvious in his wide eyes. 'Carter and the *Devil* will come aboard. We will be exposed.' Their cowering bodies are actually shivering with fear at the thought of Len Williamson.

Alison is an experienced court reporter but she is appalled at the whole concept, let alone the sights and smells. This is a travelling sales van of anguished human cargo, moving through international waters. Ghastly; gross.

The ship is scheduled to sail through the Philippines, Indonesia, Malaysia and out into the Indian Ocean. Other freighters would presumably come alongside, taking some prisoners off and adding new ones.

Ben instructs the skipper to continue his journey when they and the cargo of freed captives leave. He advises him to put in at Davao and declare what has been happening; to throw himself on the mercy of the judicial system before these videos reach the authorities. Ben suggests he'll get a more favourable hearing if they confess the names of all the people they have been working with. Otherwise, they will be caught eventually, with twenty years in an unforgiving prison being the best on offer.

Alison watches and records the captain weighing up his fear of *the Devil* against the certainty that the authorities will catch him. He will never captain a ship again. It is pathetic to watch, as his face jabbers silently – but then the sight and stench on the deck have been infinitely more pathetic and painful.

* * * *

The fishing boat is loaded. The captain and crew are left, bound by cable ties, with a knife within shuffling distance at the end of the room. By the time they have cut themselves free, Ben and his team will be well on their way through the darkness to Nagada and Madang.

Alison sits with the women on the way back, with Harry and Mike trying to communicate in a range of languages from Nuigini Pidgin – Tok Pisin; to Tagalog to Chinese. Most seem in too much shock to even understand what is happening to them. Are they just in some new form of capture?

Alison finds one Islander woman who can communicate with some English. She speaks a little at a time, small rushes of words, in a very quiet teary voice, eyes downcast, about days at sea; tormented struggles for survival; and the fears for what the future might hold after this ordeal.

Her name, she says, is Hillnah. It is recorded by the camera – a testimony for when the ship's captain and crew might go on trial.

Hillnah is holding the hand of a young man. She says he is her fiancé. He has a badly bruised eye and cheek. He keeps his gaze averted as often as possible. She says it is the shame. He hasn't been able to protect his bride. He won't be able to hold his head up in society ever again. They cannot go back to their village. They are *dead* to that world now. She wails again as she explains – personal humiliation they can handle, but not the terrible community shame.

The video camera records their torment – but the lens cannot sense the residual fear and panic. Time might wash away the stench of the captivity but the inner turmoil will always be there, in their minds.

Steve on the *Lerna*

Coral Sea. Sunday 18 February 2007

I had felt the *Lerna* move out of the Cairns bay in the middle of the night and, by morning, the Queensland coast is just a ribbon of greeny-purple on the horizon.

Sailing is quiet time for me. By mid-morning, I have completed every routine task and I join Gina on the sundeck.

She has a dreamy smile as she lies on her familiar lounger, enjoying the warmth of the sun. The jacuzzi springs into life, her security blanket, giving her the confidence that she isn't being overheard.

'You said we are heading into dangerous times?' she whispers quietly.

'The law is closing in on Roger. I think he is aware but perhaps not about how close they might be to him.'

'How do you know this?' She is watching me with curious eyes, then she sucks her bottom lip, nodding at some dawning realisation.

'Just trust me. It's coming to a head.'

'Oh, I hope so!' She has clearly taken it all for long enough. An involuntary twitch is making her cheek wink. Her lip trembles despite her efforts at control.

'What would your dream be after this is all over?' I ask.

She looks at me with surprise. 'What? My dream? You ask the strangest questions. As if I would have a choice. I've been a captive too long to think for myself.'

'Come on. What do you really want? You have done the pretty rich girl on the expensive yacht. What would you really like?'

She looks at me with a smirking grin, the nervous twitch already just a memory. 'You would only laugh. I don't want you to laugh at me.'

'Try me. You know me well enough now. I won't laugh. Come on. What would you like?'

She shrugs and looks away.

Then she whispers very slowly, almost forcefully, still looking away. 'I would like to be loved by somebody who works at just a normal job – a plumber or a carpenter maybe. I would like to be a wife and mother, needed for just being me. I would like to be helpful. I want to shop for a family in a supermarket, cook meals, clean a house, walk children to school. I want to be needed and I want to be free from all this.'

Her deep-blue eyes are watering as she turns to see my face. Her *little girl lost* expression pleads. 'But it can never be – so why tease me?'

I try to stay upbeat – this is better than her twitchy fear. 'The first part of getting things to change is to have an idea of what you want.'

She stares, a little cynically, but questioning.

'And what about you? What do you want?' she asks.

'Similar things. I've been a soldier for much of my life. It's hard on relationships when you're deployed six to eight months at a time. When you get back, it takes two to three months to get back into a normal mindset again – and then you are training to go away again.' I pause. 'I'd like to settle down. I have done travelling. I'm over it.'

She looks at me. We are both quiet. 'For me, I don't think it can ever be. But, when this is all over, I hope you get *your* wish,' she says eventually. Her blue eyes are moist.

I have no smart words. What a generous thought. I can only manage, 'Thank you. Think positive. A day at a time.'

Lady Meredith

A polished Bentley passes through the iron gates, the chauffeur guiding the car smoothly along the drive to the former stately home, set among grassy lawns and old spreading trees. It is a beautiful place for an exclusive nursing home.

Lady Meredith insists on walking slowly, with her cane, into the building. She moves steadily, with a sense of power and gravitas. A bespectacled slim doctor, in his fifties, meets her in the lobby.

'How is he today, doctor?'

'Comfortable, Lady Meredith,' is the reply.

They walk together into the downstairs room where Sir Terence lies on his bed. Quiet classical music is playing in the background. He looks clean and relaxed, hair brushed, head on a raised pillow. His eyes are open but staring ahead.

'Can you hear me, Terry?' she says quietly. There is no response. No movement of the body or eyes. It is as if there is no-one in the room.

'He can probably hear you, Lady Meredith,' the doctor assures her. 'It is important that you talk. It is possible he is registering but his brain is in such shock that he can't make anything move, like a type of stroke.'

She nods, angry that it has come to this. She holds his hand; her caring supportive husband – a noble knight, a gallant man who has treated her so well for all of the decades of their marriage. A loving husband, a grandfather and great-grandfather. The doctor leaves quietly.

She can handle him being ill, even in this detached state. Her anger is not at him or at God for allowing this to happen. Her anger is directed at the international criminals who have hi-jacked her husband's integrity; who seduced him into foolish and illegal acts by playing on his vanity, his need to feel important.

And now powerful law-enforcement agencies would expose her husband's frailties without any thought for the huge personal impact on an important family or the prestige of a nation which had made him a knight. There are bigger agenda at play. Yet, police minds can be so petty, so narrow minded.

She is now the custodian of her husband's reputation and she will not allow a good life be vilified at its end, by his foolishness. There are generations of younger Sedgewoods who need to feel proud of Sir Terence and his achievements – not ashamed that their ancestor blew all of his good works in a few moments of madness near the end of his life.

'Don't worry, Terry,' Lady Meredith chats away to her unaware husband. 'I have spoken to the key players. This mess will never reach the public arena. Your reputation will be unsullied. All you have to do is get better. Take your time.'

* * * *

An hour later, the dignified lady has cried all the tears she could muster, in private. She has maintained a long monologue without any reaction from her spouse.

She will return again tomorrow and tell him another warm story of family and happiness; from a heart that has loved him for nearly sixty years.

She kisses his forehead gently, picks up her cane, bids the doctor farewell and walks with aged poise to the Bentley.

Nagada Lagoon

There was never going to be much sleep beside the Nagada Lagoon.

The best way to reassure the captives, Ben says, is to be around a roaring fire. Warmth; light; a whole group who have endured together, sitting free of bonds; a time to talk or be silent, to hug; to feel pain or just to watch, to heal; perhaps to dream, to believe that there might be a future, beyond the torture they endured; happiness, hope.

Huts are there for any who wish to use them but no-one is leaving the circle of visibility, except to wash away the grime and taste of captivity in cleansing showers and fresh clothes.

The comforting flicker from the burning logs embodies safety, sanctuary and an emerging comfort that this freedom might be real, is true. Whispered conversations, tears, questions and occasional smiles.

Ben and his team stay in sight; compassionate; a supportive feeling of strength, of good; of reality – not intruding nor organising.

Alison is still dazed by all that has happened; the culture shock from Cairns to the release of the captives; and she hasn't slept – too much excitement pumping.

She has been resting a little, beside Ron, the larrikin Aussie; leaning against her in the tight fit of the circle. 'How did you come to be here?' she asks. 'Doing this work?' The campfire atmosphere is encouraging people to talk quietly to neighbours.

Ron seems unsure of what words to use. It is as if he wants to speak but is shy to reveal himself.

Perhaps it is Alison's manner, the soft, tired smile that gets Ron to start talking, in a whisper – of personal things. He speaks slowly, carefully, checking her reaction; as if he has always wanted to tell someone but has never felt it to be possible.

Gently, he tells how he lost his wife to breast cancer five years before, about his two boys, now aged nine and ten, living with his parents in Yeppoon in Central Queensland, and how he lost the plot when his wife died – couldn't handle the responsibility on his own.

Alison smiles encouragement. She thought that few men she had met would allow themselves to consider that personal observation. They always wanted to be seen as being so capable.

But Ron continues; he had gone to work in the mines. Big money. A fitter by trade. His chance to set up his boys.

It was at the mines that he had heard about Ben's group. The friend of a workmate had experienced *Nemesis* help, first-hand. Ron had liked the thought of helping others, meaningful work. Perhaps, he might be of use there.

In a rare rush of enthusiasm, he contacted Ben through the grapevine and he has been in New Guinea for the past three years.

'I would've liked it as it was, with my wife and boys; but that life has gone.' His eyes are dry and distant. 'Of course, I've been running away – and still am!' He gives a lop-sided grin as he speaks. 'I'm grateful my parents are giving the boys a stable childhood. Their mother would be pleased, I think. Better than a neurotic life with me. But hey! I've been helping people now. Maybe that's as good a reason as any, for me living on the planet.'

She doesn't say anything as he continues.

'I think I've been making a difference. You see them around you, just now.' He points at the freed captives 'That's got to be good. To help other people. But yes. I hope to return home eventually, a better person and a better father.'

She doesn't comment immediately.

'Do you know how Ben got into this?" she asks eventually. 'He seems very driven.'

'Ben?' His eyes seem to refocus on the present. He looks at her questioning face – soft eyes. 'I'm told Ben was Navy; special forces, a commando. When he retired from that life, he took his wife and daughter away for a year to sail the islands. He was in the Halmahera Sea in Indonesia just west of this big island that we're on at present when they were attacked by pirates.

'He'll need to tell you what happened. But it resulted in him setting up *Nemesis*. He works with international police forces to make it hard for these gangs. His special operations skills are very useful.

'You can imagine some of the raids he's been on. In recent times, he has been on the trail of the gang who organised the ship we raided tonight. He had a run-in about three years ago with the enforcer you heard the captain call *the Devil*.

'I believe he's called Len Williamson – a cruel malicious bastard from every report I've heard. He has a frozen face – can't move his cheeks to smile; the result of knife-fight with Ben on a Chinese junk. Ben's knife sliced nerves in his face as he escaped in the fight. Even after plastic surgery to hide the scars, the cheeks apparently still don't work the way they should. It will be an interesting confrontation if those two ever meet again.

'Williamson works with a man they call Peter Carter. You heard him mentioned tonight also. They both work for a more shadowy group headed, we think, by an Englishman called Roger Cavanagh.'

Alison feels the cold shivers again. Her Steve is on the *Lerna* with Roger Cavanagh – and she has heard that Peter Carter and Len Williamson have also rejoined the ship. Not good news at all.

'Ben has been trying to get evidence on Cavanagh for months,' Ron continues. 'Actions like tonight's tend to flush them out a bit; to get them to make mistakes. We hope we are getting closer to making their operations so inconvenient that the whole trade will stop.'

And Alison wonders about the story she'd heard weeks before from an old acquaintance of Brennan's. He was the one who had told her where she might find the *Nemesis* man on particular days in a Brisbane pub. He'd also spoken about why the retired special forces soldier was really in this business. He'd said that Alison looked not unlike Ben Brennan's daughter, who had died, years before, in Indonesia.

That was why he had reacted to her when she'd said, back in the Brisbane bar weeks ago, *I was told you would understand what it means to someone like me, particularly like me. That's why.*

Roger and Peter Carter

Coral Sea. Monday 19 February 2007

'Roger,' says Peter Carter, 'our watchers in Honiara tell us a pearling lugger set out from the Solomons for Milne Bay a day ago. It's crewed by homeless kids – orphans – who are learning how to work sails on a boat with no power. Do you see the potential for maintaining our product lines?'

'These are dangerous times,' his boss replies. 'There are groups chasing us down at this moment. What is the benefit for us?'

Peter always likes the way his boss talks in terms of commercial needs. He doesn't get emotional. This is a business – no place for wimps.

'We need to feed the *product* in at the bottom end,' says Carter, 'or the line will dry up. Don't we?'

'Where is the trunk ship at the moment?' Cavanagh smiles indulgently at Carter's mirroring of the *Ramas* language.

'Moving along the north coast of New Guinea. But the *Shinwuan* left Makira in the southern Solomons a day ago. It will be close to this pearling lugger before long. We could attack from the *Shinwuan*, take the *product* on board and catch up with the trunk freighter somewhere around Zamboanga in the Philippines.'

'Do you have a team?'

'Even with Len away, there's a proven team on the *Shinwuan*.'

After a minute's thought, Cavanagh boldly says, 'Go for it.'

Eavesdropping

Cairns. Monday 19 February 2007

Back in the critical incident room, Sergeant Bill Jones finalises his recording of the conversation between Carter and Cavanagh.

Another hi-jacking in the planning!

Incredible. We have them on the ropes. What are they thinking?

With a sense of urgency, he picks up the phone to advise Jeff Fowler but his boss's secure line is engaged.

The scrambler call

The pale purple flashing light on his teleconference phone is the constant confirmation to him that the scrambler is working.

Fowler can hear them clearly. He has Eileen Lewis with him. Forbes and Weston are on the line from the *NPA* along with Broderick and Kennedy representing *Versec*.

Fowler has started by giving his situation report; the Navy tracking the *Lerna*, now well over half-way to Port Moresby and the monitoring of the microphones. He has told them about Steve Flynn, the man from the *Sea Spray* being on board and how he is working with the AFP.

He has explained about Brennan's group raiding the trunk freighter off Madang and how an independent investigative reporter has the whole episode on video; the captives, the captain, the crew, the damning comments about the link to Carter and Williamson who, Jeff believes, are on the *Lerna* at that moment.

Kyle Broderick speaks about the American investigation into the GBIB board of directors. His team has established significant corporate fraud.

The directors really are rich gamblers who have apparently become bored with the routine of investment banking, and have embarked on the more dare-devil approach of betting with borrowed money on long-shots.

Their problem has been that the long-shots keep coming up successfully. Well, they are very talented in the investment business. They can read trends. They have been doing it all their lives. So, armed with a belief that they are bulletproof, they have fallen even further for the seductive persuasion of an international fraudster known only as *Ramas*.

Ramas has allegedly shown them how to launder illegal money, which gives them more fuel for their gambling. The organised crime structure is another *Ramas* gift which, on the surface, leaves them all feeling rich, corporate and protected; but it has just led to a continual escalation of their risk-taking.

Broderick also advises they have clear confessions from several directors, which confirm that the arrangement with *Ramas* goes back over thirty years and that the current communication with the leader is through their chair of the board, Sir Terence Sedgewood, who is now poorly in England.

Ramas communication has apparently always been through a conduit, never in person with the source. They can't give any clue as to the identity of the person who set it all up.

At this stage of the investigation, Broderick isn't sure whether or not the directors are protecting someone very senior in Congress or within the machinery of government in Washington. He says that it won't surprise him if there is that link – but it hasn't been established yet.

They are currently checking into Sir Terence's associates in Washington to see if anything can be established there. They have uncovered that he has made several trips to CIA headquarters at Langley, Virginia, in the past.

Broderick goes on to explain the status of the investigation into the *Sea Spray*. In his view, there is a high probability that Cavanagh's late-appointed communications man, Bob Curtis, was the inside presence on Ingrid's yacht, orchestrating the attack on the *Sea Spray*.

The *Shinwuan* checks out as the likely staging post. The inside man had cleaned out all the personal effects of the two security guards before leaving the ship in Nadi – some slack scenes of crime procedures. Maybe they thought the crime part was over. Who knows?

Broderick says that he would not be surprised if the original stolen passports surface again in illegal operations somewhere around the world. It has appeared to the investigators that whole operation has worked like a business, recycling any valuables for the next criminal occasion.

Before passing to the *NPA* report, the *Versec* chief adds, 'I'm getting a lot of heat from somewhere high up. I don't know that any of the GBIB directors have the clout to influence a congressional committee – but I'm being told to back off and leave the *DNI* to oversee things. Naturally, I've told them where to go, but it's only a matter of time.'

'Have you established any link between GBIB and Roger Cavanagh?' asks Fowler.

'Only loosely through the *Sea Spray* matter, through Sir Terence being on associated boards – but, no, nothing concrete; nothing that would nail him in a court of law.'

Angus Forbes gives the *NPA* position. 'We have a *tech* who has cracked Cavanagh's encryption code so we are aware of the messages he is receiving and sending. We can't yet establish who is sending him messages or to whom the replies are going. The sources are still being shown as *anonymous*. It is a clever security program but we're working on it. I've no doubt Cavanagh is up to his ears in this and that the Australian video evidence might well link him in tighter.

'We have learned from the decoding that Cavanagh got a warning yesterday of a spy on his ship. He didn't hear it from us so I can only assume it has come from an Australian connection. He got an encrypted message from somewhere.'

There is a long silence from the Australian end; puzzled looks and memory searching. An incredulous Jeff Fowler eventually asks, 'Do you really mean you think that someone in Australia is a party to this encryption code? I'm staggered. I would have thought that the mastermind would be the only one with the code and he would be in Britain or the States.'

'I'm just giving information,' says Forbes. 'Sir Terence is out of the picture now. I'm told he's in an exclusive private hospital and that his mind has gone. He can't even recognise his wife. Like Kyle, we're getting heat to pause our work. My supervisor is a retired Brigadier. He's received word from the Minister that we have to back off. We can collect information but no action till we are advised.'

Broderick adds, 'You're right, Angus. Some bastard has put the fix in at the political level. He must be a powerful player that Cavanagh.'

'Well, I'm not going to be pushed around,' the Scottish detective states adamantly. 'I'm a policeman first and foremost. We have a crook, almost dead to rights, and I think we should be moving to trap him. We won't get him through the courts unless we nail him in the act, will we?'

Fowler, still recovering from the shock that a leak might have occurred from within his group, reminds them, 'Our plant on the *Lerna* has microphone bugs in several areas of the ship. We've already recorded Cavanagh's voice talking about his business; the connections with the South Pacific Freight Company; and how the books are fudged to conceal his involvement. We have a lot of information and we are collecting more each day. We would be keen to hold off any trap situations till we can at least get our people out of the danger area.'

Another long pause.

'It might be too late for that,' says Forbes quietly. 'We've sent a sailing boat – an old pearling lugger I think they call it – from the Solomons as bait for pirates who might want to capture potential slaves. We have floated the word that it's crewed by young orphans; people who won't have families asking questions if they disappeared. There are certainly young people in the crew, who can draw Cavanagh into the trap. We have a couple of agents with them, who can record and photograph; to get the evidence we need. They are briefed on what the targets probably look like. We'll have photos to share with each of you, when the snatch is made – for verification purposes.'

Fowler is rarely angry but his controlled ire could not be mistaken.

'You have no bloody authority to go off making crazy unilateral plans like that! You are putting the whole operation at significant risk. There are already many people on the ground working hard to nail this man. This is a mad plan! The lugger could be attacked by any mob of pirates. Even if Cavanagh did get involved, the path to his door would be swept clean. You are more likely just to scare him off somewhere where we can't monitor him.'

The gruff Scotsman is not used to taking backward steps. 'I'll have you know, my Aussie colleague, that we don't have the bloody luxury of waiting days or weeks to collect evidence. We may only have hours in business here. I think Kyle might be in a similar situation. We need to precipitate the action.'

A short silence.

'Anyway,' says Forbes. 'The lugger sailed yesterday and the word was passed around the Honiara wharf that it was headed for Milne Bay in New Guinea.'

More silence. Angry minds using all their discipline to keep the co-operative venture moving along.

'Well, we'll just have to manage the best we can with that scenario,' says Fowler, calm again, at least in his voice. 'Can I also tell you that our man on board advises us that Cavanagh is trying to set up some insurance. He asked his directors to find him a ship which could berth at a dock in Sydney Harbour. He wanted some leverage, some negotiating power. I am sure you can each imagine possible scenarios there. We are monitoring that situation in Australia but I suspect you should both be aware of a similar threat in your areas.'

Broderick's voice comes on, speaking calmly, as a mediating influence. 'Look, we've a lot of information about a whole range of crimes – but it is a jigsaw that hasn't yet been put together. There's the *Sea Spray* hi-jack and now the slavery angle. We've GBIB directors admitting to assisting the ransom demand and it was most likely their expertise that let the hi-jackers conceal the passage of the money to the Swiss banks. They are also implicated in laundering huge sums of money which could be coming from SPFA. We have a circumstantial link with Sir Terence being the chair of the boards of both GBIB and SPFA.

'In short, we still don't have any documented evidence that Roger Cavanagh is linked into *any* of these affairs. Maybe your recordings will help, Jeff, but defence lawyers will claim it is inadmissible evidence.

'There's nothing hard, yet. We need proof – and we don't know who this *Ramas* is. So I'm not overly bothered about Angus's lugger ruse if it gets us proof. But, you're right, Jeff, it'll be bloody hard to tie him into it. He's a cunning coyote.'

There is silence.

'Well, have we all laid our cards on the table?' Forbes asks brusquely. 'Is there any more we need to share?'

Fowler says, 'No more from here. We'll keep you advised as things develop and send copies of the recordings as they come to hand. They may match something you have. We would be really keen to know the content of any encrypted messages in real time, Angus, if you can do that.'

Angus indicates to Catherine, to assure that will happen.

'We can do that,' Forbes replies. 'Kyle? Anything?'

'No,' he replies thoughtfully. 'You're up-to-date on our progress. We can't move any further with GBIB until the *DNI* approves our actions. We're keen to know anything about *Ramas*. We've no clues. Send us anything.'

The conference finishes with the usual sign-offs.

'I don't see how it is possible for someone in Australia to reveal that Steve Flynn is our contact on the *Lerna*,' Fowler says to Eileen Lewis. 'And then get that information to the source of the encryption? Bizarre and impossible. It has to be someone in the States or Britain with the encryption code. The message was sent to Cavanagh. Any more on a ship coming into Balmain?'

'Only what I have told you,' replies Lewis.

'Check with everything Bill Jones has up in Cairns. Maybe your fresh eyes will see something we've all missed. I've a feeling we are near the end game here.

'Oh, and can you check with the International Maritime Bureau in Kuala Lumpur, please. Perhaps their data bases on vessel attacks could show a correlation that might be useful. At the very least, they will need to have our information logged for future matching.'

As Lewis leaves the office, Fowler's secure phone rings. The caller ID shows that it is Bill Jones calling from Cairns.

Alison and Ben Brennan

New Guinea. Monday 19 February 2007

Alison is feeling excited and exhausted, almost simultaneously; and she has the sense that yesterday's action was only a foretaste of what life is like in the company of Ben Brennan.

The Air Nuigini flight from Madang to Port Moresby is uneventful. Tom and Ron accompany Ben and Alison back to the capital. Harry and Mike remain in Madang to start the delicate process of supporting and repatriating the captives.

Back at the hotel, Alison burns two DVDs of the video from the trunk freighter. On Ben's instruction, she sends one to Jeff Fowler in Canberra and the other to Mal Willis in Cairns. The original recording remains in the camera memory stick.

Ben gets an update from the network. The *Lerna* hasn't arrived yet but it will probably pass by Moresby on the next day.

There is word from the Solomons about a potential situation developing. A sail-training ship has set out on the previous day for Milne Bay. The word on the docks is that it is crewed by children, learning to work as a team on a lugger.

'The young people are apparently from orphanages,' says Tom as Ben shakes his head and grimaces.

'Ron, talk to Bill Jones,' says Ben. 'I want to be informed on my satellite phone about that boat – ongoing information. A tempting prize for Cavanagh's people – but, maybe, he'll be cautious given all that's going on.'

Alison hides her bewilderment.

An hour or more of telephone calls. Plans are being made.

Ben speaks with Mal Willis in Cairns, wanting to know what has been recorded from the *Lerna* microphones about the sailing lugger from the Solomons.

Willis confirms Cavanagh's approval for an attack from the *Shinwuan*. And Brennan briefs on the DVDs which will be posted to him and Fowler within the hour.

* * * *

Brennan whispers only to Alison. 'We've made video interviews before; not the raw images of actual slave ships like you have taken but still real people's voices and faces. Last year, I even hid a note in a native mask which I thought was being sent up the line to the controller of this trade – but nothing seems to have come of it.

'It gave a closed internet link to the video interview with a released slave; a moving, harrowing story. I had hoped someone on the other end would feel the tortured grief in the wailing voice and understand the pain that they cause at our level – but they probably couldn't care less. No conscience. It's all about money and power.

'But *your* video, Alison, shows the scene first hand. They'll nearly be able to smell it all from the pictures. Very powerful evidence that we can use in a court.'

Alison listens in a kaleidoscope of thoughts as he briefs her about the *Nemesis* men in Alotau, John and Karl.

She is getting used to the nicknames. She cheerfully expects each would be a Nuigini native, just as Mike has been.

The plan is to fly to Gurney Airport in Milne Bay province today and pick up a fishing boat from Alotau, the provincial capital. Ben insists that they need to be well ahead of the *Lerna*. So they will sail from Alotau to a waiting fishing boat at Samarai. That is the area which would be closest to the *Lerna's* path and they will be ready to move to wherever the action might be.

344

A fishing boat doesn't travel as fast as a freighter or the *Lerna*, but they would have inflatables on board. If they were close by, then they would have a chance.

Alison would not be travelling on the fishing boat. The danger is too great. She will remain in Alotau under the protection of Tom, whom she has come to know and trust. Ron and Ben would lead any attack party.

Alison wants to argue about getting footage as evidence.

Ben pulls her quietly to the side and says, 'I think you're a brave young woman for even coming this far. Trust me, if there is any action around the sailing lugger, it will not be as peaceful as what you saw on the trunk freighter. I need you to stay safe in Alotau with Tom. No matter what happens, he will get you out through the network to Cairns again.'

A cold shadow of dread envelops Alison as Ben talks – about perhaps not coming back. The worry must be showing on her face.

'I told you weeks ago you should stick to the court circuit.' He speaks with just a trace of a bleak smile. 'I'm really proud of what you have achieved here. In more ways than you would realise, you are very precious to me.'

Her eyes widen in the poignant silence. Then the long-awaited words start to flow. He needs to say something, to help her understand the pain.

'Years ago, my wife and daughter were taken by pirates, *pedagang budak* they are called, slave traders, over in Indonesian waters. I let my family down on that occasion and … they died. You remind me very much of my beautiful daughter. I wouldn't want you to be harmed in any way.'

For the first time, Alison can see a moist emotional glint in his eyes.

'Please.' His voice quivers. 'For me! Stay with Tom in the safety of Alotau.'

Gina on the *Lerna*

'Roger, Steve told me you received the most magnificent sapphire yesterday. Is that right?'

Gina, with a towel slung over her shoulder, is just walking past Roger in the suite office. He is stooped over his laptop. Still lost in thought, he looks round. The mention of the word *sapphire* suddenly lights up his face.

'It's a beauty, Gina,' he exclaims. 'You'd love it. Let me show you.'

He turns to the Polynesian mask on the wall and pulls it back on its hinges. Gina stands close to his right shoulder as she says, 'Terrific. I'd love to see it.'

The dial on the safe spins and Gina remembers the numbers where it stops: 20, 3, 11. The safe door swings open and Roger removes a cloth-covered package from the papers, tagged keys and money in the strongbox.

She looks at the deep blue of the cleaned part of the gemstone and lets an affected wonder come into her voice. 'Oh, it's *beautiful*, Roger. Well done! A marvellous stone. Thank you for letting me see it and touch it.' Her finger strokes the polished part.

'I'm afraid,' he says protectively, 'that is as close as you will get. It'll be faceted and sent to an important person in the organisation.'

'No worries. It's enough to see it ... and your happiness. Thank you!' She pecks his cheek and leaves her emperor feeling quite euphoric.

Nemesis planning

New Guinea. Monday 19 February 2007

'The biggest weakness in this whole process is that we can't get in touch with him.' Ben expresses his frustrations as the thoughts tumble through his mind. 'We can hear his updates but we can't tell him what we need him to understand.'

Alison says innocently, 'I have Steve's ship-mobile number. Would that work up here? We exchanged mobile numbers in Cairns.'

'You little beauty! You betchya it'll work. Ship phones work through satellite connections. As long as his phone's charged, we're in business.'

He notes Steve's number; to be used only in an emergency.

* * * *

The flurry of organising makes the time pass quickly; regular phone conversations with the network booking rooms and fishing boats. Ben needs scuba gear for at least two people.

Bill Jones in Cairns is able to brief on Carter's plan to fly to somewhere called Misima and to link up with the attackers from there.

* * * *

By ten o'clock, they have checked out of the hotel and are on their way to Jackson Field at Port Moresby Airport.

It is a short flight tracking down the southern coast of New Guinea until they swing in over the cleared slopes of Milne Bay province into Gurney Airport.

Alison is getting used to the New Guinea airstrips with their limited terminal facilities. But, once you know what to expect, they actually feel like important symbols of civilisation in a country where many still live very close to nature.

The aged vehicle which takes them into Alotau would have been a rust-heap on the streets of Cairns but here it is sparing them all a long walk from the airport to town.

Alotau is a busy provincial centre for Milne Bay. There are aromatic markets, smoky vehicles, bustling ships in port and throngs of smiling people.

Alison and Tom get settled into a two-room house with a strong thatched roof supported on wooden and woven-thatch walls. It isn't luxury but it will give shelter from the weather. They should merge easily into this rushing little centre – although she doesn't see any other women of her age or race in the streets.

Ben and Ron leave quickly, with rucksacks, scuba gear, satellite phones and weapons. They need to be on the water, heading for Samarai, closer to the shipping lanes. Samarai is the old colonial administrative centre, with commercial services like banks, a Customs base and lots of history.

The welter of activity finally passes. Alison settles down on the stretcher-bed in the house, to collect her thoughts and prepare for the inevitable new frenzy of activity when Ben returns in about a week's time.

The *Lerna* and Port Moresby

New Guinea. Tuesday 20 February 2007

Steve Flynn stands outside on the bridge parapet as the captain noses the *Lerna* towards the harbour in Port Moresby.

He can see the stilt village to the west where the houses are built out over the water – sparkling in the bright heat. The air feels moist to breathe. The tops of massive mountain ranges to the north disappear from sight into clouds. The capital city itself, has the look of a business centre with low office blocks and buildings stretching into the distance.

No-one is expecting the ship to stay long. A luxury ship at the wharf for any length of time might embolden attention from local gangs. The captain will take on fuel then register his course round the south-eastern tip of New Guinea, north through the Solomon Sea and up into the Bismarck Sea … and he will sail without delay.

Peter Carter clears his plans with Roger. They discuss them in the suite office while the mini-microphone duly beams the signal to the 'spectacle case' in Steve's soft bag and then out to an innocuous fishing boat on the horizon.

Bill Jones's listening ears and digital recorders follow every word. Bill also registers that the tracking devices are showing Alison in Alotau and Steve on the *Lerna* in Port Moresby. Everything is working as intended. Everyone on the tracking side is as informed as they can be.

Carter disembarks for the task ahead. His Air Nuigini flight is booked to the Misima Island airstrip on the island near the end of the Louisiade Archipelago, off the south-east tip of New Guinea.

From there, a fishing boat will take him out to sea for a rendezvous with a large freighter, the *Shinwuan*, sometime in the late evening.

* * * *

Gina can sense the change in Roger's mood. He is always at his most intense before big plans are about to unfold. He has been engrossed on his laptop, monitoring something – perhaps the fluctuations in the world monetary market.

She stays away from the sundeck while the boat is berthed in Moresby. No need to draw attention. There will be time enough to relax out there when they are out at sea again.

Roger has said little to her – just part of the furniture these days. Used to being ignored, she prefers to catch up with Steve. Their little chats lift her spirits. Something is about to happen. It is in the air.

She sees Peter Carter leave the ship carrying a backpack, off on another trip.

Steve routinely checks and cleans the weapons from the gun lockers. 'Force of habit', he says. But he isn't convincing. She can taste the tension.

She prepares herself mentally and physically, even putting together an emergency backpack that she can grab in a hurry if they have to evacuate.

And exercise. She has always maintained her model physique with a daily stretching routine but now she is doing sit-ups and push-ups as if she were training for athletics. The ship's gym gear is getting a workout too.

It is good to have motivation – but frightening too.

By midday, the *Lerna* casts off and is tracking down the coast towards Milne Bay.

Fowler and Catherine Weston of NPA

Canberra. Tuesday 20 February 2007

'Catherine, I needed to know this earlier! Bloody Special Boat Squadron, for goodness sake. They are the elite British forces.'

Jeff Fowler expresses the frustration of dealing with super-secretive overseas agencies. 'We have people who could get caught up in unnecessary firefights if they are not aware. The last thing we need is *blue on blue.*'

Catherine Weston has just told Fowler, over the secure phone, that there are no orphans on the sailing lugger heading over to New Guinea. Indeed, the crew is entirely SBS specialists, not just a couple of agents trying to collect evidence.

'And what is their back-up?' he asks.

'Angus's view is they will capture the attackers and hold them for testimony. He expects he might apprehend either Peter Carter or Roger Cavanagh in the sting. At the very least, he expects to get a red-handed link to Cavanagh.'

Fowler gives out an exasperated sigh as he sanitises the oaths from his words. 'Like I said on the teleconference, it's ... mad. They expect to capture an unknown number of men and just sail with them into New Guinea waters? Is the ... British Navy in the area, perhaps?'

'I haven't got that detail,' says Catherine. 'This was initiated very quickly as a circuit-breaker to being stymied in high places.'

Fowler shakes his head with frustration. 'We have *Nemesis* entering the area. They've just freed the captives off Madang. Without knowledge that it's SBS troops on board … potentially lots of friendly forces could die in the mêlée. I repeat, we really don't need a *blue on blue*. It's lunacy to have these unilateral bright ideas. Shit!'

He pauses for several seconds before continuing, 'I'll speak with the Australian Navy. They have the authority to take the pirates into custody under the 2005 protocols to the Rome Convention on Piracy. Then at least we can have some control over the legitimacy of any capture.'

Catherine remains silent.

'Are you in communication with the lugger?' Fowler asks impatiently. 'By coded transmission or radio contact? They need to know of the existence of our *Nemesis* team and of the potential presence of the Australian Navy. We'll try to get word to our people but they may already be out of contact. This is not pretty, Catherine – not pretty at all!'

'I note your concerns.' Her tone is contrite. 'It wasn't a deliberate act not to keep the Australians informed. We will try to minimise the risks to your people and ours. We will try to make the best of the situation, Jeff.'

* * * *

Fowler is still fuming as he gets through to the Deputy Chief of the Navy. He knows Catherine Weston is protecting her boss. Never apologise. But the lunacy of it all. At least the Australian Navy people seem pleased to get the extra information. They will work on how they might assist the British Special Boat Service if they come under attack or by taking captives off their hands.

Fowler then tries to phone through to Ben Brennan's satellite phone but he is unable to make contact. Satellite coverage is good but it isn't perfect. Eventually, he gets through to Tom in Alotau.

Tom is across the situation and undertakes to keep trying Ben's phone. He explains that Ben and Ron are already en route to Samarai, where they will be ready to support the lugger, with a forward base on Misima Island.

Lowering the phone, Fowler sits quietly, evaluating the potential scenarios.

He understands the intentions behind the British sting. What has already been set in motion can't now be stopped, but he needs to ensure that it is used to their best advantage.

Steve on the *Lerna*

South of New Guinea. Tuesday 20 February 2007

I sit on my bed, whispering my updates into the little microphone.

I have armed Gina and myself. I now know the code to the wall safe. All the weapons in the gun lockers are clean, loaded and ready for action. Both Carter and Williamson are off the ship, which is now making good speed towards the Milne Bay area.

I would really like to know what plans are unfolding ... but since that can't be, I can only put as many of my own plans in place for when the action starts.

Such is the life of a soldier – long periods of waiting, before fast and violent action.

Peter Carter and the *Shinwuan*

Misima Island. Tuesday 20 February 2007

Peter Carter lands at the small airstrip on Misima Island and is whisked away on a fishing boat to the *Shinwuan*, just over the horizon.

The plan is that, when the lugger is sighted, one inflatable with seven armed fighters will approach from the east under cover of the descending dark, while Carter will manoeuvre his fishing boat from the west in the sunset, between the lugger and Misima, drawing the attention of the people on board towards the land, not the inflatable.

On full darkness, the attack team will advance from the blind side and overpower the crew.

Then, Carter will bring the fishing boat alongside to take the *product* line of orphans on board. More inflatables will then transport the captives to the *Shinwuan* which is equipped to handle them until they reach a trunk ship a week later in the waters around the Philippines.

Carter has trained the *Shinwuan* team himself; the same team who accompanied him onto the *Sea Spray* so many weeks before.

For the moment, he and his two-man fishing boat crew will head back to Misima waters, throw a net over the side, pretend to fish and wait.

Bill Jones

Cairns. Tuesday 20 February 2007

The little microphones are working a treat.

Bill Jones is flat out making recordings of every conversation.

A methodical man, he now has a library of documented evidence to bring an international criminal to justice.

He is the listener and recorder – the fly-on-the-wall.

Ben and Ron

Ben receives the message from Tom as he arrives in Samarai.

So SBS troops are involved – his old unit. Just for a second, he pities the pirates who would go on board the lugger to confront those men.

For his part, he will stay in the background around Misima, in case they are needed.

Knowing the Navy is in the picture is comforting too.

His boat sails with Ron and him, leaving Karl behind to man the comms at Samarai.

They move through the magical lagoons of the Torlesses, in the northern line of the Louisiades Archipelago, towards Misima where they will await developments. He hopes his satellite phone will work well there.

The lugger

Solomon Sea. Tuesday 20 February 2007

Out on the Solomon Sea, the canvas is heavy and the rigging pulleys move slowly in the hands of the *orphans*. A passing fishing boat waves and they wave back.

The lugger is making good progress.

Just on the horizon, the sailors think they can see an island. Perhaps that would be Mount Sisa on Misima.

The sea is calm, just a gentle ocean swell. A few specks of tiny fishing boats can be seen far out in the open water. Their size contrasts with the brown bulks of the freight carriers as they plough their way ceaselessly through the warm blue waters.

The *Shinwuan*

On the *Shinwuan*, the location of the lugger comes in from a watching fishing boat.

* * * *

Carter lies underneath a shady tarpaulin on his fishing boat. His satellite-phone buzzes and he listens.

He makes some rapid calculations; position, sunlight and approaching dusk. The former Army officer completes his computations and translates them into orders for his team. The attack is ready.

* * * *

After dark, the Shinwuan team will approach the lugger with muffled oars from the darkness while, on the island side, the brightly-lit fishing boat would be making noise with drums, traditional instruments and singing. The glowing lanterns and festivities should be the focus of everyone's attention on the lugger.

Once the prize has been taken, the team will fire a green flare – the signal for the fishing boat to come alongside and more inflatables to approach from the *Shinwuan*.

Meanwhile, Carter lies back on the deck savouring the fading sunshine and remnant of the blue sky, while he processes all his information one more time.

He watches the contrail of a passenger aircraft, high overhead, as it cuts a scar across the early evening sky – an aloof technological marvel, oblivious to the timeless routine of salty netting on a fish-scaled boat deck which is being enacted so far below.

The *Lerna*

Panapompom Island, Louisiade Archipelago, south east of the New Guinea mainland. Tuesday 20 February 2007

'Let's go snorkelling tomorrow, Roger. What a super place.'

The water is so clear that Gina can see little blue fish swimming through the coral at least ten metres below the surface, even as the sunlight is starting to fade.

Captain Rodriguez has brought the *Lerna* silently into a picturesque lagoon a few kilometres short of Misima – an idyllic spot with low hills, lush rainforest, white coral beaches and coconut palms hanging almost to the water.

Gina's enthusiasm is rubbing off on Roger.

'Absolutely,' he replies with one of his rare happy grins of recent days. 'Let's have a holiday. This is a little sanctuary, isn't it?'

The attack

Solomon Sea. Tuesday 20 February 2007

The sun has set.

The lugger is close to the north-east tip of Misima Island. The fishing boat lies between the lugger and the land. Colourful, traditional lanterns dance gaily on the rigging to the vibration of two crewmen banging their drums, dancing and singing. It looks like some cultural celebration to attract fish.

Carter is sure that every eye on the lugger will be looking at the fishing boat. To any observer, it would appear that their nets are in the water but it is merely an illusion in the dark.

The boat looks magically bright as it drifts closer to the shape of the lugger, which is lit only by tiny navigation lights.

Closer, closer.

Thirty metres away, closing, and the noisy dancing continues. Carter is steering; shielded by a big coolie hat and the shadow of the darkened wheelhouse.

* * * *

The inflatable from the Shinwuan approaches. It has used a muffled engine to about three hundred metres in the darkness. Now, it is being paddled silently over the last darkened stretch – the same technique that they had used on the *Sea Spray* off Fiji.

It edges gently alongside the lugger and two pirates creep aboard; armed with clubs, pistols and machetes. Others follow quickly over the side. They can see people shapes at the far gunwale, watching the fishing boat performance and then … a flurry hurtles at them, noiselessly.

Grunts and thumps as short heavy clubs are laid into the intruders.

* * * *

A gunshot echoes, followed by a brief crackle of muffled coughs; moans.

In that time, seven intruders have been immobilised by the SBS troops. Five are secured with long cable ties and potential calls for help are cut off by gags. Two others in the inflatable are dead.

The whole action took no more than a minute. There were only a few whispers of communication.

The lugger is silent again.

* * * *

On the fishing boat, Carter is thirty metres away. He has heard the gunshot and scuffling sounds, even over the loud singing and drumming noise from his own boat.

He waits for the green flare, checking his timings and listening for more sounds that the lugger has been secured.

Some rattling, a pinhole-type light flickers and then everything is quiet.

Five seconds, ten seconds, fifteen seconds – something is wrong.

The fishing boat is still metres from the lugger and a hundred metres from shore.

Twenty seconds.

Carter turns the wheel to nose the fishing boat away when he hears a muffled outboard start. That is not in the plan. Something has gone wrong.

He tells the fishermen to steer the boat north, while he slips over the side, with his small backpack secured, and starts to swim silently for shore; away into the darkness, away from the boats, without any splashing.

363

* * * *

The scuffle on the lugger had been fast.

Five men had come over the side initially and been taken out by short heavy clubs to the head. A shot from the attackers had escaped in the darkness; the coughs of silenced weapons responded.

A sailor now goes over the side to secure the inflatable boat, with its two dead occupants.

A quick flash of a pencil torch reveals the identities of the intruders. Peter Carter is not one of the captured – nor is Roger Cavanagh.

The leader is not on the inflatable. The fishing boat? Must be.

The inflatable is deployed immediately within thirty seconds of the first action. The four SBS men on board reach the fishing boat within ninety seconds and two personnel go on board. A quiet call of 'Negative', from the fishing boat and the inflatable starts its search of the inky waters between the boats and the shore.

A powerful floodlight shines from the lugger, trying to pick up the head of a swimmer or phosphorescence from swimming strokes. A hundred metres of gently chopping sea needs to be searched.

There is nothing.

The watchers patrol in the inflatable, going straight into the shore and gradually zig-zagging their way back out to the boats. If Carter is there, he is well hidden.

* * * *

Peter Carter is not in prime physical condition. But he has more than a usual surge of fear coursing through his body.

He swims silently, slipping below the water for about twenty seconds at a time as the searchlight pans across. He has all night to cover the distance to the beach as long as he stays hidden.

Slowly he works his way south, away from the obvious short path to the shore. The current helps carry him. When he is over fifty metres away from the boats, he slowly heads shorewards, stopping regularly for a floating rest.

An hour later, he drifts onto the coral sand of the beach. Timing his movement, he moves quickly over the five metres of loose debris to the tree line – and rests, watching the activity on the water. He can't stay long. By daylight, or even before, the sailors would land on the beach and find his tracks.

Suddenly, a huge tropical downpour falls out of the heavens.

He allows the rain to wash the salt from his clothes and skin. He bends a banana leaf to collect water to drink and gradually his pulse rate slows to normal.

He knows he would be on the north-east shore of Misima Island. He is going to have to walk over the forested country to get to the southern shore. He needs to keep away from the beach and his enemies. When safe, he will contact the *Lerna* for help. Grabbing a couple of coconuts, he shakes them to ensure there is liquid inside. He puts them in his soaked backpack with his bush knife, pistol and waterproof satellite phone.

With one last look at the boats out from the beach, he moves quietly into the forest up the steep slope away from the shore.

* * * *

'Seven intruders, five captured of whom three are wounded, plus two dead.'

The lieutenant-commander of the Australian Navy patrol boat takes the message from the lugger. The patrol boat moves to within a kilometre under cover of darkness.

The crew take five captured intruders and two deceased into their custody under the 2005 Rome Convention on Piracy.

The naval commander reports to Australian headquarters, confirming that none of them fit the description of either Peter Carter or Roger Cavanagh.

The briefing is immediately beamed to Jeff Fowler who contacts Mal Willis and, by satellite phone, to Ben Brennan.

The vessel will bring the captives back to Australia under guard, pending further instructions.

Panapompom Lagoon

Panapompom, New Guinea. Wednesday 21 February 2007

A beautiful morning breaks over the Panapompom lagoon.

Roger Cavanagh has woken early and he checks his messages.

Nothing relating to Peter Carter's mission.

He walks up to the bridge where Captain Rodriguez is enjoying the peace of the tranquil setting.

'Any messages, Captain?'

'One from the freighter, the *Shinwuan*, Sir. It simply says, *Minus seven. Moving on.*'

Roger understands the freighter captain's discreet cryptic message. Not good news.

But, no mention of Peter. He would have been the eighth, if more than the inflatable crew had been captured.

Hopefully, the resourceful old soldier has avoided whatever has gone down. Or he might be evading capture. Or perhaps, it could be even worse.

Whatever, it has been Peter's grand scheme and … it has failed.

They will just have to sit tight and await further information.

Panapompom Lagoon is a better place than most to hide out of circulation. There will be plenty of time for Gina's swim – when she wakens.

* * * *

Back at the office, Roger receives a stunning new message, relayed in encryption from the captain of the trunk freighter through Mr Masa at SPFA.

Their trunk freighter had been attacked off Madang and the entire current *product line* taken off.

What? Unbelievable.

Who? The next thought.

Damn Peter Carter, not being there to ask. This is operational stuff. This is why Carter and Williamson are employed – to be across whoever might try anything like this.

When? Several nights ago. The weekend?

He tries to put together the pieces of information as he reads on.

Is it an official boarding, like the Navy? No, surely Mr Masa would have mentioned that.

So, is it some freelance group of other pirates?

What is happening? No more details given. Damn them, for not knowing more.

Why has it taken so long to inform him? Where is the operational Intelligence that any general needs? Even Napoleon couldn't operate without good field information.

Heads will roll. Trust requires a firm but fair response. This is not at the acceptable standard for their sophisticated operation. But Roger needs information – and quickly.

With Peter Carter missing in action, Roger sends a brief cryptic message by email to Len Williamson – awareness; and another to Mr Masa for follow-up details from the trunk freighter captain.

Len Williamson

The frozen face of Len Williamson is as cheery as it can ever get.

His small cargo vessel has rendezvoused with the Korean freighter at sea. The sky is still dark but the crew are either watching or working as the ship's powerful derricks lift several pallets of sealed boxes on board.

Williamson nods his approval as they are concealed in the centre of a large batch of containers.

The computer entry on the captain's laptop gives the Korean captain confirmation of a substantial sum of money deposited into his personal account.

* * * *

Williamson leaves the area on his own vessel; then offloads to a fishing boat into Port Macquarie Harbour. The final stage will be a relaxing jet flight to Port Moresby to link up with the *Lerna*.

Waiting in the lounge for his flight, he receives disturbing email news from Roger about a raid on their trunk freighter north of Madang. The *product* line had been offloaded, videos had been taken, the whole operation has been potentially compromised. He knows that freighter and the captain. He has visited them before with Peter Carter.

Len thinks it through. This wouldn't be pirates. There is honour among thieves – and fear, if that doesn't work. They wouldn't attack an SPFA freighter.

The word, *Nemesis*, flashes through his mind. It is their style.

Ben Brennan.

A strong fury courses through him as he longs for the opportunity to meet again the man who had so damaged his face. The time could be near. If Brennan is indeed the attacker of the trunk freighter, he would still be in New Guinea – the land of the legendary *Rascal* gangs. Why, almost anything could happen to a man in that lawless culture up there.

The airport speakers advise noisily that his flight has been delayed.

He relaxes; savouring the revenge he has suppressed in deference to the wishes of Peter and Roger. But now, vengeance will be in all of their minds.

His discreet email to the *Lerna* comes back with a concise guarded message that they are working on it. No mention of *Nemesis* or Brennan, not even in their usual coded language.

They are too preoccupied to see the prime culprit, he thinks.

Len's leaders clearly need his assistance; he can sense that. This is a time for initiative, to repay his leader's faith in him. Settling scores has been part of his being, ever since the early days with the London gangs. There is a dignity in vengeance; in showing others that attacks on gang members would always be punished. That had been his job with the South London mob; maintaining the discipline, the code of honour.

He had learned his craft well; skill with weapons, of course, but most of it is in the mind games. Enforcing and protection are about intimidation; moving quietly, speaking gently – and carrying a big knife. His cheek skin strains as he remembers the hard men who had underestimated Len Williamson. They said he didn't have *the bottle* to take them on. Well, they had found out, hadn't they?

His old gang boss said he was doing a service, like a public executioner *taking bad boogers out of society*. That is how Len sees it too. There is discipline in being an enforcer.

Roger understands that really well too. He wants people to be respectfully intimidated – a silent message not to step out of line. Of course, you have to make an example every so often. Len finds that he can do that easily, like flicking a switch in his mind. He has no trouble at all inflicting maximum pain on the traitor to the cause; knowing that he is a master of his dark art.

It is about honour, a pride in being an effective protector.

That was how he met Roger in the first place, recommended when the South London mob was broken up and, from the moment they met, he could tell that Roger understood. He wanted controlled enforcement.

Roger has respected him; educated him to think about his role. He talks a lot about Napoleon and he calls Len his *Imperial Guard*, the elite.

How nice it is to be valued for your craft skills, not just for being the hired muscle.

Roger had talked to him about social service. Why should Len be any less valued than the police or the prison system? They are reinforcing one system of rules. Aren't there executioners in America, China and Indonesia? Why should Len be less valued?

Roger is really good with words, with explaining things, with valuing good servants to the company. Len has learned so much about people, from his leader.

And now, Len will repay the faith by taking Ben Brennan out. He doesn't yet know what is happening on Roger's world scene but he knows there is a lot of pressure around. His boss doesn't need to be harassed by that *Nemesis* mob.

This is a time for bold action, like he has learned about Napoleon. Hit hard and hit first. This is the time for the trusted 'Imperial Guard' to look after his emperor. He can't wait for his chance to be of service.

* * * *

The airport announcer advises the new departure time for his plane. He will be in the air soon. Straight flight from Port Macquarie to Port Moresby, then a short hop to Milne Bay – only a few hours in the scheme of things.

Brennan will meet his real nemesis sooner than he might realise. Len Williamson is on his way.

Peter Carter

Misima Island, New Guinea. Wednesday 21 February 2007

The rainforest is dark. The dawn lifts the light intensity to an eerie dark gloom. It enables Peter Carter to see how to move forward. He has stumbled his way through the wet forest all night.

A rushing brook is a good excuse for a drink stop. At least there is no shortage of water. He uses his bush knife to peel the fibre shell from one of his coconuts. The milk gives him nourishment before he presses on through less dense forest near the ridge top. No view of the sea but the land slopes away in front.

He takes his sodden phone from his back pack. Will it pick up a satellite?

He dials Roger's number and it rings. His boss seems pleased to hear his voice.

After a brief summary of the failed attack, Peter asks to be picked up the next day, somewhere on the south coast near Misima.

Then he switches the phone off to preserve its life.

Fowler

Dawn in Australia finds AFP Superintendent Fowler very busy. He has advised the *NPA* and *Versec* of the failed raid on the lugger. The prisoners will be brought back to Australian waters for interview. The *Shinwuan* is sailing on. It can be intercepted, if and when necessary.

He calls Inspector Mal Willis to clarify, tactfully and discreetly, how the situation has developed.

'It is a mess, Mal. Maybe, next time, operational matters will be discussed with experienced operators on the ground. Lucky none of our people appear to have been injured or killed. So, confirm for me, Mal, the *Lerna* is at Panapompom Lagoon? We assume Cavanagh is on board? No locations for others? Do I have it right?'

'That's as I understand it at the moment,' Willis replies. 'Bill is collecting a lot of very useful incriminating info – all being transferred to DVD. We'll certainly get Cavanagh for something, and it *will* stand up in court.'

* * * *

Fowler phones Eileen Lewis. 'Any word on that freighter for Balmain, yet?'

'No new requests at all for berthing. We had one Japanese vessel leave last week. The only other vessel due is a Korean freighter and it's been booked in for months. It's now scheduled to dock in two days, a day early. No others. Strange. Maybe the tip-off was wrong?'

'Okay. Anything from the International Maritime Bureau in Malaysia?'

'Negative there too. They're working on it.'

'Thanks.' Fowler dials Bill Jones's number.

Lady Meredith

London. Wednesday 21 February 2007

Lady Meredith is meticulous as she places the original paper sheets into the safety deposit box.

'They are secure now,' she murmurs. 'Leverage. Always the leverage.'

In the quiet of the bank vault, she looks at two sets of photocopies. One would travel back with her in the thick beige envelope to the safe at the Sedgewood family home. The other is placed in a second envelope, inside another, addressed to the family's solicitors in *the city* of London – extra insurance.

She smiles as she makes her slow walk from the secure area of the bank. How lucky that she had insisted over the years that Terry tell her about the people he was working with and the diplomatic schemes in which he had become involved.

How wise she had been to have kept detailed records – the training drummed into her at Bletchley Park, when that stately home and its many huts had been the centre of deciphering in the war. And it had been a part of her disciplined life ever since.

Terry had dismissed her record-keeping as *a terrible waste of time*. He wouldn't be saying that now, if he was able to talk. But he *had* kept a journal, of sorts. Not a detailed diary but occasional names which alluded to events. She had found it in his study desk drawer – locked.

Over the years, he had told her lots of innocuous chat about the influential people; high in government, in international Intelligence; power-brokers, billionaires, leader of states and criminals. She understood that – that was the world they both inhabited.

There had been deals, coups, international manipulation, alliances and deception – but he hadn't spoken of his possible compromised involvement. Maybe he had hoped that it would resolve itself in the course of time – lost in the protected secrets of business and diplomacy.

As she had forced the desk drawer, she hoped the journal might help join some of the many dots in their shared pasts.

Indeed, her study of Terry's notes had indeed jogged her memory. Most of it was confirmation of her own records.

Then, the journal mentioned *Butch*.

Now that was and is a revelation, in many ways – a real *jewel in the crown* for the times ahead. Cliff Butcher, *Butch*, had worked with her husband in the past, in diplomatic circles, but not under that name. That was a confidential name. She knew the other names.

The pieces are clicking together in Lady Meredith's mind as she approaches the bank's ornate doors.

What a pity Terry hadn't actually told his Merri everything. He had never mentioned his concerns about the gamblers in the American merchant bank. For whatever reason – guilt, shame, misplaced pride or perhaps even someone with a hold over him – he had not disclosed his association with Cavanagh or the organisation in which he was now embroiled. He might have been spared this debilitating end to a long and successful life.

But then, men get arrogant with power, don't they? she thinks. *They don't have a woman's intuition about what could go wrong, years into the future.*

No matter. She will manage things for him now. She is in charge.

Was it ever really not so? She gives an enigmatic smile.

She is not surprised that so many people have been instantly receptive to her requests; they have far too much to lose, if this were to get out.

But *Butch* ... now *Butch* has been a coup. He makes the difference. What a surprise.

Now she can call in the favours for the deeds of years gone by and for keeping silent about things which would compromise, not just people, but organisations and governments.

She smiles as she leaves the bank. She has been used to being obeyed for a long time. After all, she *is* the lady of the manor.

Pressure on Versec

Larry Kennedy is frustrated, angry. 'I don't believe anyone could influence a congressional committee to put this investigation on hold. Jeezus, it's too important.'

'You'd better believe it.' Kyle Broderick looks tired. 'I've just come back from a meeting with the *DNI* and Congressman Legrand. We've been told to stop. They say it's just for the moment but it's a *Stop*.'

'But we've got him,' says Kennedy. 'The Australian recordings, the monitored emails, the ship in the Bismarck Sea and the captives from the British sting? If you add that to the confessions from GBIB – we have him; surely?'

'That's the cop in you talking, Larry,' says Broderick. 'I gave them all those arguments. I even suggested they send an American warship to intercept the trunk ship on its way to the Philippines. Gee, there are enough US ships in those waters, sailing out of Guam. D'you know what they said?'

Larry looks questioningly at his boss.

'They said, *What? Send an American naval vessel to intercept a Panamanian-registered vessel with a Russian crew in international waters? Have you any idea of the diplomatic furore that would cause?* That was what they said, Larry. They are covering their political bums.'

'And when I accused them of that,' he continues, 'they said, *This is much more sensitive than mere politics, Kyle. We're now dealing in the classified secrets of the United States of America; and perhaps other countries too. We are in areas we can't discuss. So, accept what you are being told. Back off. Got it?*'

Broderick groans with weariness.

'What can you say to a conversation stopper like that?' he says and sighs. 'I tried, Larry. Believe me, I tried. It's over. Take it on the chin and we live to fight another day. The first rule in policing – turn up to police another day.'

They sit quietly, dejection sagging their faces. Someone had gotten to the higher powers and pulled the plug. Wheels within wheels.

Roger's plan at Panapompom Lagoon

Panapompom Island, New Guinea. Thursday 22 February 2007

Roger's laugh resonates over the water as he floats on the crystal surface.

Gina turns to laugh back before duck-diving through the clear lagoon after a playful green turtle. She is a graceful swimmer. The turtle wins the race but appears to enjoy the game because he comes back to taunt her once more.

'How long has it been since we have laughed like this?' Roger asks, as the grinning Gina bobs up beside him. It is as if they are back in the Mediterranean, swimming off the *Ajaccio 3* in a secluded Corsican cove. How has it all slipped away?

His silent thoughts question his priorities of recent years. These are the times he has been working for – the laughs, the exclusive locations, the fruits of his wealth. He has lost his focus recently.

* * * *

I sit high above, on the rail of the Lerna, with a high-powered rifle across my knees – insurance against nosy sharks. I can see to the lagoon floor, some ten metres below the surface. From this vantage point, I would have no difficulty in picking up approaching danger.

Roger looks at ease. It is the closest I can remember seeing him match the charismatic smiling emperor who came aboard at Noumea; living the lifestyle which his wealth should allow.

Gina swims so effortlessly. I smile wistfully. She is at last having some fun. What a contrast from those many boring days when she has just lain with a book on the sundeck.

But this is relaxing time. Roger has told me this morning that the *Lerna* would stay at this lagoon for a few days and he couldn't have picked a better spot.

He wants me to take the tender to the east in the direction of Misima when he gives the word – probably around midday. Peter is in trouble and needs to be picked up. The tender will handle the short voyage easily. At nine metres, it is bigger than many of the local fishing boats. The waters would be gentle in the lee of the island and I would take two experienced crewmen.

It isn't for me to ask questions. I am an employee first and foremost, being careful not to overstep the trust my employer seems to have bestowed on me. Meanwhile, I continue to relish Gina's enjoyment in this wonderful tropical setting. She is indeed a good-looking woman … and perhaps also, a good actress.

* * * *

The captain gives me a refresher on the tender; the GPS system, sonar for the concealed reefs, radio link with the *Lerna* and the on-board emergency equipment, including a superb first-aid kit.

The weather-tracking shows no disturbances and I have offloaded some well-maintained armaments from the gun-locker onto the tender, just in case.

Gina gives us a farewell wave from the upper deck as we set off eastwards to our waiting location. It is a beautiful tropical day, with peaceful seas and the scents of lush forest plants carried on the sea air.

Peter Carter

Misima Island, New Guinea. Thursday 22 February 2007

Carter is bruised, scratched, tired and hungry. There have been plenty of clear forest streams for water but he has been living off the fleshy roughage of two coconuts.

Better than nothing – but not a lot better. With his stomach rebelling with cramps, he wonders how people survive in this jungle – and, just for a second, his admiration for the native people rises.

He's been making his way down-slope all day – no longer the fit soldier of past years. The occasional glimpses of the sea in the distance lift his spirits. He should reach the beach in a few hours. Then, he will be picked up and this torture would be over.

No recriminations. It was his idea to attack the lugger. He still can't understand what had gone wrong. Orphans on a boat? It makes no sense.

He won't complain. Roger doesn't like grumblers.

A good businessman draws a line under a failed transaction and moves on to the next venture. Only in the review of the business planning would you go back and examine the reasons why a particular transaction had not been successful.

Steve

Off Misima Island, New Guinea. Thursday 22 February 2007

The water is beautiful.

My voyage along the south coast of Misima Island is a gentle afternoon cruise. Fish jump and flap – sail fish or manta rays, at a guess. Some ocean mammals break the surface intermittently – dolphins, porpoises – a little distance away.

Forest-clad ridges rise on the left. Misima is a large island. One of the crewmen tells me that it was once important for gold mining. But the jungle looks impenetrable. An occasional native village breaks the vast greenery with huts built out on stilts over the water, small canoes tied up underneath.

We sail past the small port of Misima. My satellite navigation system shows an airstrip there. Some forest has been cleared. The tree clearing must have been the work of generations – it looks a massive task.

A few local fishing boats float idly with nets in the water. The crews give us a curious look; some wave – but we don't encourage any interaction. The fewer questions the better.

We will sit out in the water until further instructions about where to pick up Peter Carter – possibly in the early morning.

Ben Brennan

It is early morning.

Ben Brennan is relieved at the report of the comparative success of the SBS operation.

Carter?

Not captured.

Ben is already heading back to Alotau for better communication with the network and the outside world. He tries to ring Tom on the satellite phone but can get no answer.

He rings Karl, who is based down at Samarai awaiting Ben's return and gets through in three rings.

'It's funny, Karl,' says Ben. 'I get straight through to you in three rings and I can't raise Tom who is only fifty kilometres from you. Damned satellites! Get him to call me, please. I need to give him an update. Thanks.'

Off the Torlesse Islands, New Guinea. Friday 23 February 2007

Ben's phone rings. It must be the long-awaited call from Tom. It is his phone.

Brennan has been heading steadily back from Misima in the slow fishing boat. They are off the Torlesse Islands on the way back to Alotau.

'At last, Tom. Have you been asleep?'

It is Karl on the phone. 'Ben, I'm at Tom's place. He's dead.'

'Shit. Alison?' Ben has a rising dread as he asks the question.

'No sign. Definitely not here.'

'What happened?'

'Not pretty,' says Karl. 'Knife. He is messed up pretty bad. Not just stabbed. Brutal ... and something else. There are three letters daubed in blood on the mat beside him. They are L, A and F. I don't know what it means.'

'L, A and F?' Ben checks. 'LAF. Laf? Laugh! Oh, no!'

'What?'

The sense of horror is welling up inside him.

'My guess ... my guess is this is the work of Len Williamson.'

'Who?'

'A sadistic bastard who cuts people with a knife – the man who terrified the crew of the trunk freighter off Madang. He can't smile because I messed up his face in a fight a few years ago. He needed surgery and his tightened face doesn't move. Some have referred to him as *Laughing Len* since then – never to his face, mind you – because he *can't* laugh.'

The full significance of what had happened is sinking in.

'Karl, he has taken Alison captive then?'

'Hard to tell. It's possible. The hut is roughed up a bit. I'll get the network checking everything out. I'm real sorry about Tom. He was a good bloke.'

'Sure was.'

The venom of hatred laces Ben's tone.

Len Williamson

Off the Torlesse Islands. Friday 23 February 2007

Len Williamson calls Captain Rodriguez on the ship's satellite phone to get the location of the *Lerna*.

He himself is on a fishing boat, heading east, just north of the Torlesse Islands. There is a scatter of local fishing boats – some stationary, some moving with purpose.

His small boat will come alongside the *Lerna* with a package to be placed in the forward bulkhead room. He will need a couple of crewmen.

Is the tender available?

No, away with Steve Flynn to pick up Peter Carter.

Len doesn't ask questions. He'll call when the fishing boat is closer.

To Captain Rodriguez, the call is routine – a member of the ship's complement returning from an excursion.

He tells no-one else. This is captain's work – routine.

Len arrives

Captain Rodriguez watches the fishing boat approach. It enters the lagoon by sail but it is now changing to its motor – only a gentle diesel purr at that distance.

The captain speaks with Len over the phone and assigns two crewmen to assist him.

The *Lerna* basks gently in the middle of a hot day. Roger is in his suite on the laptop. Gina rests in the sundeck shade – her usual siesta.

The fishing boat comes alongside on the starboard. Len passes what looks like a long roll of matting to the crewmen. It isn't bamboo – more grassy reeds, bound together, like the flooring on the mud floors of huts.

Len leaps on board the *Lerna* and the fishing boat leaves with a wave to the captain on the bridge.

The two crewmen struggle with the heavy matting roll as Len unlocks the bulkhead storeroom. They manoeuvre the long load into the confined space.

* * * *

Gina sees the fishing boat with its distinctive sail moving into the lagoon.

A motor kicks in as it comes closer to the *Lerna*. Logical. No-one would be game to damage the glistening sapphire hull of this fine ship.

She wonders why the boat is coming so close.

Interested; she finds a spot on the deck where she can watch, discreetly.

Captain Rodriguez is on the bridge. He wouldn't normally welcome fishing visitors – and Steve is away with the tender to pick up Peter. He is the security.

She thinks fleetingly of going for the pistol she has hidden in her walk-in wardrobe. Then she sees the distinctive shape of Len Williamson on the fishing vessel. Now, she understands.

He has been gone since Cairns. How has he managed to mysteriously turn up in this lost lagoon?

Two crewmen take a long roll of matting from the fishing boat. They seem surprised by the weight. Something looks wrong with the roll. It isn't in fact a roll. It is more like a wrapping – covering something cylindrical in shape.

Gina casually makes her way down the port side. The men carry the weighty wrapping to the forward bulkhead storeroom. She stands very still in the port corridor, watching; unnoticed.

She has never seen that room opened before – but Len has a key.

She watches Len go inside the storeroom and emerge about fifteen minutes later, locking the door behind him.

How strange. Gina mulls over the scene and determines to let Steve know when he returns.

* * * *

Len has dismissed the crewmen, locking the door from the inside. Fitted cabinets and cupboards have been built onto the frame of the ship leaving a cramped floor space – a dusty place with a salty smell.

As Len cuts the ties to the matting roll, it falls apart to reveal the trussed form of an unconscious, dishevelled Alison Wood. A large bruise extends through her hairline onto the temple and past her eye. He checks for vital signs.

He wheezes as he loosens the gag to ease her breathing. He doesn't want her suffocating. This woman needs to be alive.

She is the bait to bring Ben Brennan to him. She is the woman that had a *Nemesis* agent guarding her. It was so strange for someone of her looks to be in Alotau when no cruise boat was docked. She must be very important to the *Nemesis* leader to need to be protected. Brennan won't be able to help himself from trying to save a woman in distress – any woman, let alone one that his men are sheltering. The clue in blood will get to him.

But he must be patient. Brennan's time will come.

With a chortle at his plan, he cuts the restraint and reties her to hooks in the bulkhead, placing the thick matting under her light body to muffle any movements of her wriggling body – no drumming heels to raise questions with anyone. He replaces the gag.

She is as comfortable as any prisoner of his would ever be. Satisfied, he locks the bulkhead door and heads off to the suite.

Roger would need to know he has returned safely and that the pallets have been safely stored on the Korean freighter bound for White Bay Wharf at Balmain.

His boss would be surprised and impressed by his initiative in finding his own way back to the *Lerna*. Roger is always pleased when his team think wisely for themselves. Initiative within parameters. Good training.

The captive in the bulkhead will be Len's secret, though.

He will wait until he has dealt with Brennan before he tells Roger of his brilliance. He will visit the girl regularly with water – and a bucket. What a thoughtful person he is.

Would Brennan appreciate his thoughtfulness? he wonders, with an evil chortle at the memory of his gory clue left on the matting floor of the hut in Alotau.

Carter on Misima

It has been daylight for a few hours when Carter finally drags his battered body through a tangle of vines and onto a narrow beach – not the white sandy coral of the northern shore.

The dark mud smells of decaying vegetation. But for all that, it is the most beautiful sight to his eyes. He collapses in an exhausted heap until an ant starts biting ferociously.

Stung into action, he extracts his satellite phone and calls Roger.

He believes he is somewhere to the east of the Misima settlement, shallow water. He asks for the tender to move along the coastline two hundred metres out to sea until he can spot it. He will then call Flynn's phone and guide them in.

Roger gives Steve's number to Peter.

Carter writes it in the dry mud and, so as not to lose his lifeline out of that God-forsaken jungle, he even takes out his knife and carves the number carefully into a fallen tree trunk – just in case.

His time through unforgiving jungle has knocked his natural self-belief down a notch. And yet, he knows he has done well to survive. He dozes until another powerful ant takes him to be a tasty morsel.

After two hours, Carter can see the shape of the *Lerna's* tender making its way along the coastline.

He rings Steve's satellite number and feels the rush of relief when it connects. He has been saving the battery and praying that the satellite would not let him down.

* * * *

The tender comes in as close as it can without bottoming out.

Carter wades out, thigh deep into the water.

'Swim to us.'

He forces his tired limbs … until strong arms pull him on board and he looks up into the grinning face of Steve Flynn.

'Welcome on board, Peter. Full circle, eh? My turn to rescue *you*.'

A faint smile is all Carter can manage to give his suffering thanks.

The crewmen swab him down with fresh water and start to treat his scratches with antiseptic swabs from the substantial onboard first aid kit.

* * * *

I am at the wheel, navigating back to Panapompom. I look across occasionally to the crewmen working on Carter's body. He looks as if he has been flogged with a lash. His whole body is scarred with red cuts and bites.

I almost feel some pity for him – almost.

No doubt, his story will unfold in time.

Ben Brennan

Ben Brennan is angry, very angry. He now has easy comms with Karl. He has pulled up among other fishing boats at the Torlesse Lagoon, lest they end up chasing their tails around the New Guinea islands. The network is searching for Len Williamson and a captive Alison. They will report soon.

Ben has been having flashbacks, of looking into the lifeless eyes of the two loves of his life: his wife, and the daughter who had looked like Alison Wood.

The ghost is with him again.

The same mirage – which rarely gives him peace. Two boats moored well out in the bay off the Indonesian *pulau*. He had located the *pedagang budak*. It was on dusk. Which boat held his wife and daughter? His swim to the first boat was done noiselessly, under-water for much of the way. The years of training were paying off. Gently onto the painted rail of the *perahu*. The heavy wooden boat scarcely moved with the additional weight.

The slavers were near the wheelhouse. Two of them. He could see one clearly, the other disappeared below. He attacked the first with the knife. The body slid silently to the deck; Ben's hand over the mouth to stifle any sound. There was no sound.

Then a cry, a shot. The second slaver.

Ben turned to face the armed aggressor who was emerging from a forward deck hatch. A double tap from Ben's assault rifle dropped him.

A cry from the other boat. Fifteen metres away. A gun burst, returned by Ben followed by a shout of pain and a loud splash.

His family were not on the first boat. He dived to swim the fifteen metres to the second *perahu*. Time was so precious.

He climbed aboard. One dead in the wheelhouse. Two swimming for shore. He saw them breaking the water surface. His rifle burst hit them both. No mistake – the sound of the bullet impact and blood.

Down into the hold. Empty. The memory of the splash. Over the side.

Powerful torchlight through the crystal water.

There, metres down in the clear water of the lagoon, silhouetted shadowy figures against the white sandy bottom – faint shapes.

The dive. Dragging the bound figures to the surface. Superhuman efforts to heave the still forms onto the low net-deck ... CPR. Bonds cut by the knife. More CPR. No pulse. No reaction in the blue, pale faces.

They were gone. His Sonya and his Sarah. Gone.

* * * *

He had buried them in the sands of the pulau.

It is the ever-present distress of having let his family down that drives his fanatical pursuit of the people who prey on defenceless women.

And now, he knows that Len Williamson is taunting him.

Another man driven – but Laughing Len is driven by hatred; a loathing of his nemesis. He would be reminded of Brennan every time he looks in a mirror; every time someone stares at his face; every time he wants to laugh and the tight skin on his cheeks prevents it being more than a grotesque, painful wheeze.

Yes, Ben Brennan understands Len Williamson's angry ache. Wounds delivered in the midst of a fight for their lives on a Chinese slaving ship as they tangled with each other in the dark, knives flashing in each other's hands.

Williamson had attacked him just as he had laid down his rifle to cut the women free. He only had his knife in his hand to shield himself. The fierce encounter had left the former London enforcer with many shallow slashes to the face, as he had fallen overboard into the warm ocean.

Brennan found out later that his attacker had survived and had needed extensive plastic surgery – but the doctors had been unable to restore his face to its previous condition. He would always now look like the victim of a car accident.

Yes, Brennan understands; but he does not forgive Williamson for taking out his sadistic vengeance on Tom, as well as on an innocent woman.

But he can do little till he knows where Alison is.

He has spoken with Willis in Cairns who confirmed that the *Lerna* is in Panapompom Lagoon, not far from his present location, and that Steve Flynn's tracking device shows him as being away near the Misima settlement.

They have been unable to pick up the tracking device from Alison. There are problems with satellite connections in this part of the world; usually temporary conditions.

Mal Willis assures Ben that, even if Alison has lost the device, it would still be transmitting from wherever it is. Since there is no signal from the device … it is an electronic tracking problem.

They must wait to receive the signal when connection is resumed. The chances of the tracker being broken or of Alison physically losing the device would have to be small. They must assume that it is still on her person.

And so they wait. All good information. He has been in the business long enough to know that if you listen and wait then the pieces will eventually fall into place.

He sits back to let his anger stew.

Len Williamson will pay for what he did to Tom – and presumably, in some form, to Alison.

Back on the *Lerna*

Panapompom, New Guinea. Friday 23 February 2007

I made good time from Misima with the current and tide behind us, but it is still late afternoon as we enter the peaceful Panapompom lagoon to see the *Lerna* anchored where I had last seen it.

As the tender comes alongside, I am surprised to see so many watching eyes.

Carter moves gingerly onto the ship; his fragile appearance quickly bringing crewmen to his assistance.

Roger and Gina stand together on the top deck. On the level below, there is the unmistakable figure of Len Williamson. Where has he come from? I last saw him in Cairns.

* * * *

Lying comfortably on a proper bed, Carter seems to be at peace for the first time in days.

As he slowly eats a hot meal from Marcel, I listen in the background to him telling Roger and Williamson the story of a lugger and a freighter called the *Shinwuan*. He speaks of an enemy with a spotlight searching the waters for him and his flight through the jungle to get to the southern shore.

Cavanagh glances back at me as he and Williamson listen unemotionally. Does he realize that I am hearing the detail about the raw side of his activities for the first time?

'It's a set-up,' Roger says, at length. 'A sail-training boat wouldn't have a powerful searchlight on board.' He paces the small cabin, looking just like a modern Napoleon in thought. 'Yep. A fit-up. All seven were taken. The people on the lugger were clearly searching for you, Peter. It has to have been a trap.' He pauses to think some more. 'I'd lay money on it there are no orphans on that lugger – maybe police. The orphan story was a lure – and we took the bait.'

Carter looks very uncomfortable but Cavanagh flicks his hand to put him at ease.

'Len has placed the shipment on the Korean freighter,' Roger advises, with a deferring smile to Williamson. 'So we still have some trump cards to play. We always have our leverage. Our problem is, with Sir Terence out of action, we don't have an inside track into what our enemies might be planning.

'We don't know who they are. But they are close; the trunk freighter has been attacked and the *product* released. I need to know what is going on.' His furrowed brows twitch with thought. 'It's good you are both back on board. Get some rest. I think there could be interesting times ahead.'

He gives me a strange look as he returns to his suite but he doesn't speak.

Bill Jones

Bill Jones has just listened to the conversation from Peter Carter's cabin. The meticulous monitoring of the microphones on the *Lerna* is paying off.

He is just about to rush along the corridor to brief Mal Willis in the critical incident room of the Cairns Police Headquarters, when a pinging light comes on to indicate a signal is being received from Alison Wood's tracking device.

It is very confusing. It must be a mistake. The signal matches the location of the *Lerna* and Steve's device too. Hasn't the inspector told him Alison Wood is missing? Suspected kidnap. Has he picked it up wrongly?

There is no indication from any of the microphones that Alison is on board. Why would she be? She has no reason to be on board. She has never been on the ship before.

He goes off to see Mal Willis.

It doesn't make sense to the inspector either. 'Unless ... data is impersonal. It doesn't lie. That would be like disbelieving your compass. The answer is probably somewhere else,'

They check the records of all the other microphones on board.

Steve Flynn has just retrieved Carter from being marooned on the island. Williamson is back from apparently placing a shipment on a Korean freighter heading for Sydney. Cavanagh has said that it is his trump card.

Brennan reported one of his agents had been killed by a knife attack at Alotau, where he had been protecting Alison.

She has gone missing there, on the mainland, and now her tracking device is active again, showing her to be on the *Lerna* ... but there is no corroborating evidence. Has the device been removed from Alison and carried to the ship? Williamson is the only logical carrier of the device.

Time to call Jeff Fowler.

Fowler

Fowler listens patiently to the update.

It is clear to him that Cavanagh is still guessing.

Brennan suspects Williamson has killed his man, Tom, at Alotau and has taken Alison Wood prisoner.

Yet Williamson is back on the *Lerna* and so is Alison's tracking device. If she is on the ship, why is there no other evidence of her arrival on board? No other microphone has recorded anything.

Then, there is the comment that Len has placed a shipment onto a Korean freighter as his insurance. He needs to speak urgently with Inspector Eileen Lewis and the Office of the Deputy Chief of the Navy. Under the anti-terrorism guidelines, the Navy can intercept the ship. The question is when to make a move.

Fowler has also received disturbing information from Larry Kennedy at *Versec* – they have been told to stop their investigations. Add that to Catherine Weston's advice that the *NPA* has been put on hold and there are some big imponderables happening, in South East Asia and the world scene.

He advises Mal Willis to let Brennan know as soon as possible.

For his part, his priority is to deal with the Korean freighter.

Steve on the *Lerna*

Panapompom, New Guinea. Friday 23 February 2007

I find Gina on the sundeck. Where else would she be, even with the sun almost gone? But she is not lounging. She is pacing.

The romantic in me hopes that she has had a happy time while I have been away. My parting memory was of her laughing and swimming with Roger in the lagoon. But her intense expression belies that notion.

She whispers the strangest story to me about when Len Williamson arrived back; about a roll, or more accurately a wrap of matting which he has placed in the bulkhead.

My interest is piqued. 'Only Peter, Len and Roger have keys for that room. Peter told me that. It is only used for storing records. Do you think you could look quietly at Roger's keys?' I could see her fear as I asked. 'See if any are tagged as the bulkhead storeroom.'

She pulls her shoulders back. 'I'll see what I can find out.'

* * * *

I return to my cabin to whisper a summary into the microphone, including the locked bulkhead with no access to keys. I have to trust that they are listening.

A crewman knocks on the cabin door – the accustomed beckoning call.

Roger seems quite relaxed when I enter the suite office – on his laptop as usual. It seems to be his main means of communicating with the outside world.

He glances at me over his shoulder. 'You did well to get Peter out of there.'

Accepting the praise, I say, 'He's been knocked around a bit, fighting through that jungle. Rugged-looking stuff. I wouldn't envy him that.'

I watch Roger turn slowly with his chin cradled between forefinger and thumb, as if wondering what to tell me. 'Steve, I think we are in a difficult situation at the moment. There are forces trying to shut down our operation, largely because of some illegal freight we have been carrying.'

I shrug my shoulders in question. I know that SPFA carries contraband, just not the nature or the scale of the operation.

'I'm afraid Peter made an error of judgement.' An unaccustomed admission. 'He tried to pick up a cargo off Misima Island. As you gather, he had to flee. Just got out. But he's a good operator. Few others would have survived.

'I think we'll stay here at the lagoon for a day or two. No-one knows we're here. Anyone searching would be looking farther north up the New Guinea coast on the course that Captain Rodriguez registered. So here, any search might just pass us by. We have good satellite connectivity. I can email the Board of the SPFA from here as easily as up the coast. And,' he grins, 'I like watching Gina swimming with the turtles.' A happy laugh lightens his expression. 'You have done well, getting her back to her happy self.'

I demur. 'You both looked happy swimming away together. This place lends itself to being relaxed.'

Roger

Panapompom, New Guinea. Friday 23 February 2007

Roger has decided. He needs this Australian for Plan C, if Plan B fails.

He is wary of the mole. The Bernard principle of protection that he learned at his London school never leaves him no matter how successful he has become. A leader needs people to shield him; to take the first attack. Even his idol Napoleon had his Imperial Guard.

He will continue to introduce Steve Flynn to the business, gently. It is an instinctive thing. He likes the way Steve doesn't ask probing questions. Deep in his mind, he is satisfied the mole isn't Steve. It doesn't add up that he could be.

Now, is it Peter and Len? A crew member?

He rattles through his mental checklist again, as he has been doing since he received the *Ramas* message. The crew know little, only where they have been and where they are. That wouldn't be of any more than superficial use to anyone. Certainly not condemning information for a court of law. Most of it has been on registered routes, deliberately clean – alibi quality.

That means that it is Len. He has been away. Maybe the old South London enforcer has seen an angle to work?

Roger will need to watch him; and he would have to trust that the instructions for the Korean freighter have been carried out correctly. But, to give him credit, Len *has* done well to find his way back to the *Lerna*, even allowing for his advance knowledge of their route.

A vein in his temple throbs nervously.

Suspicions.

Willis and Ben Brennan

Cairns. Friday 23 February 2007

'Alison's tracking device is signalling from the *Lerna*!'

Mal Willis is briefing Ben Brennan. 'No corroborating evidence from any of the microphones and they all appear to be working properly. We can also confirm that Williamson is back on board. We have his voice recorded. Carter has been picked up after the lugger episode and is also back on the *Lerna*, badly scratched and exhausted apparently, but otherwise alright.

'Steve has passed on a strange message – when Len returned to the ship, he placed a roll of matting in the bulkhead storeroom. Gina saw it happening and told Steve when he returned. Apparently only Roger, Peter and Len have keys for that room.'

'What sort of roll?' asks Brennan.

'Gina called it more like a wrap than a roll as if it was wrapping something cylindrical.'

'A person's body?'

'I have no confirmation of that,' replies Willis, 'nor confirmation of the length of the cylinder. But she noted the crewmen found it heavy to carry.'

'That's enough for me,' replies Brennan. 'We have no other information that she is anywhere else. My guess is she's in that bulkhead storeroom. I'll bet she's alive too or she would have just been dumped at sea.'

'You could well be right. But Ben – wouldn't it be a trap to draw you in? The letters written in the blood! Williamson would know you would try to track him. You're going into the dragon's den if you go there.'

Brennan ignores the comments. 'I need you to get clearance from Jeff Fowler for me to contact Steve on board. I have his satellite phone number. Alison gave it to me in Port Moresby. I'll need a friend on the ship to clear the way. Ron and I can get on board but I will need some Intelligence about that storeroom.'

'Okay. Will do,' says Willis. 'I'll be back in touch.'

Roger

In response to Roger's earlier request, the encrypted message reads:

No ID on the mole. Be careful.

The respondent added:

British investigation team on hold. Trap with a lugger has not achieved the results they wanted. Americans have confessions from bank directors but nothing directly linking any of us. The stop has been put on them too. May well get through this, yet.

Clearance to contact

Jeff Fowler has spoken with Eileen Lewis about Williamson placing a shipment on the Korean freighter. This is her province.

'We need to locate this ship, quickly,' he says. 'Can you get the Navy to intercept it before it enters Sydney Harbour, please? I want the crew interviewed individually till we establish what the shipment is. My imagination can come up with some very horrible scenarios.'

* * * *

Lewis has just left to handle the Korean freighter as Mal Willis phones in to relay Brennan's plan to Fowler.

'How is he going to get on board a ship in the middle of glassy lagoon?'

'He didn't say,' replies Willis. 'He is former SBS. He would have some skills in that area, I'd imagine.'

Fowler's mind runs a rapid risk analysis. His *untouchable* support groups in Britain and the States are drying up fast. This is fast reverting to an Australian operation and the threat actually appears to be against Australian interests, especially with the Korean freighter advancing on Sydney.

At some stage, they are going to have to detain Roger Cavanagh. The Australian Navy are in the area and in the loop. So what would be lost if Brennan attacked the boat?

It wouldn't be a frontal raid. He would get on the boat by stealth. If he did, he would need the support of Steve Flynn, himself Defence-force trained. But Flynn doesn't have any of the recent information from the recordings. So, it would probably be a manageable risk for Brennan to put him in the picture.

Potentially, that would give three armed operatives against a possibly passive crew and the three enemy in Cavanagh, Carter and Williamson.

There is the risk to Alison Wood, if she is indeed being held captive in the bulkhead. But is there any chance she will get out alive if Ben does nothing?

Not much, unless Steve can free her. Even then, they will still be at the mercy of the gangsters on board.

No, it is a good calculated risk to let Ben get himself and another agent on board. If his phoning compromises Steve, he can bluff his way out. The microphones will pick up any imminent danger.

'Yes, Mal. Tell Ben he has clearance to contact Steve. They are the ones in the middle of it all. Give him the go-ahead. I'll contact the Navy to see what back-up we can have in the area.'

Steve

My satellite phone suddenly rings, just as I return to my cabin – a quiet ring.

It is a surprise. Who knows the number? Roger? Carter? The captain? Why would *they* phone?

'Hello, this is Steve.'

Then I hear the words, 'Steve, Ben Brennan. Are you able to speak?'

'I'm good. In my cabin,' I whisper.

No small talk, no questions. Ben would not be phoning me for a social chat.

'I need to come on board the *Lerna* tonight in the dark. I will have one man with me as back-up. We will carry side-arms and spear guns. We could do with your help. I think it could be Alison that is being held captive in the bulkhead store.'

'Shit!'

'Williamson killed one of my men in Alotau and I believe that he kidnapped Alison. Her tracking device is coming from the *Lerna*.' He pauses to let Steve collect his thoughts. 'So, we are coming on board. Can you access assault rifles?'

'Can do. Understood. Give me details.'

'We'll scuba from the edge of the lagoon to the rear of the boat, near where the tender is lowered. Will that be best?'

'That'll work. Carter and Williamson have their adjacent cabins on that level, on the starboard side. I can meet you with rifles. They are in good order and loaded. We could access the bulkhead from the port side corridor. Least chance of being interrupted. I'll see if we can get a key to the storeroom.'

'No,' says Ben. 'If only the three enemies have keys, we want nothing to alert them. I'll have plastic explosive. We'll blow the lock, not the door. It will be a muffled concussion sound.'

'What time?' I ask.

'Aim for one hundred hours; all things being equal.'

'Give me your number in case anything changes.'

We hang up and I lie back on the bed, realising clearly for the first time that Alison is actually only a few metres away; probably in dire need of my help. This wait will be frustrating in the extreme.

I now know who is to blame for her plight.

I make myself a solemn promise that if Alison has come to any harm, Williamson will pay for it, very dearly.

Cecile and the Mohács Blue

Cecile sits staring at the Mohács Blue in her exquisite cellar; such a beautiful stone. But her research of the past few weeks has turned up strange and thought-provoking ideas.

She has always known that the sapphire was once owned by Napoleon and, before that, by Suleiman the Magnificent. That provenance is part of what makes it so valuable.

And yet, something about the gemstone is making her uncomfortable. She has had the sensation for a while. Is she going mad? Losing her clarity of thought?

How can she be? She and Douglas still run a large successful chateau and all its business interests. They wouldn't be able to do that if they were losing their thinking ability.

But, she had paid a research assistant, a Sorbonne scholar, to find out some more about the Mohács Blue. Where had the stone been from 1815, when Napoleon was exiled to Saint Helena, until it arrived as a gift to her in 1990?

The researcher had gone to primary sources. He read the original preserved letters which the great emperor had dictated to his old schooldays' friend and later private secretary, Louis de Bourrienne, at Longwood House on Saint Helena. Those notes tally with what Henri-Gatien, *Comte Bertrand*, also wrote – the Count of Bertrand was also exiled, with Napoleon, on that Saint Helena prison island.

The information is that a Romany woman had place a curse on Napoleon and the Mohács Blue. That story has always been known – she has heard it over the years. Who hasn't? Everyone who knows anything about sapphires is aware. It is on public websites – and she had, and has, dismissed it as the gossip of fantasists. Famous rulers are, and were, forever being cursed by someone or other.

But, this researcher had found detail to support the rumour.

The curse was placed on the day of Napoleon's coronation in 1805 because his men had stolen the sapphire from a Romany camp on 25 May, 1797 after the fall of Pavia in Italy.

The curse had been that Napoleon, as the thief of the gemstone, would lose all his power, be banished from the esteem of society and die in isolated ignominy. It had only been on Saint Helena that Napoleon had reflected on the significance of the curse – as it seemed that the prophecy might actually have come true for him. He had spoken to his associates about his thoughts. It is documented.

The research assistant tried to track down information about the Romany woman. He found a source document – an instruction signed by Eugène de Beauharnais, Viceroy of Italy in 1805 – that effectively imprisoned a Romany woman in an institution, near Milano, because she was mad.

The only identification was that the woman was either from the *Ćurari* or the *Kalderaš* people, originally from the western Balkans. They recorded no specific name for her. All they had was the link to a long-gone Romany camp at Pavia on 25 May, 1797.

The stone had then been sent to Napoleon's private collection, on his personal instruction, where presumably it remained, at least in technical terms, until his defeat at Waterloo. Its location after that has been variously attributed to being hidden in the grounds of a house at 6 Rue Chantereine, later to be Rue de la Victorie. Napoleon definitely stayed there in the time period – although he was often away on military campaigns and affairs of state. Another source insists that the gem had been seen in a basement at the Tuileries Palace, which burned down in 1871. Napoleon had lived in that official residence, too.

Whatever the truth, *the game* recovered it from a wealthy Russian as the Soviet Union started to finally collapse at the start of the 1990s. That man had met a grisly end, apparently, and all previous noble references to him have been elided from official national records. Had he been cursed too?

It seems to Cecile that history could be repeating with her increasing sense of anguish. She needs to get out of the *Hydra's* trap. Perhaps returning some of her treasured collection should be part of that penance – to release her.

The other pain nagging at her is the ever-present, haunting sound of women in pain – women who speak French but with unusual accents, probably South Pacific accents.

It had been like the torment of *Tantalus* since that anonymous note had arrived, hidden in a gift of a native mask – English written words, and a closed internet link to that very private video of a woman telling the price in misery to get these gifts to her. That is the wailing which never actually leaves her – the horror of what the slave trade actually means for an individual – hidden in an Indonesian *objet d'art*. Who knew to send that link to her, through the secure *Ramas* system?

The wailing woman could have been from any of the French-speaking South Pacific islands. She was being traded. Intellectually, that is not the issue for Cecile – women have been objects of possession and cultural denigration for millennia. She understands her history.

No! It was the pain in the sound of the voice – like a baby crying to a mother. Once heard, it could not be unheard. It could not be ignored. It seared through to her soul – and it had never left her. There was a chorus of women wailing behind the one woman – a choir lament, with the same pangs of distress.

That Cecile could be the cause of such anguish? Is that the cost for her collection?

So, she is forming a plan to return art pieces and jewellery to worthy previous owners or to places of protection, over time.

The latter seems to be more likely.

How could even the most skilled researcher track down the legitimate descendants of a Romany soldier at the Battle of Mohács in 1526?

Until a verifiable owner of the Mohács Blue can be found, she plans that it can be kept safe in the *Muséum National D'histoire Naturelle* in Paris. They have lots of gemstones in their Treasury vault. The sapphire set of Queen Marie Amélie is there, as is the Ruspoli Sapphire – remnant relics of past regal jewels. They could easily guard one more blue gem, especially since it has such provenance.

As for the paintings, she is working on a clever plan for them to be *found* around the country in mysterious cellars or abandoned stores. That promises to be a good exercise for her brain – to map out the processes for slowly divesting herself of her collection and, in the process, to shed the pain and the entrapment of the *Hydra*.

She looks again at the Mohács Blue. Such a pity. Such a beautiful jewel.

She adds her plan to the inventory instructions she has been building, with her wish for the Mohács Blue to arrive at the Natural History Museum in Paris, by a process yet to be elaborated.

For a few seconds, Cecile feels a sense of relief – no pain, no conscience, freedom from guilt – and then the wailing returns.

Len Williamson waits

Len Williamson has set his trap and now he waits.

He imagines the *Nemesis* people scurrying and questioning everywhere around the New Guinea islands to find out who killed their mate. But it will only be Brennan who will be able to join the dots – the missing woman and the letters in blood.

Someone will realise that the *Lerna* is at Panapompom – perhaps the fishing boat crew will let it slip. He hadn't hidden who he was or where they were going. But only Brennan would take the risk to tackle Len Williamson. Everyone else would head in the opposite direction. He chortles at the thought.

It had been luck to have heard the talk in Alotau about the white woman with the Malay man – but luck is made. All Roger's men are trained to look for opportunities.

He knew from the follow-up email report, that the trunk freighter's captain had mentioned a female journalist travelling with Brennan and making a video on the ship when the *product* was released. He'd read that when he landed at Moresby.

So, as soon as he saw the woman in Alotau, he knew she must be the woman who had been with Brennan in Madang. There could be no other white woman with her looks and age in that area. There were no cruise boats in the harbour.

And Brennan must be close too, hunting the *Lerna*.

It is all so logical.

But his enemy wasn't in Alotau when Len arrived. Brennan had clearly left the girl to be safe. He chortles again at how he has upset Brennan's plan. From there, his own course of action was simple.

He hired a boat crew who would take him out to the islands where the *Lerna* would pass. Then he made his way to the hut where he had seen the woman.

He clubbed her as he entered and stabbed the Malay in the neck. The rest was a matter of leaving a clue to infuriate Brennan and then getting out of there. It had been easy. This is how he makes his living. He is good at attack and capture.

Now on the *Lerna*, he expects the trap will snap tight on his prey. His bloody note will bring Brennan; he knows that. *Nemesis* will find out where he is, maybe from the fishermen, maybe from other sources – but Len is confident the bait will lure him out.

Carter has returned exhausted from his abortive attempt on the lugger. But Len thinks he will be angry enough at being *done over* in the raid that he will be an asset if Brennan tries to come on board – back-up if needed.

So he tells Peter to expect some action either that night or the next. He has set the bait.

'What bait?' Peter insists on knowing.

'I have the woman journalist that was with Brennan on the trunk freighter,' he wheezes round his misshapen teeth. 'She's in the bulkhead store. Alive.'

Carter doesn't know whether to be angry or pitying. What a dumb thing; just crazy! 'Have you told the boss?'

'Not yet. Not till I have Brennan for him. That bastard has caused us too much trouble.'

'Jeezus, Len.'

But Carter is very tired from his ordeal. He desperately needs sleep. He can't even think straight in his current exhaustion. And maybe nothing will happen quickly anyway.

'Alright. I need to sleep just now.'

He lies down fully-clothed in case he is needed. His cabin is next to Len's. He will be easily roused if necessary.

The action starts

They dive deep and move towards the moored ship.

Under cover of darkness, Brennan had sailed to the reverse of a headland on the edge of the Panapompom lagoon. A little after midnight on Sunday, he and Ron, dressed in scuba gear, slip into the warm waters. At 12.50 am, they are fifty metres from the *Lerna*. There is no moon.

At one minute before one in the morning, they surface under the shelter of the hull. A low bird whistle receives a very low answering whistle and the two divers look up into the face of Steve Flynn.

* * * *

I leave my cabin at 12.50 am with my key for the gun lockers. I quietly remove three assault rifles and a Glock from the port locker at the lower level. The Glock goes straight into my waistband in the small of my back, under the flap of my loose shirt.

The ship is quiet – so quiet that the sound of the water gently lapping against the hull sounds like big waves; but not much louder than my thumping heart.

The lights are out in the companionways – must be a fuse. No time to check the power board. I know every step of the corridor. Silently, I make my way to the stern to await the arrival of the divers. I check my watch. On time. They have the harder task to swim from the edge of the lagoon.

The low whistle is scarcely audible.

I recognise Ben as I pull him from the water. He is accompanied by a fit-looking man who whispers, 'Ron', in my ear. They remove their air tanks and leave them with their spear guns on the stern platform.

Ben and Ron make their way to the start of the pitch-dark port corridor. Ben's waterproof pinhole torch gives a brief flash, as a solitary confirmation of direction and clear passage, while I move to cover the starboard companionway, listening for anything out of the ordinary, especially from the cabins of Williamson or Carter.

But there is no sound except the lagoon's quiet rhythm against the hull.

* * * *

Ben doesn't need directions. The old Navy man moves with Ron along the darkened port companionway to the bow. The bulkhead storeroom door is in total darkness – not even a glow from an emergency bulb. They locate the lock with their pinhole torch.

Ben places Ron facing the stern at the port corridor exit, covering any access to the bulkhead door from either companionway; in case of any interference.

The former SBS man manipulates the plastic explosive at the lock. His gun is on the deck beside him, while he uses both hands in the darkness on the task in hand.

He is just preparing the detonator with his knife when he hears the thump and sigh from behind. He senses rather than sees Ron's body on the ground.

The wheezing chortle is all the warning Ben has as a ferocious dark form barrels into his side; a club hitting him with a glancing blow on the left shoulder in the darkness.

The knife he'd been using to prepare the fuse is still in Ben's right hand. He feels the hard edge of his attacker's knife against his wetsuit as strong muscles push him backwards ... and the sweaty smell of hatred wafts over him from the assailant's hissing breath

A ferocious dance of death begins.

418

Alison

Thirsty – desperately thirsty. Alison's head aches, a throbbing pain.

Pitch-dark; she can see nothing. A muffled thumping and grunting noise seems to be coming from beyond a door or a wall.

She can't move. Her arms won't work – tied to something behind her – and her legs are restricted. A foul-tasting rag clogs her mouth; tied in place.

Unable to wrestle with her bonds because, when she tries, she can't get her breath. Her only breath comes through her nose – no chance for big gasps of air.

It is a terrible sensation that her nose could block and she might suffocate in this darkness. She forces her mind to stay calm as she struggles to breathe steadily. Maybe it will persuade her fluttering pulse to slow down.

It has been a horror movie since she first saw the face of the man she assumes is *the Devil*, Len Williamson. He just appeared in her sight in the hut as she woke up with a splitting headache. Had she fainted? He had come from nowhere.

Her memory of the Alotau hut is sickening; her friend, Tom, stabbed, dead, covered with blood; his blood smeared all over the matting.

Horrific! A cruel *devil*. And the smell. Blood and death. Once sniffed, it could never be forgotten. Poor, poor Tom. Such a good man.

419

She is surprised that she is still alive. The memory of the terrified expressions on the trunk freighter crew roll through her mind; of that captain describing the sadistic torturer – and now she has seen for herself what he can do. She would have screamed at the time but a paralysing fear gripped her with an intensity that froze all messages from the brain.

The smell of vomit on her clothes turns her empty stomach. When did she last eat? No more left to vomit into the gag. She feels the ropes binding her where she lies. She guesses he must have tied her while she'd been in a faint. Oh, her head – the throbbing is intense.

She remembers, back at the hut, he had carried her out, wrapped in suffocating grass matting; then dumped her almost gently in a rattling vehicle which he drove down to the wharf.

Loaded onto a smelly fishing boat, they had set out to sea.

She had woken as the boat was puttering over a glassy sea. Confused. Pain in the back of the head. Very woozy. Nothing made any sense. Tied tightly round the waist to the boat spar … huge knots behind her. A rough tarpaulin, fixed to the wheelhouse, shaded her from the direct rays of the sun.

She had kept seeing images of Tom lying dead in the hut. Blood. The sticky sweet smell of the blood. The gorge had risen in her throat at the memory and she had puked all over her clothes.

One of the Nuigini seamen came by regularly to give her sips of fresh water – and to toss a bucket of sea water over her; but nowhere near enough to clean herself, to get rid of the mess, the stink.

Time passed in a daze. Only the painful pangs of hunger made it real.

She was not sure how long she had been on the boat. Her bonds had been loosened twice as she was allowed to toilet herself; into a bucket and over the side. No privacy, even less dignity, but she'd been past caring. Neither the two seamen on board nor Len paid her more than scant attention, except to ensure she was still there. The stench of vomit, sweat and dirt would have kept anyone at bay, as she lay there, semi-drenched.

Maybe it had been two days, if she had been counting correctly. Then, her arms and legs were tied again. Len had given her an eerie chortle and pinched her cheek almost playfully. Everything had gone blank again until she had woken in this darkened place.

She is still at sea; she can sense the subtle swell of the ocean beneath her.

Then, here in this new darkness, there has been this scuffling sound to her right. She thinks it might be a rat; a flush of terror washes through her as she pictures herself a prisoner in the dark at the mercy of a gnawing, filthy rodent – claws crawling over and up her trapped defenceless legs. The terror passes – so thirsty; water, water … much worse than the hunger … so thirsty. Eventually, she realises that the scuffling is outside the wall or the door.

For no conscious reason, she pictures herself shackled to Hillnah on the trunk freighter; the sense of powerlessness, fear, defeat; the shame to be lying there in the smell of one's own mess. This wasn't part of her thinking when she thought she would write an exposé on pirates.

God, is that what he has planned for her? It hit her with the suddenness of a punch to the stomach. To be sold into slavery?

She can't imagine, not even start to visualise, what that reality might be – a brothel in Thailand, a sex slave in Arabia – but her callous subconscious forms pictures for her from somewhere in the recesses of her mind.

Rape. Multiple bruising rapes. Beatings. Drugs. Humiliation. Degradation. Numbing. No identity.

No-one knowing what has happened. Parents pining, not knowing.

Ben not knowing; Steve wondering where she is, lovely caring Steve; and Tom – aargh, the acrid taste rises up her throat again.

No, breathe slowly. Don't choke! Don't vomit and block the airway!

Be quiet. No sound. No way does she want Williamson back onto the scene.

And now there are shouts, groans and grunts – still outside the door. She can hear swearing – loud oaths. She is sure it is Ben's voice. Perhaps this is the dream. She just wants it to be Ben's voice because he means safety.

Steve

I hear the scuffling and turn back from defending the starboard companionway, instinctively flicking on the emergency corridor lights at the switch box as I go forward. They work. No fuse – just flicked off by someone who knew where that manual override control was.

It is a horrific sight that greets me in the ambient corridor glow – the light at the bulkhead door still seems to be out. The fallen form of Ron lies blocking the corridor on the left. Ben lies heaving in a pool of blood to the right of the door. Directly in front and moving towards me at speed is the massive blood-spattered shape of Len Williamson.

He is roaring and spitting – a screaming, threatening banshee hurtling like a train out of a dark tunnel. No escape.

It is a reflex action from years of military training and the power of fear. The burst of automatic gunfire explodes from my rifle tearing a pattern of ragged holes across the chest of Len's shirt. The tormentor scarcely gurgles as he hits me in a shocked heap, bowling me over. The vibrating, sweaty body pinions me, onion breath centimetres from my face. His eyes are open, staring, surprised and fast dying. A last surge of bloody puke splurts from the dead mouth and soaks onto my shirt.

I ease myself from under the heavy steaming, gory corpse – heart racing and every nerve end at fever pitch.

Justice. No time to savour. It is all happening too fast.

I am taking in the images, but time has frozen for me. I process still photographs in my mind. Ron – moving, groggy, trying to get to his feet, rifle in hand. Ben – clearly still alive but blood oozing from a chest wound with a gurgling sucking sound. He needs help.

I have just started to move towards him when I hear a soft voice behind me say, 'Stay right where you are! No silly movements.'

Of course, the gunfire would have wakened the whole ship on a quiet night like this. It is the voice of Peter Carter. He has an automatic rifle in his hands and those hands are rock steady.

'Lay your weapons down ever so gently. Hands away from the triggers.'

Ron and I lower our guns, as instructed, ever so gently. I smell the waft of death and blood as we bend to the floor near Len's lifeless shape.

Ben lies on his back, semi-conscious, in no shape to do other than struggle to breathe. His hand is vainly trying to stop the flow of blood from his chest. He is close to losing total consciousness. His own weapon is out of his, and our, reach.

'And the hand guns.'

Ron's pistol is in a side holster. He places it carefully on the corridor floor. I gently slap my sides to indicate no gun. My Glock is beyond Peter's vision in the small of my back under the waistband of my trousers and under the flap of my shirt. Don't let him frisk us.

Carter looks carefully at Ben, lying and gurgling in a pool of his own blood. Clearly, assessing that the *Nemesis* leader is no danger to anyone and will probably be dead very soon, he says to Ron and me, 'Now, you two, ever so carefully, if you do not want to be shot in a painful place, you will pass me side-by-side and walk hands held high. We are going to Roger's suite. There will be some questions to be answered.'

Startled crewmen watch our walk along the corridor and up the companionway steps, then disappear quickly. The thought occurs to me that they might call for help because we can't say anything to them, without jeopardising their safety. We keep walking.

At the suite, Roger waits, pistol in hand. He ushers us all through the office and into the living area beyond. As cluttered a place as I'd remembered, filled with his collectibles hotch-potch. Too much of too many rich things. Tasteless – but this would be the wrong time to tell him.

Carter sits both Ron and me together on the couch facing towards the bedroom door, hands still in the air. He covers us with the automatic rifle while Roger lays his pistol down carefully on his coffee table to take in the scene.

'Well, what do we have here, Peter?' I have to admire his cool. Guns going off. Sleep interrupted – and his voice is calm, controlled, even casual.

'Len is dead at the bulkhead store entrance. Shot by Mr Flynn. There is a dead or dying Ben Brennan of *Nemesis* down there, knifed by our Len. I don't know this man's name but he was with Brennan and, of course, you know your security officer, Steve.' His voice is almost mocking of his boss's trust in the man that he has warned about.

Roger doesn't appear to notice the tone.

'Well, Steve?' he asks of me.

My hands are still in the air. 'I heard a noise. It's one in the morning. I went to investigate, taking a rifle as I patrolled. When I got to the companionway leading down to the bulkhead store, the night corridor lights were out. I could hear a scuffle. I switched on the emergency lights. Someone had flicked the manual control – and I saw Len, knife in hand, with a bloody man on the ground clearly with serious wounds and this man, that I have never seen before, lifting himself slowly from the floor.

'Len came at me with the knife and I shot him. It was instinctive. Self-defence. Then Peter arrived.'

'I see.' Roger turns his gaze on Ron. 'And who might you be? Are you an acquaintance of the infamous Mr Brennan who is apparently dying on my deck?'

'Piss off,' says Ron.

'Not necessarily the smartest answer you could give,' says Roger, calmly. 'Try again before I see how stupid you would choose to be. Who are you?'

'Your sadistic knifeman killed a friend of mine in Alotau. He also kidnapped a lady who is currently captive in your bulkhead. We came to free her but your madman was waiting in the dark. Did you want a kidnapped woman in your store?'

Roger turns slowly to Peter. 'Is there a woman in the store, Peter?'

Carter nods. 'Apparently.'

Cavanagh's voice is still very measured. He could be interviewing someone for a job. 'Who is the woman, Peter?'

'Len told me she's the journalist who was on the trunk freighter at Madang. He was holding her as bait to draw Brennan to the ship.'

The pause is charged as Cavanagh absorbs the information, but his facial expression scarcely changes.

'Oh, what a brilliant idea, Peter,' he says, with a serene sarcasm that goes right through his associate like a spear. 'Kidnap a journalist who knows about our activities and bring her to *our* ship, which has had no link to any of the recent events and then create a bloodbath to draw even more attention; in front of an entire crew. A really brilliant idea – totally brilliant. And you knew about this, Peter? Stunning. Absolutely stunning!'

He turns to me. 'Is he telling the truth, Steve? Whom do I believe? Or does it make no difference?'

Suddenly, Gina is behind Peter and Roger as she speaks sleepily, 'What's going on, Roger?'

Both men turn their eyes to Gina and I fire my Glock about two seconds later. The bullet catches Peter under the chin as he swung his rifle back at my rapid movement. He falls in a heap on the thick carpeted floor. I would have been very proud of that shot in the service and then, as now, I would not admit to how lucky it actually was.

Roger's hand reaches for his gun from the table. He now looks shocked rather than calm; the noise, the surprise. His gun is pointed at Gina, who he had turned to after she had spoken.

I call to Roger to lower the gun but *the emperor* is frozen in a shocked pose with the gun still pointing at Gina.

Ron starts towards Gina – an instinctive gesture to block any shot from the hand of the confused, disoriented Roger.

I fire at the gun hand – a stupid thing to do. My subconscious is telling me that this master criminal needs to be taken alive. *Don't shoot to kill* was the subliminal message.

The bullet missed, as it would – no longer am I lucky – and Roger turns like a robot, gun moving with him, to confront me.

He has a dazed disconnected expression. Gun concussion in a restricted space can do that.

An explosion comes from over Ron's shoulder and Roger is spun around like a top, clutching his shoulder in numbed shock, his pistol bouncing onto the carpet. I look at the source of the gunshot to see Gina with her Glock in her right hand and the gun pointed at her partner.

'He was going to shoot you, Steve!' Her high pitched squeal mirrors her shocked expression. She looks totally appalled at what she has just done.

Ron holds her gently as he removes the weapon from her hand. She holds on tightly to him or she would have collapsed to the floor.

'You ran in front of his gun to stop him shooting me.' She is gazing in stunned admiration at Ron. And then she repeats it as if she hadn't heard herself properly. Ron gently lowers her to the floor and lets her sit with her back against the leg of a lounge chair. She repeats her sentence again, 'You ran in front of his gun to stop him shooting me.'

I am back in control of my senses. Cavanagh has received a bullet wound to his right shoulder and needs medical aid. He is moaning; colour draining from his face, clearly in shock.

Carter is far beyond medical help. He lies in a bloody mess, his brains soaking the carpet from the exit wound in the back of his head.

'Ron, can you look after the situation here?' I pass Roger's weapon over to where the neoprene-clad hero is comforting the collapsed Gina.

'I need to see what I can do for Ben … and Alison.' I realise with urgency that she might be in a very dangerous condition. 'The key? Gina did you find a key for the bulkhead store?' I ask insistently.

She still looks and sounds dumbfounded. 'No! Probably in his safe. 20-3-11.' She gives a groggy smile to show she is pleased that she has remembered but I am already through the door and in the study, twirling the safe knob.

Three right to 20, two left to 3, one right to 11 and the door swings open.

It is a small safe with money, papers, a cloth bundle and a couple of keys. I look at them both. One has a red plastic tag reading, *Bulkhead store.*

With Carter's automatic rifle in hand, I am the soldier of old. Maybe a little rusty, but thinking and moving like a trained assault team member; past more shocked faces of crewmen, too scared to be involved with people holding guns; and I have more important priorities – along the corridor and down the companionway. The full lights are back on. Someone must have fixed the fuse, if that had been the problem.

The bloody body of Len Williamson lies where he had fallen.

I move over to Ben. He is soaked in blood, with his clawing hands still pressed against a fiercely sucking chest wound.

I flick his wetsuit hood off, tug it free and place it over the wound to make a seal – basic combat first-aid. Ben's eyes flicker open. He is not going to live unless he gets urgent help. He's lost a lot of blood and probably has severe damage to a lung, at the very least.

I place his hand over the rubber pad and gently prop him up, turning him slightly to the injured side so that the lean of the body weight would help to maintain the seal.

The sucking sound stops. He seems to breathe a little easier.

I move to the storeroom door. Plastic explosive is placed around the lock. The keyhole is clear. I push the key in and turn. The lock moves and the door swings outwards to open.

The corridor light floods in to show a confined space with a human shape, head turned away from the light. It should be Alison. But the shape is filthy, crumpled. It smells strongly of a warm animal odour and vomit.

I remove the gag while speaking quietly to tell her who I am and that everything will be alright. She doesn't speak, just gasps. I grab a bloody, fallen knife to cut the ropes on her arms and feet.

She gasps, 'Wa … water.'

'I'll get it.' I take the companionway steps in three bounds.

A frightened crewman stands in the corridor. 'A beaker of water and a glass, fast!' The man nods and leaves to do as commanded. They are a well-disciplined crew – servile, but disciplined. Another head appears.

'Call the captain to the bulkhead and get a first-aid kit, fast.' The second crewman dutifully rushes to obey.

I go back to check on Ben Brennan. His eyes are open. He is trying to speak. 'Is she … alive?'

'Yes. She's alive. She'll be alright.' I sound more confident than I feel at that moment.

He nods almost imperceptibly and a trace of a smile curls his mouth. I can see satisfaction in his grey eyes. Perhaps it has been worthwhile. If the price has to be paid …?

The crewman arrives with the water. I gently hold the water for Alison to sip. Little sips, followed by gasps.

She screams a quiet scream as she continues suffering the protracted pain from the blood coursing past where her bonds have restricted the blood flow.

'Steve. Oh, Steve!' The tears flow. I hold her carefully but closely, feeling a deep anger at the suffering she has endured.

The captain arrives at the bulkhead door, his eyes expressing his shock at the carnage around him.

'Captain Rodriguez.' I rise to my full height and speak formally, needing to assure him that the situation is not up for debate. 'Roger Cavanagh has been shot and is being attended to in his suite. Carter and Williamson are both dead. Williamson is here as you can see, and Carter in Roger's suite.' To his credit, he listens calmly as I continue. 'The man outside has a sucking chest wound. Can you get the best medical attention you can for him at present? This lady is Miss Wood. She has been held captive in *your* storeroom by Len Williamson. There is another man guarding Mr Cavanagh in the stateroom. His name is Ron. Ron and the injured man outside came to rescue Miss Wood from Williamson's clutches.'

It is a lot for the captain to take in, in one go. But, ever the cool skipper, he maintains the appearance of a composed leader of a ship's crew.

'Steve, you are in charge now.' He glances back through the door. 'The man outside is being looked after. What do you need me to do first?'

'I need you to tell your crew we have had an incident on board with two people dead and two injured. We need a methodical approach to dealing with the casualties first of all, the wounded and the dead, and then we will make contact with the outside world.

'I don't want anything touched around the dead bodies. Help the wounded with as little interference to the area as possible. Can you handle that for me?'

'Yes, Steve. I can.' He is doing what he does best, organising a ship's crew.

Alison is moving better now. The water helped.

She had listened to my conversation with the captain. 'Steve, how is Ben?'

'Badly wounded, just outside the door. He has asked if you are alright and I said you are. He smiled when I told him.'

'Can I see him please?' She groans with an effort to get to her feet. 'Please help me walk. My legs don't work.'

'I'll carry you.' I pick her up like a child and take her outside, whispering to prepare her, 'He's in a bad way, Alison.'

The crewman who is assisting Ben moves aside as we arrive.

I lower her near her injured friend. He is still breathing. The black neoprene wetsuit is soaked down the front in a slowly congealing flow of warm bright blood. She cries as the emotion releases.

'Oh, Ben! Ben. Thank you for coming for me. I'm *so* sorry.'

His eyes open at the sound of her voice. He smiles faintly through the wincing agony of his wounds.

'Alive … you're alive,' he gasps painfully, taking in the sight of battered vomit-reeking but alive Alison. 'I … didn't fail you, girl. Live a ha … happy … life … for me.'

His eyes close, face contented. I feel his pulse. Very weak.

'He's resting,' I say encouragingly, in hope rather than certainty, helping her to her feet. 'We'll do everything we can for him.'

Alison's wail is a melancholy sound as the tension of the past few days bursts out, in tears and cries. She hugs against my chest.

I pick her up and slowly carry her out of the gloom, away from the smell of the bulkhead corridor, up the steps to the fresher air of the stateroom.

I call out to Ron on approach and Gina comes to open the door. Her eyes widen at the sight of Alison's pitiable condition.

'My bedroom,' she commands with a new-found efficiency; leading me with my arms full, past the moaning Roger, who has a crewman patching the bullet wound in his right shoulder. Carter lies where he has fallen. Ron is quietly guarding the scene.

'How's Ben?' he asks.

'Not good,' I say. 'Sucking chest wound. Lost a lot of blood. Still hanging in there, though.'

I lay Alison on the bed and Gina pushes me to the side saying, 'Let me care for her, Steve. You have bigger things to handle with the whole ship. I am needed here now,' she adds with a wry smile.

I give her a quick single-arm hug and say, 'Good on you, Gina. Thank you for saving all of us.'

She grins with a quiet gratitude. This is a turning point. She knows she has taken back control of her life.

Mal Willis

Mal Willis is relieved to hear Steve Flynn's voice.

He had been woken an hour earlier by Bill Jones, phoning from the critical incident room. Goodness, he must have been sleeping there.

The sergeant had been listening to a confrontation in the suite living room where Carter had brought Steve and another man to answer Roger's questions about an incident at the bulkhead store-room. There had been shots fired. It was hard to picture exactly what had gone on. It was all recorded.

Bill had phoned Mal Willis and Jeff Fowler to inform them, in case the Navy would have to move in during the night to rescue the situation.

Mal now takes quick notes as Steve explains, over the satellite phone, the happenings of the night. In return, the police inspector gives him operational advice on securing the bodies and the crime scene, evacuating the wounded and how to progress from there.

After those immediate suggestions, he promises to get back on the ship's telephone within half-an-hour with more detailed instructions.

He concludes with a sincere, 'Well done, Steve! Well done to you all!'

Jeff Fowler

Canberra. Sunday 25 February 2007

Jeff Fowler had become instantly alert at the sound of Bill Jones's voice. Mal Willis is patched into the line. Fowler takes in all the briefing:

Two dead, Carter and Williamson.

Two wounded, Brennan seriously; Cavanagh – a shoulder wound.

Alison Wood released from captivity. Alive. Shocked, maybe traumatised, a large bruise on the temple, binding marks on ankles and wrists but otherwise no obvious injuries.

Steve Flynn and one of Brennan's men, called Ron, are in control of the ship. Captain Rodriguez and his crew have been most co-operative.

Cavanagh's woman, Gina Robér, has been credited with saving the situation by shooting Cavanagh.

Steve Flynn is seeking assistance with medical evacuation and the security of the ship.

Fowler advises there is an Australian patrol boat in the vicinity. He will contact the Navy immediately to seek orders for their support. They have the capacity to handle the emergency first-aid and the security.

He asks Inspector Willis to convey the thanks of the AFP to Steve Flynn and the others, and to advise that the patrol boat would be with them at first light, only a couple of hours or so away in those waters.

Before signing off, Fowler speaks to Bill Jones. 'Thank you for not sleeping, Bill. You are a very special sergeant. Thank you for your good work, monitoring over all these days.'

'Appreciated, Sir. Just doing my job.'

* * * *

As a courtesy to his international colleagues, Fowler sends an electronic advice to the *NPA* and *Versec* so that they are at least aware, even if they can't act.

The *Lerna*

None of the crew have slept on the Lerna. The sun washes its morning aura over the tranquil Panapompom Lagoon but, on board, it is a frenzy of activity.

Captain Rodriguez is on the bridge, in conversation with the officers on the Australian Navy patrol boat which has nosed into the lagoon, with the dawn. It is now almost alongside, armed sailors ready to board.

Alison Wood is the only guest asleep, with Gina keeping a patient watch over her. Ron is still quietly guarding Cavanagh, now patched but very pale and in considerable pain as the initial shock of the bullet wound has worn off. He is lying on his uninjured side, grimacing and moaning on the couch.

Down in the companionway, Ben Brennan has lost consciousness. The shallow breaths are the faintest indication of life, even though the sucking wound is now sealed. He is very pale, almost blue in pallor.

The bodies of Williamson and Carter still lie where they have fallen. That had been the advice from Mal Willis; leave the crime scene as untouched as possible until Navy personnel could make their assessment.

* * * *

I meet the sailors as they board to give directions on how to locate Ben and Roger, the wounded personnel. A lieutenant-commander comes on board, passing on congratulations. He then goes to the bridge to introduce himself formally to Captain Rodriguez who is, as ever, the picture of courtesy and compliance.

Within minutes, the Navy have an armed officer on the bridge, assisting the captain.

Numerous photographs are taken of both scenes of shooting action. Roger and Ben are evacuated to the patrol boat where a medical facility exists. Len and Peter are zipped into black body bags and are carried onto the patrol boat.

Armed sailors have taken over the security of the ship from Ron and me. We both head into Gina's rooms to unwind for the first time from the tension.

Alison is lost in the sleep of the exhausted; washed somehow and dressed in her hostess's designer pyjamas, smelling fragrant and clean between aromatic silk sheets.

Gina, the self-appointed nurse, has done well. She is carefully watching her resting patient with a new-found look of confidence. It is in her manner, her expression – no longer the jaded model.

I check Alison's breathing. There is a nasty bruise on the side of her head and red tie-marks where the ropes had bound her but she would recover from the physical experience. I wonder about the effect, in the long term, on her peace of mind. This has been a harrowing time – and I only know about her time on the *Lerna*. What else had happened since we parted in that Cairns restaurant?

Gina takes Ron back out to the suite office where she sits on the couch to thank him again for protecting her from a bullet.

I listen through the open door to the ever-gracious Ron pointing out that it was actually Gina's bullet which has saved us all, by hitting Roger in the shoulder. Their smirking laughs are the grins and chat of emotionally drained people.

I think of Ron realising that, since all the action, he is sitting beside a stunning red-head with a fashion-model figure who is smiling at him and thanking him – not an everyday experience for a covert warrior, I would guess.

The giggles suggest that Gina too is listening to a tousle-haired Aussie hero continuing to tell her she has done well, saved lives, and been useful. Such lavish praise, such genuineness – all to a lady who has been starved of both for so long; except from me, perhaps.

I doze as they talk and the tension of the past few hours drains out of me. My body and mind need rest.

* * * *

The naval commander radios his report back to headquarters.

His patrol boat has Roger Cavanagh in custody as well as holding the two bodies of his associates in the ship's morgue.

They have the critically wounded Ben Brennan in their sick bay with the ship's medical officer monitoring him very closely, under radioed advice from specialist doctors at Naval HQ.

The *Lerna*, its crew and guests are under military supervision as it sails alongside the patrol boat.

* * * *

Meanwhile, another naval patrol boat is also heading south with five people in custody and two in body bags from a foiled raid off Misima Island, days before.

* * * *

And at first light on this excitement-charged morning, an Australian naval frigate has intercepted a Korean freighter en route for Sydney. It has indeed been a hectic few days.

Angus Forbes

London. Saturday 24 February 2007

It is nearing midnight on a Saturday in London as Angus Forbes reads the main message of an email from Jeff Fowler.

'Bingo! The Australian Navy have Roger Cavanagh in custody. It is Sunday morning there,' he says to Catherine Weston.

They had spent their Saturday evening checking and collating all their evidence and theorising. *NPA* is a seven-days-a-week job, despite the challenges and the *stop order*. Who could sleep while thinking of all the possible permutations?

Angus Forbes sips his cup of black tea as he reads aloud the Australian's early morning report, with a wry interest.

'Cavanagh has been shot in the shoulder. Apparently, there were two gunfights on board. Two *Nemesis* agents had gone on board. Carter and Williamson are both dead – shot. A *Nemesis* agent, their top man in fact, is critical with a stab wound. They don't muck about, those Aussies, do they?'

Catherine Weston gives an encouraging grin. 'The sun will be well up into Sunday over there now. Good that they are working our hours.' She feels for her boss. The *NPA* has effectively been shut down, although they are still toiling away. Forbes's rather rash plan for using the lugger as bait had not achieved its expected catch. However, she suspects that the plan might not have been all his doing. It smacks of something that could have been foisted on him from higher up – because it strikes her as passing strange that special forces troops could be on location so effectively in such a short time frame.

No matter, Angus's Highland confidence has taken a jolt. His colleagues at *Versec* had been told to halt all their operations, too. The whole investigation is being marginalised. Angus is not feeling at his most valued.

'They should be able to join the dots, now,' Catherine says optimistically. 'They can interrogate him with the evidence in front of them.'

He nods, still thinking.

'Jeff Fowler has another comment,' he says. 'He has had the Navy intercept a Korean freighter heading from Newcastle to Sydney.'

'Goodness!' Her eyebrows rise in admiring wonder. 'Do they never sleep? What was Fowler's justification for that?'

'He's using his anti-terrorism legislation. Apparently, Len Williamson got a shipment placed on the freighter after it left Newcastle and Fowler has Cavanagh on tape as saying that this is his trump card. You'd have to expect something potentially nasty. I'm just pleased that Fowler and their Navy have the freedom to act as swiftly as that.' He gives a wan smile.

'I'll need to brief the Brigadier though,' he adds. 'They could decide in five minutes that it is *all systems go*, again.'

'I love your Scottish optimism,' says Catherine with her Yorkshire twang bringing quiet laughs to them both.

* * * *

'So Brigadier,' says Angus, concluding his briefing over the phone. 'The Aussies seem to have the case wrapped up. Cavanagh is in custody; caught in the act with the bad guys kidnapping a journalist. They have all the records of *Lerna* conversations and our technician has cracked his encryption code.'

'What?' queries the Brigadier.

'Roger Cavanagh communicated with his masters through a PGP encryption code,' explains Angus. 'Well, one of our techs has actually managed to crack his code. He was lucky, but luck favours the brave. We've been able to read Roger's messages from and to his bosses. We just haven't managed to identify the sources yet – just what is written. But the tech is confident he can crack it.'

'Well, well done!' praises the Brigadier. 'I'm both impressed and amazed at such an achievement. It is like Bletchley Park all over again with your fellows cracking enemy codes, eh?'

'Yes. Anyway, I reckon Cavanagh will sing like a canary now. He has nothing to gain by holding out further. I'm sure he will plea-bargain. Otherwise he'll be locked up forever with all the scams and killings involved.

'It's been a huge enterprise. I don't think people really understand its scale. And these bankers in the States; their money laundering and gambling on the market. That's set to blow too. It could never continue indefinitely. I don't know what they were thinking. Maybe they needed a bit of Scottish canniness with their money.'

'Indeed,' replies the Brigadier. 'There's a lot to be said for the traditional honest management of resources. Now, do you really think Cavanagh will give up so easily? He must have weathered many crises in his time. Wouldn't you expect him to have other aces to play? He would have some sort of exit strategy.'

'The Aussies have heard he reports to a person called *Ramas*,' says Angus. 'A lot of the takings appear to go to this *Ramas*, through some as yet unlocated channels. Fowler reckons Cavanagh will reveal the identity very soon and then they'll have all the pieces of the jigsaw.'

'That really would be a coup for our antipodean friends,' agrees the Brigadier. 'I didn't realise they were that close.'

'Well, you're up-to-date now, Sir. I'm sorry the lugger episode didn't snatch the big one for us. We probably should have involved you in the planning, but you were in France when it was hatched.'

'Not a problem, Angus,' he consoles. 'At least it took out seven of the enemy with no loss to us. We rattled their cage – good training for our chaps.'

The Brigadier mentions he will be going back to the chateau in France for a couple of days.

'We'll catch up next week.'

The Korean freighter

A naval helicopter brings Jeff Fowler out to the deck of the Navy frigate at first light. From there, he transfers over by ship's tender to the Korean freighter.

Inspector Eileen Lewis has been leading the interview process; but this is so critical to Fowler's anti-terrorism role that he wants to see for himself.

Lewis tells him the captain is being uncooperative. They have interviewed most of the crew. She has established that a number of sealed crates had been lifted on board at sea from a smaller cargo boat.

They have located them, sealed and marked as containing engine parts, hidden in the centre of a mass of containers. The Navy bomb disposal team has opened one crate and it does indeed contain engine parts.

So, presently, they are checking whether false information has been supplied or if they've gone to the wrong container in error.

* * * *

Jeff Fowler meets a scowling Korean skipper, being held under guard on his bridge. He is complaining in very broken English; but good enough to be understood. When asked about the shipment, he scowls and becomes sullen.

'It's no use saying nothing,' advises Fowler. 'Your crew saw the boxes being lifted on board. We have their interview statements. They took us to one container. Who asked you to bring the boxes on board?'

The captain sits and glowers.

'If we find weapons or explosives in these boxes and you haven't spoken to us, you will be in jail for many many years. I will see to that personally,' Fowler continues quietly.

The Korean captain's eyes widen. He is paying close attention.

'We will find the boxes. You know that. This ship is going nowhere. If we have to open every container on the ship, we will find the boxes.'

'What explosive?' says the captain, in his strong accent. 'Motor parts!'

'Who made the arrangement with you?' persists the policeman.

'Masa,' says the Korean. 'Meester Masa. SPFA. Motor parts. Late shipment to go to Balmeen.'

'Who brought them on board?'

'Weellamsin,' says the captain. 'Lin Weellamsin. He pay me. EFT. Look!'

The captain turns to his laptop and flicks a few keys. There is an electronic funds transfer from a company in Malaysia. 'Weellamsin pay me. Good contract. Legal business.'

'Show me the container where the boxes are stored.'

* * * *

The captain indicates the same container that the crew have already identified. He looks angry and confused. 'No explosive,' he repeats. 'Motor parts.'

* * * *

Fowler leaves the captain under guard and returns to Eileen Lewis. This is confusing. Why would Cavanagh load motor parts onto a freighter going to Sydney? How could that be his trump card?

He needs to interview Cavanagh.

443

He leaves Lewis with the naval personnel working through every crate in the container. At the lowest level of concern, the captain is guilty of taking on board an illegal shipment to by-pass proper controls. At the highest level of concern, there could be any form of terrorist device or explosive packed into an innocuous container. They will check everything.

* * * *

Fowler leaves the freighter and the frigate's helicopter flies him back to land.

He contacts the office of the Deputy Chief of the Navy. He has to interview Roger Cavanagh as a matter of some urgency. How can that be arranged, given that Cavanagh is on a patrol boat days out from Cairns?

Gina and Ron

Gina listens to Ron speak about his work with *Nemesis*.

He talks about Ben Brennan's tremendous drive to disrupt the slave traffickers.

She feels she can at least relate, in a smaller way, to a sense of imprisonment. What free people don't understand is that the true punishment is the loss of freedom and the lack of a sense of worth. It is the mental incarceration.

But the conditions of total slavery, chained in a coffle, would be beyond most human tolerance; and too hard for Gina to contemplate. Horrible!

'What a good man you are. What did you do before you started this?'

His story starts. 'I was a fitter and turner by trade. Married with two young boys.' He looks wistful. It seems a long time ago.

'So why did you change?' Gina is puzzled.

He tells her about losing his wife; and trying to bring up the boys. 'I lost it. No excuse and I make none. Weak as piss, I know, but there you are. That's what happened. I left it to my parents to raise my boys – along with my late wife's family.'

Then he speaks of joining *Nemesis*. 'I decided I might not be so useless if I could help Ben save some of these poor wretches.'

'What a sad, inspiring story, Ron,' says Gina. 'You're being too hard on yourself. What now?'

445

'That depends on Ben. Let's see how he pulls through; *if* he pulls through.'

She sits quietly holding Ron's hand.

'And you, Gina? With Roger in custody, will you have a life here?'

She gives an ironic grin. 'I don't know if I've ever had a life here really, Ron. Roger has been a man driven by business and by collecting possessions. I've always just been another collectible.

'And yet – yet, over time – there were some really fun times. Even anchored here in the lagoon, we were laughing and swimming like we used to. He was the most carefree I can remember in months. As if he knew it was all going to end.

'So no, Ron, I don't know. I come from Bournemouth in England. That's all history. I have had no contact for years. Too hard to go back to that world now.

'I was a cat-walk model before I joined Roger. I've no skills and fashion-looks don't last. I've no money. All this luxury was here to be used – but I could never take it away. It'll probably all be taken back by the authorities anyway. Just a façade; an old cracked mirror – and I don't like my reflection in it.'

He gives her an encouraging hug. 'But you're the hero of the moment. You've saved us all. Steve will tell everyone. It'll all work out.'

'I hope you're right, Ron. I really hope you're right.' Her voice is filled with a need for this all to end. 'Thanks for listening. Can we just rest here together, for a bit? Alison's asleep in my bed and I desperately need to close my eyes. My beauty sleep was rudely interrupted by you men making all that noise.'

She lays her head against her new-found friend, falling quickly asleep with a contented smile on her face.

Alison awakes

Alison's eyes open slowly in the large bed with scented silk sheets. Then she sits up and sees me, freshly-showered, at the foot of the bed.

'Welcome to today,' I say cheerily. 'How're you feeling?'

'Been asleep,' she says dozily. 'Where am I? Hello, Steve. What's happening? Where am I?'

I smile at her confusion. 'You're in Gina's bed. You've been through a hard time. You needed your sleep so I've just been checking to see you're alright.'

'Gina's bed?' she says, as she tries to recollect the earlier hours. 'Oh, Steve! What's been happening?'

'Would you like a glass of water and another ice pack for that bruised forehead? I'll bring you up-to-date?'

She nods and takes a sip from the glass I am holding out for her.

'We are sailing towards Cairns,' I tell her, as I gently place the covered ice pack on her head. 'It is Sunday. You've slept well.'

She winces and takes control of the cold pack, dabbing.

I carry on with the update. 'Ben and Roger are on the Navy patrol boat which is travelling beside us. Do you remember? Ben is listed as critical but stable. He was stabbed in the chest in a fight with Williamson.' I pause as her memory recall ends in a sad nod. 'Roger has a serious gunshot wound to the shoulder but it's not life-threatening. The Navy is in control of both ships. So we can just enjoy our luxury cruise back to Australia.'

She is silent; still looking confused. I don't want to prompt any more bad memories so I just wait. I've been struggling myself, in the quiet of the stateroom suite as I waited for her to waken. The memory of the shooting, the smell of bloody vomit, the sight of bullet-smashed bodies, the shock on everyone's faces – not least the women I care about.

I've been in firefights in the Army but as part of a trained team, never quite like the past few hours. Maybe it's easier when you're with others. But it's still not something you ever forget.

And I nearly lost it all – Alison.

I realise that now. This woman is important to me. I shudder to think what she might have been through in these past hours and days but I don't want to go there.

And it is bringing me different memories; of a drunken father, my mother cowering in fear – and of me, too young and too small to stop it, to make it all go away; of being inadequate, jumping up to help and being thrown across the room; the sense of uselessness, unable to make the difference.

I'm no hero – never have been. All that courage bullshit – you do what you have been trained to do; it just happens. All I ever wanted was to be like all the fellas I could see in the streets – normal; in happy stable relationships. They don't have to be involved with international crims. They can go to work for 9.00 am and be home by 5.00 pm to do the gardening, play with the kids, kick a footy around. No adrenalin-charged frights and fights. No doubting their adequacy. No feeling scared for themselves or their friends. Oh, how good it would be just to be – ordinary.

'Len?' she asks, with her eyes widening in fear.

'He's dead. Len and Peter Carter are both dead.'

She nods. Vague recollections and understandings flash through her memory.

'Gina?'

'Gina's with Ron in the suite office; asleep the last time I looked. She cleaned you up, put you to bed and looked after you.' I pause as she processes something in her mind, nodding at whatever she is remembering. 'And she saved the day by shooting Roger. She's one of the heroes. We would all have been gone without her taking them by surprise. Ron is Ben's offsider. He and Gina seemed to be chatting away quite happily.'

'Wow!' She speaks slowly. 'Good on Gina; shooting Roger. It's hard to imagine. Good on her. I remember Ron. I met him earlier up at Madang. He's okay?' She sees my thumbs-up. 'What a huge few days! Has it really only been a few days since we lay on the grass in Cairns? And Ben told me to go back to court reporting. I've been so scared, Steve. I've been trying to be brave – and I feel such a fool for getting into this. I should've just stayed as a court reporter, as Ben told me. He would have been safe today.'

'No.' I soothe, shaking my head. 'You know he would've continued the struggle whatever you'd said. It was his mission. He is driven to do this.'

'He said I reminded him of his daughter, Steve.' She is getting maudlin. 'And he would not let me down like he had failed her. He was torturing himself because he couldn't save his wife and daughter from being captured and drowned by pirates.'

'Is that what happened? I wondered, back in Cairns, what was driving him with this *Nemesis* business. We've never been in his shoes. He must have felt responsibility. Survivor's guilt!' I pause to think it through. 'Probably, no-one else is blaming him.'

'But he came onto this ship to save me, didn't he?' she says in a pleading tone. 'If he hadn't been trying to rescue me, none of this would have happened.'

'Now *you're* tormenting yourself. You know he would have confronted Len and Roger eventually. It was his reason for living – to bring them, and their kind, to some form of justice.'

As an after-thought, I add, 'You know, you might actually have made Ben very happy. He knows he saved you; he didn't fail. That you reminded him of his daughter might have helped. Didn't you see how happy and proud he looked, even through his pain? He has been vindicated. You've done him a service.'

'Do you really think so?'

'I do. And if he hadn't taken the lead to come on board during the night, you might still be at the mercy of that animal. You've been very brave, Alison. I don't know what has happened since Cairns but you've certainly put yourself on the line. You're a pretty inspiring woman.'

She gives a wry smile as I continue. 'Most of us blokes have been soldiers of some sort or another. We've seen some stuff like this before but you're a journalist. You deserve a badge for putting yourself out there.'

We hug on the bed as she makes a step forward out of the abyss.

'Do you believe in destiny?' I ask. 'Things happen for a reason?' She is clinging to me, her head nuzzles at my neck; shaking – crying gentle tears of relief. She doesn't reply but raises her moist eyes in question.

'If you hadn't been chasing your exposé and I hadn't been picked up by the *Lerna*, we would never have met. It's kismet!'

She smiles; her eyes doing the talking.

'It was the danger caused by our meeting in Cairns that brought Ben and Mal Willis to your motel room to protect us. There's a destiny that has brought us together, Alison. And a destiny that has saved us. We are fated to be together. Do you feel that? I feel that.'

I am pleased I'd managed to say what I'd been thinking since not long after we'd met. It is hard to find suitable words to express myself.

She just nods tearily – a small encouraging smile telling me she agrees.

We lie back, comforted by each other's warmth, strength, touch, scents – it has been a long time since we have been together; the memory of the last time is still fresh in my mind and the bed is very comfortable; aromatic and welcoming.

The sweetly-scented silk shimmers as it floats above us, settling over our long-awaited embrace.

Fowler and Roger Cavanagh

'Get me off this bloody ship!' roars Roger. 'This is illegal detainment and I won't stand for it! Get me back on the *Lerna* this minute!'

His efforts cause him to wince in pain from his wound, taking away some of the bravado of the moment.

Jeff Fowler is intrigued rather than shocked by the response. Clearly, this will be no ordinary interview. He feels the buzz in his system. Placing a digital recorder on the table, he has a strong urge to grin but ... he contains it.

'I'm in international waters.' Roger has recovered his composure. 'I've been taken from New Guinean waters by force. I've committed no crime. I demand to be released.' His cheeks are straining red.

'No crime?' Fowler gives a patient frown. 'Well, let's start with international piracy, smuggling of illegal materials, laundering large sums of money to avoid lawful taxes.' The federal policeman maintains his expression while he watches his adversary's cheeks twitch. 'Before we even touch on complicity in murder, theft, kidnap, extortion ... you name it.'

'A fantasy.' Roger snorts. 'Total shit! Show me where my name is a signatory to any illegal act. Show me any time I've been at a scene of a crime. Show me any evidence at all to link me to any of these fanciful accusations. I'm a legal trader and there are many highly-respected people who will attest to that.'

Fowler does smile now, a polite cat smile; a cat with a mouse smile. It is his natural reaction to the thrill of the contest. He is in his element.

'We have documentation of one Peter Carter – purchases, arrangements, supervision and training of people who are committing criminal acts. He is a signatory to the disbursement of the profits of illegal acts. He is implicated in acts of piracy. And he is a key associate, a paid employee of one Roger Cavanagh; your good self.'

Roger laughs derisively, then winces again from pain. Suave though he can be with his wavy blond hair and tanned complexion, he is not at his best with a 9 mm bullet hole in his shoulder. While his ability to command is a mite dulled – charm seems to be his new tack instead of bravado.

'Superintendent, dear dear me.' He teases. 'I know nothing of any illegal acts associated with anything that Peter Carter may have signed, supervised or been implicated in. Bring him in here and let him testify to the contrary.'

Fowler's expression is unmoved.

'You are well aware that Peter Carter is deceased. However, we do have recorded conversations between you and Mr Carter discussing, planning and, indeed, you approving an act of piracy off the coast of New Guinea.'

'It's doctored. Inadmissible in evidence,' says Roger smugly, barely concealing his concern at how such a recording could exist. It could only have been the mole.

Who the hell was that mole? It must have been Len, Roger thinks. He is sure of that now. When did they get to him? Was kidnapping the girl part of a sting to get him? More than likely. There is the proof that he was the mole, if any more proof is still needed.

'Superintendent, you will need to do better than that.'

Fowler patiently continues.

'Then we have Len Williamson, a notorious stand-over man and another of your employees, with an open-and-shut case of murder and kidnap at the least.'

The policeman watches his quarry carefully. Is that a flicker of uncertainty? He can't be sure.

'Oh, now you are becoming boring, Superintendent. Whatever Len Williamson did, he did of his own volition. Can you prove any link between him and me?'

Still it keeps coming. 'Then we have your association with the Boards of the South Pacific Freight Alliance and Grey Bear Investment Bank of the United States. People-smuggling, slavery, kidnap, wildlife smuggling, art theft … with the funds being laundered through GBIB.'

That gets a swift clipped response.

'I have not served on the boards of either company.' Roger is terse. 'Nor do I have any association with the operations of their activities. You know that.'

The policeman is unmoved.

'Well, it sounds good anyway, Mr Cavanagh. We have sworn testimonies from Messers Li, Gonzalez, Alatas, Masa, Esobal and Yodsuwan from the South Pacific Freight Alliance board that you are in effect the organiser of all the illegal trafficking activities in which the alliance has been involved.'

Roger's eyes are the only indicators of his concern.

'Well, haven't you done well, Superintendent?' he says. 'That is at least better. I would, of course, contest all of those testimonies in any court of law.'

'Of course,' Fowler responds. 'But the jury would hear their testimony and form a view of the truth or otherwise. The reporting in the wider *court of public opinion* would ensure that you would never work again in any position of influence or integrity. Who would trust someone indicted by so many?'

The Englishman is now looking at his police adversary with a new respect. There is a contest here for sure.

'But wait, there's much more,' continues the superintendent. 'We have the hi-jack of the *Sea Spray 2* followed by the murder of Aldo Pollock, a security guard; a ransom demand and the theft of millions by that extortion strategy.'

'You can't tie me into that,' splutters Roger, his anger returning. 'I was nowhere near that event.'

Steve? Steve had been the other guard on that boat. But did Steve know it was the SPFA team that had attacked the *Sea Spray*? No, how could he know it? He has already discounted Steve's involvement as the mole. The mole was Len.

'Not according to the testimony of the GBIB directors who told Sir Terence Sedgewood of the process to by-pass the financial tracking systems. He then informed you by encrypted message and you delivered your ransom demand in the same way.'

'Oh, and did I tell you we have cracked your PGP encryption code so we know all about the messages sent between you and Sir Terence – and, of course others. Are you ready to talk yet?'

Roger is more chastened. He sits quietly – his brain scheming on overtime. The mention of cracking the code seems to trigger another change of attitude.

'I want to be released immediately,' Roger asserts loudly. 'I have influence.'

Fowler laughs. He shouldn't have, he knows that, but the arrogance of Roger Cavanagh beggars belief.

'And your influence is?'

'I have been involved in work of a classified nature on behalf of governments. I would think they would not want the embarrassment of what I could say,' says Roger, jaw jutting in defiance.

'That avenue may have worked in other countries but it won't work here. I will not be put under such pressure. Indeed, it is our Navy which is detaining you under the international protocols of the sea.'

Cavanagh is silent again. He is such a wheeler and dealer. Fowler is enjoying the challenge.

'I might have information about a possible terrorist attack on a major city.' Cavanagh is playing his trump card. 'Information that I will not release until I am safe from your persecution.'

'Why should I believe you?'

454

'Have I ever told you a lie?' he says, with mock offence. 'I may have information about a cargo on a ship which could sail into a city harbour, causing an enormous potential threat. Do you want to know this information or are you going to proceed with your doomed prosecution of these defamatory accusations?'

'You would have to give me some information that is checkable before any such claim would have credibility.'

'Alright. I am aware of a shipment which was loaded into a container off the New South Wales coast, only a few days ago.'

Cavanagh speaks with the seriousness of knowledge about an impending tragedy. 'I will only divulge the location of the container when I am released to a neutral country with no extradition agreement to Australia or its allies.' His pointed stare strengthens his show of bravado.

'Am I to understand,' asks Fowler quietly, 'that you are threatening me to release you because you have information about a cargo which might be of danger to a city? In Australia? Are you trying to extort your freedom now, in exchange for information? Your brazenness is gob-smacking.'

'I'm giving you an offer,' says Cavanagh flatly. 'I am a dealer. There is always a deal to be made.'

'Alright. Start by giving me information that will be useful to me. To whom do you report? Who is *Ramas*?'

Angus and the Minister

Angus Forbes picks up his phone, checking his watch – Sunday evening. Monday in Australia where all the action would be happening.

It is the Minister's office. Perhaps, they are giving the go-ahead on Roger Cavanagh. On a Sunday?

The Minister comes on the line.

'Angus, terrible news, old boy. Sorry to be the one to break it to you. The Brigadier and his wife, the countess, have been killed in a plane crash off the Brittany coast.'

Angus is stunned. He remembers the Brigadier mentioning only yesterday on the phone that he would be going back to the chateau and that he would talk to him next week. That's what he had said. The Brigadier is a very experienced pilot with his own twin-engined plane. He flies back and forth over the channel every week.

'What happened, Minister?'

'These are only early reports but it seems the Brigadier went home to see the countess at the chateau. Then they both took off on a flight logged for London. Witnesses saw the plane out over the sea this afternoon, off the coast of Brittany. They said it appeared to suddenly dive and splash into the ocean. Must have been engine failure because it wasn't a stormy day.

456

'The strange thing is the usual flight path doesn't go anywhere near the ocean off Brittany. It crosses the channel north east of Normandy. Why would he be so far off his flight path? It is all very sad! Sorry to be the one to break the news but I thought you would want to hear it from me rather than any other source. Now there will be a huge funeral. The Brigadier was a national war hero and the countess is, was, enormously successful in her own right – huge vineyards, wineries, almost royalty if they still had it in France. All very sad.'

'Thank you for letting me know,' says Angus 'and my condolences to both sides of the family. Does the Brigadier's passing have any impact on the status of your *NPA* project, Minister?' he asks, never one to miss an opportunity to remind the Minister that he had actually set up the project, which is now stalled.

'No,' says the Minister. 'Keep it on hold still.'

'Okay, Minister. Can I advise my team of that?'

'Of course, Angus,' replies the Minister. 'Of course.'

Roger Cavanagh and Fowler

Coral Sea. Monday 26 February 2007

'Mr Cavanagh,' says Fowler. 'I admire your angling and dealing but, to use your British parlance, *You're nicked and you know it.* Our case will stand up in court. *You* know it. *I* know it. You are not telling me anything that is useful in tidying up all these operations you have put in place.'

'*Ramas*, eh?' says Cavanagh. 'That's what you want. Will that be the bargain then? If you get *Ramas*, we can negotiate?'

'That would be a start. You know I can't negotiate deals with people accused of crimes. I am a policeman. Plea-bargaining can only happen through the process of prosecution. You would deal with the prosecutors. I can tell you, though, that making threats is not the way to go. The only negotiating tool which has ever proved successful in the past has been to turn Queen's evidence so that the criminal activities can be stopped.'

There is a pause as Cavanagh looks at Fowler. He ponders some more. Then, he grimaces with discomfort from the pain in his shoulder.

Eventually, he is ready.

'*Ramas* is a codename for our organisation ... and for the person who set up the processes we use. She, because it is a *she*, made the template for a multi-levelled organisation where there are no links between the layers except by coded messages. Today we use encryption – but you know that anyway, apparently.

'*Ramas* developed her system some forty years ago and she engenders great respect for her abilities in understanding how to manipulate the financial systems, while staying under the radar of law-enforcement agencies.

'For an older lady, she is right across modern technology. *Ramas* is short for *ramasseur* which, as you would know, is French for *collector* – or at least a kind of collector, a dog catcher really. I think the name must have been a joke, chosen just to confuse people even more.

'Nevertheless, *Ramas is* a collector. She doesn't need money, nor does she want it. Rather, we who have learned from her, pay her a tribute regularly; beautiful things she might like, *objets d'art*; in the way that loyal subjects give gifts to a queen. I have met *Ramas* twice, once in Paris and once in London. That is who *Ramas* is.'

Jeff Fowler frowns. 'Helpful, but it doesn't let us locate the lady. Does she have a name?'

'I have never known a name for her. That is part of the secrecy of our organisation. Our two mantras are *results* and *silence*. We use coded names only, for very senior people. Real names are not bandied about.'

'Well, so far, you haven't told me nearly enough to even consider a plea-bargain. The identity of *Ramas* would be a big step forward. Otherwise, as you know, we have a catalogue of indictments against you.'

Cavanagh is trying to look calm but it makes him look more devious. Maybe it is the effect of his injury – the hunched look. No more Mr Charisma.

'Did you want to return to your threat to a major city?' Fowler is encouraging. 'Did you have anything you wanted to tell me about that?'

Cavanagh stays quiet. He seems to be considering his options.

'It won't work. I can see that now!' Roger says with a strange expression in his eyes, almost wild and then settling. He sounds resigned. 'I am a student of the Emperor Napoleon. Even that great man, Corsican you know, came to see that there are times to concede.'

Fowler says nothing. This is a time for listening and waiting.

'This shoulder is really uncomfortable,' says Roger. 'How could she have shot at me? After all that I have done for her. Ingratitude; plain ingratitude. Look. Len Williamson loaded a shipment onto a freighter off Port Macquarie.'

'Yes.' Fowler is relaxed. 'Tell me the whole story, Mr Cavanagh. Let's not waste any more time. What was the shipment? What are you alleging?'

More silence.

'Could I have a drink of water, please? This shoulder.' He winces.

Fowler passes a plastic cup of water to his left hand.

After a sip or two, a deflated Roger says, 'It was a distraction, you see. I didn't expect to be shot. I was anticipating being able to escape from the *Lerna*. I was planning my opportunity to disappear – just me and an assistant. The investigators were closing in. I thought it might be insurance – a bluff, to get us out of a tricky situation; to give us time to get away. It would give me the space I needed.

'I wouldn't need much time. A few hours and I would have been gone. The escape route is all set up – me and the Australian. I've just given him practice with sailing the tender. I have planes ready on three airstrips. I can fly – old private licence from way back – but you don't forget. We would have just disappeared. It was a distraction. You see that, don't you?' His eyes plead for understanding and then he turns his head away with a rueful shake.

He continues. 'It couldn't work with the Navy involved. I knew that much. We try to stay under the radar. I thought if we had the chance to be missing for a few hours in open sea, we might get away. It can't work now. I see that.'

He sighs a dejected, resigned gasp.

'The shipment was motor parts but delivered in such a way as to make it look more sinister. The captain was well paid. If we were cornered, we could make it look like a terrorist situation because all the crew would know a shipment was on-loaded at sea. Then there would be a search which would take you all hours and hours, chasing your tails. We would get away and the shipment would prove to be harmless motor parts. So we would have done no harm. You see that, don't you? No harm; no crime. How could we be accused of offences when clearly they were innocent parts, quite appropriate to be unloaded at White Bay?'

Jeff Fowler keeps his face as composed as he can while he watches Cavanagh's performance and thinks to himself, *This man is quite mad! He rationalises everything into his own simplistic business logic with no comprehension at all of the fear, the man-hours and the cost which his idiotic projects entail. He is insane!*

'So there is nothing of danger on the Korean freighter?'

'Ah, you knew which freighter it was.' He sounds surprised. 'You are better than I gave you credit for.'

Fowler shakes his head in wonder. The man really is quite mad. How else could he live in this delusion, which has caused so much grief to so many?

'Do you have any more information on *Ramas*?'

'I believe she is French,' says Cavanagh contritely. 'She spoke with a strong French accent when I met her. I believe she may be a countess, with a home in the Loire or somewhere close. This will get me off these charges now, won't it?'

'That will be up to the lawyers, the prosecutors, Mr Cavanagh. I am but a simple policeman. Tell me, have you ever heard of the *Napoleon Curse*?'

'A curse? On the emperor?'

'Yes. In January of this year, a prospector in Central Queensland invoked Napoleon's Curse on the people who had stolen his fine sapphire. I thought you might know since you are such a student of the French Emperor.'

'A curse? Who believes in curses?' Cavanagh says, bewildered.

'Yes. My researchers tell me it was originally placed by a Romany because *Il Gran Ladro* – that means *The Great Thief* in Italian – your Napoleon, had stolen the sapphire from the Romany people of the Balkans.'

461

'What did the curse say?'

'That he would lose all his power and be shunned by society. And it happened to Napoleon, didn't it? That sapphire was called the Mohács Blue. You must have heard of it if you have really studied the emperor. You can even find the reference on the web. You haven't been stealing sapphires recently, have you, Mr Cavanagh? As I say, I'm told that a Bosnian prospector in Central Queensland had a very valuable sapphire stolen, just last month.

'It is only that the thief of that stone mentioned that it had been stolen for *Ramas*. It is in the court record. Now the Bosnian invoked the old Romany curse. He actually called it Napoleon's Curse, by name, on whoever had stolen his sapphire, the *Balkan Blue*. How many *Ramases* are there? Could it be that the thief will be cursed ... like Napoleon? Have you received the *Balkan Blue*, Mr Cavanagh?'

'I am no thief. Nor is *Ramas*.'

But the Englishman had gone very pale.

* * * *

Fowler leaves Roger Cavanagh in his cabin. Quite mad, he thinks. A totally bizarre conversation – and it is all recorded.

He has some urgent phone calls to make; information to share – and quickly; and some advice to the lieutenant-commander of the patrol boat, who would have to deal with the irrational cunning of Mr Cavanagh during this return voyage to Cairns. No doubt he would try to compromise the situation in some way for his benefit. Lawyers can conjure up the most obscure points of legal distraction. It is critical to give him nothing to claim, especially in any form of mistreatment.

Then he leaves as he arrived; by helicopter to the frigate at sea – only now it is dark. There will be busy times ahead if they are to tie up all the loose ends and mop up this criminal mess.

Cecile and Douglas

Loire Valley. Sunday 25 February 2007

Cecile looks fondly at her husband. And so it has come to this.

She takes Douglas's hand. They no longer feel like the countess and the Brigadier – just Cecile and Douglas. He has really been the only man who has attracted her since the days of Aaron and the untimely death of the count. There had been many over the years who would have been delighted suitors, but her interest was never in the trivial; more the intellectual.

She hadn't needed intimate relationships with men. But Douglas could talk her language; well at least until he was drawn into the unforgiving vortex of *Ramas* – so sad that her imaginary game had been misappropriated and made so toxic.

She has written the farewell letter. It lies on the table in the bedroom. The police will find it, in time.

The Brigadier had flown in at lunchtime. He hadn't been expected for another day. They had sat quietly in their sitting room off the bedroom, surrounded by the rich gold and burgundy furnishings – relics of a grander age.

Douglas had told her that Roger Cavanagh had been shot and was now in custody. The British NPA had cracked the encryption code. Roger was expected to tell the police everything he knew. It wouldn't be the whole story. Does anyone really know the whole story? But it is over. They both know that.

There is a sadness but also a tranquillity. They have lived long. Of course, given their time again they would have done things differently. Nevertheless, ever the pragmatist, the game is over for Cecile – in every sense. With a lady's attention to detail, she straightens the cover on the back of the sofa and hand-in-hand they walk to the aircraft, still sitting warm on the runway from its recent flight from England.

Quietly they board the plane. Douglas checks the fuel gauge. It isn't full but there will be enough for the flight ahead. He radios his usual flight plan to London and fires the twin engines into life.

Cecile looks through the windscreen to her favourite willow tree beside the lake. The trailing branches seem to be weeping a farewell. The ducks still swim peacefully over the waters in front of the manicured gardens. The chateau looks especially grand today; the afternoon sun glints off the roof turrets.

Douglas taxies the plane into position.

'Au revoir, my ducks, my memories and my collection,' says Cecile. 'Isn't it funny that it was Merri's strange French which came up with the title *Ramasseur* for *the game*? She thought my collection of antiquities in the chateau was so quaint. Then *Ramas* became the reason for all the collection to grow.'

Douglas smiles a tolerant smile. They are at peace now but Cecile has to let go a little first.

'It was a *Hydra*, Douglas. Its breath poisoned everything just like the monster from Greek mythology ... and it had a life of its own. I couldn't escape. I couldn't kill it. I never intended it should be a force of evil. Perhaps, our action now will kill the monster's heads forever. They say the *Hydra* was the guardian of the under-world. Well, we shall soon know, won't we?'

'Cecile, we are doing what is right at last.' His voice carries a patient, resigned understanding; the proud old soldier going out on his last patrol. 'Perhaps we will now end the terror of this devil we have helped to create.'

'But it was only a game, Douglas, only a game.'

The ingenuous bewilderment in her tone reminds him of that trace of guileless fragility which had first attracted him to the aloof intellectual countess – a vulnerability which lesser men might have taken for arrogance.

'It was Aaron who made it into something more sinister.' Her voice seems distant. 'But the real pain came from the *Butcher*. He took it into new horrors, kept it going and ensured we were trapped. I don't know how he came on the scene. He is the Devil incarnate.

'I know it was he who drew my British friends into it – all anonymous, protected by the blind codes. But they were my friends from long ago. The compounded agony is that I lived through the inhumanity of the Nazis giving legal sanction to condemn so many of their own citizens as sub-human; to take away their legitimacy and exterminate them. That was where I found my integrity, my soul, all those years ago. That was what I fought against.

'Yet here am I today, ostensibly founder of an organisation which is to my eternal shame not too dissimilar from that brutish corruption of morals and values. Our game has ended up sentencing innocent people to a lifetime of slavery. No matter how we sanitise it with our language, what is the difference?

'And Douglas, these terrible nightmares I have had for the past year? Haunting sounds of women in pain? South Pacific women, calling to me on the breeze and in the recesses of my subconscious.

'It has been a torment – the horror of the slave trade, in an Indonesian *objet d'art*. I hadn't understood until that moment what Aaron, Cavanagh and the *Butcher* had done to my simple game. I sat there under my willow tree as the sounds of the women's lament floated around me. And there was no escape – caught by the *Hydra*. So many unintended consequences hidden in the secrets of the maze. May the *Ramas Hydra* and the *Butcher* rot in hell.'

The twin engines roar; the ducks fluster busily in their flight across the lake and the plane rises gracefully into the sky. It heads west, out over the Atlantic, leaving the green patchwork of the Brittany coast behind.

* * * *

Cecile reaches across and kisses her husband. 'Au revoir, mon amour'.

Together they push down on the twin joysticks and the plane plunges at speed towards the hungry waves. 'Au revoir, *Ramas Hydra*'.

Alison in fresh air

Coral Sea. Monday 26 February 2007

Alison needs to smell fresh sea air again after her long confinement.

The bruises and bumps are sore but healing – and it is so comforting to be with Steve again. Maybe he is right – that it is destiny they are together. Time will tell but it is feeling good so far.

Stars are twinkling above. She looks across the evening water from the rail of the *Lerna* and sees the lights of the Navy boat slipping steadily through the gentle swell, keeping pace with them. They are like two migrating whales moving south.

She realises that Roger and Ben are on that ship, along with the bodies of Carter and Williamson. It helps reinforce her appreciation that she is safe with the people who remain on the *Lerna*; a very reassuring feeling.

Steve walks her up to the bridge. Glowing lights from the instruments contrast with the darkened sky outside. He introduces her to Captain Rodriguez, always happy in control of his ship, even with the naval officer standing close by.

Earlier, she had heard a chopper arrive over the naval vessel. She and Steve had stepped onto the balcony to watch. A Sikorsky Sea Hawk, Steve advised in response to her questioning look. It lowered a man onto the small deck of the patrol boat in a very slick exercise. She heard the helicopter again in the dark of the early evening.

Ever the inquisitive journalist, she turns to the naval officer on the bridge to ask what was happening with the chopper earlier. She gets a non-committal, if polite, response.

'Interesting.' She shrugs; not sure whether that thought is stimulated by her interest in whatever has been happening on the patrol boat or by the familiarity of the bland bureaucratic fob-off to a questioning member of the media.

Awareness. Her brain is regenerating from the numbing horror of the past few days; senses are starting to function again.

Her arm is linked tightly with Steve's. She needs that warm strong boost; that caring comfort.

Roger on the naval patrol boat

Coral Sea. Monday 26 February 2007

'Am I in custody?' Roger asks the lieutenant-commander when he comes for an evening visit.

The skipper replies diplomatically, 'You *are* in custody, under the rules of the sea; however, I think more of a guest, getting medical help.'

Superintendent Fowler had told the skipper about his likely conversations with Mr Cavanagh, and he had advised the commander to avoid getting into any difficult or devious arguments with their guest.

Best to duck the questions. Play the diplomat as far as you can, he had said. Lock him up if you have to, but try the gentle way first. He's on a ship. He's not going anywhere. We don't want to give him any leeway to use against us later in the law courts. He will twist your words.

'So that I can get some fresh air occasionally, can I go for a walk?' Roger persists. 'I am recuperating from a serious injury. I can't stay inside all day – unless I *am* a prisoner.'

'Of course, Sir,' says the commander. 'But this isn't a cruise boat. It is a naval ship so you can't just wander. I'll get someone to escort you.'

'Bah,' says Roger. 'If you must. I just want to breathe and to see the water. I live on boats, you know.'

'Yes, Sir,' says the commander. 'How long will you want to be outdoors?'

'I *am* a bloody prisoner.' Roger gasps. 'Have your men stand with me if you must. I might want to go out for ten minutes now and ten minutes in another hour. I just want to smell the air. You are a seaman. You understand.'

'Of course, Sir,' says the commander with great patience. 'I will assign a rating to you. You can call him when you require. We can start tomorrow morning.'

'Thank you, Captain,' says Roger, inflating the skipper's rank intentionally. 'I knew you would understand.'

Alison and Steve

Coral Sea. Monday 26 February 2007

'What will happen when we get to Cairns?' Alison looks fresh and innocent as she asks the question of me.

'I would imagine the police, Customs and quarantine will go over the *Lerna* with a fine-tooth comb. We will all give statements and then life will go on. Or at least until the court cases. We may be called to give evidence at some stage … but that could be years away, in reality.'

She takes in my words. 'I have masses of information for the biggest investigative journalism piece in years. The question is, do I really want to write it now, after seeing and smelling it all first-hand? This is the story I've always wanted to write. And I know I will write it. It's just I feel a bit shaken by it all, at the moment. It is a terrible business this piracy and smuggling, isn't it?'

'It sure is. Just give it some time.' I let her roll with her thoughts – an unwinding process. For all her doubting worry at present, she looks more beautiful than ever – a warmth in her eyes, a fragile quiver in the tone and yet, that strong individuality which conveys her courage to forge ahead.

'We have time to think,' she muses. 'Let's have another walk in the sea air.'

Roger defiant

Cavanagh, accompanied by a sailor, shuffles onto the rear deck. He is hampered by his injury, walking almost Napoleon-like with his right arm in a sling and a grey Navy-issue blanket wrapped over him like a cape.

He returns refreshed after ten minutes, as promised.

An hour later he is out again; ten minutes of pleasant chat with the sailor. They talk about the sea and places Roger has visited. He is very interested in the sailor's adventure stories – and starting to move more freely. The limited exercise is proving helpful.

* * * *

'I want Gina and Steve to come to me,' Roger tells the rating. 'She is my partner, my wife. Steve is my assistant. Tell the captain. It is important.'

'The commander, Sir. Yes, Sir, I'll pass your message on.'

* * * *

'The commander said, *No*, Sir.' The rating relays the answer.

'Noooo! I demand to see the commander. Tell him I have urgent information affecting the safety of both these ships. He will regret it forever if he doesn't come to see me. There is a time limit on this.'

* * * *

'Mr Cavanagh.' The lieutenant-commander stands with an armed rating in the doorway and speaks quietly. 'If you cannot stop pestering my crew with your requests, I regret that I will have to withdraw your walking breaks and confine you to your room.'

Roger Cavanagh stands hunched and defiant, the grey blanket cape over his shoulders. He fixes the commander with a steely gaze. 'You have just over an hour to return me to my ship.'

'I see, Mr Cavanagh. And why would you suggest such a timeline?'

'Because there is a bomb on the *Lerna* ... and only I have the code to defuse it.'

'Rubbish. This is just another of your attention-seeking ploys. I can tell you that we will not be acceding to your numerous requests. Rather, you will be confined to this room for the duration.'

'There is a bomb in the ensuite of my stateroom. The hatch is to the right of the sink console. Have one of your sailors check. It needs my code entered in an hour from now or it will explode. It is preset for just such an emergency. I clear it every three days and then it resets itself. A significant bomb. You have less than an hour, should you keep ignoring what I say. I have been tracking the time. I wouldn't delay if I were you, Captain. Do you want all these lives on your conscience ... and your record?'

The commander orders the rating to secure and guard the door. 'I will check your information, Mr Cavanagh. I assume that both the hatch and the bomb will be obvious?' He gives a disbelieving querulous stare.

'Oh, they will be obvious alright. Maybe you should check with the AFP superintendent too. I am not bluffing. You have an hour, including the time to get me over to the *Lerna*.'

The bomb

Cairns. Tuesday 27 February 2007

Jeff Fowler listens to the patrol boat commander on a line relayed through naval headquarters. He has made it only as far as Cairns since his interview with Roger Cavanagh on the previous day. It has been a chance for liaison with Mal Willis and his team.

'It certainly looks like a bomb, Sir. Exactly where Cavanagh said it would be. It has a red flashing LED screen which takes six digits, with a key pad below. Cavanagh says that the bomb is always active when he is on board and he defuses it every three days. His insurance he calls it. According to him, there is about half-an-hour to go before the next deadline.'

'What has he asked for?'

'He had wanted Gina and Steve to visit him. Now he wants to be transferred to the *Lerna* and to meet with the two.'

'He's up to something. He won't just defuse the bomb and quietly resume being a prisoner.'

'Do we have choice, Sir? Time is of the essence. We can't determine the size of the alleged bomb. It is bolted under the flooring on the bathroom. Presumably it was installed for this particular eventuality. I imagine it would take out the *Lerna* at least. Perhaps our vessel as well.'

Fowler pauses.

'Alright. Take him across to the *Lerna*. Comply with his requests, including Steve Flynn and Gina ... what's her surname?

No matter. I needn't tell you that he must be watched – armed guard at all times. Keep me informed of his next request. There *will* be more. I wish you well, Commander.'

The *Lerna*

I watch the naval tender come alongside. Two sailors flank Gina and me. They have automatic weapons slung on their shoulders and holstered side-arms.

We have been informed of Roger's request. I look at Gina. She has a nervous tick in her cheek. She had thought this was all over … and now she has to meet the man she had shot, again.

Sailors surround the hunched figure as he steps onboard, grey cape concealing his right-arm sling. He straightens as much as his shoulder will allow and gives us a cheeky grin.

'Good to see you both,' he calls out. 'Come close. Help me to my room.'

As we move towards him, he says to the sailors, 'Give me some space now. My friends will assist me. Watch as you like.' And then, in a quieter voice to Gina, 'I forgive you for shooting me, my dear. All will be well.'

He turns to me.

'Steve.' His whispered tone becomes more conspiratorial; beyond the hearing of others. 'There is a bomb under my ensuite. When it explodes, it will take out the front of the ship, leaving our tender free at the rear for a few minutes before the rest sinks. The tender is fully-stocked, even has my encrypted computer program installed. We'll take it and go. Gina too. I'll give her to you.' He glances at my blank expression and adds, 'She likes you. It's a reward.'

476

Too astounded to take in what he has just said, I ignore the Gina comment with the pragmatic, 'Roger, it's broad daylight. We are surrounded by armed sailors – in the open sea with a patrol boat alongside.'

He shooshes me impatiently. 'We'll go at dark. I can reset the bomb to go off when I choose. They won't be suspecting. We only have to clear the horizon. I have powerful friends and lots of money. We can be offloaded by seaplane or helicopter. I can fly, bit rusty, but trust me. I have planned for such an eventuality.'

He turns to Gina. 'Walk on my left side, Gina. I need to hold your hand,' as we move along the companionway to the stairs. But Gina recoils.

'No, Roger. It's over. I won't be your slave any longer.'

Cavanagh gives only a resigned shrug and motions me onwards towards his suite. 'So sad. So sad.'

Gina stays at the door of the bedroom with two sailors while another armed guard and I accompany Roger into the bathroom.

A hatch has been removed in the floor and I can see a red flashing screen in the hole.

'Help me, Steve.' He reaches for support on my arm. The sailor stands watchful in the doorway, assault rifle at the ready. I give him a shrugging glance and help Cavanagh lower to his knees.

He reaches into the hatchway.

The chateau

It had lain on the bedroom table. *A l'attention de la tête de police.*

Angus reads the emailed translation, as he stands in the luxury of the Loire chateau. The French police inspector, a *commandant*, in charge of the local criminal investigation, watches discreetly.

The Ramas Hydra

It started as a game. An English friend saw my collection of antiques in the chateau and called me a 'ramasseur'. The wrong word but strangely appropriate, I think, as a collector of stray dogs. The organisation has accumulated more than a few mongrels. The joke stayed as the name for the game.

Long before I married the Count in 1953, I had a son with Aaron Rossiter, an American banker, when I worked in Washington. My son's name was Cecil Bauchet-Rossiter. I had to leave him behind to be raised by the Rossiter family. The reasons seem immaterial today. It was the decision we made at the time.

In the early sixties, I went back to visit him; when I shared 'the game', Ramas, with his father. It was an imaginary business model, a blind maze protected by encryption codes; three dimensional, self-generating. Aaron took the idea and made it into a real business.

The game set up trading companies as discrete cells. They were legal businesses which also dealt with contraband, illegal trade.

478

That was Aaron's initiative. From the start, the illegal money was banked and legitimised through an investment bank which Aaron set up for the purpose in Washington. It was called the Grey Bear Investment Bank. The directors were specially chosen by Aaron to play the money markets. The profits mixed with the illegal funds were disguised as investment revenue.

As the cells grew, a range of banks and gambling establishments filtered the money, which was then dispersed into secure repositories around the world.

Aaron insisted that I be known as the founder by the codename, Ramas, and precious gifts were sent to me regularly as part of the business model. I collected them in the cellar behind the wine casks under the chateau – our old hiding place from the Nazis in wartime. You will find everything there. It is all catalogued with my wishes as to how it should be dispersed – if you please.

Initially, I helped develop the blind alleys of the game with the codes and conduits between layers and cells so that no-one knew more than a couple of others in the organisation and the identities of the leaders were protected.

By the seventies, I realised what was happening and I wanted out but it was like the Hydra of Greek mythology. If you cut off one head, two more grew in its place. Its breath poisoned any attackers. It kept getting bigger and more dangerous.

The gifts kept coming and I realised I couldn't get out. I played no active part throughout the seventies, eighties and early nineties.

To my shame, I helped them in the nineties with transferring the old Intelligence codes into technological encryptions. It was the challenge of the code developer which drew me back. No excuses. I was too old by then to keep fighting it.

Aaron is long dead. I lost touch with my son decades ago. His father told me he had changed his name. Cecil never sought contact with me. Indeed his father told me that our child had disowned me for leaving him. Such is life.

I went back for Aaron's funeral hoping to see our Cecil but I could not recognise him and, if he was there, he didn't come near me. Very sad after all of these years – my only child.

But Ramas continued.

While I sent occasional messages, I didn't run the organisation at any time. I suspect there might have been several Ramas characters. An up-and-coming Englishman, Roger Cavanagh, added a new layer of political protection in the nineties and again a few years ago in this century, building that path-smoothing expense as a mandated requirement into the business structure.

That gave an automatic bulwark of distracting interference around the Ramas' activities. Cavanagh graduated from the Mediterranean cells to develop South East Asia. I met him twice. He may well be the new Ramas.

Another big player in the structure is an American called Cliff Butcher, known as 'the Butcher' or 'Butch'. He is a fixer and is associated with Langley in some way. I have never known how he became involved – no doubt through Aaron Rossiter. I know at least one of the conduits consulted him regularly.

The Butcher, he is ruthless – a monster. I told Aaron to get rid of him but it didn't happen.

Apart from Rossiter, Cavanagh and Butcher, the blame for the way the game grew into the Ramas Hydra is entirely mine. The others were all bit-players or seduced by the mystique of the puzzle. Blame them not!

I apologise sincerely to all who have suffered and I now pay the price.

Like Heracles of the Greek mythology, may you now kill off the Ramas Hydra forever.

Cecile Bauchet

Angus Forbes slowly lowers the email letter. A frown creases his wrinkled forehead more than usual.

Something is wrong.

The French police *commandant* is still looking away, discreetly.

If the letter can be taken at face value, then Cecile Bauchet, the countess, has played no active part in the Ramas organisation for quarter of a century. Were there really several Ramases, like the *Hydra* of old?

Cavanagh might be able to reveal more than he has told so far. At the least, his computer might let Techs find the email trail to all the political protectors around the world.

Forbes needs to send the Australians this letter and to get an update on any progress with their prize captive.

'This is my copy?' he confirms with the inspector. 'To be handled with the utmost discretion, of course. I need to share with my international law-enforcement colleagues, to help put this jigsaw together.'

'*Oui.* In the spirit of *entente cordiale* and solving this case. *Absolument.*'

'*Merci,*' Forbes says, with his best French accent. 'May I now see the cellar?'

'*Bien sur.* This way, *si'l vous plait.*'

Roger and the bomb

Roger motions me to join him kneeling at the hatch.

With his left hand, he passes a note to me. 'For Gina. For later. In case.'

He reaches his left hand back into the hatch opening. I assume he is about to key in the code to disable the explosive device. Old shrapnel wounds in my right side tingle again at the thought.

His blanket cape slips from his shoulder and he seems to lose his balance forward, his hand disappearing deep into the hatch. As I reach to assist him, his left hand emerges from the hole holding a Glock pistol. In the one movement, he twists and shoots round me at the sailor in the doorway, who falls with a red hole starting to stain the chest of his grey camouflaged *basic duties* uniform.

'Quick,' hisses Roger. 'We need to barricade in here till night-fall. Then we'll put the next stage into action.'

There is no thought in my movements. It is pure instinct or Army combat training kicking in.

As he is uttering his words and another armed sailor appears in the doorway, I swat Roger's left arm behind me and bash the hand hard against the wall to get the weapon to fall. But he holds on.

The new sailor has us both lined up, with me in front.

As Roger struggles to turn the gun towards the doorway again, I swing my right arm back, elbow cocked, with all the force of the days of pent-up tension and anger at his arrogance.

I hear a crunching snap as my elbow sinks hard into the front of his neck and I follow through, upwards towards the chin, snapping his head back with a crack into the steel stanchion of the ship's frame.

All tension seeps out of Cavanagh's frame and the pistol falls.

The armed sailor in the doorway hasn't moved, but he is poised for action.

I reach for Roger's pulse and recoil at his misshapen neck. His head seems at a very odd angle and blood is pouring out of a wound at the back of his skull. If he isn't dead, he is seconds away from it.

Gina's wide-eyed face appears over the sailor's shoulder.

I point the sailor's attention to Cavanagh's unnaturally lopsided bloody head and look at Gina. 'He's dead,' and I sink back against the ensuite wall – shivering in the realisation of what has just happened.

A second Navy man arrives to crouch and administer first-aid to the fallen sailor. More uniformed men arrive and check Cavanagh.

Gina kneels beside me. Neither of us can speak. Then, her eyes catch the flashing light from inside the hatch – the red blipping console.

'The bomb, Steve. It's still armed.'

I shake myself back into the present.

'Fuck! A phone. Fast!' I call to the nearest sailor. 'I need to speak to your commander.'

His companion is already speaking to the patrol boat and he hands the phone to me.

I blurt my words out to the commander. 'No, it's not disarmed. Do you have any idea of the code? How long have we got?'

'You probably have about ten minutes,' he suggests to me. 'I recommend you all evacuate.'

My brain has gone into military mode; disengage from danger, look for solutions not retreat, don't be discouraged by all the potential risks. 'Can you get everyone over to your boat in that time? What if the time is less? What if the bomb is big enough to take out both boats? Let me try to defuse it. It needs a code. The mad bastard might even have been bluffing.'

* * * *

The commander starts the process to evacuate the *Lerna*, using their inflatables and by launching the ship's tender.

The people could jump into the water faster but that wouldn't get them over to the naval vessel faster ... and if the bomb is large ... and they are in the water ... or even close to the *Lerna* ...?

I know I have to try to key in the code.

Gina and I open the safe first: 20.3.11. We see the rag bundle containing the big sapphire. There are stacks of money and a key for a safety deposit box. I scan through a sheaf of bank papers from Switzerland, the Caymans ... but there is nothing that looks like a six digit code to Gina or me.

How long now? Minutes?

Captain Rodriguez is calmly telling the crew over the ship's public address system to head to the tender in the stern, when Ron and Alison arrive in the stateroom.

'You stay, we stay,' says Alison, sounding much more macho than she looks. Ron just shrugs at her and then me.

'We are trying to find the code,' says Gina. 'Could it be the safe code?'

'Not six digits,' I reply.

'Looks like a birth date,' says Alison. '20.03.11'

'When was Roger's birthday?' I ask Gina.

'Twentieth of March.' Our eyes light up at the prospect.

'But he wasn't born in 1911,' says Ron. 'Maybe it was his great-grandfather.'

'No,' says Gina. 'He always used to brag about having the same birthday as Napoleon's son. It would be 1811 not 1911.'

'Worth a try,' suggests Ron.

'And if it is wrong and it sets off the bomb?' I ask.

Ron shrugs again. 'Got a better idea? Anyone?'

Alison raises her hands in resignation.

I look at the sailors still guarding the door and at Gina. 'Any objections to me trying?'

'Perhaps, just one person try, Sir,' suggests the sailor, beckoning everyone out the door. 'You others retreat into the outside corridor. The ship is being evacuated.' A superfluous reminder when the PA system is repeating the message as we speak.

I smile wanly at the retreating faces, enter the bathroom alone and kneel at the hatch.

Roger's body still lies there, pulled to the side. At least I got that right. I breathe a sigh of relief that he is gone

I key 20.03.11.

The lights keep flashing.

* * * *

In the corridor, I say, 'Wrong code. Little Napoleon didn't work. Other thoughts?'

Alison's face lights up again, 'Well, what about Big Napoleon – Napoleon Bonaparte's birthday itself? When was that?'

'All his Napoleon stuff is on the shelf in there,' says Gina leading the way.

She grabs a thick book about the life of the emperor and scans the early pages. 'Here it is. Fifteenth of August, Seventeen sixty-nine.'

'15.08.69,' announces Alison. 'Try it, Steve. I'll come with you this time.'

* * * *

I kneel at the hatch again, Alison beside me with her back to Roger's body, and I key 15.08.69.

It purrs and, in two seconds, the screen shuts down.

I count another ten before I breathe. Like bloody Afghanistan all over again.

The bomb is defused and my eyes are watering from the tension release.

* * * *

485

As the comms buzz back and forward between the sailors on both vessels, I remain sitting with Alison, slumped in Roger's bedroom. At least, we are away from the sight of his offensive body.

The ship's PA system has stopped the evacuation messages.

A sailor hands me a phone saying, 'Cairns police.'

'Mal Willis here, Steve. We've been updated. Well done! How are you and the others?'

I smile at Alison's weary, bruised face. 'We're a bit jumpy, but still here. Is it over now, Inspector? I think Alison and I have kept our part of the deal we made in that motel room.'

* * * *

As we pull ourselves to our feet to catch up with Ron and Gina, I feel the note that Roger had passed to me. I glance quickly at it. It is intended for Gina.

'Roger gave me this at the hatch in the ensuite. He wanted me to pass it on to you. *In case*, he said.'

I hold out the letter.

'I don't want it.' Gina holds up both hands as if to recoil.

Ron takes the letter. 'He's dead now. This is closure. Will I read it to you, Gina?'

She shrugs, nods and gulps at the prospect. She beckons to Alison and me to huddle with her. Then she nods again for Ron to start.

'It's rough writing but it reads:

My dear Gina

I didn't ever think it would finish this way. I am desperately sorry. I want you to know how much I admired the patient way you put up with me and my moods. You really are the most charming of ladies. How could I have been so blind not to have appreciated you more?

I forgive you for shooting me. I can understand now what has been happening – but I didn't understand at the time. I have been a terrible fool!

486

I had a long talk with the federal policeman. I don't know what I could have been thinking.

Napoleon always said: Death is nothing, but to live defeated and inglorious is to die daily.

Gina, my love, I am dreadfully sorry for the way I treated you. I must have been out of my mind.

I can't let them take me like a wounded prisoner to wither like the Emperor on St Helena. I will escape or die on my shield.

I wish you every happiness for the future.

Love

Roger'

A tear rolls slowly down Gina's cheek.

'Sorry.' She dabs her cheek, embarrassed. 'I shouldn't feel like this, after all that he has done. It's just the tension and I know he's gone now. It's just so sad,' she says. 'He was a good man once. We had fun when we first met. You know, he couldn't even stand the sight of blood and yet he let people do these terrible things. It's just so sad.'

Gina melts into Ron's arms, and then she turns to look at us.

'But he was really just a little boy,' she continues, with watery eyes. 'For all his money and influence, he was just a kid mucking around in boats who had too much power to understand what he was doing. I knew he wasn't with it in recent months – but how could you tell him? And now he knew it himself. At the end, he actually understood … that he was mad. How tragic is that? And all the pain he had caused.'

PART SIX

Arriving back at Cairns

Cairns. Wednesday 28 February 2007

We four stand on the sundeck as the *Lerna* is escorted into the naval berth at Cairns Harbour.

Captain Rodriguez relays the advice from the authorities that no guests or crew will be allowed to leave for at least a day. We will all be interviewed and the police forensic teams will go through the entire ship.

* * * *

Among the first to board are Inspector Mal Willis and Sergeant Bill Jones. Bill wants to recover his mini-microphones and I dutifully show him where I had placed them.

'They worked a treat, Steve. I'm so pleased … and you located them well.' Bill is *over the moon* that the gadgets have been so effective. 'You never know with technology. So much can go wrong and yet, so much depends on it, usually.' *A philosopher with a commentary on our modern world*, I think.

The inspector is glowing in his praise. Indeed, it is starting to feel good now that the whole saga appears to be over. He gives an update from Jeff Fowler's interview with Roger Cavanagh, without the exact words or the actual alleged identity of *Ramas* – but enough so that we knew that an identity has been established.

I take Mal aside and ask what might come out of the investigation with respect to me.

'I've been responsible for the deaths of three people. Will there be repercussions?' In truth, I've been worrying all the way back. No rules of engagement here. I could see it ending up pear-shaped in the courts ... and me being painted into another situation beyond my control.

The inspector is reassuring. 'For one of them, we have a recording of what happened and it was clearly a life or death situation. Another had an armed man charging at you – a man who had just inflicted grievous bodily harm, at least, on Ben Brennan. Self-defence. And Cavanagh had just shot a sailor and was in the process of shooting again. I think there would be fair justification in all those cases. I wouldn't expect any ramifications, unless it is a recommendation for a bravery award.'

Relief and surprise. I smile my thanks; but I am still shivering internally. It is not easy to take lives, no matter how much training you have behind you or how deserved it might be. Indeed, other faces from Afghanistan and Iraq have been flashing through my troubled thoughts. All I want is to be normal.

* * * *

The sundeck proves to be popular for Ron, Gina, Alison and me. Bill comes up regularly to give a briefing on progress.

'They found some interesting things in Roger's safe,' he says. 'There is a super sapphire, uncut, wrapped in a cloth.'

A newly confident and relaxed Gina interjects with the explanation. 'That was stolen from a prospector in the Gemfields of Queensland a few weeks ago. Roger was going to give it to *Ramas*.'

Alison sits up, surprised at a memory being recalled. 'I reported on that case in the Emerald court. It's the *Balkan Blue*. The prospector is called Drago. He'll be really pleased to see his gem again.' She grins at the memory. 'The robber was a German and, now that I think about it, he did say, *It was for Ramas*, and nobody knew what he was talking about.'

Bill nods. 'Yes, I read your column on it. Told the Super too. And Drago had put a curse on whoever had stolen it. It was called the *Napoleon Curse*. We found out that a Romany from the Balkans cursed the emperor at his coronation two hundred years ago for stealing a sapphire from the family. Napoleon lost his power and was banished just as the gypsy foretold.'

'And,' Gina adds, 'it seems the same has happened to Roger. Who would have thought that curses actually work? I don't ever want a sapphire. Who knows who would have a claim on it?'

'Stay well clear of them. No curses either.' Ron says with a grin.

Bill continues, 'They also found bank papers which probably relate to accounts in the Caymans, Panama, Zurich, and Vaduz. That last one is in Liechtenstein,' he adds helpfully. 'Perhaps the papers will give access to a stack of illegal money. There is a key there too which looks like a safety deposit key. Interpol will check it out. If there is money there, it will go to the victims of crime.'

'I think,' Alison says thoughtfully, 'some of it could go to *Nemesis* to help with their work of resettling those traumatised slaves. Those poor people I saw at the Nagada lagoon – I hope they are starting to heal. Any more news on Ben?'

'Yes,' says Bill. 'Still critical but stable. He's conscious now. He's been moved to Cairns Base Hospital. The knife seems to have missed the heart and major blood vessels so they are hopeful he will recover.'

There is a collective sigh of relief. Ben Brennan has given a lot towards resolving this whole affair.

* * * *

Bill Jones comes back up to the sundeck.

'Do you want to jump into the jacuzzi, Bill?' asks Gina cheekily. 'You're working too hard, while we just laze up here.' She is getting her sparkle back.

He laughs. 'I'll pass on the jacuzzi.' Such an old-fashioned manner – so proper. 'But, they've just been working their way through the bulkhead store. It is not old office files at all. It's a *dirt file*.

'Cavanagh's listeners were collecting compromising photos, gossip and incriminating notes on important people across much of South East Asia, for blackmail. That was how he kept people in line. There are tapes, DVDs, pictures – all embarrassing or exposing people in some way and all cross-referenced.'

The tumblers click into place for me. 'I wondered how he could maintain such a large operation with only Carter and Williamson as immediate back-up. He had everyone over a barrel. And the training courses were about digging dirt to menace as many people as possible. The *Ramas* business system had a lot of nasty tricks, eh?'

'Yes,' says Alison. 'That storeroom had a very dirty feel about it. Brrrr!' She shudders at the memory.

'Mal Willis is coming to see us all in about an hour,' Bill announces. 'That will about wrap up things here. It's been good working with you all.'

'And you, Bill,' I say. 'This was a team effort. We wouldn't be here today but for your good work. Thanks, mate! You're appreciated.'

We are all lost fleetingly in the unwanted emotion of some painful memories. It had been a close-run thing. Tendrils of individual recollections; the decisions we had made, the avalanche of events which had given us no choice.

Once on that conveyor belt, we had been carried along, to live or die in a thrashing battle of good and evil, locked in a struggle for triumph or death.

We were bit-players caught up in something beyond our rational comprehension and yet, we hadn't walked away. Sometimes deliberately, sometimes shamed by our consciences, we had stood up – and survived together.

'We'd better get packed for leaving this ship, then,' I suggest, breaking the contemplation of the moment. As if in spontaneous agreement, they all start to head from the sundeck to gather their gear.

Gina holds me back as the others leave.

'I wanted to say *thank you*, Steve.' She wears a weepy smile. The mask of the fashion model had evaporated long ago. The haughty aristocrat had dissembled in the ocean mists. This is the true lady now; the girl from Bournemouth, shaped by experience and the recent revitalisation of her identity.

'You really have saved my life in so many ways; from the first walk into town at Noumea, keeping my spirits up through the bad days; giving me the gun to stop Roger. But more than that, you got me questioning who and what I wanted to be. I think I know now; and I may have found a good person in Ron. I really like him, Steve. He's had some painful life-experiences too. Maybe ...' Her sapphire eyes plead at me for endorsement. 'I *need* someone to really need me for just being me. You know? We're both ready to be happy, just living simple lives. And two boys need a mum. You understand. I know you do. If we all get on ...? Perhaps there will be a better prize than a pot of gold at the end of this rainbow.'

I can't speak. I like knowing that she is happy but I don't like being praised. I am not worthy. Too many emotions. Without my hang-ups, we might have been an item – but then? I am who I am. Like kissing a good-looking sister?

'So thank you for being my friend, Steve. I will never ever forget what you have done for me. I don't really understand how you became involved in all of this. Why didn't you just walk away? Maybe it is because ... or in spite of, being in the Army.'

I shrug. Her observation might be more astute than she realises; but I settle for, 'It was the right thing to do.' I hadn't had time to consider my motivations. They were probably all pretty base – following a woman who had more guts than I had, redemption for my mother's treatment, not enough brains not to follow ... 'I had a responsibility.'

'There you go, Steve. What a noble sense of duty.'

She doesn't get it; but then ... no officer ever gave me a compliment like that, through all the campaigns. Hey, it is worth something to hear it, genuinely expressed.

She pauses. 'Steve, I love you in a way that is higher than what I used to think love was – more like family. Alison is a very lucky girl. I wish you both the best. I hope Ron and I can find something similar.'

Her look is wistful; the pull of those blue eyes almost hypnotic. 'Don't be a stranger after all this. We'll need some space for a while – all of us. But if there is ever anything that I can do for you? Well, you know …!'

She is holding my arm tightly – a bond of communication, of deep feeling. We had shared an experience – life and death. There is an understanding that we are about to move on – but the bond of these weeks? We would always have that.

'You'll do well, Gina. I'm really pleased you've found Ron. He's a good bloke. You'll make it work. Alison and I? We need time too. We want to see if we can stand each other's company for more than the few days we've managed to have together so far. We'll see. You're a fine person, Georgina Roberts. Don't let anyone tell you otherwise; and you saved *my* life too. That's not forgotten.'

We give each other the embrace of friends. No kiss; we have never kissed. But there is a warmth of touch, scent and heartbeat passing between us. For reasons I'm sure neither of us fully understand – I certainly don't – the animal attraction which each has felt, resisted and repressed, has been transcended. This is a friendship of *family* – the sister I never had, the interdependence I knew with some while out on Army patrol; the brother Gina has lost, discarded so callously and painfully.

* * * *

The Cairns Base Hospital is a huge place, seven storeys high, but *Intensive Care* is well signposted.

Ben Brennan is awake, with a drip flowing into him and a chest drain leading to a one-way seal, but he is out of danger. Very lucky. They have told him that the prompt first-aid had saved his life. Perhaps his bank of past good deeds has played a part too, because Len's knife missed a key artery by millimetres.

Gina, Ron, Alison and I are his first visitors, other than the medical staff – Mal Willis must have pulled some strings with the doctors to get us in there. We are all thoroughly checked over by the nurses; gowned and gloved to minimise the risk of infection.

'Well, don't you look well,' says Ron. 'You brush up okay after sleeping through a nice sea cruise.'

The big smile on Ben's weather-beaten face shows a new inner peace. He is very pale but he looks happy.

'Good to see you all. Tell me the news. Let me just touch your hands … gloves and all. Gee, it's good to see you! Just good to even be here, really. A close thing, they tell me.'

Patiently and slowly, we tell him about Roger, Len and Peter and how the Navy had brought us back.

He receives the revelations about the *Lerna* wall safe and the bulkhead store with an understanding frown. Leverage and protection had been Roger's game. The secrecy, blind alleys, codes, levels and layers of training which allowed anonymous chiefs to function within a larger structure. It really had been brilliant – maintained by a dirt file with the threat of exposure.

'The police superintendent believes that the top level of Roger's network is now gone.'

Ben just nods a cynical gesture. 'We'll see. We'll just see. I know Jeff Fowler. He's a good man and a good police officer – but we will just see how many heads roll at a high level.'

We share our personal plans and Ben promises he will stay in contact.

* * * *

The farewells at Cairns Airport are happy goodbyes.

Ron and Gina catch a flight to Rockhampton which will be followed by the short drive to see his sons in Yeppoon. There will be walks along the sandy beach and the boardwalks, with a view out to the islands.

Alison and I are heading to Brisbane. She has an investigative piece on international piracy to write, while doing the circuit of the *city* courts this time.

We have few possessions. Funnily, we can't see much merit in being collectors.

Broderick and Forbes

Kyle Broderick is sharing war stories with Angus Forbes. They have both received word that *Versec* and the *NPA* are to be closed down with their functions absorbed into the current Intelligence and policing structures.

'Isn't this just why we came into this business?' asks Kyle. 'A pop-singer called Ingrid was kidnapped and held for ransom. Wasn't that how it all started? And someone, or some group, was delaying or distracting any investigation until it was too late to follow the trail. I am remembering correctly how we were formed, aren't I, Angus?'

'You've got it right,' replies Angus. 'What would you bet it is the same dark force which has shut us down too? And why? Because the big players around the *Sea Spray* are all gone now. Cavanagh, Carter and Williamson – gone. The Brigadier and the Countess – in the drink. Even Sir Terence is gone – or at least his mind is. No doubt the directors of GBIB and SPFA will be debarred from holding directorships again – but they will most probably get off pretty lightly otherwise. Money for smart lawyers.'

The old cop in Broderick senses the missing link but can't pin it down.

'I'm not so sure we have the big player yet. It just seems too convenient to blame it all on the countess. She was well into her seventies. She may have started it up but she hasn't been controlling all of this, not as an old woman. I don't buy it! We are missing a vital connection.'

Fowler and the
international politics

Canberra. Thursday 1 March 2007

Superintendent Jeff Fowler is having difficulty understanding what has just been requested of him.

'Put all your Cavanagh files on hold,' he has been told.

His sergeant, Bill Jones, has compiled a veritable library of interview recordings from the *Lerna*; there are investigation reports from the Korean freighter – another library's worth; there are interviews completed by other national police forces around the *Sea Spray* hi-jack and from the directors of the South Pacific Freight Alliance.

Add to that collection, the interviews taken by *Versec* from the directors of GBIB; the encrypted messages from *Ramas* and others to Roger; the DVDs of the video recording on the trunk freighter; the data-matching of the International Maritime Bureau in Kuala Lumpur as well as all the incidental correlating of Intelligence across agencies. Not to mention the detailed forensic examination going on currently around the *Lerna*.

'Put it on hold? You are joking. Tell me this is a gee up.'

'No joke, Superintendent.'

'There is enough hard evidence to put away a lot of crooks for ever, even allowing that many of the major players are now dead. How can you put that on hold? What does it mean?'

He has asked the questions of his Commissioner who has explained that this investigation has moved into the classified area of the Intelligence agencies of several major countries. He himself isn't privy to that classified knowledge. Sometimes, he says, there is a bigger picture than the crime at the grass roots. You just have to trust the people at that level.

The data will not be lost. But the AFP will have to wait until the clearance is given, just the same as for all the other international agencies around the world. That is the way with classified secrets. It can be a shadowy world.

* * * *

Jeff Fowler can take orders. He believes you can't be a good leader if you can't also be a good follower. However, he doesn't like this squelch which is being placed on this mammoth co-operative international investment of people, time and technology into stopping the pirate network, with all its ramifications into the financial industry.

He is being gagged, not by the Commissioner but by mysterious people above him. He will have to explain this to his team. And he will do that, as diplomatically as he can, without compromising the integrity of all the nations who have assisted.

It is at moments like this that he realises that he would much prefer to be listening to his daughter playing with her school string ensemble.

An hour later, he is in the front row. She hadn't expected her father would be able to attend. He is always so busy. She is delighted. So are Jeff and his wife. They have a happy daughter and the music soothes his angry spirit somewhat.

Drago reunited with the *Balkan Blue*

Drago and Mick are feeling nervous as they walk into the Rockhampton Police Headquarters. They are always much more comfortable in the anonymity of the Gemfields – but this is an important meeting. They have to attend for this.

They are ushered into a room and introduced to Detective Inspector Peter Downton and Detective Sergeant Ralph Clark.

'Welcome to Rocky,' greets DI Downton cheerily.

'You have news about *Balkan Blue*?' Drago asks, intensely.

Sergeant Clark lifts a small box onto the table. 'Please open it, Drago.'

As the lid comes off, a tear forms on the Bosnian's cheek – the old rag is still protecting his jewel. With the gentleness of a butterfly opening its wings, Drago peels back the cloth to reveal a rough greeny-blue stone which, where it has been cleaned, shines with a deep gem-quality sapphire-blue.

It is like a father being reunited with a child.

'Ah, *Balkan Blue*. Thank you! Thank you! Vere did you find it?'

'You wouldn't want to know,' says Downton. 'It has been over oceans since you last saw it. But, it is here with you now. You will look after it, Drago, won't you? It needs to be kept in a safe in a jeweller's store, preferably the one who will facet it for you. Don't keep it on your body.'

Drago says, 'Tis so good to see again.' He kisses the stone. 'I vill find faceter. Can I leave it safe here, vith you? Until I find right jeweller and get you come vith me, keep it safe? Can I ask you do that, please?'

Drago's English is halting but they all understand his request.

Inspector Downton laughs. 'We're not normally security guards but, for you Drago, we'll keep it safe until you're ready. This rock has had too many journeys already.'

The old prospector dabs his eyes. 'Thank you. Ve look forward. *The Balkan Blue* vill be magnificent sapphire. You vill see.' Drago pauses. 'Oh, I told police from Anakie that I place curse of Napoleon on thieves of my stone. I vant to lift now. Not cause harm now that Napoleon Stone is safe again. You vill tell Anakie policeman for me, please.'

Downton looks at his sergeant and then back to Drago.

'We'll make sure he knows. Can't have people coming to harm because of the curse.'

'Do you really believe in that *Napoleon Curse*, Drago?' asks Sergeant Clark.

'*Da. Apsolutno.* Yes. How you say?' He looks at honest Mick for help. Getting none, he remembers. 'Absolutely. Look vhat happen to thieving Napoleon. Romany curse caught up vith him. And now *Balkan Blue* is returned to me. Tis power of *Napoleon Curse*. What not to believe. Did anything happen to thief of my stone?'

Sergeant Clark looks suitably impressed. 'Yes, Drago. Things certainly *did* happen to the thief … and thieves.'

The funeral

London. Saturday 3 March 2007

It is a huge memorial turn-out.

There are to be two services: one in England and one in France.

By family agreement, they would each honour the lives of both the Brigadier and the countess, at both.

Some flotsam from the plane has been found but no bodies for a burial. It is deep water with strong currents. The sea would be their grave.

Angus Forbes stands quietly with Catherine Weston – appropriate solemnity to honour the passing of their boss, a military hero. It is also honouring a heroine of France, in the countess.

That is what is sticking in Angus's Scottish craw. He has read the report from Australia of the interview which Jeff Fowler had with Cavanagh.

Cavanagh identified the mastermind of this huge international criminal gang, *Ramas*, as being someone called the *Countess* who had a stately home in France. She was very wealthy and the gang gave her gifts of rare or precious things for her home. She was *Ramas* and Cavanagh had actually met her twice.

There could be little doubt the French-speaking *Ramas* that Cavanagh had spoken with in London and Paris was the same Countess being *honoured* at this funeral service in England today. Forbes has stood in her Loire chateau, with the trappings of wealth everywhere. He has been told by his French police *commandant*

504

colleague that the pieces on display in the rooms visited by the public are perhaps all family heirlooms. But, in the cool wine cellars beneath, they have already found a treasure trove of jewellery, paintings, sculptures and rare antiques, none of which would ever be seen in public and most of which have been stolen from around the world.

There has been no official comment so far. French respect for the deceased might well take some time before any public information will be released – but Forbes has also read Cecile Bauchet's farewell letter.

He has seen the cellar, still with so many paintings and valuables being methodically packaged for official transport.

In Forbes' mind, this is the tribute which this *Empress* exacted from her gangs for setting up the template for their criminal operations in the first place.

So Angus has very real difficulty celebrating the life of a master criminal.

More than that, the plane crash had happened just after he had told the Brigadier that Techs had cracked the encryption coded and could read the messages.

Techs has since found the sources of some of the senders. Three have been established so far: Sir Terence Sedgewood from his personal laptop, the Brigadier from a laptop usually in his plane, and the countess from her desk computer at the chateau. The evidence is there.

They had all believed their identities would forever be anonymous but they should have known that there are few codes or encryptions that can't be cracked with a bit of luck along the way. Bletchley Park is just one example of that. They should have known.

Techs suggests there must be other sources as well, perhaps from America, and they are coming from a much more sophisticated encryption source. He would keep at trying to find the key to unlock this new challenge.

Forbes is frustrated that he can't have his master criminal brought before the courts.

Sure, small players will be charged and punished, as they deserve to be. But the big fish have escaped justice.

Sir Terence Sedgewood by most accounts had never met Ramas. He couldn't actually have been as important as Roger Cavanagh in the scheme of things – because Cavanagh had allegedly met Ramas twice, a very trusted member of the organisation, surely.

Sir Terence really appears to have been little more than a gullible player; a conduit for messages, a figurehead of importance who could sit on boards, chair meetings, argue eloquently and keep state secrets acquired from the diplomatic scene. But really he was a child in the hands of a skilled manipulator.

The Brigadier had married the countess in a second marriage. Whether or not he had been aware of her activities initially would never now be known, but he certainly must have known of her business affairs in later years and allowed himself to be a party to the scheming, which falls far outside the officer's code.

The master-schemer clearly must have been the countess, apparently with an amazing talent to charm her disciples to her code of *results* and *silence*. She had brought her business management skills to restructure criminal operations – the language of business; because it brought a sense of formality and respectability to activities which most thinking-people would consider utterly reprehensible.

How much more dignified it always seems to speak of *investments* rather than *bets* or *money laundering*? How much more respectable to speak of *product lines* rather than *coffles of slaves*?

Yes, Angus and Catherine are both finding it hard to come to terms with the shroud of secrecy which is enveloping this memorial. Never speak ill of the dead, yet this pair are being treated as heroes.

Goodness! They committed suicide when their illegal deeds were about to be exposed.

No, it doesn't sit right with professional police officers.

The Minister sees them both and comes over to speak.

'What a marvellous celebration of two fine people,' he gushes. 'Their families must feel very proud, despite the tragedy of their double loss.'

'Yes, indeed, Minister,' says Angus, with a civil servant's diplomatic grace.

'Do you see that lady walking towards us?' says the Minister. 'That is Lady Meredith, Sir Terence's wife. I'll introduce you. Marvellous lady she is. Was one of the boffins at Bletchley Park during the war. Cracked the Enigma Code, they did. Some of that work has only just recently become public knowledge. She can keep a state secret, that lady.

'Good afternoon, Lady Meredith. How lovely to see you, despite the sadness of the occasion.'

'Oh, hello Minister. Nice to see you too,' she answers.

'May I introduce Angus Forbes and Catherine Weston, Lady Meredith. Both worked closely with the Brigadier.'

'Pleased to meet you,' says Lady Meredith, with polished charm.

'And how is Sir Terence?' asks the Minister.

'Just as usual,' is the reply.

The Minister nods and changes tack. 'Marvellous service, really. Great to see such a celebration of two fine people,' says the Minister.

'Oh yes. And such a good turn-out,' she says.

'I'm so pleased you were able to be here to support the Brigadier's family,' says the Minister, acknowledging that Lady Meredith is not as mobile as when she was younger.

'Oh, I'm here for the countess too,' she says sweetly.

'Really,' says the Minister. 'I didn't know you knew the countess.'

'Oh yes. I have known her since the fifties. We worked together, you know. We go back a long way!'

There is a mysterious tone in her voice and intrigue in the smile as she takes her leave and makes her slow dignified walk back to the Bentley.

Angus and Catherine are stunned. Their jaws are still dropped as she reaches her car. Had they heard correctly?

Wheels within wheels.

The Minister goes off on his cheery way while the police officers return to cross some more 't's and dot some more 'i's.

The chase is not over

Forbes has been thinking for a while since the memorial service. They are angry thoughts.

Back on the secure phone line to Washington, he says, 'Kyle, I think some investigation into the countess's past might not be astray.' He pauses as he brings his Scottish ire under control. 'She has a connection with Lady Meredith Sedgewood that I hadn't appreciated previously. Maybe there are other connections too, even in the States?'

'We're out of it now, Buddy. Closed down.' The American is not happy.

'Unless we keep going, my big American friend, in a canny way; the way a Scot would approach it. Do you think we could just discreetly explore what visits or acquaintances that the countess Cecile Bauchet might have had in the States? Just two quiet investigators. Listening and not frightening the horses. What do you think, Kyle? This is what we are good at.'

'Mmm. I'm just angry enough to try your suggestion, Angus. Nobody will have shut down the people-trafficking, although it may slow for a while. We could have blown it right open; all of them – the sponsors who buy the slaves, right through all the lines of distribution – and it is the poor Filipina, Chinese, Islander or Thai woman who suffers. It stinks! Yes, my Scottish friend, maybe we can keep the pot of enquiry bubbling gently. I think you're right. I still think we've missed the mastermind. I'll ferret around a little.'

'I'm bloody frustrated that the political will has gone,' says Angus, 'but quietly, quietly, might just unearth something.'

'Mind you,' says Kyle. 'Jeff Fowler down in Aussie land seems to get a freer run than us. He's had the Navy to back him up. I wish we had that latitude here.'

The Scotsman gives his measured assessment. 'Don't bet on the Australian freedom being as great as you think. For my money, I think this whole thing will be quietly hushed up down there too. They've got their key players. They're dead.

'The Navy will put the exercise down to the training budget – excellent practice for them. The hours of recording and cross-referencing will be filed for experience and no story will be allowed to see the light of day. Mark my words.'

'I'll be in touch!' says Kyle with a renewed sense of purpose.

London. Monday 5 March 2007

'Angus,' the big American's voice is quiet on the secure phone line from Washington. 'I have a connection. Cecile Bauchet worked at the CIA in Foggy Bottom from 1950 to 1953. She was in Intelligence gathering, using her French Resistance credibility from war time.'

'Interesting,' agrees Angus. Some pieces are falling into place. If they had appreciated earlier that the countess had such a role they could have been on to this weeks ago.

'There's more. As you noted from Cecile Bauchet's suicide note, while in Washington, she was involved in a relationship with a young merchant banker called Aaron Rossiter. It seems to have been quite a serious affair. Our cross-referencing matched Aaron Rossiter as the first managing director of the Grey Bear Investment Bank.'

'Chink, chink, chunk – the numbers are falling into place.' Angus smiles. Had this whole business started from a love affair?

509

'There's more.' Kyle Broderick likes dramatic tension. 'Aaron Rossiter is long dead but we have confirmed that there was indeed a son, Cecil Bauchet-Rossiter. We have found birth records and some school reports. Could he be playing any part in this? I'm on the trail.'

'Well done, Kyle! Bloody well done! It matches what the French found in her parting note. Where is the son now?'

'Don't know yet. One more thing.' Broderick pauses. 'I'm being tailed. Someone is on to me. Maybe I'm not as invisible as I thought. I could have stirred some bats in a long-protected cave. I've put what I have on paper and sent it to you. Just in case. I don't trust the electronic mail.'

'Take care, my friend,' Angus says. 'Better to back off and fight another day.'

'We'll see. It may be too late for that. But the cause is just, my Scottish friend. We don't walk away. I'll be in touch.'

Angus flies home

Homecoming is always good. Angus feels that nostalgic stirring as the plane circles out over the grey-blue waters of the Firth of Forth.

The islands of Inchkeith and Cramond appear to stand guard over the two mighty Forth bridges: one a reddy-brown cantilever and the other grey-white suspension, spanning the water from Edinburgh to the *Kingdom of Fife*.

It has been an interesting project being involved in the *NPA* – but bloody frustrating too. He will be glad to get back to the real world of policing, where the law is above manipulation.

A yellow envelope with USA stamps waits for him as he enters his office. Throwing it onto his desk, he opens his list of email traffic first. Top of the list is an urgent message from the Minister, Norman Brown.

It reads: *Kyle Broderick killed today in Washington. Please call my number when you get in.*

The Minister answers his private number immediately. They sharing condolences and the Minister expresses his strong wish for Angus to look after his personal safety.

He reiterates that the *Ramas* case is closed. He expresses his concern that Broderick's death might have been a result of his continuing to investigate matters around the *Versec* and *NPA* enquiries.

Angus puts the phone down slowly. It is a conscious effort, lest a slamming phone be noticed by others. His friend and colleague

511

has just been killed, on the trail of evil, and all that the powers in charge want to do is to walk away.

Well, up them! How could he not be angry? Kyle had not been prepared to just do nothing.

Stewing in renewed frustration, Angus picks up the yellow envelope and carefully slides out the pages of Broderick's quiet investigation.

He reads parts of information that he already knew and some destined to enlighten him.

Cecile Bauchet had worked in Foggy Bottom from 1950 to 1953. The CIA didn't move to Langley, Virginia until the late fifties.

She had been in a relationship with a merchant banker called Aaron Rossiter; a relationship which had produced a son, Cecil Bauchet-Rossiter in 1953. Aaron Rossiter had been the first managing director of the Grey Bear Investment Bank, the conduit of the massive money laundering for Ramas.

Then Kyle wrote about a shadowy person known as *Butch* or the *Butcher*, who seemed to be coming up in very guarded conversations in the corridors of power. He had been on the trail of *Butch*.

He had established that Lady Meredith Sedgewood had flown to Washington just after Sir Terence had taken ill – a big trip for a lady in her eighties. The word had been that she might have been visiting *Butch*, perhaps at Langley – and very likely other people in that big complex. What the connection was, he hadn't yet established.

Kyle had also heard that *Butch* was a pseudonym for a person working in clandestine operations. He had been searching for any link with the Brigadier or Sir Terence – probing a relationship from their overseas diplomatic activities.

Ted Hayes, the CEO of GBIB, had heard the name but claimed to know no more than the name. He had heard Aaron Rossiter refer to it at some time. Kyle doubted that Hayes actually knew much more than he was telling. The CEO was definitely frightened, though. Presumably that could be because the whole bank had been so exposed.

Kyle had even checked into Aaron Rossiter's funeral. Cecile Bauchet had been there with the Brigadier, as had Sir Terence Sedgewood and his wife, Lady Meredith – but it had been a big funeral and the four had returned to Europe immediately afterwards. No-one had carried out surveillance on the funeral because none of this conspiracy had been known at that time.

The last comments from Kyle were to the effect that someone had been accessing his computer. His computer had a very high level of security on it, but someone with an even higher level had been into his files. He didn't elaborate how he knew that.

He also sensed he was being physically tailed. He was an old cop. He would have a sixth sense about those matters.

* * * *

Angus sits reflecting, so saddened over the death of his colleague; a physical poignancy as a rare tear forms in his battle-hardened eyes. He thinks through what he now knows, working from evidence as a good copper must, into hypotheses which he could later test. Is he any further forward in solving the *Ramas* mystery?

In the letter left by Cecile Bauchet, she had disclosed her part in the *Ramas* organisation. The confession had been more innocuous than Angus had expected. Undoubtedly, she had set up the structure, perhaps with some help from her English friend from the Thames House days – and Lady Meredith had admitted that connection at the memorial service.

The existence of the son, Cecil, had been revealed; as well his apparent rejection of his mother.

The driving force of Aaron Rossiter had seemed to be the power behind the success of the *Ramas* venture. She called it a *Hydra* – a monster with a life of its own. Despite her claim to have made attempts to leave, she had chosen to help in the nineties after she had been out of it for decades. So, who had been running the show during those intervening years?

Aaron Rossiter was still alive at that time and in the process of handing over the chairmanship of GBIB to Sir Terence Sedgewood. Did Sir Terence know about his wife's connection with Cecile or was that part of the deep secrecy which was ingrained into those Bletchley Park women?

Did the enigmatic Merri know all along that her husband had been embroiled in the aftermath of their little anti-boredom game?

Cecile had mentioned Roger Cavanagh as the up-and-coming star. Was he the *Ramas* of the late nineties? Someone was sending messages to Sir Terence to pass on. Was that Cecile? Or had the Brigadier taken that role? And who is Cliff Butcher? Cecile clearly had no time for him. What is the link? She hadn't elaborated. Ah! The secrets that people take to the grave.

Angus decides to call Larry Kennedy, at the very least to express his condolences over Kyle, but maybe Larry might know something more.

Tomorrow would be early enough.

Ted Hayes

Washington. Wednesday 7 March 2007

The velcro straps pinning his arms to the chair look as if they should be easy to break. But, try as he might, Ted Hayes has been skilfully pinioned to the stout oaken chair in his home study.

It is a plush room as would befit the very successful CEO of a wealthy investment bank – a huge oak desk, deep pile carpets, luxurious silk wall hangings as well as a bar stocked with expensive spirits and liqueurs from around the world.

The focus of Ted's attention, however, is on the quietly-spoken bearded man who has so expertly restrained him in the chair. There is no-one else in the house; no-one to call out to. The thick furnishings and strong doors would muffle any cries anyway.

The man is in the shadows. The light from the desk lamp shows a speckling of grey in his dark beard. His eyes seem to glow dully, even in the shade of the eyebrows and hairy cheeks.

Ted can see that the man is angry. It is in the tense way he carries himself. The intruder hasn't introduced himself but Ted can guess he is probably the elusive, secretive *Butch*.

In a way, he has been expecting him to appear sooner or later. The *Butcher* had been the apparition behind the scenes since old Aaron's times; a trace, an innuendo, a suggestion, the source of a deep-seated fear.

Ted is feeling fear too as, at that moment, he is looking down the barrel of his own American Eagle .38 Special, held in the rock-steady hand of his captor.

'The mantra is?' The voice comes from behind the beard.

'*Silence* and *results*,' replies Ted.

'Have you followed the mantra?'

Ted's mouth is dry. He can hardly claim his bank has achieved results in recent times. The auditors are even now still going through all the fudging and deception that he and Aaron had orchestrated over the years.

And then there have been all the police interviews. Over and over. Checking. Drilling into inconsistencies. Broderick! He has just worn him down with his incessant picking away.

'You have been talking, Ted.' The voice is quiet, but with an edge.

'I had to co-operate. They just keep coming back and back. They have all the books. We can't argue black is white.' Ted is past feeling a need to justify. His life, as he has known it, is finished. He can never survive the ignominy of this banking fraud. Surely the man can see it.

He has moved round behind his chair.

'Are you *Butch*?' He might as well get it out into the open.

'You see, Ted. You talk too much. Where did you hear a name like that? And what right do you have to mention it? Who did you tell that name to?'

'Only Broderick. He just keeps asking more questions. I have to co-operate. I can't just sit like a dummy.'

The man moved closer to stand at Ted's left side.

'The whole truth. Only Broderick?'

'Yes. Only Broderick.' The tiredness and dejection are clear in his voice.

'Well, Broderick will not ask you any more questions. I will guarantee that.'

Ted's spirits lift momentarily at the comment. Perhaps he has given the right responses.

'And you won't be giving any more answers. Will you, Ted?'
Ted feels the round barrel of his own gun against his left temple.

* * * *

The man removes the straps from Ted's limp arms. Carefully, the gloved hands lift the lifeless left fingers and place them firmly on the butt and trigger – then they let the gun drop to the floor. It had been worth checking that Ted was left-handed before the visit. It is always the detail that lets people down.

The man stands and looks at the vapid, bloodied corpse. He needed someone to take out his anger on. The plane crash in France has annoyed him more than he would like to admit. She is gone. All of his life he has been trying to live up to his father's ideal image of his mother. It had been a love-hate relationship. She had left him at birth; just walked away to a life of grandeur – and left him.

He had seen her twice since then. Once, she had come back to see his father when he would have been just nine. She was aloof then, this French lady – almost cold, not knowing what to say; not wanting to get close. He didn't understand why. Then she was gone again.

His father would talk of her genius. He was still in love with her. After years and years, he was still in love with her – or his ideal of her, at least.

His father had been his teacher; training and channelling him into a life of secrecy as an agent, just like he claimed his mother had been in the war and afterwards. He had schooled him in the *family business* too; the secret codes, the mantras, the subtleties of the maze – the need to send her gifts through the blind channels.

And he had done all of that. Dutifully.

He had learned the *Ramas* operation but he remained concealed in the secret world of espionage and covert missions. His world was one of multiple personalities – at Langley, he was known as John Pensecola, special operations – an important man, living out his father's vision in a double life but it was always really for his mother.

517

Then, she had walked away from the business; no longer interested, decrying its illegal activities, denouncing its great successes.

Such rejection! Coldness! She had vilified *Butch*, a leading player in the company. His father had told him that; and she didn't even know who he really was. She had expressed such hatred for the cruel organisation that *Ramas* had become; ashamed of those who had ruined her precious game.

Could she not see that a business needs to be cold and analytical? Hard things need to be done – and Cliff Butcher was, and is, quite capable of doing them in so many different situations. She should be proud. Goodness, his country has honoured him often for doing very much the same in dangerous *dark ops*, under many aliases, where diplomacy has needed the sharp edge of fear to cut through the bullshit.

She had asked his father to eliminate him from *the game*, called him a monster – and **she didn't even know who he was**.

He could never speak with her again. The bubble had burst. There was honour at stake – pride, dignity insulted. Deep pain. After all his efforts to live up to the ideal – to be rejected out of hand, for being successful, was too much.

He would never receive any communication from her again. However, he would assure, for his father's sake, that the tributes continued to flow to the inventor of the system – *Ramas*, as far as anyone might know.

He had watched the elderly French woman come to his father's funeral. The pain was excruciating; to see her, to match the ideal and the reality, to endure again his sense of unworthiness within a rich career of camouflaged achievement. He had been unable to approach her, to say who he was, so ingrained had the discipline of *the game* become in his mind.

She probably wouldn't have acknowledged him anyway. And it was *she* who had invented the whole bloody system; she and that English fool's wife. Merri was clever – still is – very astute, easy conversationalist, an ideas lady. But her husband? – a pompous fop;

someone with whom circumstance had decreed *Butch* must work over the years and maintain pleasantries.

How fitting that his deluded knightly brain had overcooked.

But it had been Cavanagh's mad pirate scheme that had blown the whole brilliant operation apart. Why had the *Ramas* organisation agreed to let that happen? Why had *Butch* agreed? The GBIB board were on a high, believing absolutely that it would work without a hitch – and it nearly did.

Hubris? Anger? Frustration? All of the above.

Even more so now that the woman *Butch* had always tried to impress had flown herself into the sea with that English soldier – before she had even understood what a talent she had created all these years ago in him; and had left him, alone, unrecognised, unacknowledged and unappreciated.

He is Cliff Butcher who, through that quiet pseudonym and a dozen other covert and overt identities, is one of the most skilled political manipulators on the planet. He is a craftsman. He makes things happen without others even knowing that they have happened – a stiletto knife between the ribs; hit and gone before the brain has even known. And she didn't even know of his success.

Yes, he is angry. Hayes has paid the price. So has Broderick.

His index finger taps against the barrel of the Sig pistol in his pocket; reassurance, just in case another needs to move on from this mortal world.

Larry Kennedy

Washington. Thursday 8 March 2007

Larry Kennedy is a good cop, hurting badly, as he takes the call from Angus Forbes.

'The first rule in policing is that you turn up for the next day,' he says sadly to the Scotsman. 'I don't know who said that first – but I heard Kyle say it often.'

He tells Forbes that it appears that Broderick had been staking out in one of the seedier parts of Washington. A gang area. His gun was missing as was his money and badge. It was a knife that had killed him. Lots of knife wounds actually. A gang trademark.

'No-one really believes it was a mugging but it was certainly a cleverly disguised kill if it was anything else,' he says. 'I'll keep looking. I owe it to him. Someone was after him. He told me that.'

'There aren't many left to ask now,' says Angus. 'Maybe Ted Hayes might know something he is not telling us.'

'He won't be telling us anything either,' Kennedy informs him. 'Suicide; yesterday. His own gun, in his own study. Looks like a clean case.'

'So we really only have this Cliff Butcher left? Is that it?' Angus asks.

'Well, he's a shady character too from what I gather,' Larry explains. 'That is probably not his name; and if he really exists, he must be in some undercover role. Maybe government. Maybe overseas ops. Not an area where we can just go in and ask for him.'

'I agree, Larry. Kyle gave his life for ferreting around in this area. Just listen quietly to any chatter but don't put yourself in danger.'

'No sweat, Buddy. I'll keep you informed if I hear anything. You take care over there too. That *Ramas* monster might have long tentacles.'

Angus and Jeff

Edinburgh. Friday 23 March 2007

Angus had been delighted to hear from his Aussie counterpart in the *Ramas* affair, a week ago. Jeff Fowler was coming over to London for an anti-terrorism think-tank and would have a day free to come to Edinburgh.

'Jeff, it'll be really good to see you. There'll be a grand Scottish welcome awaiting you with accommodation at my place.'

Now together in Edinburgh and by the second single malt from the top of the vat, Angus and Jeff are relaxed in each other's company.

The two policemen are mulling over the evidence that has absorbed them so much in recent weeks. They have a lot of *bits and pieces of the jigsaw* as their late American colleague liked to put it.

The Scotsman has formed some ideas. 'I think *Ramas* was actually an arrangement, rather than a person. It worked with its parts being independent and anonymous; a charade where the participants thought they were being controlled by some larger organisation or a single leader. But,' Angus pauses. 'they weren't really under that sort of control at all. It was an illusion.'

'Classic con job, eh?' Jeff smiles. 'Even the founder wouldn't know who was running things.'

Angus continues toying with the evidence. 'I think Cavanagh played a larger part in recent times than we may have suspected initially.' He pauses again. 'In fact, it was his amendments to the structure that provided the finances for the political buy-offs. It was he who ensured all participants had to contribute through their business plans. Once he had the influential people compromised, they believed they had to continue running interference for *Ramas*.'

'You're right, Angus. We found him doing exactly that in the Pacific. He had an enormous dirt file in his ship on influential people from every place he traded.'

The Scotsman is on a roll. 'Well, all of that gave Cavanagh a false sense of confidence to engage in mad schemes.' Angus claps his hands. 'It's the arrogance that gets them in the end. They had a process which kept them low profile but the *Sea Spray* incident was right in the radar. That blew the whole thing open. Maybe we didn't do so badly after all, eh?'

Jeff smiles. 'Using that logic, the irony is that the fix continues even after Roger is gone. It is still in because the troops don't realise the organiser is dead. His or her role has always been anonymous – codenamed. I'll bet there's still someone sending *Ramas* messages through the systems. Maybe your Techs will stumble onto some it?'

The dour Scot sips another whisky, very slowly. 'It is a good drop, this Scottish water. D'you want a top up?' He doesn't wait, but adds some more whisky to Fowler's glass.

'I think you could be right, Jeff, about that bloody evil business continuing just as before. We've stepped away from cleaning out a nest of vipers. And that's what annoys me most.'

'Angus, I take your point about Cavanagh being more powerful than people might have credited him. But I'd hate anyone to have good thoughts of that bastard. I met him – interviewed him. He was a dangerous madman. He created misery for thousands – and always at arm's length from the dirty stuff.'

'The countess called it the *Hydra*, didn't she?' Angus replays his understanding. 'So the organisation is still continuing; just like heads cut off the *Hydra* but new ones regrowing in their place? SPFA is wound up but the trunk ships still sail and payments continue through the automatic system which Cecile and Aaron devised all those years ago; and which Roger refined to its present form. Am I right?'

Jeff nods sagely. 'That might well be how it works,' as Angus pours two more beautiful malts. The great universal truth about Scottish whisky is that each one gets smoother as you sip more.

'But what has gone, though, is the training,' Angus says, while savouring the amber spirit. 'The trainers are dead, are they not? Will the structure not wither away, without the training? With no encrypted messages, will the system be sustained?'

Jeff responds. 'Well, if they are indeed autonomous groups, they will regenerate using the *Ramas* model. All that has really changed is that a few heads have been removed. Maybe the new leaders are already in place, operating under the radar.'

The whisky *is* tasting better as they debate.

'And they have taken us – the bloody radar – away,' snarls the frustrated Scot.

Jeff Fowler and Ben Brennan

Brisbane. Tuesday 27 March 2007

'Ben, have they let you out of hospital yet?' asks Jeff Fowler. 'I think I know how it was all done. I'm in Brisbane for a couple of days. Can we meet? Somewhere quiet. Not over the phone.'

'Yeh. Been back in Brisbane for a week. Recuperating down at Moreton Bay. How does that sound to meet down there? Manly jetty?'

* * * *

'I'm just back from Scotland, Ben; catching up with Angus Forbes. I think I have the whole mess clear in my head now. See what you think?'

Ben Brennan still looks frail as he sits on the Manly jetty wall. He clearly likes being near the salt; there is a jaunty set to his grin. The tide is in, rolling its greeny-blue mask over the sea-grass beds. A stone-grey shape of a mammal surfaces in front of them and snorts from a trunk-like snout.

'Dugong!' says Ben. 'Good to see them. No fear. Nature at its best. So tell me your story, Jeff. We'll see how our ideas match.'

Fowler steeples his fingers to emphasise the logic of his thinking. 'The organisation was called *Ramas*, after a French countess Cecile Bauchet. She had a chateau in the Loire Valley, filled with all the memorabilia of a stately home. An English friend chose the

525

term *ramasseur* to describe her collecting habit. *Ramasseur* is not the correct term in French. But, to the two friends in the late fifties, inventing a game to overcome their boredom, *Ramas* seemed an appropriate joke, which took on a more sinister meaning.

'I need to go back a little. Cecile was just a child when the Nazis invaded France and her chateau was taken over as officers' barracks. She and her family hid their heirlooms and treasures in the cellars, behind huge wine barrels. Then she ran messages for the *Resistance* – a brave young girl at that time. After the war, she didn't like the idea of playing the role of a docile little lady. So she took off the States – to Washington DC.

'Her wartime credentials got her a job in Intelligence in the old Foggy Bottom E-Street complex of the CIA. Routine work, but interesting to a girl weaned in occupied France. While in Washington, she fell in love with a young banker, Aaron Rossiter, and they had a son together, Cecil Bauchet-Rossiter. But the relationship strains over raising the son.

'After three years, the relationship could not last as it was. Cecile needed to go back to being the countess eventually, and Aaron wouldn't leave the States. That's my best guess. Who knows what goes on in relationships?

'Headstrong, she leaves her son behind and moves to England initially where her American experience gets her a start at Thames House with a section of MI5. Cecil remains with his father, where Aaron's extended family support presumably promises a brighter future for a young boy growing up.

'In London, Cecile meets up with Meredith Sedgewood who had been a cryptographer at Bletchley Park during the war. The two become friends and dream up *the game* together.

'*The Game* was an imaginary international business model in a fantasy world within which goods were traded and transported across national borders under a subterfuge of coded messages. At that stage, it was just two bored women seeking an innocent outlet for their intellects and imaginations.

'By the end of the 1950s, Cecile has inherited the chateau on the death of her father. She has married appropriately and settles down to running the family vineyards and wineries. The marriage apparently was happy enough but it was not a lasting venture because the Count died in 1962 in a tragic climbing accident.

'Cecile, in her grief, makes contact with Aaron Rossiter again and together they hatch the financial structure for *the game*, which is now known by the name, *Ramas*, after Meredith's incorrect French, *ramasseur*. It merely adds to the confusion which is all part of the mask of the puzzle.

'Then, *Ramas* changes from a piece of imagination to a real, if disguised, trading entity. Through the 1960s, the clandestine group actually does trade successfully as a number of discrete self-sustaining modules – each with its own training capacity and each funnelling excess monies back through the financial institution of which Aaron is the founding managing director, Grey Bear Investment Bank.

'By the end of that decade, the business interests have expanded into a lucrative trade. Recruitment of personnel has a focus on those who aspire to a higher lot in life and who are susceptible to the brainwashing training which the organisation is using to convince its members of the merit of wealth over human values.

'Cecile opts out. She isn't happy with the real-world version of her fantasy. Anyway, she has more than enough to do running a chateau and its interests – but the *Ramas* organisation won't let her go.

'Aaron Rossiter has built a commission component into the financial structure, including payment for favours; and it includes presents for the owner of the original idea, Cecile. All the presents pass through blind routes so that a mystique grows about *Ramas* and who he or she is.'

Brennan is now staring intently at Fowler, no longer glancing out to the bay. He flicks his hand for Fowler to continue.

'For her part and to her shame, Cecile accepts the gifts while purporting to discourage the practice. She had an extravagant cellar at the chateau where she displayed all the treasures, for her own eyes only. Despite her stated attempts to distance herself from this new *game*, it is like the mythical *Hydra*, as she said in her farewell letter. If you cut off one head, two would grow in its place. The *Ramas* model was self-generating. It fed on itself by creating and servicing new and old markets, all under the cloak of *silence* and *results*.

'Aaron Rossiter died just as new technologies were emerging. Roger Cavanagh filled a gap and helped build the protection culture to a new level. He sought Cecile's help with encryption for the new era and the challenge was again accepted – she loved the intellectual spur of solving problems.'

Ben shakes his head. 'No. Do you have any evidence that Roger developed the new encryption? He only met Cecile twice, didn't he?'

'But he could have used the anonymous communication,' Jeff argues. 'She wouldn't have known who she was dealing with. She would assume it was the person who had been running the organisation since she had left.'

Ben shrugs. 'Maybe. Maybe not. Go on anyway.'

'You could well be right, Ben. However, perhaps another player in America has arrived to take on Aaron Rossiter's role as the real *Ramas*. There was a person known as *Butch*, Cliff Butcher. My colleague in America, Kyle Broderick, was on the trail of *Butch* when he was killed. Kyle knew he was being followed. He took the precaution of sending his written notes to Angus Forbes in Edinburgh. It was there that we have been piecing together the recent parts of the puzzle.

'Go on.' Ben flicks his hand again to encourage faster progress.

'Kyle had gone back to investigating the GBIB board. He believed the key had to be there. He discovered that Ted Hayes, the CEO, had handled all the operational aspects of the bank. He'd been a star recruit of Aaron Rossiter.

'While ferreting around with the help of the auditors, Broderick actually uncovered many of the trails and blind alleys which had been set up to launder the money, to pay commissions and buy protection.

'But Hayes was saying nothing, holding out for the investigation to be called off. That was the way it had always happened in the past. He nearly succeeded with the stone-walling. And we, the investigators, have all been put on hold.

'Anyway, Broderick went back into Rossiter's past and to the relationship with Cecile Bauchet; and into the past of the son, this Cecil Bauchet-Rossiter. Cecil had followed his mother's genes into Intelligence work, CIA or an offshoot of it, where he operated clandestinely – a dead end.

'The auditors of GBIB discovered the *Ramas* costing structure had been amended five years ago at the instigation of the SPFA, read Roger Cavanagh. He was the kingpin of the South East Asian operation. He built in the provision for protection money to become an automatic pay-off for high-powered political clout. And he reinforced the policy of gifts to Cecile Bauchet as respect for her development of the concept.

'When Broderick confronted Ted Hayes with all of this, he revealed what he knew of the system's set-up by Aaron Rossiter and the refinements of the encryption.'

Brennan wrinkles his face as he considers the scenario. 'Keep going.'

'Now we come to the catches in the story. In her farewell note, Cecile advised that, apart from an occasional warning or advice, she had scarcely sent an encrypted note in the past twenty years. The messages which Sir Terence and others were relaying had not come from her. Aaron was dead. Ted Hayes only sent routine messages within the confines of his encryption authority.

'Broderick then assumed that Roger Cavanagh must have been the big player. Indeed, the former London pauper had shown a tremendous aptitude for learning, improvising and setting up self-sustaining systems.

'What he had never learned though was how to control his impetuosity. The *Sea Spray* episode was the venture which would blow the whole system apart.'

Ben rubs his chin. 'So, are you saying that Roger was actually *Ramas*?' He shakes his head. 'I can't buy that. He wouldn't send encrypted messages to Sir Terence for him to send straight back. What about Terence's wife, Meredith? She was in at the start. Is she still involved? She would make as likely a *Ramas*, surely?'

'She's over eighty, Ben. She may have had a ghost-operator's role early on but I doubt she would set up her husband for the fall that he was always going to take.

'Then again, she might know a helluva lot more than she lets on. I wouldn't doubt she has influence in mysterious circles, even today. I'd bet she knows a lot that many would like to keep covered up; but I can't see an octogenarian running this complex show.

'No-one has implicated her in anything beyond the 1950s – and it was just an innocent game back then. No, I think Kyle found the solution.

'Kyle went hunting for *Butch* and then someone or some people got onto his tail. He knew his time was limited so he contacted Angus and posted his information. Kyle was killed the next day in a failed mugging in Washington.'

Ben raises his eyes upwards in exasperation. 'Well, anyone who believes that believes in fairies.'

Jeff smiles bleakly in agreement. 'The notes were sent to Edinburgh, with all the strands of the mystery pointing towards someone high in the United States, someone who could intercept Intelligence and put obstructions in the way – the very protection that Roger always thought to be so important.

'Kyle believed *Butch* was that key protector – the organiser who arranged for the fix to be put in whenever suspicions were raised about *Ramas*. So Angus puts Kyle's information together with Cecile's farewell note to come up with the solution.

'She had written of her lost son not being called Cecil anymore. He had changed his name. But perhaps he still had traces of the original name.

'Angus's *Versec* contact, Larry Kennedy, found the name Cliff Butcher being remembered. Cliff Butcher – Cliff Bauchet – Cecil Bauchet-Rossiter? Could it be?

'If Cliff was indeed the son of Cecile and Aaron then he would be in his early fifties today. He would have been trained and groomed by Aaron. He would also have been in the US Intelligence community for a couple of decades at least. Just maybe he could have inherited his mother's problem-solving creativity to master-mind the whole process while shedding a mysterious distraction in the direction of the Loire Valley.'

'Sounds better,' agrees Ben. 'So they have picked up this Cliff Butcher or what ever alias is known by?'

'No,' says Jeff. 'The man he might be goes by the name of John Pensecola, a senior *dark ops* man – which is saying something at a place like Langley. He is missing. Presumed drowned. Boating accident off the coast of Massachusetts. A week ago.'

'How convenient.' He shakes a tired head. 'No body? Maybe he will rise from the dead like Steve Flynn did.' Ben is wearing his best cynical expression.

'Funny you should say that because Cecile referred to the *Ramas Hydra* in her farewell note – whenever you cut off the *Hydra's* head two more grow in its place. That was her justification for not being able to kill *the game* off.

'If we are to think we have killed this thing off because Cavanagh and his henchmen have gone, just consider all the people that have been trained across South-East Asia, not to mention the Caribbean and the Mediterranean.

'And, because of their blind message routes, none of them know who the senior players are. They only know code names or pseud-onyms. The *Hydra* will rise again; ominous thought though it is.'

'Ah?' queries Ben, 'Even with main heads lopped? Aaron, Cecile, Sir Terence, the Brigadier, Roger, GBIB … even with all of them gone? You reckon?'

'But we haven't got Cliff Butcher; and no doubt there were other Rogers in the other areas of operation. Peter Carter told Steve

Flynn that he was about to lead the operation in Thailand. And then, who else was on their secret payroll in very high influential places? I think there's a lot we don't know about. The next iteration may not be the *Ramas Hydra* but it will grow its heads again. We need to be vigilant.'

Ben looks out over the tranquil waters, yachts with people at play – a relaxed scene.

How many people would be motivated to rock such a peaceful life? he thinks. *How many would stand up and be counted, if the going got tough?*

'There needs to be the will for that to happen – the will at the highest level.' He shakes his head. 'Too many vested interests, deals, alliances, self-interest, greed. Until people are prepared to take the hard decisions, I agree with you, Jeff, the *Hydra* could well rise again.'

Alison, Steve and Ben

Brisbane. Thursday 28 June 2007

'Guess who's coming to dinner?' asks Alison, as I come in the door.

'Pass. Tell me!' I grin. She has that effect on me. These have been a happy few months as we find our way together in this new life.

She laughs back at my unwillingness to guess. 'It's none other than Mr Ben Brennan!' She pauses for effect. 'He phoned today to say he's in Brisbane and could he look us up? He will be here at six-thirty.'

'Terrific! I'll have a shower and be ready in time.'

* * * *

We open the door to a slimmer Ben Brennan, but the weather-beaten face still shines with alert experience. He has a couple of bottles of merlot in his hand and greets us both with a friendly hug.

'Ah ha! You *do* drink after all.' Alison jokes at the old memory of him sitting at a bar with an untouched glass of beer. How long ago that image seems. So much has happened since.

* * * *

We enjoy a light meal as we talk through happenings since the farewell at Cairns Hospital – a few months of rehabilitation for Ben; walking, eating well, physiotherapy and more walking. He is fit again. We'd had only occasional brief communication since. He'd never been a talker.

But he's been to Yeppoon.

'I caught up with Ron and Gina there. You wouldn't recognise Gina now. Her hair is short and a quiet ginger-brown, not the red you would remember. But still the same good-looking lady with those deep-blue eyes. She said to tell you she loves walking the boys to school; shopping in the supermarket and cooking for them all when they come home. Said you'd understand.'

I do. I have a spontaneous smile at the memory of her on the *Lerna* sundeck explaining her dream. I feel good for her.

Ben continues. 'Oh, she said she'd made contact with her brother in Bournemouth. Maybe it's not all lost on that front either. She said you would understand that too. I assume she must have spoken to you about that part of her life?'

I nod. 'Yes. Good. A hopeful sign. Ron?'

'He is at an engineering works in Yeppoon – fitter and turner work. He's content. Family life is his wealth and treasure now. His mum and dad are pleased to be just grandparents again, just watching the view. They all looked happy. The boys are full of enough energy to keep them all on their toes.'

I watch Alison top up the wine glasses. This is good, listening to Ben. I sense how very close Alison feels to this man. She'd told me he had said, *I will respect you as my daughter.* She hadn't fully realised the circumstance nor the depth of meaning in that casual remark at the time. But she certainly does now.

She – we – owe a lot to Ben Brennan.

'Now what about you two?' he asks. 'How are things with you both?'

'We're doing well, Ben,' I respond. 'This lady never stops smiling. You can't help but be feeling great around her.'

Alison gives an embarrassed grin.

'I'm working in security,' I tell him, 'doing risk assessments. No frontline patrols; more back-room. It pays the rent. I don't need anything high pressure just at the moment.

'Jeff Fowler has been talking to me about liaison work with the AFP – analysis mainly. He has suggested some training courses.

I'd get recognition for prior knowledge. It sounds interesting – and useful. I think I could be alright at that. But, really, for the moment I just want to be *ordinary*. I've had enough adventure for two lifetimes. You understand that better than anyone. And besides, I've an investigative journalist to look after.' I give my girl a hug.

'And the exposé of international piracy? How is that progressing?' asks Ben of Alison.

'Funny you should ask, Ben.' Her expression suddenly becomes more serious. 'Do you remember you said, *We'll see!* up in the hospital in Cairns, when we said that Roger's network was all gone and everyone would be brought to justice? Do you remember saying that?'

'I do.' His face is taking on a patient, pained look.

'Well, I wrote up what I thought was an honest balanced account of how that piracy network was organised,' she says. 'It took me a few weeks, tying my research in with all the things I saw with you both. Then my editor said they couldn't touch it – not *wouldn't* touch it, but *couldn't* touch it. When I asked why, I was told there is an embargo. It touches on classified material. I can't use the names or the incidents.'

Ben gives a tolerant smile – no surprise in his eyes; they merely tried not to be judgemental and signal, *I told you so.*

'So what are you going to do now?'

Alison is at her feisty grinning best. 'If I can't tell the real story, I have decided to write a novel – a work of fiction which, coincidentally, will be about an international piracy ring which kidnaps people either for ransom or for sending them into slavery. How do you think that will go?'

Ben laughs at the idea.

'Where would that appear on the bookshelves?' I joke. 'Readers will think it's fantasy not fiction.'

'No! I'm serious, Steve. Publishers can't be restricted in printing a fictional story. There can be nothing classified about a work of fiction, can there? It's a piece of imagination. All the disclaimers.'

'You could be onto something,' says Ben encouragingly. 'Certainly worth a try. I wish you well. I'll be pleased to read any drafts you produce. But you *will* write about the frontline action, won't you? You'll put it in language people can believe? That it really happens.'

She pouted cheekily at me. 'Of course. Steve thinks people won't believe it. I'll show him he's wrong.'

Ben raises a challenging eyebrow. 'Well, if they want proof, I have a nicely healed scar on my chest, testimony. It actually happened.'

More merlot appeared in the wine glasses.

'And you, Ben?' asks Alison. 'How are *you* going?'

'I am going well. Despite the injury and the rehab, I am probably in better nick now than I've been for years. I walk a lot, eat sensibly and don't take part in any of the action I used to.

'But more than that,' he continues, reaching out for Alison's hand. 'I think I got rid of some of my demons on the *Lerna* that night. Seeing you safe, seeing your worried smile as I lay on the deck; I think I've at long last been able to believe that I'm not a complete failure. I didn't let *you* down. That might sound easy to you … but it hasn't been for me. Not if you'd been in my mind. It's been a dark unforgiving place for so long. Sandra and Sarah were my wife and daughter. I loved them dearly and they trusted me to protect them on our idyllic sailing trip through the islands. The *pedagang budak* got the drop on me, knocked their protector out and they were gone when I came round. I was too slow.

'But I've come to terms with it now. Time heals. And to see you both so happy now – so positive about the future. Yeh, I think I'm going well.'

We each ponder personal thoughts.

'Oh, I nearly forgot,' he adds with enthusiasm. 'Harry sent me a note. You remember Harry, Alison. You last saw him at Nagada. We left him to get the captives repatriated. He sent me an email to say that, at last, all the women, girls and boys have returned to their homes. It took a lot of time and patience to get over the worst feelings of humiliation, rejection. There's a lot of healing to happen still, but at least they've gone back. It's a start. They'll need years for the trauma to ease – if it ever does. And he's received three notes already, with the women writing how they are trying to get their lives together again. It is working already for some.

'And one said …' He pauses, strange emotion in his old grey eyes. 'You will remember her. Hillnah is her name; she said, *The lady with the camera? Will she tell our story? Will people know what happened here?* I thought that summed up the importance of our *Nemesis* work and your courage in standing up to be counted; in coming with us onto the trunk freighter. You shone a light into that miserable business. You've given them hope, Alison; a meaning to go on.'

She is holding Ben's hand tightly. There is a tension in the air as the significance of the words is absorbed. I move round to place my arm around her shoulder. I understand her pain, the sentiments, the passion, and the thinly-interred memories which are being resurrected.

I can read Alison's face; I've heard this tale before. She is picturing Hillnah – the captive's shamed look as she told her story of that desperate ordeal. The scents, the sounds, the sights wafting in from her memory.

Tears well in her journalist eyes but they don't fall – they just bead there, defiant, refusing to drop. Her jaw takes on a firm line. The reason for stepping up to the mark, for not just turning away; it is so obvious at this moment.

'I *will* write the bloody novel,' she says with a quiet vehemence. 'I *will* tell their story. Whether or not people think it's a fantasy, I *will* get their story out there! I will make it something about *Napoleon's Stone*. Stealing Drago's sapphire got the curse invoked … and it was part of the reason we were on their trail and maybe why Cavanagh fell. I might even call it *The Napoleon Curse.*'

'Oh,' Ben says. 'That's reminds me. The curse that the Balkan made actually comes from a Romany woman giving the hex to

Napoleon, at his coronation in Milan in 1805. Napoleon had stolen a stone called the Mohács Blue.'

'Yes,' we both say. Waiting.

'Well, Jeff Fowler told me that the Mohács Blue was been found in the cellar of the chateau of the *Ramas* countess in France. She left a farewell note explaining all her sins and she had even been doing up an inventory so that the treasures could be returned to their rightful owners.'

'Yes.' We both repeat. He is building to something.

'She wrote in her note that she had been haunted by wailing women from a video of a slave woman. I sent her that very video link in an Indonesian mask a couple of years ago. It worked. You hope something like that might have an effect but I didn't know that it had. I thought the leader of that slave trade wouldn't give a damn. Maybe that's part of the effect of the curse – a conscience keeps plaguing them every hour of their life.'

'Good on you, Ben!' I feel like giving him the praise he so rarely accepts. 'So how do they give back the sapphire that a Romany woman owned two hundred years ago? To the one who placed the curse on Napoleon?'

'It has apparently been sent to the Natural History Museum in Paris – at the countess's request. They have a vault there for precious stones – very secure. There are other gems from the old French crown jewels kept there. Maybe the curse has used up its power now. It got Napoleon in the end and a lot of *would-be-Napoleons* in the *Ramas* network.'

We sit silently for a few minutes, sipping Ben's merlot and just letting all the ramifications percolate through our thinking.

'So, Alison, write your novel.' urges Ben. 'People deserve to know what is happening out there. And the victims deserve it for their closure. They need to know that society cares.'

The novel

Brisbane. Saturday 15 September 2007

The mass media has gone crazy.

Apparently, some investment bank in the USA is about to collapse and the government won't bail them out. They say it could blow into the worst crisis in decades – affecting every financial institution across the whole globe. I don't recognise the name. It is not GBIB but it sounds like the same sort of over-hyped craziness.

Evidently, it has been coming for a few weeks with international banks ceasing involvement in the hedge funds that underwrite many of the US mortgage debt. Probably caused by fools with too much money and too little sense who are gambling with everyone else's lives – almost *Ramas*-like.

But I have other priorities. I have just read the current draft manuscript of Alison's novel. She had the bulk of it already written for the rejected non-fiction version and has been spending night and day transposing it into novel form.

The editors seem happy with it all at this early stage. They think the market will buy it.

And she has written it beautifully – all these years of journalist reports. She has a way with the written word and can make a story interesting. I hope it sells well. It is a tale that needs to be read.

I marvel at how we came through all that alive but I also wonder if we wouldn't just get caught up in the same scenario if it all happened again – drawn into it.

It seems somehow ordained that clever manipulators can play a chess game with our lives, as the current financial crisis seems to be showing us ... with staggering consequences for the ordinary people who are losing their life's savings.

It's as if powerful people play by different rules and speak their own version of coded language; whereas we, the pawns, are guided meekly, blindly, and curtseying to our fate.

It has never really been a matter of choice. The deterrents to prevent us straying from the beckoning path are so much less convincing than the captivating allure of just following along. So easy to be bewitched – and then be trapped.

I should've been receptive to the signs, to understand the bigger picture, to feel others' pain in my journey through life.

It is all there to hear and see. But we get engrossed in ourselves, and people close to us. We don't see. Even worse, we just look away ... because it is all too difficult.

But perhaps, some of us actually have to live it to understand, to sip from their cup – and make a difference.

All that is necessary for the triumph of evil is that good men – or women – do nothing. Some old Irish philosopher is supposed to have said that. But the luring siren call of power is so enticing. We are snared before we realise.

Samar

North Queensland. Saturday 15 September 2007

He looks every bit the grey mariner. Port Hinchinbrook marina teems with small craft which spend their months just cruising the spectacular Queensland coast.

He drops a soft bag and a laptop case into the car that has been left waiting for him.

One more trip back to the yacht; a casual, confident stride down the boardwalk. The last thing he wants is to look like a tourist or even someone trying to enter the country surreptitiously.

The dress-denim shorts, loose checked shirt, the designer-seaman's cap, the cheery *G'day* and the wave to the others tying up boats. He fits; he belongs.

He is just another Aussie boatie, with a hint of some accent and a bit of money, loving the salt and the sea.

But then, he has always fitted. He has always been able to morph – the chameleon, the master of adaptation.

He places another soft bag in the car and stops to look out to the peaceful impressive Hinchinbrook Island. Wisps of cloud are gathered at the tops of the high forested peaks. Mysterious. They look almost out of place in the mainly blue sky. Sparkling azure water spreads north from Cardwell to Mission Beach and the Family Islands. A beautiful place.

The man rubs the chin where a thick beard used to be. A very different view from the one he used to see from his window over to the Virginian landscape.

Cavanagh's demise had created a vacuum.

It would surely be foolishness to leave the whole system leaderless and rudderless.

He has ignored the rumours that Cavanagh had fallen because of an alleged *Napoleon Curse* – that was the word around, but clearly just the superstitious twaddle of a Romany legend; the opiate of the weak.

He smiles a self-satisfied smirk. He might even call his new enterprise, *Samar.* That would have appealed to his mother's quirky humour. Then again, he doesn't need to be noticed; and he is past trying to live up to someone else's dream.

Beneath the radar, *silence, results.* But adapted for a new age.

* * * *

The car drives almost silently out of the marina resort; insignificant, merging into the column of vehicles; an infiltrator, heading south on the road to Townsville.

Cicadas are calling out, angry at the car. Their harmonising clicks sound almost like a wail; like aural spectres of lost souls screaming their defiance.

Waves of cicadas pass their message fast from one tribe to the next along the route. They wait noisily for the car, ahead of its passage; in protest. Who can hear them?

Who is listening to those translations of stolen spirits; those ethereal sounds that are floating on the breeze?

'Who is receiving our message?' the agonised lament seems to say.

'Who even knows what is happening? Do you hear us yet? You? Insulated in your comfortable complacency?'

'Tell them our story!' The wail is getting louder, sounding like women in grief, in pain.

'Tell them what is happening here!'

The birds slow to listen curiously to the breeze and then they fly on, puzzled, feeling strangely guilty.

'Do you know who we are? Don't turn away! Here! You can hear us! We know you can hear us! Over here! Help us!'

About the Author

Jim Reay is a former high school principal and senior public servant; now a writer of short stories and mysteries, based in Brisbane, Australia.

Born a Scot, he brings a range of perspectives to his stories; from Europe and Australia – as well as his love of history, learning and culture.

www.jimreaywriter.net

Other titles by Jim Reay

Novels

Roller Coaster (2016)
ISBN: 9781875872930
Two thousand and thirty AD – fiction
Detective and mystery stories

The Run (2016)
ISBN: 9781875872916
Espionage – fiction, Suspense –fiction,
Spy stories

Searching for Siobhan (2016)
ISBN: 9781875872893
Missing persons – investigation – Queensland – Brisbane –
History
Detective and mystery stories

The Chess Board (2015)
ISBN: 9780994377807
Detective and mystery stories
Suspense – fiction
Stereotypes (Social psychology)
Aboriginal Australians,
Queensland – fiction

Young Adult

Catching Legends (2015)
ISBN: 9781875872886
Official secrets – moral and ethical aspects – Fiction

For more information and to read samples, visit:
www.jimreaywriter.net